HERE COMES THE SUN

CELIA ANDERSON

Boldwood

First published in 2014 as *Little Boxes*. This edition published in Great Britain in 2025 by Boldwood Books Ltd.

Cover Design by Rachel Lawston

Cover Images: Rachel Lawston

A CIP catalogue record for this book is available from the British Library.

Paperback ISBN 978-1-83678-206-3

Large Print ISBN 978-1-83678-207-0

Hardback ISBN 978-1-83678-205-6

Trade Paperback ISBN 978-1-80635-308-8

Ebook ISBN 978-1-83678-208-7

Kindle ISBN 978-1-83678-209-4

Audio CD ISBN 978-1-83678-200-1

MP3 CD ISBN 978-1-83678-201-8

Digital audio download ISBN 978-1-83678-203-2

This book is printed on certified sustainable paper. Boldwood Books is dedicated to putting sustainability at the heart of our business. For more information please visit https://www.boldwoodbooks.com/about-us/sustainability/

Boldwood Books Ltd, 23 Bowerdean Street, London, SW6 3TN

www.boldwoodbooks.com

PROLOGUE

LATE OCTOBER

The box lay on the bed waiting to be opened. Small, square and shiny, it was the colour of dark sapphires and covered in stars – the sort of glitzy thing you buy when you want to make a bargain present look classy. Tucked inside its wrapping was a pale green envelope with the words 'Read me first. The box comes later' written on the front. The writing was swirling, flamboyant, and unmistakeably Shaun's.

Blinking away the sudden tears that never seemed far away these days, Molly ripped open the envelope. As she pulled out the sheet of notepaper, a light shower of glitter fell onto the duvet and she caught a waft of Shaun's favourite sandalwood after-shave. Unfolding the page, she took a deep breath, swallowed hard, and began to read.

When you open this, I'll either be soaking up the sun on Bondi Beach or glugging cold beer in a bar. I know you said you couldn't cope without me now Jake's gone, but you've got work to do and it starts today.

Here goes. Remember that old film we watched last year – you know, the one you loved and I hated – about the guy who sends letters to his wife after he's snuffed it, giving her all those missions and jobs that she's sup-posed to complete? And you said the book was better than the film, and I said it couldn't be any worse? Well, this is my take on that story, only mine's much cooler because I'm still here (although after the bender Si and me went on the night before we left, it's a wonder) and at the end of your quest, you'll know... well, wait and see what you'll know.

All I'm saying is, if Jake's still a mystery to you, he won't be for long. You've had what must seem a long time without him now. I think you must be ready to take the next steps.

See you when I'm done with exploring

Planet Earth – love you more than kangaroo burgers (don't ask – not good).
 Shaun xxxx

Molly dried her eyes on her t-shirt and re-read the letter. She might have known Shaun would have something like this up his sleeve. Best friends like him didn't come along every day. She missed him desperately. It had been the middle of October before she had accepted that he really was going away. His round-the-world trip with his partner, Simon, had been in the planning stages for months. Jake had said they'd all be applying for their bus passes by the time Shaun and Si managed to leave, but as it happened Jake had beaten them to it. Molly had never felt so lonely in her life.

Picking up the box, she gave it a shake. There was a rattle and a muted ringing sound. The lid was taped down securely and took a while to undo. To begin with, all that was visible was a heap of shredded tissue paper. She put a finger into the middle of it and felt something hard and shiny. Carefully, she parted the strands to reveal a silver bell and a tightly folded note.

1

SIX MONTHS EARLIER

Tom sat on the beach in the spring sunshine, eating cockles out of a tub and gazing grimly at the incoming tide. If it came much closer he'd have to abandon his painting for the day. It always took a good twenty minutes to pack up and get back to his car on the promenade.

As he licked his fingers and screwed up the seafood carton, there was a scrunch of pebbles and a whoosh of air as a small boy thundered past, whooping at the top of his voice. He was followed at speed by the most beautiful woman that Tom could ever remember seeing in this small seaside town. It was his Lady in Red; the one who had been cropping up in his dreams far too often since he'd first seen her on the beach. Her hair was an explosion of dark curls, and she wore tight orange jeans with a wildly clashing crimson sweater that came down almost to her knees. Tom opened his mouth to say hello but he was too late.

'Max! Don't you dare go near the sea. I mean it!' she bellowed, skidding straight into Tom as she chased the boy across the pebbles. 'Sorry, sorry... have I hurt you? Is your painting wrecked? Oh, wow. It's good, isn't it? You can tell it's meant to be the pier. I'm really, really sorry...'

Tom hauled himself off the ground and put his painting chair the right way up again. 'Hey, stop apologising, it's okay. I was getting tired of being up-right,' he said, grinning into her startlingly green eyes. 'You get a whole different perspective when you're lying on the shingle.'

She blinked and looked away. Shielding her eyes with a hand, she scanned the beach for the boy.

'Where's he gone, the little toad? Ah, there he is, he's making something out of a heap of stones. At least he's not paddling fully dressed like last time. Look, you don't even know me and I've already wrecked your work. I'm Molly. I think I've seen you here before, haven't I? Let me fix your painting.'

She bent down to see if she could repair the

damage and Tom held out a hand to stop her trying to brush bits of sand and small stones off his picture. 'No, honestly, it's fine, I'll sort it out. I'm Tom, and I've seen you, too. You're easy to remember.'

'Am I? Why?'

'Lots of reasons. You often seem to be in a hurry, you always wear something red, you've got lots of kids, you look amazing.' Tom stopped in confusion.

'Amazing? Me? Do you need your eyes testing or something?' Molly blushed again and looked at him properly for the first time. 'I'm sorry, that was really rude,' she said. 'My mum's always telling me I don't know how to take a compliment.'

'Don't worry, maybe you just need a bit more practice.' Tom bent to carry on sorting his painting kit out. He couldn't help noticing how her eyes rested on his forearms as he finished tidying up and, clearly aware of his scrutiny, she reddened even more.

'You're very strong, aren't you?' she blurted out.

Tom laughed. 'I guess I have to be, don't I? If you've seen me before, you'll know why.'

'I don't want you to think I've been staring at you, Tom. It's just that you're... um... different to most of the men round here.'

'Tell me about it.' Tom slung his bag over one shoulder and heaved himself out of his folding chair.

'Can I help you at all?' Molly asked, standing on tiptoes to get a better view of the shoreline. 'Oh, look, here are the other two Musketeers. They can carry something for you, if you like.'

'I don't need any help, thanks.' Tom bit back the familiar feeling of irritation and smiled up at a pair of girls, dressed entirely in black, who had stopped next to him. The taller one had multiple piercings. Both girls were scowling.

'Mum, what's going on?' said the pierced one. 'We saw you knock the paints all over the place. You're so clumsy. Have you seen what Max is doing now?'

Molly looked again. The small boy had been jumping off his pile of stones and had landed awkwardly the last time. He began to wail. 'Max! I told you last time not to do that. Hang on, I'm coming,' Molly shouted.

The girls sighed and rolled their eyes at Tom as they watched their mum skid away over the stones to the sandy stretch by the sea, where Max was now hurling the biggest rocks he could find into the waves. The pierced girl turned to the smaller one.

'Bloody hell, why doesn't she just leave him alone for a bit? The only place he can go is into the sea.'

'But he's only little. He can't swim yet.'

'Exactly.' The older girl smirked as they wandered off down the beach.

Tom sighed. Another opportunity lost; still no nearer to finding out more about his dream woman. Oh well, at least he knew her name now. On the other hand, it didn't take a genius to work out that she was already taken. The wedding ring gave it away, even if the children didn't.

* * *

Molly, breathless and pink in the face, came to a halt next to her youngest son and wondered why he was turning out to be so uncontrollable. Her eldest, Sam, had been completely different – happy to play with his Lego for hours, or draw endless pictures of his tortoise. Mind you, there hadn't been all this open space available to go wild in when Sam was small. They had still been living in the little village on the outskirts of Leicester where she and Jake grew up. Theo and Hattie had been brought up there, too – it was only Max who had this giant beach playground to trash.

Bribing Max with promises of ice cream, she herded her brood back towards the promenade. The girls were sulking again. She could see Tom making his laborious way over the stones – a clever balancing act involving two sticks and a lot of muscle power. He was placing each stick carefully each time he was ready to move forward, picking the biggest, steadiest stones and testing them for steadiness as he went. A folding easel stuck out from Tom's bag, and he was weighed down by his picnic chair and painting sack. It must be an enormous effort for him to get from A to B, Molly thought, flushing again as she remembered how she'd let herself down by ogling him.

She'd always had a weakness for strong, tanned forearms, and Tom's were definitely worth looking at. In fact, his whole upper body looked amazingly toned. Molly watched him swing himself over the stones with only the occasional pause to balance. How blue his eyes were – piercing and yet thoughtful, looking right inside her as if he was able to read her soul. It was a good job he couldn't.

Molly had noticed Tom painting on the cliffs for the first time last winter, and had been trying to think what she could do to get to know him ever since. There was something intriguing about his level of concentration and the way he set his jaw when he was painting. You would never dare to interrupt someone who cared so much about their work.

What kind of man would brave the bitter cold to paint such fresh, clean pictures day after day? Molly had stood in the shelter of the Ferrymead-on-Sea lighthouse on that first morning, muffled to the eyeballs in scarves and a woolly hat, but Tom's short blond curls were unprotected by any sort of headgear and he had nothing thicker than a battered leather jacket to protect him from the icy east coast wind. Molly had wondered whether to offer him some coffee from her flask, but had chickened out. He'd looked as if interruptions would definitely not be welcome.

'Mum, look at that man you were just talking to – he's very brave, isn't he?' said Hattie as Tom, reaching the concrete of the promenade, picked up speed and reclaimed the wheelchair that he'd left chained to a lamp post.

'Hattie, you're so wet. And you'd better not let him hear you say stuff like that, either,' her sister replied, giving her a shove.

Hattie righted herself and glared at Theo. 'Why not?'

'Duh, it's obvious. He'll think you pity him 'cos he can't walk without sticks. Even I know you should never do that.'

Hattie stuck out her bottom lip and watched Tom

bowl away out of sight. 'He's fast though, isn't he, Mum? He could do Paralympics or something,' she said after a moment.

'He really gets a move on,' agreed Molly, trying to banish the unfamiliar ripples of lust that were making her slightly breathless. 'Come on, we said we'd go and have an ice cream with your dad at the bistro. He'll think we've abandoned him.'

They clambered over the last heap of stones and began to wander along the promenade towards the small restaurant that Jake had opened when the family had migrated to the coast last summer. Molly had been dubious about the move for lots of reasons, but a clean break had been necessary after their marriage was looking very much as if it was over. And by and large, it had been successful. Hattie and Theo had soon made new friends, and Molly had landed a job teaching music around the local schools, thanks to her aptitude both for playing a range of instruments and for ignoring the fact that most of her pupils would rather be doing something – anything – else.

'Is Daddy having dinner with us tonight? Only he promised he'd help me make a kite for my homework. He said he'd do it yesterday, too,' grumbled

Max, kicking a discarded drink can and making a nearby elderly lady jump.

Molly apologised automatically to the lady and said that, no, Daddy would probably be working again tonight. She fought a sudden urge to go after Tom and ask him if he ever felt as if life was passing him by. He obviously wasn't a man built for self-pity. It was probably only people like herself, blessed with a lovely family and a house by the sea, who indulged in such thoughts.

Sighing, Molly put thoughts of Tom firmly out of her mind and headed for her husband. If she was going to have lustful thoughts, they ought to be about Jake. But what was she supposed to do when the thought of sex with her husband was about as enticing as a bag of cold chips?

2

After the day of the capsized chair, Tom began to feel seriously disappointed if he didn't bump into Molly at least once a week. Sometimes she waved, but usually she was too preoccupied with trying to hold on to Max.

Tom thought she was absolutely beautiful. He often wondered what sort of man would be lucky enough to live with his Lady in Red. Maybe she was married to someone who worked away, or had a job with unsociable hours? Or maybe she was on her own with the children, struggling to make ends meet? He speculated as he painted, watching for Molly out of the corner of his eye, ready to look busy whenever she appeared, aware of her every move.

But then one day in June, just when Tom had decided that Molly must be a single parent waiting for a new partner to come along and sweep her off her feet, Tom spotted Theo, Hattie and Max walking along the promenade with a gangly, spiky-haired man. He was urging them forwards with quick movements of his hands, frowning at Theo who stuck her tongue out at him and hissed something under her breath. They all laughed at this, and Tom heard the man shout, 'Theo – your mum'll go mad when she hears what you just said.'

'But you won't tell, will you, Daddy?' said the little boy, catching hold of the man's hand and swinging it to get his attention.

'No, don't, Dad – she didn't mean it. She's in enough trouble already this week,' Hattie chipped in.

'Well, whose fault's that? She should never have got that nose-ring. You knew how your mum felt about it, didn't you, Theo? After last time, I thought you'd have had more sense.'

'It's only a little one. She loves gold earrings. I didn't think she'd mind.'

The man sniffed. 'Come on, Mum'll be waiting for us at the restaurant by now so we can eat together for once. She won't like being kept hanging around, will she?'

Tom hadn't painted that day but had been sitting looking out over the sea thinking about the future. He turned his wheelchair and kept within earshot of the family, feeling uncomfortably like a stalker but following at a discreet distance until they came to a doorway under a striped awning. A sandwich board stood outside with a short chalked menu.

As he stopped, Tom was horrified to see Hattie point to him, whispering something to her sister. They both waved and smiled as they disappeared under a sign that said *Jake's Bistro*. Two bay trees in blue glazed pots sat either side of the door and, wheeling himself nearer so that he could peer into the restaurant, Tom could just see the corner of a shaded, cosy-looking room. A mouth-watering smell of garlic and basil curled its way out and he thought about going in for dinner, but changed his mind at the last moment. He was meeting Sasha later and she would expect to be fed after a long day working for him in the gallery. Today his feisty assistant had been doing the accounts, and it was never her favourite job.

In any case, seeing Molly with her family all around her was not on Tom's list of things to make the day go with a swing. He turned his chair round and sped back down the promenade, biting back a wave of resentment. It was no one's fault but his own if he hadn't got the sort of life that Molly's man must be enjoying. If it hadn't been for the stupid accident... but there was no point in going over old ground – the past was set in stone. Pushing the unwelcome thoughts away, Tom headed back into town. If he couldn't get motivated to paint, at least he could buy some flowers for the long-suffering Sasha.

* * *

The next afternoon, Tom was sitting in one of his usual places on the beach with a canvas propped up on his knees, trying to make something new and interesting of the view of the promenade, when suddenly Molly was beside him, all breathless and apologetic again.

Although summer had officially begun, it was one of those days when a brisk sea breeze was making concentration difficult. Whipping up the waves, it sent stray pieces of seaweed and sweet wrappers scooting over the pebbles and, like a few others on the beach, Molly was wrapped up as if the weather was still chilly. She wore a huge soft scarf in shades of russet, green and blue today, and a long, flowing red cardigan with the sleeves casually pushed up. She dangled a dog's lead from one hand and scanned the horizon as she spoke.

'Excuse me, I'm really sorry to bother you... Tom...' He put down his pencil as she asked, 'Have you seen a little dog go past? Sort of brownish, with a black patch over one eye? And a bent ear?'

Tom couldn't help noticing the rise and fall of her chest even under the layers of cardigan and high-necked t-shirt – it was mesmerising. He gulped and opened his mouth to answer, but she rushed on. 'I think the dog might be on heat, that's the trouble; I shouldn't really have brought her out. I'm only looking after her for one of my neighbours, but it looked so quiet down here, and the poor thing was desperate for a walk.'

Tom took a deep breath and cleared his throat. It seemed hours since he'd spoken to anyone. The last person must have been his landlady, a comfortless woman whose legs didn't meet at the top and who looked as if she'd been sucking a lemon.

'Erm... so, do you like dogs?' he asked huskily, anything to keep the conversation going. She raised her eyebrows.

'Oh, yes, I love them, especially spaniels – we always used to have a dog when I was little, but Jake won't let us have one.' She paused, biting her lip.

'Is Jake your husband?'

'Yes.'

The silence lengthened until Tom was thoroughly uncomfortable. 'So... why not?'

'Huh? Why not what?' Molly jumped slightly, looking totally confused. She must have been miles away in her head, but where?

Tom persevered. 'Why won't Jake let you have a dog?'

Molly flushed. 'I don't really know. He won't say. It's not worth another argument.'

'Do you argue a lot then?' Tom wondered if he'd gone too far with this question – it seemed much too personal a thing to ask someone he'd only just met properly, but Molly shrugged and grinned.

'Oh, you know – not more than most long-married couples, I guess. We've been together since we were at school. You change, don't you?'

'How do you mean?'

'Well, we were too young to know what we really wanted out of life when we first got together, and now...' She broke off, blushing. 'Listen to me, rambling on about Jake and you don't even know me. You must think I'm off my head, wandering around talking to strangers.'

'I'm not a stranger now, though, am I? You could

stop and chat if you see me again. I'm quite safe.'
Tom glanced down at his useless legs and grimaced.

'Yes, that'd be nice. Anyway, back to the problem
– have you seen the puppy?'

'No, I'm really sorry but I'm sure no dogs have
come along here in the last few minutes.' Molly's face
fell. More than anything Tom wanted to reach into
his haversack, produce a small brown dog, and make
her day right again.

'Never mind. I bet she's gone back to look for
the kids,' she glanced over her shoulder, 'but Mrs
Henderson will kill me if I've lost the dog. Her
mother's a pedigree cocker spaniel who escaped
and got into a one-night stand situation with a
lurcher. That's the dog's mother, not Mrs Henderson's.'

She grinned, and Tom thought how amazingly
pretty she was, especially when the worry lines disappeared. He tried to think of some other way of
stalling her, but after a few seconds' silence, she said,
'Anyway, I'd better go and leave you to your painting
– sorry to bother you. Oh, look, she's here! You bad,
bad beast, Sheherezade. I've been looking for you
everywhere.'

A wet and muddy puppy thundered out of
nowhere and hurled itself onto Tom's knee, covering

his canvas with paw prints, then bounced down and drank the remains of his paint water.

'Oh, no! Sorry, sorry, sorry.' She hauled the puppy off and it sat down next to Tom, looking up at him adoringly. He laughed.

'I think the little dog's got the right idea. Sit down for a bit, if you've got time, Molly. You look as if you need a break, and Sheherezade's a hell of a name to carry around when you're not very big. She must be knackered.'

Molly bent to pat the puppy's head and put her lead on, then sat down on the stones, wriggling to get comfortable. 'You've got a point. And shouting, "Where are you, Sheherezade?" really gets you noticed. Mrs Henderson calls her "Sherry" because she's the colour of the best sort of Tio Pepe, apparently. I don't know much about sherry. Or dogs, as you can see. Do you like animals, Tom?'

'To eat, or to have as company on dark winter nights?' He wondered if he'd gone too far – maybe she was vegetarian, or even a vegan who thought eating things with faces placed you one step away from a cannibal. 'I've never owned a dog,' he added hastily, 'but I had a budgie once.' He fell silent, wishing he could rewind the last few sentences. Why couldn't he have invented a macho sort of pet? Or even something with the 'aaaah' factor, like a lop-eared rabbit or a kitten?

'A budgie? What was its name?' At least Molly seemed interested now, and had stopped looking as if she was about to escape up the beach. Tom decided to press on.

'It was called "Perky" actually.'

'And was it?'

'Was it what?' Tom rubbed his face, feeling as if he'd dropped into the early pages of *Alice in Wonderland*.

'Was it perky?'

'Oh... not very. It died a horrible death of a heart attack. I wrote a poem to be read at its burial, actually.'

'Did you? How did it go?'

'Well, it was obviously quite depressing, but...'

'No, not the burial – I mean, how did the poem go?'

'Oh, sorry. Let me see if I can remember it. Right, here we go. Are you sure you're ready for this, Molly? I don't want to spoil your day.'

'Go for it. I'm all ears.'

Tom cleared his throat. 'Okay – here goes.'

'I have a little budgie,

His name is Perky Joe.
And when I try to tickle him,
He waggles to and fro.'

Molly appeared to be struggling with some sort of strong emotion. Her shoulders began to shake. Tom pressed on.

'He is so green and yellow
With a bit of indigo.
And when it comes to night time,
To dreamland he will go.'

There was a short silence and then Molly began to giggle. Deeply relieved, Tom joined in and soon they were both laughing hysterically. Sheherezade bounced from one to the other, licking whichever of them she could reach and barking madly. After a moment or two, Molly tried to control herself, wiping her streaming eyes and sitting up straight. Gradually, they both calmed down, until only Sheherezade was letting out the occasional yelp.

'Right. Well, you're a man of many talents, Tom,' said Molly, hiccupping slightly. 'An artist and also a poet. What else are you good at?'

Tom glanced at her as she sat with her arms

around her knees, noticing for the first time how long her eyelashes were close up. She had a faint smattering of freckles across her nose, and her lips were soft and achingly kissable. He tried not to stare, but their eyes locked and he couldn't look away. Molly was the first one to break the spell.

'I didn't mean that to sound flirty, honestly,' she said, stroking the puppy's head as if it was an important job that must be done properly.

'I know you didn't. Let's start again. So... ahem... what do you do with yourself all day, Molly?' Tom asked.

'Oh, it's not very interesting, really. I'm a music therapist in schools. I travel around trying to persuade kids that playing an instrument will solve all their problems. I get kicked a lot.'

'You're kidding? The kids kick you? Why?'

'Oh, these are the ones with really big problems. There's one who only has to catch sight of me and he shouts, "You! Fuck off." Good job I'm only part-time.' She sighed and changed the subject suddenly. 'I love this beach, don't you? But my favourite part of Ferrymead is the stone jetty, with all the tractors and fishing boats, and that rank fishy smell.'

'Yeah, me too,' said Tom. 'The whole town's perfect, as far as I'm concerned. Some people might say it's a bit seedy and old-fashioned in places, I guess.'

'Would they?' Molly frowned.

'Well, obviously no one with any sense would say that.' Tom saw Molly's shoulders relax again and thought it was safe to continue. He must have touched a nerve there. Why was she so prickly all of a sudden? 'Anyway, I've driven quite a way down the east coast when I've been looking for new places to paint,' he said, 'right from Berwick-on-Tweed to the bottom end of Suffolk, but this part of Norfolk is just so chilled out and beautiful.'

'I know. When we moved here, some of my friends thought it was crazy to leave a place where you could so easily get into Leicester – there's so much to do: bars, theatres, shopping. But I feel safe here.'

'I'm glad you like the jetty. Most people don't like that area so much. The stink puts some of the tourists off – that's got to be a bonus.' Tom knew he shouldn't hate the trippers so much; his best-selling pictures were those traditional big-sky-and-sea-type landscapes – they couldn't get enough of them. He longed to burn all those pictures one day in a wild beach bonfire and begin painting something else. Anything else. Something good.

Molly turned to smile at him. 'Do you ever get the urge to paint something different, Tom? Like portraits, or that stuff that's just big coloured shapes?'

Tom blinked. Was she a witch? He nodded wordlessly. Molly looked at her watch.

'Oh, no, I'm going to be really late for fetching Max and Hattie from school.' Before Tom could stop her, she jumped up and checked that the puppy's lead was attached properly and began to drag it up the beach, looking back over her shoulder as she went. 'Next time I see you, I'll buy you a drink, Tom. I mean as a thank you, I'm not trying to pick you up or anything... not that I... oh, sod it, I'm off.'

'Wait a minute, don't go just yet,' Tom shouted back, but she'd disappeared up the steps and along the promenade towards the town, almost stumbling in her rush to get away.

3

After this, the summer progressed badly for Tom. Although his mind was full of ideas for a new style of painting that could break boundaries and shock the art world into taking him seriously as an artist, he was filled with a sense of limbo. Every day he would go through the motions of being a successful part of the tourist industry, churning out the perfect examples of windmills, seascapes and wide-open skies that the tourists found so collectable. In the evenings he would fill a sketchbook with his plans for the future, drink too much red wine, and dream of Molly.

In the gallery, Sasha seemed concerned about him. She was still only twenty-two and found his lack of a social calendar very dull. Tom knew that his strange mixture of lethargy about life and excitement about Molly was making him an uncomfortable person to work with, and the intermittent drizzle of the miserable weeks of July and August made painting on the beach and cliffs much less of a pleasure than usual.

'Don't you have any mates, Tom?' Sasha asked, as he headed off for another night alone in his flat.

'Yeah, I've got mates – lots of them. It's just that they don't live round here.'

'Why not?'

'Well, most of them are either old school friends or people I met at art college. We keep in touch by email and on Facebook, stuff like that.'

Sasha looked at him sideways. 'What about girl-friends?'

'Nah. No one at the moment.'

'You should get out more. Come down to the pub tonight for the quiz – it's always a laugh, and you could help with the old music round.'

'Old music? You cheeky kid, I'm only thirteen years older than you.'

'So you'll come then?'

'Not tonight, Sash.'

She shrugged, and they finished packing up the shop before heading out into the deserted, rainy

streets of the little seaside town. Tom had lost interest in being sociable and he couldn't bring himself
to care if Sasha thought he was some sort of Billy No
Mates. He'd spoken to Molly only briefly in the last
months. She had taken the children to see a friend
on the Isle of Wight for several weeks of the school
holidays – apparently Jake couldn't get away from
work – and when she *was* around, she only waved, or
passed the time of day very quickly. Tom had gone
over and over their last proper meeting in his mind.
Had he put her off by being too intense? Had the
stupid budgie poem made her realise that he was
actually a complete lunatic and not to be trusted?

Maybe Molly was secretly feeling the same
yearnings as him, he thought hopefully. But the
more he agonised, the more Tom came to the conclusion that he had only imagined the way she'd looked
at him. Or even if she *had* been a bit interested, she'd
probably backed off because she was a good wife;
dutiful and faithful. Even if her husband did sound
as if he was a grumpy sod. What sort of man
wouldn't let his wife and kids have a puppy, for goodness' sake? What sort of bloke wouldn't make an effort to go on holiday with them all? What a tosser.

At last September arrived and, as if to make up
for the fiasco that had been the summer months, it

was warm and golden from the very start. There was a last flurry of trippers who bought up Tom's entire stock of local paintings, and the autumn sunshine continued well into the new school term, much to the irritation of the town's children. One Sunday in late September, knowing that he had very little to sell but still not quite ready to start something new and radical, Tom reluctantly made his way to the beach with his painting gear. He had always hated Sunday afternoons.

Even at this time of year, the beach was heaving with visitors running around and looking all healthy and motivated with their stupid dogs and delinquent children. There were even more couples than usual today, holding hands and gazing at each other and then doing that 'Oh my God, it's so cold' squealing thing as the waves lapped at their toes – smug gits. He wished Molly was here. Sighing, he settled himself more comfortably into his chair and glanced at his watch. The days were getting much shorter now that September was well underway. He would paint for two hours and then he really ought to be going back to the gallery to get his latest work hung, ready for tomorrow's last influx of trippers.

Packing away took longer than setting up, as usual. As he finally finished clambering back over the stones at the top of the beach, Tom raised his head sharply, hearing the wail of an ambulance approaching along the promenade. He was just in time to see it weaving through the light traffic, closely followed by a huge pick-up truck. His jaw dropped as he spotted Molly sitting in the passenger seat of the truck, twisting round to speak to a heap of children in the back. Tom couldn't see the driver clearly, but it obviously wasn't the man he'd seen with the children at the bistro. As Molly turned back to face the front, Tom caught sight of her face – it was streaked with tears.

Horrified, Tom looped his bags and easel over his shoulder more securely, and picked up his sticks. Getting over the sloping pile of stones to the promenade was never easy, but somehow he had to find out what her problem was. His wheelchair was where he'd left it, chained to the usual lamp post. At top speed, Tom whizzed off towards his car.

* * *

Molly had been tempted by the morning sunshine on that September Sunday, and had escaped with Max to the beach. She had known this would be frowned upon – understandably, Jake liked her to be at home on Sunday, as it was his one complete day off – but the warm breeze and the hazy blue of the sky had been impossible to resist. At first she and her youngest son had squelched around harmlessly in the dank-smelling sand under the pier, but after a while Max began to threaten a group of nasty-tempered seagulls with violence for eating a dead crab. In desperation, Molly suggested the lifeboat museum.

'Will you buy me something from the shop, Mum?' Max asked, kicking a pebble dangerously near to the gulls.

'You can have a pencil.'

'I had a pencil last time.'

'How about a rubber then?'

'Don't want a stupid rubber.'

'Well, we could get some of those nice playing cards with lifeboats on them?'

'Don't want...' He had seen Molly's expression at this point and followed her quietly.

An hour later, Max demanded food, so they fetched some hot, sugary doughnuts from the stall at the end of the pier and carried them to the sea wall near the jetty. Molly caught the seaweedy smell from the upturned fishing boats and sighed happily. She wondered if Tom was around today. Her cheeks flamed as she thought of the way he had looked at her on that day when Sheherezade had escaped. His dark blue eyes had seemed to cut right through her sensible maternal image, to see the person she'd been before the children swamped her. Molly had suddenly longed to touch Tom's cropped blond curls and to feel the strength of his arms around her.

She pulled herself together with difficulty and reminded herself that she was a married woman with four lovely offspring, one of whom was tugging at her sleeve right now. But as she helped Max to push the doughnut wrappers into a bin, everything began to go pear-shaped. The phone in her pocket chimed – a text. Frowning, she rummaged for it and read:

> Come home now. Fed up with gardening on my own, not feeling great.

'It's your dad,' said Molly. 'He was in a mood this morning because I bunked off helping him with the outside jobs. Oh, well, we'd better go back, Max. There's still time for me to do a bit of weeding, or something.'

As they hurried up the road, Molly thought

about pouring a long, cold gin and tonic. She could almost hear the tinny *pffff* of the tonic can being opened, and the rattle of the ice cubes in the glass. The girls would still be out with their friends, and Max would disappear upstairs to play on his Switch 2 as soon as they got home. She could steal the time to sit in the garden for ten minutes and have a drink, surely? The freshly sliced lemon would smell sharp and clean, and the gin trickling over the ice would have that wonderful juniper wedding-reception tang.

Molly and Max trailed back up the street, peacefully hand in hand for once. They reached home and Max, with a spurt of energy, headed for the freezer and his own supply of ice pops. The back door of the pleasantly shabby Victorian semi was open; maybe Jake was still outside raking leaves, thought Molly. He was due back at the restaurant in a couple of hours, so he couldn't be far away. More than ready for a row, she kicked bits of moss as she walked down the path to the hidden part of the garden. She hardly ever took a day off to go to the beach. It was nearly time to start thinking about dinner. She supposed it would be her turn to cook again. What use was living with a chef if he never cooked for his family?

She raised her voice. 'Jake? What are you doing?' Silence. Pausing briefly to listen for mowing noises or the crunch of a spade, she could smell the peaty soil and the rich scent of leaf mould. She ducked under a low branch into her favourite part of the garden – the bit behind the raspberry canes, where the compost heap steamed in the afternoon sunshine. The heat was intense and a bee buzzed and bumbled past her ear.

'Jake? Where are you? I got your text, what's the matter?' Molly stopped suddenly, almost tripping over the two large feet in Wellington boots on the ground. Jake was lying on his back as if he'd been taking a nap, with his phone lying next to his outstretched hand. His favourite old gardening shirt was twisted up around his waist, and his hair was full of leaves. A stray branch was digging into his side. Molly knelt and shook him, gently at first, then harder. She saw a trickle of dried blood coming from the place where the piece of wood had caught. It looked painful. Moving the offending branch, she began to shake.

4

Tom lurched into the car, bruising both knees in his hurry. The ambulance was already out of sight, but he could hear the siren wailing and it didn't take too much detective work to guess where it was heading. He drove there on autopilot – no stranger to the hospital – and slipped into a parking space right near the entrance, slapping his disabled card onto the dashboard. He knew there was no point in rushing the tedious job of getting the wheelchair out of the boot.

It was so easy if there was someone with him who knew what they were doing, but on his own it involved sticks, a balancing act, very strong arms, and patience. Today a friendly pensioner stopped to help, so everything took even longer – by the time Tom was in his high-speed, go-faster chair again, he felt ready to rip the man's head off.

'No, really, I can manage now. Thanks for all your help,' he said through gritted teeth, hurtling towards the front door of the hospital and narrowly avoiding an elderly lady who was sneaking outside for a cig-arette. She glared at him and swore as she joined the group sitting under the 'No Smoking' sign by the main pathway. The crowded bench was surrounded by soggy cigarette ends, and several people coughed mournfully as Tom wove his way through the re-volving doors. They had his sympathy – he'd been a smoker too, during his defiant 'get your ear pierced, cut your hair as short as possible, and get a tattoo' phase. The earring, tattoo and short hair had stayed, but he'd given up smoking after he accidentally flicked a lighted butt into a jar of turpentine and nearly set fire to the street.

Tom didn't spend much time thinking about his image these days. Sasha was always saying he looked pretty gorgeous, especially in his faded jeans and with a t-shirt that showed off his muscles, but as Sasha's taste usually leant heavily towards the gothic, he could never be sure if her approval was a good thing.

'You just need to lighten up a bit, Tom,' she'd said only last week.

'Me, lighten up? It's you that'll only wear black, and your make-up's enough to frighten Dracula,' he'd thrown back. Tom had never gone in for smiling much – not to be cool, he just didn't think he'd got much to smile about – but Sasha reckoned that women were always checking him out.

'I know you don't like the black stuff, but I have to work hard at looking like this. It comes naturally to you, doesn't it? You've really got the mean and moody look sewn up,' she'd said. 'And you can see women wondering about you, looking you up and down... you know what I mean?'

'No – you're talking bollocks,' Tom replied, glowering as he went through the endless process of cleaning brushes.

'There you are, you're doing it again.'

'Doing what, woman? You're off your head.'

'Ooh, don't stop. You're even making me shiver, and I know what a grumpy bastard you can be. They all want to know if you can still... you know... even if you're in a wheelchair.'

'If I can still what?' asked Tom.

'Don't be dim. If you can have sex. They're all wondering. So am I, if it comes to that.' She stared at him in horror. 'Oh, bugger, did I say that out loud?'

Tom frowned even harder. He didn't believe her. Why should any woman be clocking a guy in a wheelchair? And his sex life was nobody's business but his own.

At the hospital reception desk, Tom realised that he didn't know Molly's surname so there was no way he could find out where she'd gone. He sighed, and the girl on duty flicked her hair back, leaned over, and beamed down at him.

'Can I help you? Are you looking for someone?' she asked loudly, bending further and giving him a flash of her tanned cleavage.

'Hi, I'm Tom Cavendish. I was following an ambulance, and...' This was definitely sounding dodgy, even to Tom.

'Oh, right – are you saying you're looking for someone who's been brought in to A&E?' The girl stood up straight again, glancing down the corridor.

'I think so... I mean... I don't know...'

'Could you be a bit clearer?'

Tom lost patience and turned to wheel himself towards the sign saying Accident and Emergency, muttering, 'Thanks anyway,' over his shoulder. As he flicked off the brakes, he heard the girl murmur to the other receptionist, 'Wow, he's hot, isn't he? Got to be the best-looking man we've seen for ages. What a pity.'

Bloody hell, another woman feeling sorry for him, thought Tom, getting away as fast as possible. Now what? Should he just wheel himself into the middle of A&E and shout, 'Molly? Are you okay?'

As he hesitated, blocking the corridor, a small group of people came out of a side room and squeezed past his wheelchair. With a rush of relief, he recognised Theo, Hattie and Max. A tiny lady with wild grey curls was shepherding them forwards, making soothing noises and holding on tightly to Max's hand. The girls were pale and strained, both towering over the lady, who Tom guessed must be their grandmother by the way she was organising them.

'You'll need to hurry up, so,' she said to the children, almost pushing them along, 'The nurse said the café's closing in half an hour and this wee man's hungry.'

'Sorry, I'll get out of your way,' Tom mumbled, and ran over the lady's toe. She let out a howl, and began to hop up and down on one leg, shouting a stream of words, most of which seemed to be 'fecking' or 'idiot'. Max looked as if he was about to cry but the girls started to giggle and were soon completely out of control, tears running down their faces as their grandma teetered around the corridor. Tom decided to make a speedy exit.

'Um, sorry again, I really am going now. See you, folks,' he said, as he did a neat racing turn.

'Bye, man,' said Max. 'Gran said "feck" – I heard her. Mum said she wasn't allowed to say that again.'

'Hey, you're the man from the beach!' said Hattie, still giggling and gasping for breath as Tom tried to disappear discreetly.

'Yes, he's Tom the artist – the one Mum fancies,' whispered her sister.

'She doesn't fancy him, does she, Theo?' Their stage whispers were beginning to annoy Tom.

Theo sniggered and looked Tom straight in the eye, as she murmured, 'Well, she says she doesn't, but I know different.'

Heat flooded Tom's face – now what? Should he go for a friendly, uncle-type approach, or a hip, all-mates-together style? These girls were scary. He rubbed his chin and discovered way too much stubble. He must look even more like a stalker than usual; he should have shaved this morning. Meanwhile, the older lady regained control.

'Girls, leave that poor young man alone, for the

love of God! He's got enough to cope with already... I mean... he's more than likely in a hurry.'

The girls looked at each other in embarrassment. 'We were only kidding, Gran,' Theo said. 'This is one of Mum's friends. We know him. Sort of.'

Their gran stared at Tom intently. He glanced up and down the corridor. 'So, where is your mum?' he said to the children.

'She's in a room with Dad somewhere; she said he had a bit of a funny turn in the garden. He does that sometimes. It usually means he needs a beer.' Hattie grinned. 'Your name *is* Tom, isn't it? We see you a lot. Mum thinks your paintings are wicked... I don't think she'll be long if you want to wait to say hi...'

Hattie's voice petered out as she realised no one was listening. A stern nurse was waiting to speak to their gran, just on the edge of their circle.

Tom watched as the little group turned towards the nurse, feeling more useless than he'd ever felt in his life. After a moment, the grandma put a hand on his arm. He could feel a faint tremor in the thin fingers, even though no other sign of fear showed and her shoulders were firmly braced. She edged him away from the children.

'Look, young man, are you really a friend of my daughter?'

'I think so. We kind of bump into each other on the beach quite a lot.'

She hesitated, then took a deep breath. 'I don't suppose you could possibly... just for five minutes? No, of course not. I shouldn't be doing this on my own. If my useless lump of a husband was here it would be a different matter.'

'Could I possibly do what? Do you need me to help you?' he said, frowning. 'Erm, what can I do?'

The old lady leaned closer. Her scent was a subtle mixture of lavender, soap, and hairspray. Tom's eyelids prickled and he blinked hastily. His own grandmother had smelt almost exactly the same, but with a hint of humbugs. She was whispering now.

'Well, it's just that I think this lady wants to speak to me. It's not looking good.' She swallowed hard. 'You see, Theo and Hattie didn't catch sight of their dad in the garden – we kept them inside, and Max was playing upstairs. But I saw Jake. I wondered if you could... I mean the children seem to know you... Perhaps you could just mind them for a few minutes while I go and have a word.' Her face suddenly showed all its years, a ghastly colour under her make-up.

'I'm really hungry. Could we all get a burger, do you think?' Theo asked, exchanging glances with her grandmother.

Tom pulled himself together. 'Definitely. I'm starving, too. Let's go, guys. There's a restaurant just along here.' He wheeled his chair round, this time avoiding toes and other stray limbs, and began to trundle down the long corridor. Amazingly, the girls followed, towing their brother, who blinked but only murmured, 'Chippies?' half to himself. Their grandma bit her lip, and Tom gave her a wave and a thumbs up, which seemed suddenly inappropriate as the silent nurse waited in the background.

So that was how a man whose experience of children had previously been restricted to glaring at the ones who lay on the floor and screamed in Sainsbury's found himself seated at a grubby table, surrounded by cartons of red sauce, with a tired small boy on his knee, trying to avoid the nosy looks of the other customers. And actually, he was having fun. Sort of.

5

The days leading up to Jake's funeral were hideous. Afterwards, everything was blurred, but Molly knew she would never forget the gut-wrenching pain of telling the children what had happened. She couldn't understand how they'd got through the rest of that first day. Their neighbour with the truck had fetched them home from the hospital, unable to meet Molly's eyes, and Max had immediately retreated to the play-room to watch back-to-back films, clutching his teddy.

'Is Tom coming round later?' he asked, pausing on his way out of the room.

'Tom?'

'Painting Tom, you know who I mean.'

'Oh, right. Your gran said he was at the hospital, but I didn't see him. No, he's not coming round. Not unless you invited him?'

'I didn't know if I was allowed. He's nice, isn't he? Tom bought us chippies,' said Max.

'Yes, he's a kind man to look after you and feed you all. I don't know his phone number or I would ring him to say thank you.'

Max sighed and left the room, shoulders sagging. Hattie followed him. Her older brother would be here soon and she wasn't his favourite person at the moment, having dropped his mobile in the bath on his last visit.

Sam arrived soon after, white-faced and stunned, having cadged a lift from his college fifty miles away. Unable to sit still, he went straight out to cut the hedge. Molly tried to get him to calm down.

'Look, love, you don't need to do that. Come and have a drink and talk to us?'

'I just want to get this done, Mum. It looks like Dad meant to do it – the shears are already out and he's... he'd started hacking away at it already.'

'But why now? We can do it tomorrow, or next week. There's no rush.'

'Mum, just let me get on with this, will you? I need to, that's all.'

His voice tailed off as he fought the tears that were never far away from any of them. They kept going on pot after pot of tea, but somehow Molly couldn't face any wine later or even the brandy that several people tried to press on her. For a woman who felt very much at home with a glass in her hand, this was odd.

The only explanation Molly could come up with was that she'd always associated alcohol with fun, and her throat closed up every time she looked at Jake's carefully stocked wine rack. She had memories of him putting it together – a self-assembly kit with instructions that seemed to be in Arabic. He had cursed and muttered for hours, and the whole thing still had a kind of Leaning Tower of Pisa air about it. So many memories. A whole marriage full of them – lots of happy ones, but some that didn't bear thinking about.

In between making tea for her visitors and trying to persuade everyone to eat, Molly worried vaguely about what they should all wear for the funeral and whether the girls would be able to look half-decent. At least *they* had plenty of black to choose from. Eventually, she dug out her grey interview suit. It had a fitted knee-length skirt and a long, flowing jacket; perfect for looking smart but very boring. She couldn't resist adding a soft crimson scarf.

Jake had never approved of dark, depressing clothes for funerals. She remembered him just before his dad's service, announcing his decision to wear a red checked shirt and beige chinos. His mum had been mortified but he'd just shrugged and said, 'Look, it won't bring the old sod back if I go and buy a black suit, will it?' And in the end they'd all followed Jake's lead and worn something bright. It had helped a bit with the general gloom, but Molly had never been able to decide if he'd done it as a celebration of his dad's life or for reasons of his own.

There were too many phone calls in the days before the funeral, all beginning in the same way. Unutterably weary, Molly trotted out her standard list of responses.

'No, we just can't believe it, either.'

'No, he wasn't ill.'

'Well, yes, it could have been a stroke. We just don't know yet.'

'Yes, everyone will really miss him.'

'The children are doing as well as possible, in the circumstances.'

'Yes, of course I'll call you if we need anything.'

She didn't call them. Often, in those early days,

she listened for the door. He would be home soon, surely? She thought she heard the creak of his computer chair, and his tread on the stairs as he went in search of night-time biscuit supplies. The people she really wanted were the ones who turned up unannounced, brought a cake or a shepherd's pie, and went away when they could see that she'd had enough.

The very best of these visitors was Molly's favourite-ever friend, Shaun. She had never been very good at forging strong friendships, but Shaun was different. Skinny-hipped and elegant in his tight black jeans and shirt, he went a long way towards saving Molly's sanity. He was sparing with his sympathy, even though he'd loved Jake for all of his adult life. This had never worried any of them; as far as Molly knew, Jake had always been relentlessly straight and Shaun's sexuality had never been an issue. Jake had teased him relentlessly about his constant string of boyfriends, but once Simon had come on the scene, everyone had realised that Shaun was at last settling down.

Now, drinking copious amounts of Earl Grey, Shaun and Molly struggled to create a funeral that would do Jake proud.

'It's going to be awful, and then there'll be the bit

afterwards – that'll be the worst,' said Molly, stretching her aching shoulders and trying to concentrate.

'What bit?'

'You know, when everybody lines up to kiss the bereaved family.'

'Oh, Molly, loosen up a bit, can't you? People just want to show you they care.'

'I know, but I don't want to be expected to kiss everybody just because they've bothered to turn up.' Her voice broke. 'I wish my dad was here.'

'Yes, I was meaning to ask you about Geoff – your mum told me he'd run off with the floozie from the pub. What's that supposed to mean, and why didn't you tell me?'

Molly thought about this for a few moments. Why hadn't she discussed her dad's defection with Shaun? She supposed she'd been embarrassed. Her parents' marriage had been unstable for years. They had relocated to Norfolk to be near Molly and the family, and for a while things had improved. But since Geoff had taken the regular folk singing slot at one of the local pubs, he'd become a different person. His sudden decision to leave with the ravishing Thai barmaid had shocked everyone who knew him, and Molly was finding it hard to forgive him, although her mum only seemed to miss him for his skills in erecting shelves and planting tomatoes.

'It's a long story. He's living in Vietnam and finding himself, apparently.' Molly snorted. 'I hope it doesn't take too long. Mum's dying to get her hands on his pension, but he's managed to stop her so far.'

Shaun sighed heavily and rolled his eyes. 'Anyway, where were we? What about that nice poem about being in the next room?' he suggested, leafing through one of the books he'd brought with him.

'No. Jake thought that one was way too creepy; they had it at his dad's funeral. He said he kept imagining his dad in the kitchen, trying to float through the wall. Where have all these books come from, anyway?'

'Oh, they're Simon's. He's got a weird obsession with death at the moment. He really loves walking around graveyards – he especially likes the ones in places like Italy and France where you get a photo on the top of the marble plinth.'

'But isn't that... er... maybe a bit of an odd hobby?' Molly had never been too keen on Simon; in her opinion, he took advantage of Shaun's kindness by constantly arriving at his flat distraught and drunk in the early hours of the morning, borrowing money and clothes, and generally taking without giving. On the plus side, he did have a very cute bottom.

'Well, it keeps him off the streets, and there are lots of other poems in here,' said Shaun, 'or I could write one myself. I'd make a better job of it than this lot.' He waved a hand dismissively over the heap of books on the floor.

Bacon sandwiches and chocolate biscuits seemed to make the whole family feel a bit more human, so they all lived on those for most of the time that week. In the end, Molly and Shaun managed to finish the Order of Service just in time to get it printed. The picture on the front showed Jake pointing at the camera. He was wearing a battered trilby with a feather in it – his favourite hat.

Molly didn't know where the old photograph had come from. She had rummaged through their entire collection of snapshots during the last few days, but a lot of them seemed to have got lost over the years. She was sure there should be more. Jake had always refused to part with this particular one; it had always sat in a frame on the mantelpiece. He was holding a brimming glass of red wine, and his eyes twinkled out of the photo, making Molly's heart squeeze.

Her emotions were all over the place, but a weird and unreasonable anger that Jake had left her without warning was threatening to overwhelm everything else. She had loved him for so long, but after all they'd been through and the pain that they'd both inflicted on each other, she wasn't sure how much of the love was left, and how much of the ache in her heart was guilt rather than loss. Whatever the history between Jake and Molly, there was no doubt that her head was in a mess. The children and Shaun were suffering deeply, and the thought of getting them all through the funeral was almost too much to bear.

Molly finally decided that they would all follow the coffin into the church as the organist played 'Blackbird', one in the medley of Beatles songs Jake had sung to his babies when they wouldn't go to sleep. She had wanted to have a recording of it, but Shaun had told an awful tale of a funeral Simon had recently 'popped into' where Spotify had seized up at the crucial moment and the procession had entered in eerie silence, with feet shuffling and sniffing noises being the only sounds heard.

In the event, the service went quite well in a sur-real kind of way. No one was completely prostrate with grief, the waterproof mascara lived up to its promise, and Theo's intentionally laddered tights made her gran sigh with shame, but on the whole,

Molly thought Jake would have been pleased with his family. Despite her bacon sandwich diet, she'd somehow managed to lose half a stone, and Shaun said she looked quite good in a blotchy sort of way.

Louisa, Jake's deputy chef at the bistro, managed a few kind words about her irascible boss before she broke down in tears, and Molly remembered to thank everyone nicely for coming. She'd been touched to see Tom amongst the mourners, in a black jacket and what were obviously his best jeans, short blond curls still wet from the shower. He'd held her hands for a moment and some of his electricity had flowed into her, giving her the strength to deal with the remaining queue of people.

'Are you okay, Molly?' he'd said. 'Well, no, that's a stupid question. As if you'd be okay. I don't know why I said that.'

'I'm not so bad, really, what about you?'

'I feel a bit of a fraud being here – didn't know your bloke, but I just wanted to see if you were managing. There's nothing much else I can do, seeing as you didn't ask me to write you a poem for the service.'

She'd smiled at him, suddenly overcome with a longing to be wrapped in Tom's strong arms.

Bending down, she'd surprised herself by whispering, 'I just need a hug, Tom. Hold the poem, though.'

'Well, I can manage both those requests,' he whispered back. 'Here, or would that be a bit tacky?'

Molly laughed and hugged him for as long as she dared, then stood up ready to face the rest of the long line of well-wishers. After that, energised, she developed a new set of useful phrases.

'Yes, thank you, a lovely service. Jake would have been proud of the children.'

'Yes, Max is with his childminder. No, I don't think he'll feel as if he missed out when he's older, really; he is only six, after all.'

'No, I'm not going back to work for a week or two. Yes, I know keeping busy helps but I can't think straight yet.'

'Yes, they said it was a massive stroke. I know... totally out of the blue. No, there hadn't been any signs.'

'Yes, of course I'll ring you if you can help in any way.' And so on, until the hideous day ended, and Molly curled herself into a tight ball in the empty bed, heart aching too much to cry.

* * *

After the funeral, life seemed very quiet. Even though he'd felt out of place on the day, Tom had known he must go to the church – and Molly's hug had been his reward. He thought how brave and calm she'd managed to be; even when her daughters sobbed into her neck, she just wrapped an arm around each one and stared straight ahead at the huge display of flowers on the coffin.

Now the days dragged into October as Tom struggled to motivate himself. Most mornings he thought about going along to the bistro to see if Molly was there. Who would be running the place now? Someone must be there to keep the money flowing in, surely? But when he finally made it to the promenade and wheeled himself into the little restaurant for lunch, he could see that there was no need to worry. The thin, dark-haired lady who had spoken about her boss at the funeral was clearly in charge, ordering the waiters around and cooking up a storm.

'Louisa, table three, garlic prawns and a side order of tomato and basil salad,' the waiter shouted, and the reply came back immediately.

'Okay, Baz. We've got freshly baked ciabatta with basil if he wants some?'

The waiter raised his eyebrows at Tom, and he nodded eagerly. The smell from the little kitchen was heavenly, and the sizzling sounds were making his stomach rumble. Jake's manager, although scary-looking, was holding the fort beautifully.

Back at work later that day, Tom took a fresh look at his own empire. His studio was tucked away in the back streets of the town, on the ground floor of a large Victorian terraced house, with the shop and gallery on the front and enough of a ramp to make access easy. Sometimes he painted inside, but more often than not he left his gallery in Sasha's capable hands. He would haul his painting kit to the cliffs, the pier, the shops, the market, or anywhere else that the tourists might like to remember when they were back home.

The studio was usually the one place where Tom was completely at peace with the world. Hidden from the customers' eyes, at the very back of the building, was his workroom – organised chaos and great to come back to and take stock after a day outdoors. It was strange that lately its magic had waned. He tried his usual trick of putting the paints in order, rainbow-style, but even that didn't touch his apathy. Sasha flitted in and out, skinny as a liquorice stick in her long black dresses and biker boots, bringing stewed tea and Jammie Dodgers, wiping already clean surfaces and generally pissing him off.

A few customers stopped by to escape the drizzle, but left fairly quickly – gloom seemed to hang in the air like smog. One or two bought greetings cards to stay out of the rain, but on the whole the punters seemed to feel that even the disgusting weather was better than the chilly atmosphere in the shop.

So now what? Tom was seeing Molly every night in his sleep – long, feverish dreams where they ran along the beach, unhampered by his useless legs, the shingle, or mad dogs. How could he find a way to get to know her properly? His timing couldn't be worse. The last thing she would want at the moment would be a lovesick hanger-on. He could feel himself getting seriously morose – even Sasha was concerned.

'Tom, why don't you take your stuff and go down to the pier? You need some fresh air and you can paint under cover there. We could do with some of those great little pictures of the crab fishermen; they go really well with the visitors,' she said, hopefully.

'Look, just stop interfering. I don't want bloody fresh air and I don't want to paint anything else *cute*!' The words were out of his mouth before he realised how true they were. Against his better judgement, he had restocked, and the shop was full of nice safe pictures. He wanted to paint dangerously now – to splash colour around in great nose-bleeds of red, and tarry masses of black. He wanted to use clashing bile greens and hot pinks, and layer the paint on with a huge spatula. He wanted to live dangerously for a change.

'So... don't.'

'What do you mean?' Tom stared at Sasha. Her arms were folded across her chest. He'd never seen her looking quite so stern, even in her grumpiest moods.

'You want to make changes, so go ahead and make them. Take some time out. The storeroom's full of your cute stuff, as you call it. I'll restock every now and again and take care of the shop. My sister Jodie can keep an eye on your bedsit. She's always saying she wants to come for a long visit. She's sweating over her dissertation, and she can do that anywhere.'

'But where would I go?' Tom's heart had begun to pound. If he went away, he'd lose the chance to get to know Molly better, but maybe space was what she needed too. Space and time to grieve.

Sasha was waving her arms about now as she thought aloud. 'Find somewhere with a craggier kind of vibe. Lashing waves, storms at sea, that kind of thing. Go to... hey, I've got it. Let's do this thing properly. You know Jodie lives quite near to one of the wilder stretches of the Scottish coastline? You could do a flat swap. Shall I message her and see if she's up for it?'

Tom took a deep breath. The passionate desire to experiment and to see if he could really achieve his dream fought with the equally strong urge to be with Molly. Common sense won. He'd take two risks. To possibly fail and to miss the opportunity of being with his dream woman. There was only one way to find out if he could do this.

* * *

The following months seemed to drag for Molly. Tom's brief message to explain why he wouldn't be around for a while hit her hard. She hadn't realised how much she was enjoying getting to know him until he suddenly wasn't there any more. Some days just the effort of getting the children organised and making herself go to work seemed way too much, and the grief for Jake came in huge, unexpected waves. Sometimes she felt as if she was coping quite well but then another breaker would hit her and down she'd go again. There was no rhyme or reason to the process. Time passed, punctuated by fairly regular emails from Tom. He was painting day and night, apparently, and his stay in Scotland kept being extended. It was hard not to envy him and resent his freedom as Molly battled through the endless days of routine and sadness.

But then right at the end of October, when the shops were full of Hallowe'en masks, the fireworks were already going off in the parks and Tom had messaged to say he was finally back in his old flat, the first box arrived to weave Shaun's magic.

Molly read the enclosed letter twice, found the folded note and the bell, and was just about to investigate further when Theo's voice from downstairs made her jump so hard that she bit her tongue. Cursing to herself, she heard the insistent cry of, 'Mum. Muuuuuuuum!' and pushed everything under the duvet, rushing out onto the landing before Theo could think of coming upstairs to find her.

'I'm here. What's up?'

'Hattie and Max are fighting! Tell them, Mum.'

'You tell them, Theo – or get Netflix on, would you? I'll be down in a minute.'

Silence, then, 'Okay. Can I borrow ten quid? Nat texted me, she wants to go to the cinema.'

'Help yourself. My purse is in my bag.'

'What's for dinner?'

Molly thought for a moment. Who cared what was for dinner? 'What about pizza?'

'We had pizza last night.'

'Hmmm – Chinese then?'

'Mum, when are you going to start cooking properly again? We're fed up with takeaways.'

'Theo, you're plenty old enough to do some cooking yourself. You and Hattie can cook tonight. Take an extra twenty and get some proper shopping.'

'But Mum... I only know how to do pasta bake.'

'That'll be fine if you make a salad to go with it. See you later.'

Molly held her breath and waited for the explosion, but after a couple of minutes, the muffled swearing stopped and she could hear Theo crashing about looking for the purse. Heading back to the bedroom, Molly sat down and uncovered her loot. The little indigo box seemed to glow, shiny with silver stars and full of secrets. Somehow, the disturbance had cleared the air and she didn't delay the moment any longer, but opened the folded paper with shaking hands. She looked down at it, blinking hard at the scrawl of writing.

Hi Moll,

Here's your first clue, and I'm making it easy to begin with. I'm warning you now, they're all going to be in rhyme, because...

well, because I can. I'm doing this for you –
hope you'll see why eventually. Never forget
how much I love you, and don't waste time
being angry with me. I know you'll wonder
what all this is about and probably question
my motives, but they're all good – honest!
   Shaun xxx

   So you're right on the brink of your
        quest,
   Will your courage be put to the test?
   To find out about Jake,
   The first step you must take,
    Is to turn your face now to the west...

(Or in other words, call this number and ask for
Dot.)

Quest? What was all that about? Molly looked
down at the sheet of writing paper. Was she going to
be plagued from now on by men who wrote terrible
poetry? Was her life about to become even more
complicated? Since the awful day in September
when Jake had gone forever, she felt as if she had
been spiralling further and further away from anything resembling normality. If only she could ring

Shaun and ask him what he was playing at, but he'd told her at the outset that he was going to leave his state-of-the-art phone at home, and wasn't even going to try to pick up his emails.

'I'm going native, Molly,' he'd said proudly. 'Simon won't agree to it; he still wants to be in touch with everybody, but I reckon if we're going travelling, we should do it properly.'

'But what if there's an emergency?'

'There won't be. And anyway, if there was, you could ring and leave a message on Si's phone. But what could I do stuck in the middle of nowhere?'

'You could talk to me? Is that too much to ask?' Molly cursed herself for sounding like her mother, but she had never felt so lost.

Shaun had sighed heavily. 'Look, you know that if I can be contacted, my mum'll expect me to ring her at least twice a week and she'll be texting me every day. Then if I don't answer, she'll alert the emergency services.'

'True. It's just that I'll miss hearing your voice.'

'You'll find things to distract you.' Shaun had refused to meet her eyes when he said this. He must already have been planning this box idea, Molly thought grumpily. Shivering, she reached for the phone on the bedside table. There was no point in ringing Simon, he always let his phone go to voice-mail anyway. And there was also no good reason for putting off calling this mystery person, Dot – one of the things that had driven Jake mad about Molly, she remembered with a pang, was her lack of decisive-ness. She tapped in the number written at the very bottom of the note and the call was answered on the second ring.

'Hello? Who's that?' The voice on the other end of the phone sounded young, female, and not too pleased to be disturbed.

Molly took a deep breath. 'Hello. Is that Dot?'

'Who wants to know?'

'Erm, I'm Molly... Molly White. Sorry to bother you – this is a bit of a weird question, but does the name Jake White mean anything to you?'

Even saying Jake's name had been an effort, and it was a few seconds before Molly realised that there had been no reply. 'Excuse me, are you still there? Hello?'

'Yeah, I'm here. Why do you want to know?'

'I just wondered if you were going to speak to me. I'm Molly White,' Molly said, bemused at the question.

'Duh! No, I mean why are you asking if I know Jake?'

Molly hesitated. Why exactly did she want to know, and who was this rude girl? She had an overwhelming urge to slam the phone down, collect the remaining children, and head for the beach. Who cared if Jake had been hard to understand? He'd gone, he wasn't coming back, and this was all a complete waste of time. Despite herself, she began to cry – great heaving sobs that hurt her throat.

The girl gasped. 'No, don't do that, I'm sorry, you just took me by surprise. Look, can we meet? *Stop crying, will you?*'

Her shout made Molly sit up straight and grope for a tissue. She gulped and sniffed a few times, then croaked, 'Yes, please.'

'Okay, can you get down to the seafront or shall I come to you?'

'Do you know where I live? Do you... it sounds as if you already know who I am?'

'Of course I know who you are. I could meet you on the pier in half an hour if it's important? Is it important, Molly?'

The girl's use of her name was somehow reassuring. Molly thought for a moment.

'Yes, I can do that, but give me an hour. I have to sort someone out to be with the kids. How will I recognise you?' This was beginning to sound like a very bad spy movie. The girl laughed.

'Oh, you'll spot me – I'm fairly obvious. I'll meet you by the old theatre at the end of the pier. See you soon.'

Molly held the phone tightly. 'Wait, I...' But the girl had gone. She sighed.

Somewhere along the line, she seemed to have accepted Shaun's quest. Maybe if she began to find out everything there was to know about Jake then this terrible tightness in her chest and the painful lump in her throat would begin to subside. But why *had* Shaun decided to do this? He must have been up to his eyes in packing, sorting out his flat, putting his four cats in the cattery, and generally preparing for the biggest adventure of his life. It all seemed completely mad. In character, she supposed – Shaun had always liked a mystery – but when had he found time to set Molly a treasure hunt, and what on earth was the point of it all?

She crashed around getting organised, bringing her ever-helpful next-door neighbour, Edna, in to stay with the children, putting on extra layers, and putting off thinking about the coming meeting. Finally she was ready, and the rush to get to the seafront warmed her up and distracted her even more.

The pier was quiet today. A blustery late-autumn day on the east coast wasn't a good time to enjoy the seafront, thought Molly, grimacing at the sight of the churning sea through the wooden slats. She could feel the boards shaking under her feet as she hurried along, the wind buffeting the pier's ancient supports. Getting nearer to the theatre building, she saw the girl, who seemed to be standing as close as she could to the meagre amount of shelter. There wasn't much respite from the wind anywhere today. Lifting a hand in greeting as the girl turned, Molly froze. Her heart began to thump. There was something all too familiar about the figure by the wall.

6

The girl's hair – a mad explosion of turquoise and green dreadlocks – blew around her face, and she grabbed at it with both hands as she watched Molly approach. She deftly twisted it into submission and flipped a large scrunchie around it. She was huddled into a sheepskin coat that reached nearly to her flowered Dr Martens, and her nose was blue with cold.

This girl was Sam's double in female form, but much smaller than Molly's lanky firstborn. She had the same dimple in her left cheek, identical freckles over her snub nose, and a smile like sunshine. Molly tried to move but her feet refused to obey her brain.

The two women looked at each other for a long moment. Molly's stomach clenched and she felt a slow wave of anger breaking over her head. Christ, it hurt. There were so many questions that would never be answered. Why had Shaun done this to her, when she was so full of hurt already? Wasn't he supposed to be her best friend? She supposed she should have expected a surprise like this – Shaun had known Jake so well and he had always had a slightly malicious streak. No, she corrected herself, it was probably more of a sense of drama and a liking for impact. But whatever Shaun's intentions, she was totally thrown by the sight of this beautiful creature who was now reaching out towards Molly. She took the girl's hands almost absent-mindedly, still mesmerised by the dazzling smile.

'It's good to meet you at last, Molly,' said the girl. Her voice was like Sam's, too, but higher and almost musical, as if laughter wasn't usually far away. Today, however, her eyes were shadowed.

'So you're Dot?' asked Molly. The girl nodded.

Molly continued, feeling her way. 'And obviously, you are Jake's daughter?' The girl nodded again, and Molly saw that her huge blue eyes were full of tears.

'Don't you mind? You don't seem angry. I thought you'd flip when you saw me. Dad said I was a chip off the old block.'

'Yes, you sure are. And yes, I think I'm going to be

extremely angry soon. I just don't know how to take this, that's all.'

'I know. I'm sorry.'

'Don't apologise. There'd be no point in being cross with you, would there? I'm just reeling at the thought of... well, your existence, I guess. You must know I had no idea. And how did Shaun know about you? Why didn't he tell me?'

The girl took Molly's arm and gently guided her to one of the rusty benches that lined the outside of the theatre. Molly had often sat here with Jake and the children before they'd moved to this town, when they were just holiday visitors. The view of the little town and the harbour misted over. Dot passed Molly a tissue, and Molly was surprised to see both their hands shaking as she took it.

'I didn't want you to find out like this. Dad always said he was waiting for the right moment to talk to you about me, and I respected that. Then, after he... he died so suddenly, I couldn't just turn up and introduce myself, could I?' Dot said, as Molly blew her nose noisily. She had never been able to cry like a romantic heroine – there was always mess.

'Right. And Shaun?'

'He sometimes drinks in the pub where I've just got a job. I noticed him staring at me one night. He was totally wasted, or I don't think he'd have said anything. But I seem to look just like one of your sons? He said he'd got something really important to tell me and asked for my number, then he rang me the next day when he was more or less sober.'

'Do you give every bloke your number just because they ask?' Molly could hear the disapproval in her voice, and saw Dot flinch.

'No, course I don't, but there was something about the way he was looking at me – there were tears in his eyes. I was curious, that's all... and I needed a distraction. Life's been a bit of a bitch lately. And you've got to admit, he's a cute guy?'

'Oh, yes, he's cute all right. And funny. And he's got a terrifically kind heart. Maybe you just sensed he was one of the good guys?'

'Maybe. Anyway, Shaun said he'd been doing some thinking.'

Molly nodded. If you ignored the dreadlocks and make-up, she could see why Shaun hadn't taken long to notice the family features; he had known all the children since they were born. She glanced across at Dot, who was biting her bottom lip and staring at the toe of one of her boots as if it held the answer to everything.

'Look, don't look so tragic, it's not your fault. I was

just a bit taken aback,' said Molly, thinking that this could qualify for the understatement of the year. 'I don't know where to start, though. Is it okay if I ask you some questions?'

'Be my guest,' said Dot. 'I've wanted to meet you and your children ever since I tracked Dad down.'

Molly took a deep breath. 'So... well... how long have you known about Jake?'

'It was just before my mum died early last year.' The girl rubbed her eyes. 'Mum knew she only had a little while left, and she wanted to make sure I had someone of my own in the world. I'm an only child – at least, I thought I was.'

'I'm so sorry to hear about your mum. But who was she? And... how old are you?'

Dot looked at the floor. 'It's okay, Molly – it was before you married him. I know I look like a teenager, but I'm twenty-two. My mum met Dad when he came on holiday here with his parents. They had a bit of a fling, but they didn't keep in touch. She never even told him she was pregnant. She said there was no point.'

'What do you mean?'

'Well, he told her right at the start that he was serious about someone at home. She knew she was just a holiday romance for him. But it wasn't like that for Mum – she always loved Jake. She never met anyone else who matched up, so she said.'

Molly sat in silence for a few moments, trying to get her thoughts together. Even for Jake, this was a ruthless, self-centred way to behave, starting a relationship with someone when he was supposed to be with Molly, and getting the other girl pregnant. Even if he hadn't known about the baby, he had obviously not taken much care to avoid it.

And now here was Jake's daughter – the children's half-sister. Molly well remembered the time when Dot must have been conceived. She and Jake had had a minor fall-out because Molly had wanted to go with Jake's family on holiday but it would have meant them sharing a room and his mum had said a resounding 'No'. Molly had thought that Jake should have stayed at home as a protest but he had gone off quite happily and come home brown as a berry. Now she looked back, Molly remembered with dawning realisation that Jake had definitely seemed a bit smug. She took a deep breath.

'You haven't told me how you tracked him down.'

'Oh, it was on Facebook. I found him really easily, and when I rang him, he said straight away that we should meet up. He always meant to tell you,' she said, seeing Molly's expression, 'and he wanted me to meet you all. He did, honestly. I'd been feeling a bit lost since Mum started being so ill. I was so happy to find him.'

'So where did you meet?' This seemed to be hurting them both more and more. Why had Shaun done this to her? Why did she even need to know about Dot? And now that she did, how could she walk away from the pain in the girl's eyes?

'He came to meet me at the church on Green Lane.'

'Church? But Jake didn't like going to church.'

'No, it wasn't like that. I'm a member of the bell ringing club. A campanologist,' she said proudly. 'Dad came to watch us practise and joined the club straight off.'

'He did? That's bizarre.'

'Why?'

'He wasn't the joining type.'

'No, I guess he wasn't. But he wanted us to have the chance to get to know each other, so maybe he was prepared to change.'

Molly blinked. This girl was just as direct as her dad had been. 'Hmm. So, when did your club meet?'

'Thursday nights.'

'He told me he needed to get fit and he was going to go for a good long run once a week.'

'Well, he was – he ran to Green Lane. And back.' Her grin was infectious, and against her will, Molly started to laugh. She pulled the little silver bell out of her pocket.

'You're my first clue, Dot. Don't look so worried – I'll explain later – it's a kind of treasure hunt, I think. I just hope the other ones aren't this spectacular. I'm going to have to start drinking again if they are.'

'You've stopped drinking? I was just going to suggest buying you a large glass of wine at The Anchor. I've got so many things I want to ask you. Sometimes I can't believe he's gone. To find him like that and then to lose him again so quickly...'

Molly patted the girl's arm, trying to swallow a violent rush of resentment at the way Jake seemed to have been building up a cosy relationship with his daughter in secret. 'Who told you about Jake's death, Dot? You must have been devastated.'

Dot blinked. 'Don't start me off. It's bloody typical. All these years of wanting to meet him, and now just when I thought we could get to know each other, he goes and bloody dies on me.' She looked sideways at Molly. 'After Dad didn't turn up at the club, I was worried about him. I went to the bistro and said I was an old friend of the family.' She rubbed her eyes. 'No, I'm not going to cry today. I decided when I got up, this was going to be the start of the new me. But I daren't come to the funeral. I thought you'd flip. Dad showed me some photos so I knew how much I looked like Sam.'

'I probably wouldn't even have noticed you. I was even weirder than usual that day.'

They sat in silence for a few moments. The wintry chill seemed to have soaked right into Molly's bones. She longed for hot chocolate, preferably laced with a very large brandy. Even more than that, she wanted to escape from this stark reminder of Jake's faithlessness. 'Look, I've got to go now,' she said, 'the kids are only with my neighbour until she goes to bingo. I take advantage of her good nature far too much already.'

'But there's still so much to say. Don't go!'

Molly stood up and wrapped her scarf more warmly around her neck. She shivered, overcome by her own and Dot's pain.

'I'll ring you when I've had time to think about all this. Next week, maybe.'

'Will you?' Dot's voice wavered.

'Yes, I promise. Dot... do you mind me asking, what was your mum's name?'

Dot met Molly's eyes fearlessly. 'She was called Ginny, and she was beautiful.'

Molly turned and walked away, before Dot could see the tears streaming down her cold cheeks.

* * *

As Tom splashed away in his studio, throwing paint at the enormous canvas, he felt properly alive for the first time in years. All the pain of being unable to walk seemed to be flowing out of him and pouring into his latest wild, hideously exciting seascape. He had never dreamed that letting go could be so mind-blowing.

As he painted a small boat, tossed on the crazy, multi-coloured sea, Tom thought about Molly. On the side of the brave little craft, he wrote her name, in red and gold.

The canvas was finished. Tom sat back in his chair, wiped out with exhaustion but full of a growing sense of purpose. Up until now he'd felt a fraud; an artist, yes, but only in name. Now, the picture in front of him glowed with colour, life and promise. A few more like this to go with the ones he'd completed in Scotland and he could set up a whole new exhibition in his gallery. And then he'd reconnect with Molly.

But maybe she would have moved on by now.

Why would a grumpy guy in a wheelchair stay on her mind when life had given her such a kick in the teeth? Her emails in response to his over the last few months had been friendly but no more, and he'd deliberately kept his own light. Could he risk finding out that this was all just a one-way crush?

7

Over the course of the next week, Molly changed her mind several times a day about phoning Dot. On the one hand, she was deeply curious. What had Dot's mother been like? Had she ensnared Jake? Or had he just been out for a good time and gone out of his way to sleep with someone else? Had Jake deliberately set out to be unfaithful with Ginny? And why had Shaun kept all this to himself? Why not just tell her, for pity's sake? She missed her best friend's teasing and his off-the-wall way of looking at life – this was just the sort of thing they would have discussed end-lessly if he'd been here.

Several times a day her hand hovered over her phone and then withdrew. What was there to say?

Molly's anger, usually slow to come to the boil, now consumed her and she raged at the unfairness of being unable to challenge Jake or even to ask Shaun what his game was. Once, in a fury, she rang Simon's mobile, but a tinny voice told her that it had not been possible to connect her. No surprises there, she thought bitterly.

Watching for the postman also became part of Molly's daily routine, but the lack of new deliveries was frustrating. What sort of quest was this, if it only had one clue? She wondered if Shaun, knowing her tendency to put things off, had expected it to take longer to pluck up her courage to ring Dot. He had always teased her for procrastinating. She wanted to show him that she was capable of changing, but to do that she would have to contact Dot and make a start on a new sort of relationship.

The old Molly would have flatly refused to even consider dealing with the product of Jake's cheating, but now, as the days slowly passed, she felt herself questioning her own logic in pushing Dot away just because Jake had been less than perfect. Finally, when the younger children were busy painting in the kitchen with Theo, Molly retreated to her room and rang Dot's number.

'Do you want to come round, Dot?' she heard herself asking.

'What, to your house? Now?'

'Of course to my house. Come for coffee in an hour, if you're free. I'll send the kids down to the park for a little while. I don't know if I want them to meet you yet.'

After that, things happened very quickly, as if once Molly had taken the brake off her usual restraint, she was freewheeling out of control towards a future where new children appeared and were painlessly absorbed into the nest like baby cuckoos. In the space of a fortnight, Dot had met Theo, Hattie and Max – who had all pronounced her 'well cool' – and she had FaceTimed with Sam. Out of the whole family, Sam's reaction had been the most dramatic. He'd seemed as bowled over as Molly with their physical likeness, and had even asked Dot if she had any baby photos so that they could compare notes.

Max had looked at Dot long and hard, and then nodded thoughtfully.

'You look a bit like my daddy,' he'd said, causing everyone to sniff hard.

'How do you wash your hair?' asked Hattie, gazing at the colourful halo around Dot's head.

'I don't,' she answered.

This reply pleased Hattie so much that she shared her bag of crisps with Dot, and got out Jake's handwritten book of favourite recipes to show her. Theo was a bit harder to impress, but finally cracked when she noticed Dot's tongue piercing.

'Did your mum actually let you do that?' she asked, leaning in for a closer look.

'Nah – just did it. Wouldn't do it again, though; it hurt like hell. The belly button one was a doddle, though.' And she raised her t-shirt to reveal a neat bar with a diamante 'D' in the middle.

After this, Dot dropped in at the house every few days, and was sitting drinking tea and dunking chocolate digestives in the kitchen on the first day of December when the postman finally brought the next parcel. After much soul-searching, Molly had already told Dot about Shaun's quest, and Jake's first-born had been fascinated by the idea, endlessly speculating about what the next one would hold.

'This is wicked, Molly, maybe there are more of us. What if every box has got a trail that leads to another brother or sister for me and the others? How great would that be?'

Molly wasn't bowled over by this idea, but the sound of the doorbell had her out of her seat and at the door before the chimes faded away. The second package was just as brightly wrapped as the last one. She brought it to the table, sat down, and placed it between them. The Others, as Dot called them, were all at school, so there was no need to rush upstairs. But Molly wasn't at all sure if Dot should see the next clue before she'd had time to check it out. Dot got to her feet.

'I know, I know. This is the time when I make a quick exit, but you'll ring me later, won't you? I can't wait to hear what it says.'

'I will. It'll be good to have someone to talk to about it.' They hugged. Dot's arms felt as strong as Sam's, and her firm embrace made Molly want to cry. Had Shaun guessed what a shock and yet a comfort this girl would be in such a short space of time? Molly had never been very keen on the random hugging that most people seemed to indulge in, but Dot had sneaked into her heart without warning and she was amazed at the feeling of closeness that was building between them.

As the door slammed behind Dot, Molly started to peel the tape off the parcel. This box was a deep forest green, with the texture of embossed silk. It was the colour of the best sort of Christmas tree. She thought about Christmas without Jake and resolutely pushed the thought away as she lifted the lid.

Inside was more shredded paper – silver this time – and Molly tipped the contents onto the kitchen table, holding her breath. There was the familiar folded pale green paper, and under the nest of silver was a tiny piece of plastic mistletoe. This time the message was painfully clear.

> *There's nothing quite like an old mate*
> *Catching up with their news can be*
>   *great*
> *And the time is just right*
> *So don't put up a fight*
> *Go to Leicestershire now, and find*
>   *Kate.*

* * *

(Go on, Moll – you've put it off long enough. You know you want to. This is therapy, and there's lots more to come. I've always fancied myself as an agony aunt. Sx)

Molly screwed the paper up and threw it at the wall, shocking herself by giving a wild banshee scream. Therapy? This one was going to be impossible. Kate – her friend since their schooldays, and the world's biggest scheming bitch. Molly's mind flipped back to the village where she and Kate had finally parted company. They'd always been closer than sisters; bingeing on cheap cider, flirting shamelessly with the sixth-form boys, knowing all each other's secrets, and eventually going through marriage and childbirth alongside each other. As Molly sat chewing her thumbnail, the phone shrilled. She snatched the receiver up.

'Hello? Oh, Dot. Yes, I've opened it. No, not another brother or sister for you this time.' She sat up straighter and made a decision – maybe Shaun was right and she did secretly want to do this. 'Erm, are you doing anything at the weekend? Do you fancy a trip to Leicestershire, by any chance?'

* * *

In Tom's studio, the December chill was getting depressing. He hated switching the heater on because it seemed to affect the way the paint dried, especially now he was using such vast quantities of it. The new canvases were ranged around the walls, madly colourful. Every time he looked at them, Tom felt a leap of excitement that was completely new to him. It was a primitive, heart-thumping jolt of passion. He wondered if he would ever feel that way with a woman.

Instantly, his mind flew to Molly; soft, sweet-smelling Molly with her wild tangle of curls and her smooth skin. He longed to touch her – to just hold her close and kiss the hollow of her throat, to nuzzle the curve of her neck. He moved restlessly in his chair. He'd been reading about sex on Google over the last few days – not just random things, but specifically for people like himself who felt strong and vital and seemed to have everything in working order but were terrified of risking failure. He thought for a moment and then reached for the phone.

'Hello?' Molly said breathlessly, answering after only two rings.

'Oh, hi, it's Tom, I was just wondering... erm...' Why hadn't he thought this through?

'Tom – I've been meaning to ring you. Max wants me to ask you round for tea sometime now you're back from your travels. We've... he's missed you. Could you stand it?'

'Well, tea would be great, but I just thought if you were free tonight, maybe you'd like to go for a drink?'

'Mmmm, if you only knew how tempting that sounds. But I can't ask Edna to sit again yet.'

'Edna?'

'My neighbour. She's getting on a bit so I try not

to ask her too often, and there isn't anybody else I can get at short notice. Is there a reason?'

'How do you mean?'

'For us going to the pub. Are you wanting to celebrate? It isn't your birthday, is it?'

'No, but I've just finished some new paintings, and I wanted you to see them. Never mind, it was a crazy idea.'

'Not crazy – I really wish I could come out. Another time?'

'Sure.'

As Tom put the phone down, he realised that Molly hadn't asked him round for a specific day. It must have been just another of those meaningless invitations. He sighed, and began the laborious process of going home.

8

The A47 was quiet as Molly and Dot sped westwards. Molly had thought about taking the train, but the station was a long way from the village where Kate still lived. The thought of having to rely on buses or taxis, and being stuck without an escape route, had made her swallow her sadness and get Jake's ancient Land Rover out of the garage for the first time since his death. Her own car had recently given up the ghost and had to be scrapped. She held her breath as she turned the key, but Jake's pride and joy had been well looked after in the past and after only a short, apologetic cough, it started first time.

'Wow, Molly – great wheels,' said Dot, as they ne-

gotiated Wisbech and headed for the outskirts of Peterborough. 'Bit tatty, but I love vintage.'

'I'm glad you like it, but it's so big,' Molly answered, distracted by a tractor almost blocking the
road.

'Go on, you can overtake in a minute. There's
nothing coming and that sign says there's a crawler
lane just ahead.'

Molly closed her eyes briefly, said a prayer to the
God she had neglected for years, and pressed her toe
to the floor. The car lurched forward and Dot
cheered, waving to the tractor driver as they cleared
the brow of the hill.

Switching the radio on, Dot relaxed into her seat
but Molly gasped as the CD player kicked in instead
and Jake's choice of music flooded the car. That was
one thing she'd always loved about the age of the car.
When she and Jake went out in it together, they'd
always played their old CDs. This one was a compilation that she'd spotted in a charity shop and given
him for his last birthday. He'd seemed unimpressed
when he opened it, and Molly had thought the CD
had probably been abandoned somewhere. She'd
been hurt at the time. Now, the sound of the music
from their early years together filled her ears – a
backing track for impromptu parties, their wedding

and the newly married months before Sam had been born.

'This track's great, what's it called?' asked Dot, reclining her backrest and putting her booted feet on the dashboard.

'Your dad wouldn't have let you do that,' Molly snapped, realising the music had changed to the song she and Jake had had their first shuffling dance to at their wedding.

Dot flicked a glance at Molly and put her feet back down. 'I know this one – it's "Truly Madly Deeply". Did you ever see the film with that title? My friend's mum made us watch it once, but it made us both cry.'

'Mmm,' Molly grunted, trying to stem the flood of memories that were washing over her. Where had the years gone? And had Jake been reminiscing, too? She thought back. The Land Rover hadn't been taken out very often, with Jake working so near to home – the last time he'd been anywhere in it must have been when he went to the wholesalers to chase up an order in the August before he died.

Molly remembered the date well. She had wanted him to take the day off so they could all go to Norwich to buy new school uniforms, but she'd ended up dragging the three younger children there on the train. It had been a hellish experience and Jake had annoyed her intensely by returning late in the evening, when dinner had been kept warm for a very long time. But he must have been listening to the CD that day. She remembered him breezing in, bringing an expensive bottle of red wine for them to try, and swinging her around the kitchen, trying to kiss her, until she'd pushed him away, frazzled by the children's bickering.

Molly blinked hard at the memory and resolutely put all this heart-searching out of her mind, concentrating on getting to the outer rim of Leicester. She needed her wits about her to get through the middle of the city and safely out the other side and was relieved to see that Dot's eyes were now closed, so there was no need for conversation. The village where Kate lived was the same one where Molly and Jake had grown up. In the heart of the coalfields, it had been a safe haven, but very dull. Molly's mum and dad had run the village store, and her mother-in-law had been a stalwart of the Methodist chapel. The children had gone to school there. Molly shivered as she remembered the reasons why they had left.

After a while, Dot stretched luxuriously, sat up and looked around, rubbing her eyes. She had been sleeping for the last half hour, head pillowed on her jacket.

'Are we nearly there?' she said.

Molly laughed. 'Yes, you've been very good, you can have some sweeties when we stop.'

Snorting, Dot took a big swig from her ever-present giant bottle of water. 'What do you want me to do while you go and visit your friend, Molly? I bet you'll need quite a bit of time to catch up. I'll go and have a walk if you drop me somewhere with a view.'

'Okay, that'd be great. We'll park near Kate's house and I'll point you in the direction of the canal – it's lovely down by the lock; you can watch the boats go by, and there's a pub right on the waterfront. But don't walk down the canal path on your own, there's a much safer way.'

'You sound like my mum.'

'Oh, I'm sorry...'

'No, it's lovely. I miss having someone to nag me.' She grinned. 'Anyway, you can text me when you're done chatting and maybe we can go somewhere for some dinner?'

'I don't think I'll be as long as that, love. We won't have all that much to say to each other.'

'Won't you? But you haven't seen her since you left here. I bet you'll be gabbling away like crazy.'

Molly shrugged. 'Maybe. At least Kate's expecting me. I rang her so I wouldn't have to face her looking shocked when she opened the door.' Molly wished now that she'd told Dot a bit more about her relationship with Kate. She wondered how Shaun had known that she needed to come here; Jake must have confided in him, she supposed. It had been a pretty big secret at the time, but once they had left Leicestershire and were living by the coast, perhaps Jake had felt safe enough to talk about the whole thing.

Dot misunderstood. 'Yes, I know – I hate dropping in on people, too. You never feel quite sure if they'll be pleased to see you. And if they make a big fuss of you, you think they might be just trying to make you feel better. Oh, are we here?'

Molly had pulled up at the entrance to a very up-market estate at the edge of the village. The huge wrought-iron gates across the main driveway were firmly closed, but there was a speaker at the side of them so that you could announce your presence.

'Bloody hell, what does she do, this friend of yours?'

'She runs a high-class furniture store, and her husband's worked his way right up through the ranks at the local brewery. They work long hours and don't see each other much... or they didn't when we lived here. I suppose things might have changed now. They must be mortgaged up to the hilt to afford this place.'

'These houses are massive. Do you call this sort of thing Mock Tudor? All those little diamond-paned windows?'

'Yep, I guess that's what they are. A bathroom with every bedroom, three living rooms, and a swimming pool and hot tub in the back garden.'

'Whew! No sauna?'

'Yes, that's in an annexe. And a mini-gym. Kate goes for the "buns of steel" look.'

'Great. Oh, well, let's get on with the show. Which way to the canal?'

With Dot safely dispatched, Molly walked up to the gates and pressed the buzzer. A tinny voice asked her who she was visiting and the gates swung open, well-oiled and soundless. Molly climbed back into the car and drove in, parking on Kate's drive just as the glossy front door opened.

Kate stood framed in the doorway, heels as high as ever, hair just as short – red and spiky as Molly remembered – eyes narrowed as she gazed at her one-time closest friend. They had gone through primary school together as an exclusive gang of two, both uncomfortable with other female friendships.

Kate's given reason for concentrating all her affections on Molly was that all the other girls were mean to her. Looking back, this was debatable, thought Molly.

Kate had been the toughest in the class, male and female competition included. She had taken possession of the best table in the class on the first day at school, even though their teacher had had other plans. After a few minutes, Kate had waved her hand in the air imperiously.

'Mrs Johnson! Mrs Johnson!' she'd shouted.

The teacher had frowned over her glasses. 'Katherine, dear, you mustn't shout out in class. If you put up your hand, I will speak to you.'

'But I did, and you didn't, Mrs Johnson.'

'Patience is a virtue, Katherine.'

'What?'

'Never mind. What is the problem?'

Kate had stood up and elbowed the small, rather dribbly child in the seat beside her. 'I don't want to sit next to this boy, Mrs Johnson. He smells. And he's wet his pants. I want *her* to come and sit in this seat. After you wipe up his wee.'

Their teacher had looked at Kate's pointing finger as it selected Molly as her desk-mate, and then down at the floor to the puddle that had indeed formed under Kate's table. She had sighed and gone to fetch a bucket and mop. From that day on, Molly and Kate had been inseparable.

Kate hadn't much liked other people joining them, either for schoolwork or play, and Molly had been happy to go along with this rule most of the time. As a shy child, she loved Kate's protection against name-callers, and she had always been one for an easy life. Moving up through secondary school, the bullying had been harsher. Without Kate's intervention, Molly would have been constantly known as Fatty Mullholland, a name that still gave her unpleasant flashbacks.

Now, looking the adult Kate straight in the eye, Molly swallowed hard and stepped forward, teeth clenched.

'Hey, you,' said Kate quietly.

Molly cleared her throat, but couldn't seem to get any words out. She held out the piece of plastic mistletoe. Kate stared.

'Where the hell did you get that? I wondered where it had gone. Oh, I get it. That bastard Shaun took it. I told him all that stuff in confidence, but he never could keep his trap shut.'

'Shaun came to see you? When?'

Kate frowned thoughtfully. 'I guess it must have

been at the beginning of October. Yes, it was just after my birthday. Well, are you coming in, or what?' she asked, opening the door wider and exposing the thick emerald-green carpet of the hallway.

Molly followed Kate into the house, marvelling at the pristine white paintwork and the giant wall canvases that exactly matched the carpet and the orange walls.

'You've decorated again,' she managed to mutter.

'Well, it was getting very tired-looking. You know me, I hate shoddiness.'

'Really? You could have fooled me, Kate. What you did to me was about as shoddy as it gets.'

Kate raised her well-plucked eyebrows. 'Oh, so the gloves are off at last, are they? I thought we were never going to discuss it.'

'I was half expecting you at the funeral.'

'I didn't think I'd be welcome. I wanted to come. I wanted to be there so much.'

Suddenly they were both crying, and Kate took Molly's arm, leading her into the enormous kitchen. 'Here, sit down. I was going to be all posh and make a tray of tea and little cakes, but what we need is brandy.'

'I can't, I'm driving, Kate.'

'Sod it – can't you stay over? We've got a lot of talking to do.'

'No, I need to be back for the kids, and anyway, there's Dot.'

'Dot? Dot what? What's Dot?'

Molly was catapulted back down the years, to silly jokes, midnight confessions and no need to be serious about anything. But this was no time for nostalgia – there were scores to settle. She drew herself up to her full height.

'Kate, you're a two-faced cow. Stop trying to be all matey with me. You slept with my husband. I trusted both of you.'

'But you were giving him the big brush-off at the time. The poor bloke was frustrated. You were never much of a one for wild nights of passion, let's be honest.' Kate put up a hand to stop Molly's outburst. 'Anyway, I loved him, Moll. Really, really loved him. I can't bear to think he's never coming back, the grumpy, big-headed sod.'

'You loved him even though he was grumpy and big-headed?'

'Well, didn't you?'

There was a silence, broken only by the sound of Kate's black cat miaowing around their ankles. After a few moments, Molly nodded slowly. 'So, what's the deal with the mistletoe?' she asked.

Kate looked at the floor. 'It was from that Christmas party we all went to. You remember, my Steve's work do, when Jake and Steve were both still at the brewery? Jake was just about to kiss me under a big bunch of this stuff. Tacky, plastic crap, but it does the same job as the real sort, I guess.'

'You said he was just about to. What happened?'

'You happened, as ever,' said Kate, with a bitter laugh. 'You came and took him away to dance with you.'

'I guessed something was going on at the time – you both looked so jumpy. But you got your own back later, didn't you, Kate? Big style?'

'It wasn't like that. It wasn't about you.'

'What was it about then?'

'It was... well... I was hooked on him. Always had been, always will be. From Jake's point of view? I'll never know now. But he loved you, Molly. He loved you way more than you deserved. And he would never, ever have left you for me, if that's what you're worried about. Just ask Shaun.'

'I would if I could get hold of him. There are a lot of things I'd like to ask Shaun.'

Kate nodded sympathetically and began to pour

the tea. They drank in silence for a few moments, and then Molly took a deep breath. 'I just wanted to ask you a few things,' she said, looking down at the highly polished pine of the table and drawing a J in the tiny puddle of tea that had formed by her saucer.

'Go on then.'

'I don't know how to start.'

'Well, I can't help you there, can I?'

'No. Okay, so you and Jake.'

'Yes?' Kate was leaning her chin on her hands now, and watching Molly's artwork with the tea.

'How was it for you?'

'God, that sounds like a line from a cheesy porn film from the seventies,' said Kate.

'I mean it, Kate. Help me out; this is hard.'

Kate sniggered. 'You're doing it again.'

'Look, I'm serious. Cut the crap and just answer me!' Molly shouted, banging her fist on the table and overturning her cup.

There was silence as Kate, open-mouthed, stared at her friend's flushed face. After a few seconds, she picked up the cup and reached for a cloth.

'Leave the teacup, Kate,' said Molly, more quietly. 'This isn't about spilt tea. It's about you and Jake. You and *my husband*. Was it good?'

'Was what good?'

'The sex. Was it good with Jake?' Molly was crying now, great gasping sobs that hurt her throat and made her feel sick.

'Of course it was good. I wouldn't have risked the whole thing if it hadn't been good, would I?' Kate was looking down at the table again as she spoke, and Molly reached out and grabbed her by the shoulder.

'Look at me, will you? Was it perfect, you and him? Did the earth move, and all that stuff?'

'Course it bloody did. Why wouldn't it? Didn't you think that, Molly? He was gorgeous, was Jakey.'

'Jakey? Don't you dare call him that.'

'I can call him what I like. I've known him as long as you have.'

'Yes, but he was mine. My husband.'

'Yours, was he?'

'Yes.'

They looked at each other at last, like wrestlers mid-fight. Kate took a deep breath. 'This is going nowhere. You know I loved Jake and you know I slept with him. I'm not answering any more questions. If you don't want a brandy, we'll have to have more tea. And then we'll talk about something else, shall we?'

'Like what?'

'Like the kids. Like life? Like whether I need

those amazing crocodile shoes I saw online this morning?'

When Dot returned, laden with stems of berries from the canal bank and swaying slightly from the two pints of bitter she'd drunk at the pub, Molly and Kate had their elbows on the table, mirror images of each other with chins resting on hands, just like they used to sit in Molly's mum's kitchen when they were stuck with their homework.

Hearing the doorbell, Kate pushed herself up wearily and went to usher Dot into the kitchen, grinning at the girl's open-mouthed stare. Kate and Molly had both cried away their make-up, and Molly had run her hands through her hair so many times that it was a mad birds' nest of curls. Kate's spikes stood on end, and her shoes had long since been kicked across the floor. Molly caught Dot's glance and thought that she and Kate must look as if they'd done ten rounds in the boxing ring. She stood up reluctantly.

'We're going to have to make a move, Kate,' she said. 'I've only got Edna babysitting till seven, then she's off to bingo, and it'll take us ages to get home at this time of day.'

'Ring her up – you can sort something, can't you?

I want you both to stay, we haven't nearly finished yet.'

But Molly had had quite enough emotion for one day. She and Kate hugged, and Dot and Molly drove back out through the gates, out of the village, and back onto the main road. After half an hour of silence, during which she'd sneaked in another short nap, Dot roused herself and said, 'So, are you going to tell me what all that was about, or is it a secret?'

Molly smiled sadly. 'I suppose it is still a secret but you have a right to know about your dad if you want to understand him, warts and all.' When Dot nodded, Molly continued, 'Kate loved Jake right from when we were all teenagers, but I didn't realise until it was too late to do anything about it.'

'So, you're telling me my dad had a thing going with *her*?' Dot sounded incredulous.

'Well, yes, but not a "thing" – more of a fling, I suppose. We talked about it properly today. I would never let her speak before because I felt betrayed, but I kind of get it now.'

'Go on.'

'We – Jake and me – we weren't getting on very well at the time. He was about to be made redundant from the brewery, and he was really stressed. He'd always wanted to retrain as a chef, but we couldn't afford for him to go back to college while the kids were little.' Molly paused while she negotiated a particularly nasty bend in the road.

'Yes? Don't keep stopping, it's really annoying.'

'Sorry. He said he was going to use his redundancy payment to finance a new career and to set up in business. I was jealous of him following his dream, and I was just bored with my life, I guess. We drifted.'

'It happens,' said Dot, tersely.

'Yes. Anyway, to cut a long story short, Jake fell into the old trap of finding that people you've known for a long time and who fancy you rotten are much easier to sleep with than strangers. They chatted on Facebook. It wasn't long before they moved on to texting, then long phone calls, and finally into bed.'

'But when did you find out? What did you do? I'd have killed him, or worse.' Dot's eyes were flashing now and she had twisted around in her seat to face Molly properly.

'I found out when he left home to go and stay in his mum's old caravan in Norfolk.'

'With her?'

Molly couldn't help laughing at the outrage in Dot's voice. 'No, not with Kate. He just needed to get away. From me.' There, she'd faced it at last. She'd partly driven him away herself. She hadn't given him what he needed, either in or out of bed. Blame, always put squarely on Jake's shoulders, had subtly shifted in the last hour or so. Now she was sharing the guilt, and the cold, hard lump of resentment was gradually beginning to melt away. Shaun had been right. But it hurt to know that Kate had apparently enjoyed being in bed with Jake so much. What had been wrong with Molly that sex had so often seemed a bit of a chore?

'Well, you're a damn sight more forgiving than I could ever be,' said Dot, squeezing Molly's arm. 'Now put your foot down and let's get home, I'm starving. Don't forget you promised us all chips tonight. This music's driving me nuts, what else have you got?'

Dot began rummaging in the glovebox and soon unearthed a different CD. She ejected the last one, slotted her choice in and turned up the volume. George Harrison was singing about being handled with care. Molly had always loved this song but maybe the time had come to get over feeling wary of the pain. She had to stop expecting everyone to handle her with care. It was time to face the past. She was sure there would be more to deal with now Shaun had got into his stride, but she was a big girl. Bring it on.

* * *

Tom sat in the consultant's plush office in the private clinic above the hospital. He had always hated the idea of private medicine but this was urgent, and the NHS couldn't seem to help him – or, not this side of the next millennium.

'So, Mr Cavendish... oh, I'm sorry, you asked me to call you Tom. Your question is, how likely is it that you'll be able to form a lasting sexual relationship? Am I right in thinking that you haven't been sexually active so far in your life?'

Tom blushed. However many times he'd rehearsed this, it was always going to sound like an episode of *Jeremy Kyle* or *Oprah*. 'No, I've never slept with a woman. Or a man, for that matter.' He laughed nervously. 'I wasn't a precocious teenager.'

'I beg your pardon?'

'Well, I had my accident when I was only fifteen. And I hadn't quite managed to get anyone into bed with me by then.'

'Ah, I see. But that was twenty years ago – surely over the course of time you will have experimented? You were a healthy young man otherwise, I'm assuming?'

'I only experimented on myself, if you know what

I mean. I was too nervous to try with a girl for ages, and when I did, I got so far and bottled out. I think there must be something in my head holding me back.'

The consultant leaned back in his chair and looked at Tom over his glasses. There was a silence that seemed to go on much too long. Tom squirmed. Weren't doctors supposed to be rushed off their feet? Why was this taking so long? Finally he gave in.

'Okay, I guess I know what the real problem is. When I was in hospital after the accident, I was drifting in and out of consciousness for the first few days, but I could hear everything that was happening.'

'Go on.'

Tom sighed. 'I heard one of the doctors discussing my case with a couple of nurses. One of the girls was saying what a shame it was, and asking if I'd ever be able to lead a normal life if I recovered. She meant sex; I could tell by her voice. The doctor said it was unlikely. The other one asked him if that meant I could never have children. They were walking away by this time, but I'm sure it was a no.'

'I see. Of course you know that this was only one opinion, given when you were still very sick. But, if you don't mind my asking, why has the issue become important to you now? You are, I see from your notes, thirty-five?'

'Well, I've met someone fairly recently. And I want to know if I can ever offer her a normal relationship. Maybe even a baby. I need to be able to satisfy her.'

'So you've never made any concerted attempt to have sex since your accident? May I ask why not?'

Tom cringed. 'I know it sounds weird. Just scared, I guess. I've been close to it a few times but I backed off when it came to the... er... crunch.'

'I see. Well, I very much wish I could help you, but unfortunately this is out of my field of expertise. However, I do know a place where this sort of problem can be addressed. If you speak to my secretary, she will make you an appointment.'

'Thank you. Will it be fairly soon? Only, I really need to know one way or the other.'

'Oh, yes, I think we can help you reasonably quickly. And Mr Cavendish – Tom?'

'Yes?'

'May I just wish you the very best of luck? Although I have to say, looking at the facts, I don't think luck will be needed.'

The two men shook hands and Tom wheeled himself out towards the outer office, feeling more positive than he had for months. Was this all it was going to take to make mad, passionate love to Molly? A bit of bravery? A few appointments? A specialist who cared? Tom watched the consultant's pretty secretary wiggling her way down the corridor in her skyscraper heels and was consumed with sheer red-blooded lust for a moment. She turned, saw Tom watching, and grinned at him wickedly. It was a complicit look that said, 'I know what you're thinking and I don't care. I want you to look at my legs and my tight little backside.'

Tom shivered slightly. It was so going to happen with Molly. It really was. He was going to get over his stupid hang-ups and act like a proper man for a change. Wasn't he?

9

Molly waited with a mixture of excitement and trepidation for the next parcel to arrive. Shaun had referred to *all* the boxes in his first clue, but how many should she expect? And how many nasty surprises were in store? She was still feeling the after-effects of her meeting with Kate, but on the whole, Molly was able to think about the horrible Kate and Jake thing without too much pain now. It was a huge relief.

For a long time she had shied away from the issue, except in the middle of the night when, sleepless, she had not been able to resist torturing herself that Jake had apparently preferred Kate. But during the intense time of soul-searching in Kate's kitchen,

Molly began to accept that Kate had always felt the same sense of being second best.

She and Kate had chatted on the phone several times since Molly's trip to Leicestershire, and had arranged to meet after Christmas to talk some more. It was difficult not to be resentful after the first flush of forgiveness had worn off, but Molly was determined to try and put the whole thing behind her, even if waves of rage still threatened to engulf her in the wakeful small hours.

When she and Dot had got back from Kate's house, Molly had decided to do a proper job on getting the whole Kate issue out of her system and had forced herself go into the study to check if Jake's laptop was hiding any more secrets of his relationship with Kate. She had shied away from this room since Jake's death, feeling strangely uncomfortable in there, and had only been in briefly to fetch some necessary paperwork.

Jake's computer was usually kept in the locked middle drawer of his desk – he had been very security conscious. Molly took the bunch that held all Jake's keys and found the smallest one, slipping it into the well-oiled lock. The drawer opened smoothly and she stared. The laptop wasn't there.

After a few seconds of panic, Molly breathed

again. Of course! Jake had taken it to work when the accountant visited last time. Why hadn't she remembered before? But it had never occurred to her to look for the laptop – she'd always had her own computer and had never needed to access anything on Jake's. She reached for the phone.

'Louisa, it's Molly. Sorry to bother you, I know you must be busy, but is Jake's computer still at the bistro? It is? Can I fetch it tomorrow then? What? He did what? Oh. Okay, I suppose I'd better contact the insurance people tomorrow. You might have told me, though... yes, I can see you didn't want to upset me, but... oh well, never mind.'

Molly put the phone down, cursing the trainee waiter who had spilt a whole jug of water into Jake's laptop before it could be returned. Tears filled her eyes as she realised that she would never know the full story of Kate and Jake's fling. Their emails were lost forever now. She sighed. Oh well, maybe it was for the best. Reading other people's private letters was pretty low, and whatever she'd found, it would have been bound to hurt. It was probably better this way.

* * *

At last, just before Christmas, the postman arrived with a parcel for Molly. Hands shaking, she fell on the package, taking it to her usual refuge upstairs. She had tried to make the main bedroom into her own place rather than just a room where Jake no longer slept. Her pillows were piled up in the centre of the bed, and she had finally got around to moving Jake's heap of 'to be read' books from the bedside cabinet. His clothes had been bagged up and taken to the charity shop – Dot and Theo had helped, and the three of them had cried their way through Jake's wardrobe, ending up with just a few special things. They'd kept a soft blue Coldplay t-shirt, a checked shirt faded with age, Jake's favourite Levi 501s, and a torn and battered denim jacket from his student days. Molly had folded and wrapped them carefully and put them in the attic. There was no need to make anyone feel worse by unexpectedly coming across the clothes.

Strewing shreds of wrapping paper all around the bed, Molly could see that the latest box was red and gold. It was flat, oblong in shape, and covered in tiny holly leaves. She sighed. Christmas was only a few days away, and she still hadn't finished shopping. The green envelope was also decorated with holly, hand-drawn with Shaun's gold pen. The words

'Happy Christmas' were written above her name. Molly opened the envelope.

Hi sweetie,

    So, did you see Kate? And is the delightful Dot as much fun as Jake said she was? I guess you're coming along with the quest nicely now, if you've followed my first two pointers, but this one is from me to you.
Happy Christmas, gorgeous,
    Shaun xxxxxxx

Gorgeous? The only other person who had ever described her that way was Tom, thought Molly, with an involuntary shiver. She had always laughed when Shaun said nice things about her appearance, but if they both used the same word, maybe she wasn't so ordinary after all. She pulled in her tummy, which was much more streamlined than it had been in the past, and looked for the rhyme. A separate piece of notepaper had been hidden under the envelope, neatly folded, and almost covering something even more intriguing. Molly read the words out loud to the empty room.

An adventure is waiting for you

And a journey both retro and new
To complete your next quest
Find the one who'll know best
Why your dearest wish never came
     true.

Underneath the note was the most beautiful Christmas card Molly had ever seen. It was a hand-painted Victorian scene of a family gathered round a roaring fire. A black Labrador lay along the hearth, two children were opening presents, and the mantel-piece was festooned with striped stockings hanging in a row. A glittering Christmas tree stood at one side of the fireplace, and a little table was laden with mince pies and sherry. Molly opened the card.

Inside, Shaun had written:

I know it's a bit twee but next year I'm ex-pecting a Christmas just like this one. Keep the faith, best buddy. Love always – S x
     PS And remember what my mum always says – what doesn't kill you makes you stronger. xxx

Molly picked up the note again and re-read it, frowning. Shaun was getting obtuse now – the first two challenges had been easy to understand, if difficult to face in lots of ways. Who was the one who knew best? And what was her dearest wish anyway? She grabbed the phone. Dot was definitely needed here.

Two days later, with her second Christmas as a widow looming ever closer, Molly was no nearer to guessing the riddle. She and Dot had talked until they were hoarse, but neither of them could come up with anything sensible.

'But you must know what your dearest wish is, Moll?' said Dot, as they ploughed their way through the other last-minute shoppers in the town, collars turned up against the biting wind and rain.

'No, I don't. I've had lots of wishes over the last few years but none of them had anything to do with adventures. Last Christmas, I just wanted life to go back to how it was before. That was a pointless exercise. We muddled through but we were all still numb, I think. I'm going to make sure this year's better.'

'What other things have you dreamed of, then? I'm intrigued.'

'Well, I used to want to be a writer – I finished a novel just before we left Leicestershire.'

'Did you?' Dot's eyes sparkled. 'So why don't you do something with it?'

'Oh, it's probably rubbish. I can't face sending it out to people who'll only reject it.'

'Write a better one then! It's time you had a hobby.'

Molly's shoulders sagged. 'I can't write any more. I feel as if my brain's full of soup. And there's the Christmas shopping to think of, anyway. This ridiculous present buying's getting in the way of working out Shaun's stupid puzzle, and all I can think about is that Jake's gone. He's really gone, Dot. I think it's only just sinking in properly, after all these months. People seem to think I should be reasonably okay by now, but it doesn't seem to work like that.'

Tears began to pour down Molly's face. Dot looked round anxiously. People were beginning to stare. She glared ferociously as a woman pushing a double buggy tutted at Molly for blocking her path. Christmas lights were everywhere, and from the depths of a nearby shop Wizzard were singing about the snowman bringing the snow.

'Come on, let's get out of this madness,' Dot said, steering Molly into the nearest doorway. Blessed silence fell for a moment, as the door of the little shop closed briefly behind them and then flapped open again in the breeze. Shivering, they moved further away from the street into a well-lit room that smelt of vanilla and cinnamon. Looking round, Dot could see a thick red candle burning, the source of the wonderful scent. It had four wicks, all lit, and the flames were wavering in the draft.

'Could you close the door, please, ladies? It's freezing out there,' said a voice from the back of the shop. 'Come in and have a look round. I'm doing mulled wine today if you need warming up a bit?'

Molly wiped her eyes hastily on her mittens and looked down. A skeletal girl, dressed from head to foot in black, was adjusting a canvas that stretched from the skirting board almost to the ceiling. Her hair was long and straight, and her eyes were thickly lined with kohl. She smiled with unexpected warmth and carried on with her work. The painting was of a storm at sea, and Molly was momentarily shaken out of her gloom. The waves were multi-coloured, every shade of purple, navy, kingfisher blue and silver that she could ever have imagined. Cresting the highest wave was a tiny fishing boat, almost standing on its end. She moved closer. In tiny letters on the side of the boat was a single word.

Molly stared, blinking in the glare of the strong spotlight that beamed onto the picture. Was this

some sort of weird sign? She had come in out of the
cold and rain for refuge, tired and sad, and here was
her own name. What did it mean?

Dot had been prowling around the small
gallery as Molly gazed at the giant canvas. Turning
slowly, Molly opened her mouth to share the news
about the little boat but Dot was far too excited to
notice.

'Look over here, Moll – these are amazing!
They're all storm pictures,' she said, standing back to
get a better look. 'Are they by the same person?' Dot's
question was directed at the girl, who was now on
her feet and pouring steaming liquid from a pan that
had been keeping warm on a primus stove. She had a
tray of thick pottery beakers waiting, and she filled
two of them to the brim, handing one each to Dot
and Molly.

'Here, have a sit down and get that inside you; the
pictures are still going to be there when you've finished. You look shattered,' the girl said to Molly,
passing over a box of tissues. 'Have you come in on
purpose, or were you just getting out of the cold?'

'It was my fault. I pushed her in here to get away
from the gawping shoppers. Some people have got
nothing better to do than stare at a woman who's obviously having a bad day,' said Dot, downing her

mulled wine and looking hopefully into the empty cup.

'Have a top-up?' asked the girl. 'I'm Sasha, by the way. I don't usually fill the customers with free plonk but it's the first time Tom's let me display his new paintings, and I wanted to celebrate.'

'Tom?' said Molly, jolted out of her contemplation of the huge storm scene. Just hearing his name filled her with a sudden excitement, a leap of the heart and a lurch of the stomach that took her breath away for a moment. 'That wouldn't be Tom who paints on the beach, would it?' she asked Sasha. 'I thought he usually did pictures of the pier and the sea and the lighthouse, and boats. He's never told me where his gallery is, for some reason.'

'Well, these have all got sea and boats in them,' said Dot.

'Yes, but...'

'I know what you mean, they're way different from his usual style,' finished Sasha, grinning. 'I told him to paint some more of the ones that the tourists go for, but he insisted on doing his own thing. He said he was sick of wishy-washy stuff for the visitors and it was time he let rip. So this is what he came up with, bless him. All those months in Scotland paid off.' Sasha stood back and looked at the biggest painting, a mixture of pride and worry on her face. 'I just hope we can sell them, that's all. It's hard enough to keep going as it is.'

Her face changed as she heard a whimper from the room at the back of the shop. Dot smiled, too. 'Is that a dog I can hear?' she said.

'It's my German Shepherd. He's overdue for a walk, but I've got to wait for the boss to get back. I usually go down to the beach about this time and give Gnasher a good run. I don't know where Tom's got to.'

'I love dogs; can I see him?' said Dot.

'Course you can, I'll fetch him. Do you like dogs, too?' Sasha asked Molly.

'Oh, yes. I always wanted a dog when I was a child, but my mum said she was allergic to them. And then, when I was married, Jake just flatly re-fused to have one in the house. He would never say why. I was gutted. I thought at least when I had a house of my own I'd be able to have a puppy.'

There was a short silence. Dot was looking at Molly strangely.

'Was it your dearest wish?' she said.

'Was it my *what*?'

'Your dearest wish?' Dot said meaningfully. 'And

who would know why you never got it? Why your dearest wish never came true?'

'What are you two babbling on about?' asked Sasha, bringing in a bouncing Alsatian.

'Oh, nothing, we need to go home, we've got some talking to do. We'll be back again to look at the paintings properly, though, Sasha. Come on, Moll, you need to get your brain in gear.'

Sasha thrust a piece of paper at them. 'Hang on, leave me your phone number if you like the pictures. Then I can text you when I persuade Tom to have a proper exhibition. You'd come, wouldn't you? And ask your friends?'

'Oh, yes,' said Molly, scribbling her name and number down. 'I'd love to see Tom have some publicity – the new paintings are amazing. Give him my love, won't you? Hopefully we'll see him soon.'

Molly and Dot waved to Sasha and left the gallery with their heads down against the now driving rain, just as Tom approached from the other end of the street. He wheeled as fast as he could, but by the time he was within shouting distance, his quarry had disappeared down the alley towards the car park. He rolled into the gallery, as Sasha galloped past him.

'Where have you been? Gnasher's desperate for a pee.'

'Wait – Sasha – did you... I mean, was that Molly just leaving the shop?'

'Haven't got a clue. Her name and number are over there. She said she knew you, *and* she really liked your new stuff,' shouted Sasha, as she raced towards the beach. 'Especially the big one. And she said to give you her love.'

Sasha's voice died away, and Tom sat very still, looking at his newest work. So Molly had approved of the pictures. And sent him her love? He felt a rush of confidence, closely followed by desire. Maybe the consultant had been right. Perhaps all he needed was to let go?

10

Back at Molly's house, Dot flicked the kettle on, got out the red and gold box again, and put the clue and the Christmas card side by side on the kitchen table. As they waited for the tea to brew, Dot and Molly stared at the picture. Dot read the verse aloud.

'*Think*, Moll – look at the picture on the card and think what your dearest wish can be? Isn't it right there in front of you?'

Molly gazed at the idyllic scene. Of course! She'd always wanted a puppy, and this traditional scene summed up the whole cosy, dog-in-front-of-the-fire image. She vaguely remembered discussing pets with Shaun after a row with Jake when Theo had been mad keen to have a dog and Jake had once again put his foot down. Molly had been angry with him for weeks. She had desperately wanted them to do this together – to choose a puppy, maybe go to dog training classes, have family walks on the beach with their beautifully behaved dog, and generally to do what she'd never been allowed to do as a child.

Dot grinned. 'So – next step. Who would know why you were never able to persuade Jake to get a dog?'

Molly poured two mugs of strong tea and absent-mindedly opened a packet of ginger nuts. The obvious person to ask would have been Jake's mum, Daisy, but she'd had a stroke and died just before the move to Norfolk, and his dad had been dead for years. Aha – Jake's brother might know why the dog issue had been so important.

'I suppose I could ask Matt,' she said doubtfully, 'but he's eight years younger than Jake. He might not know anything useful.'

'Is that the one who lives in Brighton?' asked Dot. 'You said he came over for the funeral but then went straight back home. I'd really like to meet him – he *is* my uncle, remember.'

'Yes, that's Matt. He's lived there for years, and

Shaun knows him quite well, in fact they... but let's concentrate on the clue. I'll ring him.'

Dot fidgeted as Molly found Matt's number and had eaten three biscuits by the time the call was over. 'Well, that didn't sound very illuminating,' she said. 'All I could hear was loud music.'

'He was in a bar in town with a gang of his friends and he couldn't hear me properly, but he said he'd been planning to drive over here on Boxing Day with our presents, anyway, so we can ask him then.'

'I can't wait that long,' said Dot. 'The suspense is killing me. And don't you mind if he just turns up like that? My mum would have had a fit if someone had announced they were coming to visit us without any warning, especially at Christmas.'

Molly shrugged. 'No, I don't mind. Matt's really easy to be around, and Boxing Day will be better than Christmas Day itself, because my mum's going to stay with my brother that morning.'

'What difference does that make?'

'She doesn't approve of gay men. Or women, for that matter.'

'Oh, you never said Matt was gay. Has he got a partner?'

'Yes, they're married; they had a civil ceremony

last year. Matt and Gordon run a really great bed and breakfast place together. Jake was best man at their wedding.'

Molly thought back to that warm sunny day on the south coast. The guests had all gathered on Brighton beach after the official part of the wedding and taken lots of silly photographs. Molly had worn a long floaty dress patterned with poppies, and the men had all hired white suits, kingfisher-blue waistcoats and Stetsons. The children had been allowed to choose their favourite clothes, however bizarre, and the barbeque had gone on for hours, with the whole party staggering back to Matt and Gordon's B&B in Kemptown afterwards for more champagne and a giant cupcake decorated with blue and white icing. The hangover had been well worth the suffering, if only for the enormous, delicious breakfast.

Dot had lost the thread while Molly was reminiscing. 'But I thought your mum loved Shaun?'

'What?'

'Well, Shaun's gay – how come he got away with it?'

'Oh, Mum thinks Shaun's just waiting for the love of a good woman. She's sure he'll find her eventually and then be "cured". In the meantime, she turns a blind eye. But Matt's a different kettle of fish, she says.'

'How come? He sounds fun.'

Molly laughed. 'He's fun all right, but he's very over-the-top camp – think Graham Norton with attitude – and he can be quite bitchy. He teases Mum; says she's come straight out of *Father Ted*. He can't stand Catholics. I think he had a bad time at school when he was trying to come out.'

Dot stood up to make more tea. Molly could see that she was finding it hard to take in this ready-made family circle, all knowing each other so well and with a huge bank of shared memories. Life with Dot's mum didn't sound anything like as relaxed, from the snippets that Dot had dropped over the last few weeks. Molly knew that Shaun had always thought she was as uptight as you could get about some things, but Ginny sounded even worse.

'Well, anyway,' she said soothingly, 'you'll meet Matt very soon. The urgent thing is that we need to think about meals. Matt and Gordon are as hot on cooking as Jake is... was.' There was a silence as the past tense caught up with them both. Then Molly reached for a pad of paper. 'Come on, Dot, I want inspiration. There's a fridge and a freezer full of food here, all we need to do is write the menu.'

'Are you going to ask anyone else?'

'Like who?'

'I don't know, just thought we might make it a party. It feels as if you need to do something spectacular, if last year's Christmas was grim. Mine was too, come to that. How many can you sit round your dining table?'

'Ten, if I put the extension bits in. It would be great to have a really good do on Boxing Day. Jake never liked having a crowd here. I suppose because he was always catering for other people at work, he wanted some peace and quiet on his days off.'

'The kids might like it. Christmas is still going to be very weird for them this year. We're all missing the people we've lost.'

Molly thought for a few moments. It would have to be just the right mix of guests. No stress, and nobody who'd mind if they all got emotional after the wine had been flowing. Could she? Dared she? She took a deep breath.

'I know,' she said brightly. 'What about Tom?'

'Arty Tom, do you mean?'

'Yes. I don't think he's got family round here. Shall I ring him?'

Dot put her head on one side and fixed Molly with a piercing gaze. 'Hmmm. And why are you so keen to see Tom all of a sudden? Is there something you want to get off your chest here?'

Molly felt her face flame. She began to doodle on her notepad as if she'd suddenly thought of urgent things to add to her list. Dot waited. Finally Molly looked up and met the twinkling eyes of her step-daughter. 'It doesn't mean I'm not really sad about your dad, but I can't seem to stop thinking about Tom.'

'Are you expecting me to mind, or something? It's a free country. If you want to fancy the pants off a gorgeous bloke, then why not?'

'But what will people think? They'll say it's too soon after Jake, surely?'

'Who gives a stuff what they think? And *what* people, anyway?'

'Oh, I don't know. The kids, mainly. My mum, and the neighbours? Talking of neighbours,' she added hastily, 'maybe Edna from next door would like to come for dinner on Boxing Day – you know, the one who babysits for me? She told me she was supposed to be going to her sister Lily's house, but she can't go now because Lily's got flu.'

'Don't change the subject,' Dot said.

'I'm not, but we've got to get this sorted. So, Tom and Edna?'

'Brilliant! A proper grown-up dinner party. Go on – do it!'

Molly exhaled, suddenly aware of the tension in her body as she'd waited for Dot's response. Would he come? There was only one way to find out.

* * *

Tom sat in the studio staring at the phone on the desk in front of him. He'd started to ring Molly several times since she'd left her number with Sasha earlier, but the more he thought about her, the more he was sure he would make a mess of the whole thing as soon as she answered.

He'd already bought Molly a present – an elegant little dragonfly brooch with scarlet enamelled wings. He didn't know how he'd expected to give it to her, but at this rate he might as well present it to Sasha as a thank you for hanging his canvases so beautifully, and forget any thoughts of Molly. He'd planned to spend Christmas Day in his rooms – his landlady had gone to Benidorm for a week, muttering about special turkey'n'tinsel deals and warning him about having the heating on too much – but Sasha had insisted that he come to her parents' house, at least for lunch.

'There'll be twelve of us altogether, my brothers and their wives, Mum and Dad, and all the grandchildren. It'll be chaos, but you can't be on your own, Tom.'

'Why the hell not? I usually am.'

'But just because you haven't got a family of your own any more... I mean...'

Tom had sighed and given in. Brought up by his elderly grandmother, it had been years since he'd been involved in a family Christmas. After Gran had died, he'd preferred to just buy plenty of wine, stock up with frozen dinners, and sit it out until the rest of the planet returned to normal. He looked at Molly's present, wrapped in gold paper, a red ribbon tastefully tied around it. Oh well, it would have to be a New Year's surprise. He wheeled himself into his bedroom just as his mobile began to ring. Seeing the illuminated name, he snatched it up.

'Molly? Oh, really? Boxing Day? Yes, I think I can. Yes, that'd be great. What time? What's your address? Shall I bring anything? Okay, that sounds great. See you then. Bye.'

Tom disconnected and put down the phone slowly. He shook his head. Had that call really happened? It was more than he could ever have wished for. A family party, yes – but hopefully there would be time to get Molly alone. And then... and then he would make his move. Everyone expected to get kissed at Christmas, didn't they? Tom moved uncomfortably in his chair, a sudden wave of lust rendering him dry-mouthed. He glanced down. At this rate he would have to wear a voluminous jacket for the Boxing Day party, and keep it on all day.

11

Boxing Day dawned mistily, but very quickly turned into the most perfect type of winter morning. Frost sparkled on all the trees, the air was cool and still, and the sun gradually began to warm Molly's tense shoulders as she shrugged a duffle coat on over her dressing gown and wandered into the garden with a mug of steaming black coffee.

She turned as Dot came out onto the lawn after her, dressed in Jake's wax jacket, wellies and an old nightshirt of Theo's. Dot had arrived to stay for Christmas with bags full of gifts but no nightwear. She had been amazed to find that Christmas Day in the White household involved everyone wearing their pyjamas for as long as possible – in Max and Hattie's case, all day long.

'My mum would have had a fit if I'd not got dressed for breakfast,' she said, 'but it's a great idea. Can I borrow something? I feel a bit over the top with all my clothes on while you lot are all comfy, and I haven't got a nightie or 'jamas.'

'But what do you wear to go to bed in?' said Max, eyes wide in horror.

'Nothing but a smile,' replied Dot, demonstrating the grin but fortunately not the rest of her bedtime outfit.

Max and Hattie looked scandalised but Theo was impressed.

'I'm going to sleep naked in future,' she said. 'Clothes are over-rated. It's naff to wear pyjamas.'

'Well, you needn't think I'm keeping the heating on all night just so you can play at being liberated,' said Molly, poleaxed by a sudden, sharp memory of Jake and his warm, smooth body beside her in bed. Their sex life had often been uninspiring since the children had started to arrive, especially once there were teens in the house prowling around at all hours, but she so, so missed the cuddling. Jake had never been too hot or too cold, and had always been ready to hold her in his arms in the night time.

Now, outside in the garden, Molly pasted on a smile for Dot and tried hard to focus on this particular moment. Life was trundling on regardless. Jake's comforting presence in their big double bed was a thing of the past, but here was his eldest daughter waiting for her breakfast. Dot had recently developed a real taste for the full English, thanks to Max's tuition. She could manage to eat bacon, eggs, beans, black pudding, hash browns, fried bread and sausages without putting on an ounce. Even so, today's cooking was going to be all about their lunch party. Breakfast would have to be something quick. Reluctantly, Molly took a last glance at the frosty garden. If she had a dog, she'd have a great excuse to take off for the beach at this point and leave them to get their own breakfasts.

Maybe today would be the day to think about a puppy of her own. And whatever else happened, she'd definitely be seeing Tom again. She felt the all-too-familiar fizz of excitement. It must be wrong to be like this at the thought of seeing Tom when she should be dreading the thought of another Boxing Day without Jake, but the way her husband had cheated on her with Kate was still fresh in Molly's mind, and a burn of resentment was building up again. Pushing the unwelcome thoughts away, she pondered on what to wear later. Something kind of sophisticated, but with a hint of cleavage? Grinning, she gave herself a mental slap and headed for the kitchen.

By three o'clock, the dinner table looked like the aftermath of an explosion in a cracker factory. Bits of glittery paper, plastic novelties and food remains were scattered over every inch of Molly's best red and green Christmas cloth.

Hattie and Max, bored with being on their best behaviour, had taken themselves off to watch a film; Sam and Theo had escaped to try out Sam's new tablet; and the rest of the party were finally free to sit back, pour themselves large glasses of Baileys or brandy, and have a proper chat. Edna stood up.

'I'll go and make a start on the washing up, dear,' she said to Molly.

Molly groaned. 'Edna, don't you dare. If you go in there, I'll have to come and help you. We can do it later.'

Tom began to wheel himself away from the table. 'Come on, Molly, we can just load the dishwasher and stack everything else – I'll go through. You sit down and... and rest your legs, Edna.'

'How can *you* help?' asked Edna sharply. 'And

why do you assume I need a rest? I'm not in my dotage yet, you know.'

'Nobody's washing up until much later,' said Dot. 'Settle down, all of you.'

'I'll just clear the glasses then,' said Edna. Molly rolled her eyes at Dot. There was no point in arguing.

Gordon undid the top button of his trousers. 'Molly, that was the best Boxing Day dinner I've ever eaten,' he said, 'and it even beats my mum's parsnip roulade with onion marmalade and Matt's beetroot risotto.'

'It's a good job you rang up and reminded me about you being vegetarian,' Molly answered, shuddering at the thought of the hog roast that she and Dot had originally settled on. 'Is it because you hate animals being slaughtered for our benefit? It's very high-minded of you.'

Matt laughed. 'Nah, he just thought he was eating too much fatty stuff and it was time he lost weight and got fit. Didn't work though, did it, Gordy?'

'Nope. I didn't realise how many things you could make with cheese and cream,' said Gordon with a heavy sigh. He patted his stomach sadly. 'It doesn't help having to cook a fry up every morning for the guests. I start off thinking I'll just have muesli, but even the smell of those vegetarian sausages drives me crazy.'

'Who does the cooking for you, Tom?' asked Edna loudly, glancing at him sideways as she filled a tray with dirty wine glasses. 'I expect you're a veggie, too, aren't you?'

'No, I'm too obsessed with red meat for that,' he said, ignoring her first question and adding hastily, 'although I love what you and Dot cooked today, Molly, it was amazing. I'm so full I might never fit back into my wheelchair.' He raised his eyebrows at Edna, and she blushed.

Molly racked her brains to think of a way of bringing the subject round to dogs. After a moment, she stood up. 'I know – let's go for a walk. We could all do with burning a few calories today. It's a shame we haven't got a dog, then we'd have a good reason to go out in the cold.'

Dot grinned and took up the baton. 'Yes, dogs are great for motivating you to get outside when you just want a nap. Have you ever had one, Matt?'

'A dog, or a nap? I quite fancy a snooze in front of the fire, now you mention it. It's so cool to have a whole day off with no cooking to do. Oh, sorry, love, I didn't answer your question,' he said, noticing Molly still looking at him intently. 'We did have a dog once, when I was a kid. Long time ago, though.'

'So why haven't you had one since? Is Gordon a dog-hater, or something?' Molly asked as casually as possible, starting to clear the table as the men hadn't exactly leapt at the idea of a walk.

'Oh, come on, Moll – you're not telling me you don't know why I don't have a dog?' Matt said. When Molly didn't reply, he shook his head in amazement. 'You really don't know, do you? I can't believe Jake kept it to himself.'

'Kept what to himself?' said Molly, suddenly nervous.

'About that time when we had our old Staffordshire Terrier? His name was Ringo – you must know about this, surely? The day of the Marmite?'

There was silence as Dot and Molly looked blankly at Matt. Eventually, he continued, 'It was meant to be a joke, or so Jake said. I was about three and he was six. Jake pinched my favourite cuddly toy while I was playing one afternoon. It was a dinosaur called Rex, and I never went to bed without it. After I'd screamed the place down for half an hour and Mum and Dad were going absolutely mental, we realised Jake hadn't been seen since teatime.'

Matt stopped talking and looked across at Gordon, who was frowning slightly.

'Go on,' said Molly. She couldn't think why she was feeling so sick. This was long ago. It couldn't possibly have any relevance now, could it?

'Well, after a while, my dad heard Ringo growling downstairs under the kitchen table. He went down to see what was up, and found my dinosaur in about a thousand pieces. Ringo had eaten some of the bits, but the ones that were left were covered in Marmite. It was Ringo's all-time favourite thing to eat.'

Molly picked up the tiny plastic puzzle from her cracker and examined it, feeling Tom's eyes on her, and not wanting to hear the rest.

'Anyway, it turned out Jake had spread the Marmite all over the dinosaur and left it for the dog to find. I remember screaming even louder when they had to tell me where Rex had gone.'

'But where was Jake all this time?' asked Dot, wide-eyed.

'He was hiding in the coal shed. I'm sure he only did it for a laugh. He said afterwards that he thought Ringo would just slobber over my dinosaur for a bit.'

'So what happened next?'

'Don't look so tragic, Moll, it was only a toy. Dad

dragged Jake out and made him say sorry, and then he took him downstairs and thrashed him until he begged for mercy. Jake couldn't sit down for a week.'

'You're joking?' Molly gasped. Neither of her parents had ever given her more than a tap across the back of the legs, and that was for really serious naughtiness.

'Nope, no kidding; my dad was a stickler for good behaviour. He never forgot anything you did wrong, either. The rest of the punishment was that Jake had to clean up every bit of dog mess that Ringo ever did in the garden from that day onwards.'

Matt seemed to sense the waves of disapproval coming from all quarters of the room, even from Gordon. He shrugged.

'Come on, lighten up, guys. It was all a long time ago and, luckily for Jake, Ringo was already on his last legs and he only lived about another year; the dog curled up his toes in his sleep when he was fifteen, or so my mum told me when I asked her about it after Dad died. I always wondered... but no, Jake would never have... don't listen to me, I'm rambling now. Blame all that wine.'

Molly and Dot exchanged horrified glances. At least they knew why Jake had never wanted a puppy

in the house. Molly wondered if Jake had ever forgiven his dad for the beating. By the sound of it,
Ringo's dinosaur massacre hadn't been the first or
the last time he'd been thrashed. A vision of Jake
putting a cushion over a sleeping dog's face flashed
into her mind, and she shook herself. What a ridiculous idea – Matt couldn't really think that Jake had
helped Ringo on his way, just to get out of cleaning
up after him, could he? Of course not. Jake had often
been bristly on the surface, but she'd always thought
of him as a softie underneath.

Molly sighed, wondering if it was pointless to
think about making her dreams of racing along the
beach with her own floppy-eared spaniel come true.
But why should it be too late? Hard as the story had
been to listen to, as Matt said, it was in the past. And
denying herself a dog wasn't going to help anyone
now. But why had Shaun wanted her to know about
Ringo? Was he trying to turn her against Jake for
some reason?

She itched to get on the internet and do some
research. As soon as everyone went home, she would
make a start. Maybe Tom would stay behind and
help her? As Dot gave up and joined Edna in
clearing the rest of the crockery, and the other men
joined in with even less enthusiasm, Tom wheeled

himself round to where Molly was sitting. He waited until the others had all left the room and then rummaged in his pocket.

'Molly, I want to give you this,' he said, handing her a tiny package. 'It's just... I saw it in town last week and thought of you. It's not much.'

'Oh!' Molly's involuntary gasp of horror had made Tom's colour drain away quite dramatically and she could feel Dot's eyes on her, so she quickly tore off the wrapping to reveal the jeweller's trademark burgundy case. 'It's from Warner and Sons,' she said, hardly daring to open it. 'You shouldn't have bought me a posh present, Tom. I haven't got you anything at all. You've got the gallery to run, anyway – you can't afford this sort of thing, surely?'

He flushed a deep red, and Molly cursed herself for her tactlessness.

'I'm not that hard up – I can manage to buy a Christmas present for a friend,' he said. 'And I didn't expect anything from you.'

'Yes, I know. It's just that I don't get jewellery very often.'

'Didn't your husband give you surprises?'

'Not really. He was so busy at the brewery in the early years, and then later in the bistro he was run off his feet. He always used to moan that he didn't know what to buy me for birthdays and Christmas, anyway.'

'Right. Well, are you going to open it, or what?'

Molly looked down at the little box and smiled, blinking away the treacherous tears that were never far away these days. She lifted the lid, revealing an elegant, glossy dragonfly.

'Tom, it's magical. And it's red, too. Oh, thank you, it's absolutely perfect.'

Tom beamed as Molly pinned the brooch to her jumper and then they both started as Edna came back in with her empty tray at the ready. For a moment, the older lady stood and absorbed the sight of Molly's bright eyes, the crumpled wrapping paper, and the little brooch. Then she turned and walked out of the room again.

'What was all that about?' asked Tom. 'What's wrong with Edna?'

'Goodness only knows. She can be a bit peculiar sometimes.'

'Doesn't she like me?'

'I don't think it's anything personal. The whole wheelchair thing seems to be freaking her out a bit, that's all.'

'Right. Well, I can handle that. So long as it doesn't have the same effect on you?'

Their eyes met and locked. Tom lifted a hand to brush away some glitter from one of the crackers that had somehow transferred itself to Molly's cheek.

The door swung open again. 'Cup of tea, anyone?' said Edna. Tom sighed.

12

With Christmas fading into the distance and the prospect of a new puppy to look forward to, Molly wasn't quite so keyed up about waiting for the next box. Even so, when she saw the blurred red shape of the postman through the stained glass of the front door, her heart flipped. What could Shaun have thought up for this one? So far, he'd managed to provide her with a new daughter, given her an old friend back, and set her on the hunt for a cocker spaniel puppy.

'Hello, love – is it your birthday again?' said the postman, checking out Molly's cleavage. She realised she'd forgotten to put on her usual baggy jumper this morning and her red shirt had a few too many buttons undone, but it was too late to do anything about that now.

'No, my birthday's in August – maybe it's a late Christmas present, or it could be just another of those annoying gifts from admirers,' she answered, batting her eyelashes. 'Isn't it hell when they just won't leave you alone?'

The postman looked puzzled and held out the parcel. Signing for it with what was becoming a familiar flourish, Molly practised a sexy wiggle as she went into the kitchen. The postman wasn't a catch by any stretch of the imagination, but he was definitely taking more notice of her these days so maybe she was beginning to give out a bit more 'oomph' than she'd done for months. She knew she was dressing more carefully, with the aim of Tom seeing her and being impressed.

Would Tom like the new, slightly improved Molly? She wondered for about the fiftieth time what he really thought of her. His face didn't give much away, but there was that single word on the boat in his picture. Molly's name. It couldn't be a co-incidence, could it?

She wished she had a female friend to talk to about sex – Kate didn't really count, even though they were now in touch on Facebook. You could hardly have that sort of discussion with someone who had cheerfully screwed your husband while your back was turned.

Itching to open the next box, Molly put the kettle on and thought about phoning Dot. After a moment, she decided to be on the safe side and check out its contents first. With the children at school, Molly had two hours before she needed to be at her next music session, so she settled herself at the kitchen table and began to slowly unpick the Sellotape.

Shaun had really gone to town on this one, with what seemed like extra-strong tape and double layers of brown paper. When the outer layers fell away, Molly could understand why. The box inside was wrapped in another sheet of paper – this time rainbow-coloured tissue – but it was less robust than the others had been. Gently removing the final piece, Molly saw that this container seemed to be made of thin recycled cardboard. It was a rather uninteresting shade of brown, and when Molly lifted the lid, she found a small earthenware plant pot. A scroll of writing paper was rolled up tightly inside it, tied with thick brown and green ribbon, with the words 'Robin's Nest' printed along it in gold. She opened the letter.

They say that those who can, do
And the others (who can't do) should
   teach.
But when even that gets too much,
It's tempting to head for the beach.

(And sometimes the ones who can't do – well,
they open garden centres instead, or so I'm
told.)
   You might not like this one, sweetie, but it's
got to be done – trust me. Sometimes ghosts
just have to be laid (so to speak – oo er,
missus!).
   S xxx

Molly stared at the letter. Garden centres? Plant
pots? Ghosts? Had Shaun lost the plot completely
this time? She looked more carefully at the cardboard container, turning it over and over in her
hands. On the underside was a printed label. It said:

Robin's Nest – all your quality plants, at a
price you can afford. Orchids are our speciality. Barnards Way, Keddleford, Suffolk.

It couldn't be him, surely? There was only one

Robin whose name had ever made her spine tingle like this, and she'd left him far behind in Leicestershire. Hadn't she? Molly reached for the phone to ring Dot. Hearing the engaged tone, she moaned with frustration.

* * *

In his studio, Tom had been eating his way through a huge bag of Kettle crisps to take his mind off the constant longing to see Molly again. His latest painting was coming on well – earlier that day he had almost given himself frostbite by sitting on the pier for too long, but the wild explosion of colour in front of him was his reward. The boiling sea, tinged with purple, gold and indigo, seemed to be empty of life until you looked more closely. Then, one by one, you could pick out a crazy mixture of creatures swimming in the waves. Some were obviously mermaids and mermen, but others were so bizarre that even Tom couldn't name them. They had flowed from his brush, their delicate, silvery faces almost obscured by the crashing breakers. Here and there an arm was raised as if in triumph, or maybe as a cry for help – who could tell? Tom flipped the top off a bottle of lager and looked again. The mermaid nearest to the front of the picture had Molly's face.

Who could he talk to about this crazy obsession? Sasha was way too impatient to understand his fears. She would just tell him to stop being such an idiot and go for it. He thought for a moment. What about Dot? She seemed increasingly close to Molly. Could he trust her? She was very young, but she had a thoughtful look about her. He reached for his phone. Hattie had helpfully programmed the whole family's details into it for him on Boxing Day evening, when she'd been stuck for something to do. He found Dot's number and pressed 'call' before he could change his mind.

'Hello? Who's this?' Her voice sounded frosty, and Tom's heart sank.

'It's me. It's Tom.'

'Oh – hi, Tom. What's up?' That was better; the warmth and enthusiasm was unmistakeable now. He decided to be as open as possible from the start.

'Dot, I really need someone to talk to. It's about Molly.'

'Molly? Why, is she ill?'

Tom heard the underlying panic in Dot's tone and cursed himself for worrying her. Molly had told him about the loss of Dot's mum. She must be constantly afraid that she would have to go through more grief. He had felt the same when his own parents had been killed.

'No, it's nothing like that,' he said reassuringly. 'It's me. I mean it's about how I feel about Molly.'

'Ah.' Tom could sense the smile in her voice now. 'Go on, I'm listening.'

Tom felt his shoulders begin to relax for the first time in days as he began to unburden himself. This was bliss.

* * *

Half an hour later, as Dot finally answered her phone, Molly began to gabble.

'Dot, it's me, I need you to come to Suffolk with me now. Can you? I can't do this one on my own.'

'Hey, calm down, love. When do you want to go?'

'As soon as possible. I want to get it over with. I feel sick just thinking about it.'

Dot sighed. 'Are you going to tell me what was in the box, or have I got to guess?'

'Um... it's... a bit embarrassing.' She paused, biting her thumbnail.

'Look,' Dot said, with admirable restraint, 'you rang me, Moll, I didn't ring you. If you don't want to tell me, that's fine, but I've got to go to work in a minute.'

'Yes, but... oh, maybe I should bite the bullet and do this one by myself.'

'Molly, just *make your mind up*!'

'Right, sorry. Okay, well, it all happened when we were still in Leicestershire. There was a man.'

'A man. What sort of man?'

Molly began to twist strands of hair round her fingers. She stood on one leg, then catching sight of herself in the long hall mirror, realised that she looked about ten years old. Taking a deep breath, she blurted out, 'He was the head teacher at the village school. His name was Robin. I had a real thing about him. I thought I loved him, if I'm honest.'

'And did you... erm?'

'Oh, yes, I certainly did.' Molly heaved a sigh, remembering the one, rather disappointing time she'd slept with Robin. Well, not slept, obviously – absolutely no sleeping had been involved. It had been a strange night, to say the least. Her beloved mother-in-law, Daisy, had been seriously ill in hospital and Jake had been unavailable to share the worry. It had turned out that he'd fled to the coast after his unexpected fling with Kate. Molly tried to think how to explain all this chaos to Jake's daughter without completely tarnishing his memory or making Dot think she was just a middle-aged tart.

'Anyway,' she continued, 'Shaun seems to know all about it. I guess Jake must have told him, although it's not like Shaun to have kept quiet and not asked me about Robin – he's so nosy. But there's no other way he could have found out, so maybe Jake made him promise not to tell. And now Shaun's got some mad idea that I should go to Suffolk and track Robin down.'

'Have you seen him recently?' asked Dot. Molly could hear her crashing around in her kitchen getting ready for work, swearing as she stubbed her toe.

'Oh, no, not since Jake and I moved to Norfolk. Well, actually, it was before that, because Robin and Lydia – that's his horrible wife – left before we did. He gave up teaching, but I didn't realise he was going into market gardening, or whatever it is he does. The advert mentions orchids. Lydia was always keen on those.'

'Look, I've got to go now, I'll be really late as it is. I'll see about swapping my shifts around at the pub and you decide if you want to drive over there, and when. Will your mum or Edna look after the kids?'

Molly bit her lip. Her mum had made it quite clear that the children wore her out the last time she'd had them overnight, and Edna was recovering from a bad cold.

'I might get away with it one more time with Mum if I play my cards right, but I'm going to have to find an alternative if Shaun sends me on any more of these long-distance quests. Doesn't he realise I can't just drop everything and dash around the country? And it's costing me a fortune in petrol.'

'Shaun's a childless man, busy travelling the world. I'm guessing a big fat "no" to that one. Ring me later, Moll – I'll do my best to come. Apart from anything else, I'm dying to see the guy who got you all fired up.'

Molly heard Dot's giggle as she put the phone down, and blushed scarlet. Fired up? Yes, she'd been fired up all right; but not enough, as it happened. What would it be like to see Robin again? What was the point of stirring it up again? She squared her shoulders and dialled her mum's number.

* * *

Tom looked up from his book as the bell on the shop door clanged. His eyebrows rose sharply but he sat up straighter and gave his friendliest smile. Standing in front of him were Hattie and Theo, clutching a tattered piece of paper.

'Oh, hi, girls,' Tom said, aiming for an all-mates-together-type tone. Molly's daughters looked him over curiously and he reddened despite himself. He knew he must look a bit freaky in his paint-spattered overalls, but Sasha had suddenly remembered she needed to go to the bank before closing time, and Tom had had to leave his latest painting at a very messy stage. Theo grinned.

'Nice romper suit,' she said, dimpling. Hattie nudged her sister.

'Don't be so rude,' she hissed, coming forward to put herself between Theo and Tom. 'Hi, Tom. We were going to text you but then we thought we'd just call in. We were wondering if you'd like to sponsor us for our sleepover – it's for a good cause,' she added hastily, 'Cancer Research. Everyone likes to support that one, don't they?'

'Sponsor? Me?' he said. What was this all about? Tom didn't even know that Hattie and Theo were aware that he had a shop.

'Yes, we're sleeping over at Theo's friend Natasha's house tomorrow, and you have to sponsor us for every hour we can stay awake. If you want to, that is...' Hattie tailed off, seeming to realise that she'd maybe been a bit too forceful. Theo took over.

'And we were just passing your shop and we thought, seeing as you're friends with Mum, you might want to help? Maybe? Dot told us where you hang out.' She smiled down at Tom, and he suddenly saw how like Molly she was – same wild hair, same green eyes, but with a much more forthright approach.

'So what charity is it really in aid of?' he said. 'I'm getting the feeling that Cancer Research wouldn't really be your bag?' The girls glanced at each other.

'Erm... actually, it's for our school funds,' said Theo.

'Is it really?'

There was a silence. 'No,' said Hattie, after a while.

'So what are you really trying to con me for?'

'It's not a con, honest! It's a proper fundraiser. It's just that it's for sport for the disabled and Theo said not to tell you that in case you thought we were being patrimonious.'

'Patri-what?'

'She means patronising, I think,' said Theo, grinning at Tom. 'We thought you might be offended if we said the D word.'

Tom laughed despite himself. It was true that he hated the disabled tag, but the PC alternatives were much worse.

'Okay, I'll sponsor you,' he said, digging in his pocket and coming up with a car park ticket, a till receipt and a button. Hattie's face fell.

'Never mind,' she said sadly. 'It's okay.'

'Look, I'll just have to owe it to you. Put me down for a tenner.'

'Ten quid? Wicked!' shouted Hattie. Theo looked dubious.

'You sure you don't mind?' she asked. He shook his head, turning quickly as a new customer came into the gallery. 'Well, we'll go now, thanks for that. You're ace,' Theo mumbled, picking up one of Tom's business cards from the desk. 'Look, I'll text you. I bet Mum'll ask you round for tea one night. She fa— er, I mean she likes you. And she might be a bit boring sometimes, but she makes a mean curry. Would you come? It was ace when you came at Christmas.'

As Tom nodded, trying to look like the sort of person who was always being asked out for tea, Theo and Hattie slid past the lady with the shopping trolley who was probably only killing time until the last bus came. They left the gallery, waving.

Molly's family seemed to quite like him, which was cool. Or those two did at the moment anyway, thought Tom, frowning. Would they be quite so friendly when they found out that all Tom could think about was getting much, much closer to their mum? He winced. This was all turning out to be even more complicated than he'd anticipated. To disappoint these trusting kids would be unbearable but to distance himself from Molly was just as unthinkable. Tom turned to greet the new customer, who was actually showing a gratifying interest in one of his new paintings. At least one area of his life was beginning to move on. As for the rest... only time would tell.

13

The sight of the wintry fields made Molly's teeth chatter as the Land Rover bowled its way into Suffolk. There had been a sprinkling of snow in the night and she'd been tempted to cancel the trip, but Dot had stood firm.

'Don't be wimpy, Moll,' she'd said. 'If we put this one off every time it gets a bit chilly, it'll be May before we go, and I really want to see your bloke.'

'He's not my bloke – he never was, really. I only borrowed him.'

Dot looked thoughtful, taking a few moments to slot another of Jake's glovebox CD collection into the machine. The sound of Brahms came flooding out of the speakers, and she laughed.

'There, I bet that surprised you. Did you have me down as a heavy metal girl?'

'No, more of a folk-type; beads and flower power, and stuff,' said Molly vaguely. She had just spotted the sign for Robin's garden centre and was wishing they had stopped for the loo when there had been a chance. She slowed the car down to a crawl and turned into the narrow driveway. The view was breathtaking. Endless green fields, with stark trees making black silhouettes against the high skyline, and not far in the distance, a tantalising glimpse of the sea. Robin had chosen well, if this was his permanent home. Molly couldn't help thinking that even this idyllic spot wouldn't make up for having to live with bloody Lydia.

'Right, do you want to do this on your own?' asked Dot, winding down her window and pulling out a battered paperback as Molly pulled into the car park next to a cluster of farmhouse buildings.

'Hmmm, probably. I'll go and see how the land lies,' Molly answered, 'but I can see a toilet block there, so I'm going to nip for a wee first.'

She climbed down from the Land Rover and set off across the gravel, but before she could reach her goal, a shout stopped her in her tracks. A tall, broad-shouldered man in wellies, pressed jeans, and a rather new-looking wax jacket was loping towards her, arms outstretched.

'Molly! Is it really you? I can't believe it. I was only thinking about you this morning,' he yelled, before breaking off and looking back over his shoulder towards the entrance of the garden centre. Reassured, he turned back towards Molly and came towards her at a gallop, picking her up and swinging her around. She laughed, breathless, wishing that she'd managed to reach the loo before Robin had spotted her.

'Hi, Robin.' Her voice came out as a feeble croak, and she cleared her throat. 'Erm, could you put me down a minute, I just need to... er...'

Laughing as he saw her agonised glance in the direction of the toilets, Robin gently lowered Molly to the ground and motioned for her to go ahead. 'As soon as you've finished, come inside and meet me in the café, Lydia's having a bit of a lie down, so we can have a cup of tea and a chat.' Robin noticed Dot looking out of the car window as he spoke, and broke off, confused. She wound the window down and grinned.

'It's okay, I know when I'm not wanted,' she called. 'I'm just going to read my book – you can bring me a sticky bun when you come back, Moll.'

Five minutes later, Molly and Robin sat at one of the small rustic tables in the restaurant area, knees pressed uncomfortably together, pretending to be absorbed in the tea-pouring ritual.

'Do you take sugar?' asked Robin. 'I don't think we've ever had a cup of tea together, have we?'

'No, I guess we haven't. Champagne, yes, but we never got round to hot drinks.'

They were both silent. Molly opened a packet of biscuits for something to do, and then put them down, knowing she wouldn't be able to swallow anything.

'So, it's really good to see you, Molly, and looking delightful, if I may say so. But why are you here? I mean,' he blushed, 'I didn't intend that to sound ungracious, you are very welcome, of course you are.'

For the first time, Molly looked at Robin properly. She had forgotten how pedantic he could sound. His once-sandy hair was greyer than she remembered, although still very short, and the glasses on the end of his nose gave him the air of a slightly crazed professor, which was an image he'd always seemed to cultivate.

When he had been head teacher of their little village school, Robin had always worn baggy linen suits complete with waistcoats and striped granddad shirts. The mums had all thought he was wonderful, even the younger ones. Now he seemed faded, and his country gentleman outfit took away the authoritative look he'd previously had.

'So how is Lydia these days?' she asked, watching Robin flush again.

'Oh, you know...'

'Well, no, I don't – that's why I'm asking.'

Robin scratched his head, screwing his face up in a frown. Molly was reminded sharply of the times when seeing this little mannerism had filled her with tender affection. Now he just looked like an overgrown schoolboy with nits.

'I suppose you heard that Lydia was hospitalised for some months after we left Mayfield?' he said eventually.

'No, why would I have heard that?' Even to herself, Molly was beginning to sound waspish. 'What was the problem? Was it her migraines? She was always a martyr to those.'

'Funnily enough, the migraines stopped when we came here,' Robin said. 'No, it was a rare form of impetigo, actually.'

'Really? How... erm... unsightly.' Molly fought a childish urge to punch the air.

'Yes, she was very self-conscious for a long time.

She couldn't bring herself to be with people for quite a while.'

'That must have been inconvenient.'

'How do you mean?' asked Robin, looking even more like a bewildered little boy.

'Well, weren't you trying to set up this place? That must have involved mixing with rather a lot of people?'

Robin heaved a gusty sigh. 'It did, Molly. But poor Lydia couldn't help it – she was a recluse for several months. Complete bed rest was the only thing that seemed to help. Of course, now we're up and running, she's much better.'

'Yes, I suppose she is.' There was an uncomfortable silence and then Robin grabbed Molly's hand. Startled, she knocked over her teacup, and the next couple of minutes were spent mopping the table. He tried again, and this time captured Molly's hand successfully. It seemed like only yesterday, thought Molly, when just the touch of Robin's fingers had sent shivers down her spine, and she had longed to get him alone to tear off his suit, shirt, waistcoat, not to mention everything else. She met his gooseberry-coloured eyes and could see the same thought reflected there.

'Molly,' he whispered, 'do you remember that

night at my house when Lydia was away? When we made love, and you said I was the most exciting lover you'd ever had?'

'I do remember that night, actually. I'm not sure why I said that. You were only the second person I'd ever slept with so I'd hardly done an intensive survey and we didn't exactly set the world on fire that night, did we?'

There was a stunned silence. Molly got to her feet clumsily.

'Look, Robin, it was a mistake coming here, and I'm going to leave now before Lydia comes back. I had such high hopes when we went to bed together. You made me feel very special for a little while and it was good to see you again. It's cleared up a few things that I've been wondering about.'

'But Molly, I thought...'

'What did you think, Robin?' she asked, picking up her bag and wondering if he knew that he had a biscuit stuck to his sleeve.

'I thought you and I were made for each other. I thought I took you to places where no one else had taken you. You were my everything.'

'Bloody hell, have you been listening to cheesy seventies love songs?'

'Don't swear, Molly, it doesn't suit you. And I thought you liked the music I played that night.'

'I'm afraid Barry White and Diana Ross have never really done it for me, Robin. Anyway, I must go. You've got a nice little business here, I hope you and Lydia will make a go of it and...' she took a deep breath, 'be very happy together.' There, she'd said the right thing at last. Patting him on the shoulder in lieu of the kiss he was obviously expecting, Molly all but sprinted to the Land Rover, jumped in, and shot off down the drive before Dot had even managed to put her seatbelt on. They were five miles nearer to the Norfolk border before Dot plucked up the courage to speak.

'So, was it worth the drive?' she asked.

Molly began to giggle, and once she'd started, couldn't stop. Her heart felt lighter than it had done for weeks. 'Oh, yes, definitely,' she said, reaching for a mint imperial. 'Now all I've got to do is tackle my other issues.'

'What issues are they?' Dot looked nervous.

'You don't want to know. I think it comes under the heading of "too much information",' said Molly. She wished more than anything that she could have half an hour with Shaun. Had he known about her inadequacies in bed? Surely even Jake himself had never realised how bad she felt about not being able to really let go? Molly had always put in a great effort, made all the right noises, done all the wriggling, tried not to be uncooperative, or to make it obvious she'd rather read her book. She'd rather clean the bathroom, if she was perfectly honest. Her mother, clearly still locked in the dark ages of sex after having grown up in a stern Catholic family, had told Molly the day before she married Jake that it was a wife's duty to keep her husband completely satisfied.

'How do you mean, Mum? Are you saying I should never say "no" or have a headache?' Molly's knowledge of relationship problems and carnal delights had mostly come from watching *Friends* and old sitcoms. Her mother had never been one for deep discussions, and the much more adventurous Kate's comments were more designed to shock and show off than to be helpful.

'Well, I'm assuming that, even though I've tried to bring you up properly, you and Jake have already...' Peggy had shuddered delicately as Molly hung her head. She was feeling decidedly queasy that day, and already suspected that she might be pregnant. At eighteen, this thought was less than welcome.

Jake had promised to get some condoms but had bottled out. Their usual fumbling had taken a more serious turn since Jake had come back from his recent holiday with his family, and Molly was relieved that they had already arranged their wedding. Her friends were all pairing off and she wasn't the first of the gang to plan to 'tie the knot', as her father jovially put it. But she guessed she was probably the only one to have technically still been a virgin on her eighteenth birthday.

'Anyway, Molly, be that as it may, you must start as you mean to go on. A hot meal on the table when he comes home, a clean and tidy house, a well-stocked larder, and compliance in the bedroom.' Peggy busied herself wiping down her already spotless work surfaces, an indication that the matter was closed. But Molly knew that if she didn't continue this painful conversation now, she might never pluck up the courage to do it again.

'Mum, do you find sex enjoyable?' she blurted out.

Peggy sucked in her breath and began to polish the taps. 'Molly, I'm surprised at you. That question is unnecessary. You'll be wanting babies, I hope?'

Molly nodded rather dolefully. Her stomach lurched and she felt beads of sweat appear on her upper lip.

'Well then.'

'Well then what, Mum?'

'I'll be honest with you. The bedroom part is sometimes tiresome, but you must be a good wife, Molly. Jake is just a man, after all. He has needs. Now, I don't want to talk about this again. Off you go and ring the florist to remind him to deliver our order first thing tomorrow. I'd hate you to walk down the aisle with no bouquet.'

The Land Rover trundled on towards home, and silence fell. Molly looked at Dot, fast asleep with her feet on the dashboard again, as relaxed as Molly had been uptight at her age. Perhaps it wasn't too late to change. She could start again from scratch, if she dared. Molly adjusted her seat and turned off the music. She had a lot of thinking to do before they reached home.

14

Later the next afternoon, Tom took his courage in both hands, put on his favourite faded Levis, his old leather flying jacket and a red t-shirt, and got into his car. As he drove to Molly's house, he rehearsed his lines over and over again. He had to strike just the right note or he'd frighten her off before he could get to know her properly.

He pulled in behind the Land Rover, which looked as if it had been abandoned rather than parked, and swung himself out of his own, intending to reach for his sticks. Before he'd had a chance to organise himself, Hattie came flying out of the front door.

'Tom! I saw you from my window – I sleep at the

front – no one else likes it because it's a bit noisy but I like to see what's going on in the street, and I saw you. I've got my own room now. Have you come to see how we did in the sleepover?'

She paused to breathe and Tom started to manoeuvre himself out of the driving seat.

'Do you want your chair?' Hattie asked, going to the boot. 'I can do it, I know how.'

At that moment, Molly emerged from the house, and Tom was struck dumb by her beauty. She was wearing one of her floating-type ensembles, layer upon layer of crimson, burgundy and russet material over skin-tight leggings. Her hair was tied up on top of her head, and curls cascaded around her face. She opened her eyes wide when she recognised her visitor, but rallied quickly and came towards him smiling.

'Tom, this is nice. I was going to come into the shop again to see your new paintings properly.'

'Hi, Molly, I was just passing and I thought I'd bring in the girls' sponsor money.' There was an ominous silence and Hattie became very interested in the toes of her boots.

'I tell you what, we'll talk about that inside,' said Molly, glaring at her youngest daughter. Hattie sprang into action, wrenching the wheelchair out of the boot, opening it up deftly and bringing it to just the right place for Tom to slide into. He grinned at her.

'You've done that before,' he said, settling into the chair.

'Yes, I've got a friend at school who's d—' She stopped suddenly, exchanging agonised glances with her mum. Tom laughed.

'Who's the D word,' he finished. 'You don't have to walk on eggshells around me, sweetheart, I've been in a wheelchair for a long time. I'm used to it.'

'But why?' Hattie ground to a halt again as Tom began to propel himself towards the house. The step was tiny, and he easily got through the wide doorway. Over his shoulder, he said to Hattie, 'You can ask me anything you like, if you give me a cup of tea.' Hattie shook her head, biting her lip.

Soon Tom was relaxing in one of Molly's most comfortable chairs, with a brimming mug next to him and a slice of Hattie's flapjack, made that day at school. He had never felt so at home in someone else's house before. Usually it took him more than one previous visit to grow accustomed to a new place. There were practical issues, such as whether the loo was accessible, and if the floors were laminated – major slipping hazard – and whether the homeowners tried to make too many allowances for his needs.

Here, all was calm. Or almost calm; Molly was jittery about Theo going out with her new boyfriend later. But even that was refreshing, because it wasn't Tom's worry. All he needed to do was to lend a friendly ear. After a while, sensing Molly's exhaustion, Tom offered to treat them all to a takeaway – this idea was greeted rapturously by Hattie, and also by Max, who was hovering around hungrily. They spent a happy few minutes poring over the curry menu before declaring themselves in complete agreement.

'Does Max really like chicken tikka?' asked Tom, incredulously. In his limited experience, children only ate chips, burgers and nuggets.

'I like everyfin',' said Max, bouncing in and doing three circuits of the room before leaning against Tom and hugging him hard. Then, red-faced, he made a quick exit.

'He's been a bit hyper this week, Mum,' said Theo. She was lying on one of the huge squashy sofas and had narrowly missed being trampled by her brother.

Molly frowned. 'I know – he's getting worse. His teacher says he's being strange at school, too. Last week he refused to get off Anthony's knee – you know who I mean, the young student in the class? Anthony's really kind-hearted, but he can't work with a hefty seven-year-old wrapped round his waist.'

'Maybe he just wants to be near a man? He misses Dad lots. And he's not the only one.' Hattie blinked and Theo shot her a warning glare.

'Don't wail again, you'll set Mum off, and then Max'll hear and there'll be no getting him to sleep tonight. It's all right for you, your room's right at the other end of the house. He's next door to me and once he starts, he never shuts up.'

Tom looked round the room. Gloom had descended. He heard the doorbell and thanked God for the curry delivery. Getting out his wallet and waving away Molly's protestations, he wondered how he could possibly help. It was all so grim for these kids, losing a father and still trying to get used to their new, smaller unit.

Over dinner, everyone cheered up and it began to seem more like a normal evening, although Tom had never been used to cosy family nights in. They sat round Molly's enormous kitchen table with the takeaway containers spread around and a big jug of Ribena in the middle. Tom had been offered beer, but he never drank when he was driving – his licence was vital to him and losing it would be a disaster. Molly had looked long-ingly at a half-full bottle of red wine on the worktop but seemed to decide against it. Tom wished suddenly for the chance to take her out to eat, or even to be living in the sort of place where he could cook a fabulous meal and have soft candlelight and cool jazz playing.

After dinner, he stayed at the table while Theo and Hattie cleared away the debris. Max was on his knee with a book by this time, warm and sleepy, with a thumb tucked into his mouth. The soft, confiding weight of the little boy filled Tom with a rare sense of peace as he read aloud. Max took his thumb out every now and again to join in with the familiar words about the Gruffalo's child. Tom met Molly's eyes, feeling that life couldn't get much better than this.

Much later, when all the children were upstairs if not actually asleep, Tom and Molly sat down by the fire for a final cup of coffee. A log settled in a shower of sparks and Molly threw on more wood, refilling Tom's mug and passing him the biscuit tin. He sighed, stretching luxuriously and helping himself to the last piece of shortbread.

'Molly, I've been wanting to ask you – how's it go-ing, really? I mean, being a... you know...'

'Widow? It's okay, you can say it. Well, I'm not sure how it's going. Some days are so bad that you just want to stay in bed and hope the world goes away, and the pain of losing the person you've been with forever just makes you feel sick, and scared. I feel so sorry for Jake. He's missed out on everything; he'll never see his kids grow up.' Her voice grew husky and she stopped.

'It sounds bloody awful.'

Molly took a deep breath. 'Yes, but the thing is, Tom, on other days I sometimes get a mad feeling of excitement. I know it's wrong. It's probably too soon to feel like this.'

'It makes you feel guilty, I guess?'

'Yep, Jake didn't deserve to die. He was a good dad, even if...'

There was a long silence, and Tom drank his coffee, waiting. After a while, Molly sat forward and busied herself putting the tin lid back on, and tidying the tray.

'Tom,' she said, so quietly that he could hardly hear her voice. 'Can I tell you about my quest?'

'What? Did you say quest? You can tell me about anything you like. Is that some sort of Harry Potter-type question, though?'

'No, but it feels a bit like it. Sure you don't mind? It might take a while.'

Tom grinned and made himself more comfortable. 'Go ahead, I'm in no rush.' As Molly told him her story, his eyes widened, but he managed to keep quiet until she ground to a halt, rubbing her eyes.

'So, in a nutshell, the quest's all about finding out what made your husband tick? And facing up to some of your own demons at the same time?'

'That's about it. I loved Jake, I really did, Tom. But sometimes I think I didn't know him at all. He could be funny, grumpy, fiery, gentle, bloody-minded, and all in the same few minutes – that wasn't always easy to live with.'

'No, it wouldn't be,' said Tom, wondering where to go from here. This was thin ice. His brain was reeling at the thought of both Molly and Jake having affairs; he'd had them down as a normal, everyday couple. But maybe there were secrets like these in lots of marriages. How would he know? Tom thought about the time he'd seen Jake on the seafront. Not a very relaxing bloke, to say the least. Jealousy at the thought of Molly with yet another man besides the crabby one hit Tom like the first wave of a fierce spring tide. He took a deep breath and shut his mind to the unwelcome images crowding in on him.

'Anyway, I'd better get home. You've probably got to be up for work?' he said, hoping Molly would say that she was in no hurry to go to sleep and that they should maybe have another drink.

'Yes, I have. That must be one of the good bits about being an artist, no early-morning alarm?' Molly got to her feet and looked around for Tom's wheelchair, but he had already got the message and found his sticks, beginning the journey to the hallway. She hovered as he made his way to his chair, but he was relieved that she didn't try to help. At that moment, he would have given a great deal to be able to say a proper goodbye to her in the doorway, with a huge hug and lots of warm, night-time kisses. Sighing, he hefted his chair into the boot and used his sticks to reach the driver's side.

'Right, see you again soon,' Tom said, as he levered himself into the car, 'and next time the dinner's on me. I can't cook for you at my bedsit, but we could go into town? The Italian's good; you know, that one near the station?'

'It depends on babysitters. Maybe Dot would come.'

'Let's make it one day next week, I've got loads of questions to ask you about the boxes, and you might have another parcel by then. Try anyway.'

Tom held his breath, but Molly nodded. 'I'll do what I can, it was really good to get all that stuff off my chest. Thanks, Tom, you're a sweetie.'

A sweetie. Oh well, it would have to do for now. Molly leaned into the car and kissed his cheek, closing the door with a clunk and waving until he was out of sight. Tom drove home with the heady scent of her all around him and disturbing thoughts ready to keep him awake far into the night.

15

February 14 dawned cold and rainy. Molly lay snuggled under the duvet, listening to her radio in the precious early-morning quiet. She wondered if the postman would call today. There would be nothing for her from Tom, she was sure. They had seen each other a few times recently, both at Molly's house and out on the seafront, but somehow they were never alone. Just as they began to chat, someone would always burst in, or a passer-by would stop to chat, or it would rain just at the wrong moment. Their relationship seemed doomed to stand still. She sighed.

Soon Max and the girls would wake and there would be doors slamming, the shower running, and a fight for toast and cereal. The DJ was playing back-to-back requests this morning for lovers of all ages, and Molly wondered what all the fuss was about. She and Jake hadn't sent each other Valentine cards since their schooldays. Jake had never been one for grand romantic gestures at any time of year, especially not when he thought it was expected of him. But then, neither had Molly. As she drifted back to sleep and into a warm and sensual dream involving Tom, a bottle of champagne and a deserted beach, the door-bell chimed.

'Muuuuuum, the postman's here,' yelled Hattie, on her way to bag first shower.

Molly clambered out of bed and slipped into her dressing gown, padding down the stairs as she tried to get her hair into some semblance of order. She opened the door and the postman held out a parcel and a small pile of cards, refusing to return her smile.

'Oh! Thanks – I wasn't... I mean...' she said.

'No, this must be a first,' he answered, thrusting out a pad for her to sign.

'Can I ask you something?' Molly asked.

'S'pose.'

'Do you get some sort of kick out of being so rude? And do your bosses know about it?'

The postman's jaw dropped and he muttered something about people getting the wrong end of the stick sometimes, before scuttling back down the driveway. Molly grinned to herself. It was definitely time to try a bit harder not to be such a doormat.

'Was that the post, Mum?' shouted Theo. 'Is there anything for me?'

Molly put the parcel into the hall cupboard and flipped through the rest of the letters. 'Yep, three for you and one for Hattie.'

'No! Really?'

'You must have been busy, Theo. I thought you said you were having a break from boys after the disastrous night out with Ashley.'

Theo laughed, and came halfway down the stairs, holding out her hand. 'That was last week. Hey, fancy Hattie getting a card, bet she'll be really embarrassed. Let's see.' As Theo took her heap and rushed back upstairs to investigate, Molly dived for the cupboard. With one ear tuned to what was happening upstairs, she took her package through to the downstairs cloakroom and tore off the wrapping.

The fifth box was bigger than the others had been and looked extravagantly tacky. It was heart-shaped, shocking pink, and trimmed with paler pink ribbon. Sequins decorated its sides, and its glossy finish was so shiny that Molly could see her face reflected in it, blurry and distorted. She eased the lid off. Opening the cloakroom door a crack to check the children were still busy upstairs, she lifted out the now familiar envelope.

Hi Babes,

How's it going? So, we're well underway with the quest. I'm guessing you know a bit more about Jake now, and maybe a bit more about yourself, too. You might have been wondering why I'm doing all this stuff? Well, it's complicated, but I honestly couldn't think of any other way to help you to begin to move on. Not to forget Jake, but to start to live with the memories – and to do that, the memories have to be accurate, I guess. The February box is all about luuuuurve, I'm afraid. Happy Valentine's Day, my lovely buddy. One tip – get the bus or take a taxi this time. xxxxxxxxxxxxx

Molly listened again. Hattie's TV was blaring and she and Theo were conducting a shouted conversation over the top of it. She could hear Max singing in the bathroom, a high-volume rendition of 'Jingle Bells', which he had perfected just before Christmas and refused to drop. It was safe to carry on reading Shaun's latest verse.

> *Some men wear their heart on their*
> * sleeve*
> *But I'm not sure what that would*
> * achieve,*
> *And the one you loved best*
> *Loved you more than the rest*
> *Although sometimes his words might*
> * deceive...*

Inside the heart-shaped box was a tiny package wrapped in pink paper. It felt light in Molly's hand, and she tore the wrapping off, intrigued. Jewellery? Had Shaun gone all soppy on her? But all that was inside was a Yale key, labelled with the number 247.

Later that morning, with the younger children safely at school and Theo at college, Molly and Dot met by their usual bench at the far end of the pier.

'So what does it mean? Have we got to find the door that the key fits? It could be anywhere,' said Dot, looking down despairingly at the key in the palm of her hand.

'Don't worry, Shaun's been kind to us here – 247 is the number of his flat. He only lives about five miles down the coast. We can get a bus there in a few minutes, I checked.'

'But why would he leave you his key? Don't you have one anyway?'

'Yes, I've got one for emergencies, but this must be symbolic – it's all new and shiny. Always one for the grand gesture, that's Shaun. His neighbour Suzie's looking after the flat and keeping his post for him while he's away, so he'd know I wouldn't go there unless he asked me specifically.'

'And why can't we take the car?'

'I have no idea, but the bus'll make a change, and anyway, the Land Rover's making weird noises, and I need to get it seen to.'

'Come on then – I can't wait!'

As the bus bowled down the coast road, Molly thought about all this Valentine's Day malarkey. Sometimes she'd been green with envy when her friends had huge bouquets of red roses and gilt-edged cards delivered, but mostly she'd thought the whole thing was a big waste of time and money unless you had a secret passion for someone.

'Did *you* get any cards this year, Dot?' she asked, suddenly aware of how pretty her almost-daughter looked today, with her blue and green dreadlocks flowing down her back and a tapestry-style fitted coat with a fur collar making her look like a sixties film star.

'Might have,' said Dot, blushing.

'Hey, go on – tell!'

'Anonymous, nothing to tell.'

'You must have some idea who it's from?'

But Dot just shrugged and looked out of the window. Molly put that question away for later as they pulled into Shaun's village. As the bus rolled to a stop, Dot turned to Molly.

'Did you think of sending any cards this year?' she asked. Molly raised her eyebrows and said nothing. Dot grinned.

The flat was in the east wing of a rather seedy country house, and could only be approached down a narrow lane. The early-morning rain had cleared to leave behind a bright, cold day, with enough pale sunshine to make the walk a pleasure. But after they had twice been nearly ploughed up by passing tractors, Molly began to wish they'd taken the taxi option. She'd definitely call one for the return journey, she decided.

'Here we are,' she said at last, stopping by a pair of enormous wrought-iron gates. They were ajar, and Dot's mouth fell open as she and Molly turned into the driveway and began to make their way through the avenue of tall trees towards the house.

'Wow! Is Shaun loaded or something?' asked Dot. 'This place must be worth a fortune.'

'No, he just rents part of the attic – the old servants' quarters, I suppose. He's made it look great, though. Come on, I know the code to get us into the lobby.'

They emerged into a large, square hallway and began to climb the stairs, each landing less impressive than the last. As they reached the attic floor, one of the doors in the corridor opened and the tip of a permed head of blonde hair was visible.

'Oh, hello, Suzie,' said Molly. 'How are you?'

'Molly! I've been meaning to phone you but I kept putting it off.' The lady came right out into the corridor and hugged Molly, glancing at Dot with interest.

'Why? Is everything okay with the flat?'

'Yes, dear, it's all fine. I just wanted to see how you were doing. I promised Shaun I'd keep an eye on everything.'

'And that includes me, does it?' Molly grinned.

Suzie laughed. 'Well, he didn't leave instructions for you, but I know he'll not have stopped worrying even if he's all those miles away.' The women exchanged smiles. Shaun was a big part of Suzie's life – she'd always been a substitute older sister/aunt to him. Molly suddenly missed her friend with a painful intensity, blinking away tears as she chatted to Suzie about the likelihood of Simon persuading Shaun to emigrate somewhere hot.

Finally, aware of Dot's fidgety presence behind her, Molly said her goodbyes and turned away from Suzie, motioning Dot towards the next door along the passage. She got out the shiny new key and let them into the sunlit space under the eaves. Shaun had done wonders with his home.

The floor was sanded to a satin finish and, although he had a minimum of furniture, Molly knew that each piece had been lovingly chosen. A basket chair stood next to a huge, squashy sofa and the coffee table was polished to a deep shine. There was greenery everywhere. Suzie had obviously been working hard to keep the forest of plants flourishing.

'What are we looking for?' whispered Dot.

'There's no need to whisper, we're supposed to be here, you wally.'

Molly looked around and spied on the dining table a pink-wrapped parcel with her name on it in capital letters. It was large, rectangular, and quite thick. Some sort of book? She approached it warily. It was strange being in Shaun's flat without him, and she began to understand Dot's whisper.

'Go on, open it,' said Dot, coming to stand beside her. Molly began to pick away at the sticky tape. 'Hurry up!' hissed Dot. 'Just tear the paper.'

In seconds, Molly revealed a dark red photo album. It was embossed with gold and had the word 'Memories' etched on the front cover. There was a note with it.

This was Jake's book, but I always looked after it for him. For some reason, he didn't want to keep it at home. I told him you'd love to see it, but he said it was private. His own special memories. You might want to help yourself to what's on the sideboard – this could take some time.

Love you xxx

Dot looked around the room. 'Oh, look what he left for you. That explains the bus or taxi suggestion.'

On the oak sideboard stood a bottle of what looked like rather expensive red wine, a corkscrew, and half a dozen glasses. Was Shaun expecting her to throw a party? There was also a bag of Twiglets (Molly's favourites) and a jar of anchovy-stuffed olives (ditto). Molly sighed. Shaun seemed worlds away at this moment. Why had he left her to do all this emotional stuff on her own?

'Let's open the bottle and get comfy,' she said. 'I think we might be here for some time. Look, he's left a box of tissues, too. That's not filling me with confidence.'

Dot deftly uncorked the wine and filled two glasses, while Molly put Twiglets and olives into the two little bowls that Shaun had also thoughtfully provided.

'It's like an exclusive cocktail party, isn't it? Very posh. Are you ready, Moll?' said Dot, settling into a corner of the sofa.

Molly sat down and took a deep breath. She opened the album and gasped at the cover sheet. Jake's spidery handwriting had usually been a challenge to read, but he seemed to have made a special effort here.

This is my book. It's not to share; it's very personal, and if you're looking at it, you'd either better have asked my permission or have been given it already. Either way, enjoy.

Molly shivered and turned the page.

The book was, like her husband's moods, completely random. Pictures of Molly and Jake as children were interspersed with family groups, newspaper clippings of their engagement and wedding announcements. There were certificates awarded over the years, teenage snapshots, and later, assorted photographs of Sam, Theo, Hattie and Max. Many of the photographs that Molly had been looking for were here in this book – the best of the lot.

Now and again there were shots of Jake's school and college friends. Shaun featured heavily, and there was a whole page devoted to what must have been a holiday abroad, judging by the strong sunshine and azure sky. Tall horse chestnut trees formed a backdrop, and two very good-looking boys – one dark and one blond – each had an arm around Shaun and Jake's tanned shoulders. They were leaning on the wall of what looked like a beer garden. In the background could be seen chalets with window boxes full of scarlet geraniums. Jake was holding an enormous tankard and the boys were all laughing.

'I've never seen these before,' said Molly. 'It looks a bit like Switzerland or Austria. Jake didn't say he'd been to either of those places.'

'Could it be Germany?' guessed Dot. 'There's someone there in the background with those funny leather shorts on. I did a project on Bavaria for school once. It looked a bit like this in places.'

Molly bent to study the two strange boys in the photo. 'It's weird to think there are people in here that I didn't know anything about.'

'It's his whole life,' breathed Dot, leaning as close as she possibly could and pointing to various other people, asking question after question. She was enthralled by this collage of background information, and Molly thought Shaun had probably meant the book to be as much for Jake's daughter as for herself. That is, until she turned to the final page in the album. There were still several pages unfilled, but this was the last complete one. In the centre of the rectangle, Jake had pasted a shiny pink heart, obviously cut from a magazine.

All around this were pictures of Molly, each cut into its own heart shape. There was Molly in her wedding dress laughing up at her dad, as a snub-nosed little girl in a gingham frock, holding the new-born Sam with an expression of utter bliss on her face, in denim dungarees painting a room in their very first house, and finally – in the very centre of the pink heart – with Jake at the bistro. She remembered that picture well. It had been taken on his opening night, towards the end of the evening. The day had been fraught with small disasters but everything had finally come together and Jake had triumphed.

There was a caption on this main photograph, again in Jake's scrawl.

My Molly. You make it all worthwhile. Happy Anniversary.

There was a long silence. After a moment, Dot said, 'When's your anniversary?'

'June. But it's not a special one. I don't know why he'd do this for me,' answered Molly, swallowing a huge lump in her throat.

'Did you know he loved you this much?'

Molly shook her head, the album swimming before her eyes. She supposed deep down she had felt cared-for, but the day-to-day irritations and worries of raising four children, getting over her own and Jake's infidelity, moving to a whole new area, and starting a business had taken its toll on the couple in the picture who had held hands and faced the world together. She blew her nose and turned back to the first page, beginning to go through the photographs, and explaining more of them to Jake's daughter as she went along.

She marvelled at Jake's patience. When had he done this? It must have taken hours. Had he been collecting things gradually and then put the album together all in one go, or had he been working on it for years? She longed to have time to ask him – just half an hour... ten minutes... to tell him how much she appreciated this magnificent gesture, and how unbearably touched she was that he'd wanted to document their life, and to end with that visual love letter.

As she finished the book for the second time, the tears overwhelmed her, and she felt Dot's strong arms encircle her as they both cried for the man they hadn't known nearly well enough.

16

The next few weeks passed without any sign of more boxes. Tom fretted that he wasn't hearing from Molly much – somehow, the agreed-upon meal hadn't happened and the odd text, the occasional quick phone call and snatched meetings for coffee in the town were leaving him anxious and wanting more.

If it hadn't been for Dot, Tom didn't know what he'd have done. Her phone calls always seemed to come when he was at his lowest ebb, and she never failed to cheer him up.

'Come on, you old misery,' Dot said one morning. She'd called Tom after he'd texted her to see how Molly was doing, moaning that it was days since she'd been in touch. 'You've got to give her some space for a little while.'

'But I want to see her. She'll forget about me.'

Dot laughed. 'Oh, I don't think that's likely, do you?'

'Has she said something to you about me? Dot, tell me what she's been saying? Please?'

'Look, calm down. It's not all about you at the moment. Molly's wondering if the next box hasn't come yet because Shaun's giving her time to get her breath back – finding out how much Jake must have loved her has been mind-blowing, and she still feels sort of disorientated.'

'But she's okay, isn't she, Dot? She's not sick or anything?'

'No, she's definitely not sick, but it's hard for her just now. She seems to lurch between total exhaustion and getting really wound up with the kids when they rub her up the wrong way.'

'What about the photo album? How does she feel about that?'

'She keeps it with her all the time.'

Tom felt unreasonable jealousy building up as Dot spoke. He tried to shake it off – it was ridiculous. How could he resent a dead man? 'Dot, I'm going to come round later. I've got to see her. We could maybe have a takeaway?'

'Good idea. Maybe she'll show you the album. But don't hold your breath, she hasn't even told the kids about it yet.'

As Dot had suggested, the precious album was brought out that night for Tom to see, after dinner was over and the children were busy upstairs. He had to grit his teeth and smile, even though the bitter taste of envy made it hard to look at.

Sharing the photographs with Tom seemed to help, and Molly told Tom that she had decided it was time to share it with the rest of the family. She called them down, and they were very excited to find themselves featured in their dad's book of memories.

The only thing that made them sad was that Jake hadn't put many pictures of himself in there, so Dot helped them to sort out their favourite snapshots of their dad and to arrange them over the last few pages. This took several happy evenings, and was when Tom really began to feel part of the family.

He soon got into the habit of shopping online for tempting things to cook and would then meet Molly on her work nights to save her taking the big car into town. There was very little parking space at most of the schools where she worked, so it was easier for her to walk between them or catch a bus. But by the end of the day she was usually shattered, and the offer of a lift home was always well received.

Then, while Molly bustled around and organised the children, Tom would settle himself at the kitchen table and chop, slice, and prepare their supper. Later, they would cook the meal between them and all eat together, swapping their day's news, moaning about various people who had annoyed them, and eating vast quantities of Tom's favourite recipes.

Max's favourite was chilli – he had very sturdy tastebuds for a six-year-old – Hattie loved Tom's prawn risotto, and Theo was addicted to his baked cod in butter, with spinach and fluffy mashed potatoes. Dot blossomed, too, in this atmosphere of happy families. She often fetched the younger children from school and joined them for dinner. Tom could see that Molly was appreciating this new way of coping. Jake had left an enormous hole in her life and she and the children were suffering in their different ways, but it was good for them to have a change of routine.

Tom suffered, too, in a different way. He was in no doubt now of his feelings for Molly. Just the sight of her black hair flying as she ran towards his car was enough to set his heart pounding. She had begun to give him a quick kiss on the cheek as she climbed in, and he found himself waiting anxiously in case she forgot one day.

Once, he had accidentally turned as she leaned towards him, and their lips had met for a moment. They had both pulled back, pink with embarrassment, but the feeling of excitement had stayed with Tom all evening, making him tingle uncomfortably. He was positive now that he could make love to Molly whenever he got the chance. But would it ever happen? She still seemed subdued after the revelation of Jake's album. Dot said that Molly was beating herself up, and that she felt she hadn't loved Jake enough.

'Do you believe that, too, Dot?' he'd asked.

'It's hard to say. I never really had the chance to get to know him, but it sounds as if he could be a right bugger when he chose to be. There were good things and bad things about their marriage, I guess.'

'Like what?'

But Dot wouldn't be drawn on this one and just shook her head sadly.

Then, one evening, while Tom was slicing onions for a cottage pie, listening to the rain beating against the windows and feeling deeply contented, he heard Molly cry out from the hallway.

'What's up, Moll?' Dot yelled, as she loaded the washing machine with the children's wet and muddy school clothes.

Molly came slowly into the kitchen. She was holding a letter, and her hand was shaking.

'Are the kids upstairs?' she asked.

'Yes, I sent Theo up to bath the others before we eat; they were freezing after we got caught in that storm. What's up? Is it a bill?' Tom knew that Molly had been worrying about money. There never seemed to be quite enough. Jake hadn't been insured and, although the bistro was still doing well under Louisa's rule, wages had to be paid, and Molly's own salary was pitifully inadequate to run a family house. She shook her head and put the letter on the table, wrapping her arms around herself.

'I just found this on the mat. It must have been delivered by hand, so it's from somebody local. That makes it even worse.'

Dot reached the letter before Tom had a chance to drop his knife.

'What's this all about? It's filth,' she exclaimed, having scanned it in seconds.

'Read it to me, would you, Dot?' said Tom. 'My hands are all oniony.'

'*This is to say that we know what you're up to, you*

dirty bitch,' read Dot. '*Your husband is hardly cold in his grave and already you're sleeping with the cripple.*'

Tom sat very still. He hadn't heard that word for a very long time. It took him back to the playground, and large boys with sneering faces. He swallowed.

'Could you... could you pass me some water, please?' he asked.

'Oh, God, Tom, I shouldn't even have read it out. It's disgusting,' said Dot, filling a glass at the sink. 'Molly, have you got any idea who could have sent this? We need to go to the police.'

Tom squared his shoulders. 'There's no need for that, surely. It's just some local gossip trying to stir it up. You have to ignore stuff like this, otherwise they've won.'

'Well, it's someone who knows how to spell and do apostrophes,' said Molly. 'Sorry, that sounded really snobbish, I just mean it's not some ignorant yob.'

'I don't care who it is, they can't go around saying that sort of thing, can they?' Dot began to tidy up manically, almost throwing Tom's heap of onions away before he grabbed her arm.

'Look, I don't suppose it matters really, does it?' he said. 'We don't want a big fuss – it'd upset the kids. They'd be bound to find out. I don't want them to think of me like that or I'll have to stop coming here.'

He put his ingredients on a tray on his knee and wheeled himself over to the cooker. Making dinner would take his mind off this nightmare. Who would want to make trouble for any of them? They weren't causing anybody a problem, were they? Tom seethed as he fried onions, garlic and mince, crashing pans around dangerously.

Molly came over to stand behind him and put her hands on his shoulders. Tom almost dropped his spatula. 'It must be just some busybody with a bee in their bonnet about how widows should behave,' she said soothingly. 'I was shocked when I read it, but really it doesn't matter.'

'Doesn't matter? Are you mad?' Dot stared at Molly. 'You can't just sit back and let a random stranger make accusations about you two. As if you'd ever do anything like that? I'm going to check on Max – it's gone very quiet up there.'

As Dot left the room, Tom stirred his pan carefully. Molly began to lay the table, avoiding his eyes. After a moment, she said, 'I'm sorry for bringing you into this mess.'

'Are you kidding? I love being here. I don't care what people say for my sake, it's just the rest of you

I'm worried about.' He paused, dreading her answer but knowing what he had to ask. 'Molly, do you want me to stop coming round?'

'No!' The word exploded from her mouth, and she reddened. 'That's the last thing I want.'

'Well, that's okay then, and anyway, as Dot says, we wouldn't dream of doing anything like that, would we?' He smiled up at her and she looked steadily back, unblinking.

'Erm, no. No, we wouldn't, would we?'

Max burst into the room, followed by Hattie. They did two laps of the table before Molly could stop them, collapsing in giggles on the floor by the back door as they ran out of steam.

'I win, loser,' crowed Hattie, pulling a hideous face at Max.

'No, you don't. Tell her, Mum. She's a great big fat cheater.'

'Give it a rest and let's go and FaceTime Sam, shall we? I think he said he'd be at home about now,' said Dot, bringing up the rear with Theo. The rest of them followed her out, leaving Tom and Molly alone again. Molly switched on the radio. It was tuned to her favourite station that played a constant selection of nineties hits, and the sound of one of Tom's all-time favourite songs filled the room. She turned it off again.

'No, leave it, Molly. I love that one,' he said. 'I know you were just trying to fill the silence, but Paul Weller's as good a way as any to do it. And he's right – you definitely do something to me.'

She grinned. 'Really? Something good, or something horrible?'

'Well, I wasn't going to mention it tonight, but... sodding hell, the onions are burning!'

The rescue operation took several minutes and by that time the others were back, chattering madly about Sam and his new girlfriend. Hattie was totally bewitched. 'We actually saw her, Mum, she's got long blonde hair, she's dead pretty—'

'She's not that pretty,' said Max scornfully. 'She's got goofy teeth and braces.'

'Max! Don't be so rude,' said Dot. 'She's lovely. Sam likes her, and anyway, it's none of our business.'

In the argument that followed, Tom and Molly were able to get back some semblance of normality. Theo got her phone out to select one of her latest Spotify playlists and started to dance with Hattie. As the children got noisier, Tom kept an eye on Molly but she seemed calm again, and only mentioned the letter obliquely when she came out to the car with him.

'Let's just forget tonight, shall we, Tom?'

'What – all of it? I'm not sure if I can.'

He slid into the driving seat and waited to see how she would say goodbye. After a moment's hesitation, Molly bent and kissed him quickly and very gently on the lips. Before he could respond, she straightened up and looked around at the deserted street.

'There you go – if anybody's watching.' She raised her voice slightly. 'I just kissed this good friend of mine. Ha! Feel free to take photos.'

Tom grinned at her and closed the door before he was tempted to scoop her onto his knee. Enough for tonight; they had come a long way already. He raised a hand in farewell and drove away. He was way too fired up to sleep; he would start a new painting. It was time to branch out. He'd never tried portraits, but tonight he was going to paint the woman of his dreams.

17

'Have you done anything else about getting yourself a dog?' asked Dot, as she and Molly walked along the promenade. It was over a week since the anonymous letter, but there had been no more deliveries and Molly was beginning to think it was just a one-off burst of poison from someone with too much time on their hands.

The morning was so beautiful that she couldn't bring herself to think about spiteful people. Although the wind from the sea was chilly, the sun was trying to break through, and Molly felt an unexpected bubble of happiness as she watched the children throwing a Frisbee to each other down on the shore.

'I emailed a few rescue places and put my name on their lists,' she said, 'but they have to check you out. So it might be a long wait for a cocker spaniel.'

'Why does it have to be one of those? Are you a dog expert all of a sudden?'

Molly laughed. 'No, it's just that I always wanted a cocker – I love their big sad eyes.'

'That's silly. Why would you want something with depressing eyes? Now, what I reckon is, you need a cheerful sort of dog. One with character. A fun dog. With a bit of attitude, maybe? And long waggy tail. Spaniels always used to have their tails docked, does that still happen? It seems a bit cruel to me.'

Dot was walking slightly ahead of Molly and didn't turn round as she spoke, so Molly couldn't read her expression. She tapped Dot on the shoulder. 'Is that a random opinion about dogs in general... or not?'

'Ah... well, it's just that a sweet old lady up the road from me has gone into a care home a bit suddenly, and she's had to leave her dog with her son, and he hates dogs, and...'

'Dot, I don't just want any old pooch. I've been waiting to be able to choose my own dog for years.'

'Oh. Okay.'

There was a silence as they reached the end of the promenade and turned to go down onto the beach. Molly sighed. 'Well, what sort of dog is it, then?'

'Ah. It's hard to say really. I think it's got sort of an Airedale Terrier look about it – she, I should say. Her name's Marian. My friend's mum had an Airedale. They're very good with children, apparently.'

Molly tried to sort out this glut of information in her mind. 'Marian? The old lady or the dog?'

'The dog. I know what you're going to say, it is a bit of an odd name but apparently she reminds Mrs Brookes – that's my friend – of her dead Auntie Marian, who was always getting into trouble. Erm, I mean—'

'Right, so you want me to give up my dreams of a beautiful thoroughbred spaniel and adopt a mad beast that's always in trouble and isn't any particular sort of dog?'

'Well, if you put it like that. But Marian's going to have to go to the RSPCA place if no one wants her, and they put them to sleep after a while if they don't find owners, don't they?'

Molly carried on walking in silence until they reached the edge of the sea. She was wearing wellies, because they had decided to tramp the long way over the muddy cliffs. And as the waves began to lap against her booted toes, Molly wondered why nothing in her life was ever straightforward. She couldn't even manage a decent bout of grieving widowhood without gaining a daughter, a dog with behaviour issues, and a rapidly developing passion for a gorgeous man who always seemed to be just out of reach.

'Mightn't you just want to come with me to see Marian? They'll understand if you don't like her, and we needn't tell the kids,' said Dot in a small voice.

'Oh, yeah, right. I go round to meet the family of this deranged animal, get their hopes up, and then take one look at it and go, "Nah – don't like that sort of dog, sorry." Get real, Dot.'

'Yes, I see what you mean. Oh well, I expect they'll find somebody with a kind heart, eventually.'

Molly stuck the next period of silence for as long as she could, skimming stones into the grey sea and wishing she had decided to defrost the fridge, or clean the toilet, or anything but suggest a walk with Dot and the children. Luckily, Hattie and Max bounced up to her to demand chips just as she thought she couldn't hold her tongue any longer.

'Okay, come on then. Where's Theo?' Molly said, looking round to include Dot in the invitation.

Dot smiled at her in what could have been an attempt to look winning, but came off more as an insane grimace. 'She just texted me to say she'd met some of her friends by the pier and she'll be home later, but I'd like chips, please. I reckon the best place is the chippie near my house, and then you could come all and have a cup of tea afterwards.'

This was unprecedented. None of them had ever seen Dot's home. Max began to bounce up and down on the spot and Hattie hugged Dot round the waist, nearly overbalancing them both. 'We thought you didn't want us to come to your house, Dot. I said it was because you didn't like hoovering, but Mum said—'

'That's enough, kids,' interrupted Molly. 'We'd all love to come. Shall we take our chips there or have them outside first? I don't mind either way.'

'Oh, we'll take them back with us. I... I don't usually have visitors. It's only that Mum didn't like people coming round, it made her edgy, and I've never really got into the habit.'

They scrambled back up the beach and headed for the town. Molly was intrigued. What sort of place would Dot's house be? Cosy? Ultra tidy? Minimalist, or chintzy and cluttered? As they walked down one of the long streets leading away from the seafront,

Dot waved frantically to a man coming the other way.

'Hey, John!' she shouted. 'It's great to see you. And look, Molly, here's Marian.'

Molly stopped and stared. Coming towards them was the strangest dog she had ever seen, dragging an angry-looking man behind it. The dog was brindled grey, black and brown, with wild side whiskers, and gleaming, liquid brown eyes. Its tongue hung rakishly out of the side of its mouth and its long legs looked delicate and spindly, as if a newborn calf had been crossed with some sort of wolfhound.

'Hi, John,' said Dot, bending down to pat the dog when it was close enough, 'and how's Marian today?'

'Blooming nuisance,' said the man. 'Just ate most of one the missus's slippers and then sicked it up on the rug. Off down to the pound with her now.'

'What's a pound?' asked Hattie, wide-eyed.

'Place where you take useless mutts like this one, to get rid of 'em once and for all,' said the man.

'Useless? That's not very kind, is it, Mum?' Max said, tugging on Molly's hand. 'Dogs aren't useless, they're lovely. Don't you want your doggy, John?' He stared at the man, planting his feet slightly apart.

'Want her? Why would I want this stupid lump? She ain't mine, anyway; she's my ma's.'

'But doesn't your ma want her, then?' asked Hattie.

Molly glared at Dot. 'Sometimes people can't look after their dogs, and they have to find new homes for them, Hattie,' she said, willing Dot to back her up. 'I expect the RSPCA will soon find a really good home for the dog, won't they, Dot?'

Dot shrugged.

'But, Mum, what if nobody wants her?' wailed Max, starting to cry. 'She's going to be really sad.' The dog sat down and put her head on one side, holding up a paw towards Hattie.

'Oh, Mum – she's so clever, look at her trying to shake paws. Hey! Mum, *we* could have this dog, couldn't we? We've got lots of room in the garden, and—'

'Hattie, you can't just help yourself to someone else's dog, just because it can do one cute trick,' said Molly.

'It's okay by me, love. You can have 'er if you want 'er. My old ma would be tickled pink if she was adopted by some nice kids.'

Dot, Max and Hattie gazed at Molly. Marian whimpered and stood up, coming to lean against Molly's legs.

'So I guess resistance is useless?' said Molly.

'What?' Dot frowned, and Molly was hit by yet another horrible moment when Jake would have known exactly what she meant and spotted the reference. The shared language of their marriage was one of the hardest things to lose.

'It was what the chief Vogon used to say in *The Hitchhiker's Guide to the Galaxy* – resistance is useless? Oh, never mind. Has Marian got a bed, or special bowls, or anything? What does she eat?'

For a moment, no one seemed to register the second part of what Molly had just said but soon Dot, Max and Hattie were hugging her, patting Marian, and whooping with delight.

'Sam and Theo are going to go mental when they see our dog,' yelled Max. 'Let's get her stuff now, can we?' he asked John.

'By all means, son.'

They followed John back down the road, but Dot seemed uneasy. 'Would it be okay if we eat first, John, only I think Marian could get a bit excited when she smells chips?'

'Okay, just give us a knock when you've done; the wife'll be over the moon. Right then, that's great. It's soon going to be "So long, Marian".'

'What did you say?' asked Hattie, frowning.

'It's a song, love. "So Long, Marianne"? Leonard

Cohen?' John looked around at everyone's blank faces. 'Oh, forget it, you're all too young. I'll see you later.'

As they queued for their lunch, Max slipped his hand into Molly's. 'Thanks, Mum,' he said.

She looked down at his round, freckled face. What would his dad have said to this? But Jake had gone, and Shaun had known how much Molly had always wanted a dog. Just... not this dog.

* * *

At five o'clock, Tom heard Sasha closing the shop, and put his brush down with a satisfied sigh. He sat back and gazed at the portrait. He had painted Molly's back view, sitting on the pebbly beach with her knees drawn up under her chin. She was wearing the cherry-red sweater and a pair of old jeans tucked into boots. Molly's hair was loose – a wild cloud of dark curls around her shoulders.

'Why didn't you paint her face?' asked Sasha, putting a steaming mug of coffee by his side. 'I thought you'd have wanted to do her full justice?'

'Nobody could do Molly justice,' said Tom.

'Jeez, you've really got it bad. Does she know you fancy her rotten?'

'Yes. No. I don't know.'

'Well, that covers all bases, I s'pose. Why haven't you come clean about the way you feel?'

'It's not like just fancying somebody, Sasha. It's much more than that.'

'You luuuurve her, is that it? But you don't want to get into her knickers? Yeah, right. But still, why can't you just bloody tell her?'

'I don't know. I'm scared, I guess.'

'Scared of what?' Sasha gazed at Tom, wide-eyed. He wondered what it must feel like to be so confident of your own sexual powers that any sort of qualms were incomprehensible.

'Well, I can't expect you to get it, Sasha. If you like a bloke, you just eyeball him and ask him if he's up for a shag.'

They grinned at each other, and Tom thought of tonight with a spasm of terror. He'd phoned to ask Molly out and they were going somewhere for dinner for the very first time. Dot was babysitting, and Molly had said he could pick her up at eight.

'I need to make sure they're all behaving themselves, even if Hattie and Max won't go to sleep if they know I'm going out,' she'd said. 'And there's Marian, too, now for Dot to manage.'

'Marian? Have you had another baby without telling me?'

She laughed. 'No, it's a long story, I'll tell you later. But my gang do take quite a bit of organising.'

'Have they always been like this?'

'I never really went out much before, but they're definitely worse since Jake... since Jake died.'

She seemed to be finding it easier to say those words these days. And tonight they'd have some time to talk without being surrounded by her family. Tom was getting more and more attached to Molly's brood, including the feisty Dot, but he longed to have her to himself.

He'd booked a taxi so they could both have a drink, and had even bought a new shirt – soft sea-green material that went well with his favourite black jeans and grey linen jacket. He wondered if Molly would even notice what he was wearing tonight. At least he'd be able to see if the electricity that had sparked between them on the night that she'd kissed him goodbye would still be there.

18

The restaurant wasn't quite what Molly had expected. From the outside it looked fine, with soft lighting, small tables, candles, and a big chalkboard with the day's specials listed in beautiful copperplate writing.

What neither of them had realised was that Tom and his wheelchair wouldn't fit down any of the gangways, because most of the tables were occupied and everyone seemed to have spread themselves out. Chairs were pushed back, bags were on the floor, and some people had even kept their coats with them and draped them over their chairs. The restaurant manager clucked around them, obsequious but adamant that health and safety rules must be obeyed.

'I know you want to sit at a table on a *normal* chair, sir, but we have to have our fire exits clear and your wheelchair is very wide. I have no room to store it, I'm afraid,' he said, when he'd been summoned from a back room by an anxious waiter.

Molly was horrified to see that Tom's jaw was clenched and he was deathly pale. His voice could have chilled ice cubes. 'So what are you suggesting?'

'Well, if you'd like to have this table over at the side...'

'The one right next to the toilet, you mean?'

'Handy for the cloakroom, yes... which I'm sure would be useful.'

'And why might it be more useful to me than anyone else? Are you assuming I'm incontinent?'

'Tom, I don't think—' Molly interrupted, putting a hand on Tom's arm.

He shook her off and glared at the manager. 'So, if I *do* agree to sit with my guest at the table with the excellent toilet access, where will my wheelchair go?'

'It would fit nicely under that table, sir, saving you the bother of transferring to a less comfortable chair.'

'And do your other customers not mind being given these "less comfortable chairs"? Are their back-sides less sensitive than mine, for some reason?'

Molly was scarlet with embarrassment by now, but felt a giggle about to burst out. She bit her lip and studied the shiny laminate flooring. She mustn't laugh. This was serious. Was it usual for Tom to be treated like this? All the other diners had stopped eating to listen, and the silence that followed Tom's last question was painful.

'Right, we're leaving immediately,' said Tom, 'but you'll be hearing from us again very soon, probably through the local paper. This definitely comes under the heading of discrimination. Goodnight.'

The manager rushed to open the door for them as Tom hurtled out onto the street. Molly nodded to the man, torn between sympathy for the verbal trouncing and anger at his treatment of Tom. They carried on down the street, covering at least a hundred yards before Tom began to slow down.

'Oh, God, Molly, I'm sorry. Where am I going to take you now? You must be starving. Is there anywhere else decent around here?'

'I don't know, but I think that place might be out of bounds from now on. We're definitely off his Christmas card list.'

They looked at each other and began to laugh, all the tension slipping away. It didn't matter where they went – Molly had a feeling that tonight was going to be significant. There was a buzz in the air, and she noticed for the first time how good Tom looked. When the taxi had collected her, she'd been so pre-occupied with settling her strange new pet and trying to find an un-laddered pair of tights – Marian was already proving to be a bouncing-all-over-you type of dog – that she hadn't even looked at him properly.

Molly tried hard to stop herself from staring. Tom's cropped curls were still damp from the shower and she could smell the lemony tang of his after-shave. A sprinkling of tiny blond hairs was just visible at the open neck of his shirt, and his eyes were glinting with mischief.

'I know, let's go to that pizza place by the market square,' she suggested, giving herself a mental slap. 'I love dough balls.'

'I bet you say that to all the blokes.'

Molly began to snigger again, and Tom led the way through the quiet town. The pizza restaurant wasn't far away but there were some places that were awkward for him to propel himself along. Without a word, Molly took hold of the handles of his chair and took over the steering. Looking down, she had an overwhelming urge to stop and kiss the top of his head, to nuzzle the short blond curls and to inhale the sheer maleness of him.

Panicking that she was going to let herself down, Molly speeded up, almost colliding with a couple coming the other way.

'Molly, slow down, it's not a race. We're here now, look,' Tom said, grabbing the railings outside the pizzeria to stop Molly's flight.

The door was already open for a group of chattering teenagers who were gradually making their way out. The last one held it open for Tom and Molly. Molly hoped Tom wouldn't find this patronising, but he only smiled his thanks and wheeled himself inside. She held her breath, waiting for a repeat performance of the previous place, but the waitress that came towards them was a different breed altogether.

Quickly and efficiently, she showed them to a table that had plenty of room all around it and busied herself taking Molly's coat while Tom got himself organised. Then she folded up his wheelchair and stowed it where it was unobtrusive but easy to get at. Molly breathed again.

'Can I get you guys some drinks while you look at

the menu?' their waitress asked, bustling around with clean water glasses and napkins.

'I think we deserve one. Wine, Molly?'

'I never whine on a first date.'

For some reason, this pathetic crack had them both in hysterics again. The waitress smiled sympathetically. 'Bottle of house white? And some water? Fine.'

She left them alone and Tom reached for Molly's hand. 'I don't know what to say.'

'Say "Would you like to see my dough balls?" That always works for me.'

When their waitress came back, Tom and Molly were hiccupping gently, trying to calm down. She poured the wine and Tom approved it, sniffing and tasting expertly. Their glasses were soon beaded with condensation. The wine was delicious – cool, fragrant and with a hint of pencil shavings, thought Molly, reminding herself of a pompous TV connoisseur. She giggled again, and then had to tell Tom why she was laughing.

They spent the next five minutes making up even better descriptions, and were still engrossed in this game when the girl came back for their order.

'...skittish, slightly malevolent, and with a light touch of macadamia nuts and seaweed,' said Molly.

'I think you'll find it has more of a nuance of cat food, gently tinged with the dew collected at daybreak from the fleece of Spanish goats,' answered Tom. 'I'm also getting overtones of squid.'

The waitress raised an eyebrow. 'So I'm guessing you two will need another few minutes to choose?' she asked.

Molly grabbed the menu. 'No, don't go away. I'm sorry, we've just had a bit of a strange few weeks and we're a bit demob happy tonight. I'll have the four-cheese stuffed crust extravaganza with extra pepperoni. What about you, Tom?'

'Hawaiian thin and crispy, please. And double dough balls.'

They began to splutter again and the waitress left, rolling her eyes.

'Do you want me to fetch us something from the salad bar? Or does that sound as if I'm babying you?' asked Molly, glancing round to calculate the mechanics of Tom getting round three tables and in between two giant cheese plants.

'I'm not that neurotic, am I? No – you go. But you need to remember that I hate beetroot even more than coleslaw. And those nasty little croutons are only okay to flick at people on other tables.'

As she wove her way through the obstacles,

Molly reflected that this was going rather well. They knew quite a lot about each other already, thanks to the time Tom had spent in her kitchen recently, and there had been no uncomfortable silences so far. In fact, she couldn't imagine there ever being a time when they didn't have lots to say to each other.

They were almost at the end of the second bottle of wine when Molly had an epiphany. 'Tom, why don't you come and stay at my house with the kids if Shaun sends me off somewhere again? It would save me asking my mum, and Edna's really getting past childminding.'

'What's brought this on?' Tom blinked and reached for both of her hands. 'You mean, you think I'm capable of looking after the kids without you and Dot to weigh in?'

'Oh, I shouldn't have asked. You probably think it sounds like the idea from hell. And now there's that bizarre dog, too.'

'No, not at all, I'm just... I can't believe you trust me that much.'

Molly tried to speak, but the warmth of his fingers was doing magical things to her insides. She held on tightly, suddenly aware that she was quite drunk. It had been a while since she'd had this much wine in one go, and all the upheavals of the evening hadn't helped. How was she going to get out of this place without falling on her face? Tom began to caress her fingertips with his thumbs, and Molly's nerve endings went into overdrive. He lifted her left hand and kissed it gently.

'That's very French, Tom,' said Molly, desperately trying to get her mind off the sight of his forearms. He'd rolled up his sleeves, and Molly couldn't help staring – his arms, as always, almost unbearably turned her on. He must be incredibly well-muscled all over his upper half, she thought, wondering how it would feel to be lying down with him, so that their height differences didn't matter. Eye-to-eye, they could take their time to get to know each other a whole lot better. He touched her wedding band.

'How long will you carry on wearing this, do you think?' he asked huskily.

'I don't know. I've wondered that myself. Am I still married to Jake?'

'I suppose the "till death us do part" bit says no, but do you still feel married?'

'Sort of – yes and no. Would it be letting him down to take my ring off?'

'You could try it... just for a few minutes.'

'What, right now?' Molly looked down at her hand, lit by the glow of the candles on the table. She had never had an engagement ring – they'd been saving for a house, and Jake had thought it would be a waste of money. Her wedding ring shone in the flickering light. She let go of Tom's hands and began to ease it off. It stuck slightly over her knuckle and she struggled for a moment. Tom watched, expressionless. At last, the ring slid free and she put it on the tablecloth between them.

'So how does it feel?' Tom said, after a moment.

'I don't know yet. Scary. Sad. Treacherous. Exciting?' She stopped at the last word and gazed at him, horrified.

'Let's get the bill and go,' said Tom.

In the back of the taxi, they leaned together, holding hands tightly.

'Are you coming in for coffee?' asked Molly, half hoping that he'd say no. It would be hard to act normally with Dot around; her eyes were way too sharp. Tom shook his head.

'I'll need to drop you off so the taxi can take me home,' he said. 'I don't usually drink this much, and I've got a customer coming to meet me first thing about a commission.'

'Oh. Right.' The taxi was already slowing down outside her house. As they pulled onto the drive, Dot flung open the front door and Molly's heart lurched.

'What's the matter? Is somebody ill?' she gasped, jumping out of the car and heading for the door.

Dot held up a hand. 'Hey, calm down. No, nobody's ill.' She reached into her pocket and produced a letter. The handwriting looked very familiar.

19

Tom cursed the writer of that vitriolic letter many times over the next few days. Molly had been disgusted with this latest piece of spite and hadn't wanted him to see it at first, but Dot had insisted that she show him. He'd spent a sleepless night after their pizza date, waiting for Molly to call about what had been said this time. But it wasn't until, in desperation, he turned up on her doorstep the next morning that Tom read the second anonymous note.

In the kitchen, he reached for the mug of coffee that Molly had placed in front of him and unfolded the letter. The words shocked him to the core, even though he'd thought he was ready for anything.

YOU THINK YOU'RE GOING TO GET AWAY WITH THIS, BUT YOU WON'T. WE KNOW WHAT YOU'RE DOING, YOU FILTHY, CRIP-PLE-LOVING WHORE.

It was handwritten in capitals, carefully and tidily presented. The neatness of it seemed to make it even more shocking.

'What do they mean, *get away with it*? I'm not doing anything,' Molly said, folding the letter up again with trembling hands. 'Look at me, I'm shaking, Tom. How can I let them rattle me like this?'

'I know you're shocked, but you've got to get this in perspective. Whoever's written this is the one with the problem, not you. It's just some bitter and twisted idiot who's got nothing better to do than stir up gossip where there isn't any.'

'Yes, but there's not just us to consider; what about the kids? If this keeps happening, they'll be bound to find out, and then they'll look at me as if I'm... I'm...' Molly burst into tears, and Tom wheeled himself over to her.

'Look, the girls already think you... erm... fancy me,' he said. 'Hattie's mentioned it before, and she didn't seem in any way traumatised.'

'What?' Molly's face flamed, and she flinched as Tom tried to put his arms around her.

'Molly, I'm only giving you a hug. Please don't push me away,' he said.

She folded her arms and shook her head. 'I think we'd better not.'

'But that means the letter writer has won!' he shouted.

'Shhhhh, Theo's upstairs. She's on study leave today.'

Tom sighed, and turned for the door. 'I'm going to go home now. Ring me if you need to talk later. This is ridiculous.' He hoped she would try to stop him, but Molly just held open the front door and wordlessly waved goodbye. He could see her in his rear-view mirror as he drove away. She was glancing up and down the street nervously.

Back at his studio, Tom couldn't settle to anything. Eventually he flopped into his favourite chair and seethed. Didn't Molly realise that he was a flesh and blood man? How could she keep him at arm's length like this? Sasha brought him tea and some of his favourite ginger biscuits, but found them untouched an hour later when she came back to check on him.

'What's up, boss?' she asked, frowning at the sight of his drooping shoulders.

'Ah, nothing much. I just wish people would mind their own business.'

'Hey, you miserable git, I only said...'

'Not you, Sash. Look, ignore me. I'm just in a lousy mood.'

'No, really?'

Tom laughed. 'Okay, I get the message. Look, this is a waste of a fantastic day and we could both do with a break. We've had no customers for the last hour, everyone's gone to the beach now the sun's out. Let's shut up shop and take Gnasher for a walk, shall we?'

'Brilliant, I love this time of year, especially in the woods. The spring's only just getting going and everywhere looks really fresh and clean. Where shall we go?'

'That place up the coast and inland a bit, where the paths are wide and I can park near the entrance? You know, the country park?'

'Okay. I'll just cash up and then I'll be ready.'

As Tom drove north with Sasha and the wildly excited Gnasher, his heart ached for Molly. He knew she was upset, but why was she being so prickly when he only wanted to cheer her up? He sat up straight and tried to be decisive. Okay, if she didn't want to let him near her, he would keep away for a while to give her some space. Max might miss him, at least.

He felt rather than saw Sasha glance at him as he stared straight ahead at the busy road. She sighed. Even Gnasher was picking up on Tom's mood and began to whine in the back. The breeze blowing in through the car window was filled with the heady scent of wet earth and the sun shone through the still-bare branches of the trees, suggesting the possibility of warm April days to come and new leaves. But today was definitely not shaping up as one of their best outings, thought Tom bitterly.

* * *

Molly had hoped that work would take her mind off the letters, but she was struggling to focus on the grumpy seven-year-old boy who was currently murdering 'Three Blind Mice' on the recorder. At least he'd brought his instrument with him today, and had even remembered his music. This was almost unheard of in Molly's world of disillusioned, badly cared-for children, who would usually rather be any-where than school. She smiled at him encouragingly.

'That's brilliant, Kane. You've really been prac-tising this week, haven't you?'

He took the recorder out of his mouth briefly. 'Only a bit.'

'Oh, well, you're lots better, so something must be working.'

'It's 'cos me dad's left.'

'What, left your home? For good this time?'

Kane shrugged. 'He wouldn't ever let me practise. Said the noise makes him want to strangle me. My mum reckons he's a heartless bastard and he de-serves a good kicking.'

'Right.' Molly's heart twisted at the thought of Kane's miserable home life. She hugged herself, sud-denly chilly. Kane had nothing to look forward to, and neither did she. Just same old, same old. Cook-ing, cleaning, ferrying everyone about, getting gradu-ally older and more bitter. Molly looked at the child's pinched, pale face, and cursed herself for her lack of sympathy for him. He had no choice in what hap-pened. He hadn't asked to be born into a loveless marriage. 'Okay, Kane,' she said, attempting a smile. 'Let's try the next one, shall we?'

He shrugged again. Molly looked at her watch.

Only three hours till home time. Would Tom come to fetch her? Probably not, after the way she'd given him the brush-off. He might not come round at all this week. She was shocked at the intensity of the wave of misery that hit her at the thought of no Tom.

_____

20

When the postman arrived with the sixth box, Molly was wallowing in a very deep bubbly bath. She'd left Dot downstairs making breakfast pancakes, and a delicious buttery smell was just beginning to waft its way into the bathroom. It was the start of the Easter holidays and Molly was trying, without much enthusiasm, to make plans for two weeks' worth of fun things to do with her family. As the doorbell rang, she heard the sounds of Marian trying to escape from the kitchen, and frantic scuffles as the dog was restrained.

'Muuuuuuuum, the postman says you've got to sign for this parcel. Do you want me to do it?' Theo bellowed up the stairs.

'Oh! Yes, please, love, I'll be down in a minute.'

Molly heard Dot come through from the kitchen and take over from Theo, then light footsteps coming up the stairs.

'It's okay, I've got it, Moll. I told them it was probably an early birthday present from your Auntie Maisie in Bournemouth,' Dot hissed through the closed door. 'I'll put it in your bedroom. But hurry up! I can't wait to see what's next.'

Molly dried herself hastily and struggled to get her still-damp body into leggings and a baggy t-shirt. She looked down at herself, aware that clothes-wise she was losing the plot. Now Tom had stopped visiting, she didn't seem to have any enthusiasm for choosing what to wear.

Maybe she'd ring him today, to tell him about the box. Perhaps he'd rush straight round. But on the other hand, would the problem of her fizzing attraction for him come back as soon as he was sitting at her kitchen table again, looking as if he belonged? Thoughts of being in bed with Tom were haunting her sleeping and waking dreams daily now, but the gut-wrenching fear of failure was even more scary than the thought of a life without sex. There couldn't be many mothers of four who had never felt the earth move, could there? And if she got it wrong again, Molly would definitely have to admit defeat.

Kate had been able to have a fantastic time in bed with Jake, and Robin must be doing something right for Lydia to still be with him, surely? So it must be Molly who had the big problem, mustn't it? Sighing, she hurried across the landing to find Dot sitting cross-legged on the bed, chewing her nails.

'You took your time. Get a move on, this is driving me crazy. I need to see what's inside the lumpy parcel.'

Molly picked up the package and shook it gently. It was rather an odd shape this time, vaguely oval and obviously well-padded. She began to tear off the brown paper, revealing another layer of bubble wrap and then inside that, a shining yellow and blue cardboard Easter Egg with a bright blue bow round its middle.

'Wow!' breathed Dot, coming closer. 'I've never seen an egg like that before. It's fabulous, just like one of those expensive Fabergé ones, even though this one's made of cardboard. Look at all the gilt twiddly bits. It's gorgeous. Open it, go on.'

Molly undid the bow and eased the lid off the box. Inside was the familiar sheet of pale green writing paper, and underneath, a gold envelope. She unfolded the paper.

> *This quest's more than half the way*
> > *through,*
> *Are you wondering what more you*
> > *must do?*
> *Well, it's time for a break*
> *So decide who to take*
> *(My advice is to try someone new!)*

A break? With a family of four – now five, actually – and a dog to consider? Was he mad? Molly lifted out the gold envelope and ripped it open it with a finger. She pulled out a voucher for two for one night at a Majestic Inn near Peterborough. Whyever would she want to go on holiday there? There was also a note.

> *Now there's no need to worry about this if you really can't do it – I know it's hard with the family and stuff. If you can't afford all the petrol, I left some spare cash with Suzie – just ask her for the emergency envelope and she'll hand it over. I won this very desirable voucher in a raffle just before I left, and it runs out at*

the end of April. Simon turned his nose up at it but I've got a soft spot for Peterborough; we used to take our caravan there when I was a kid. There's a water park where you can walk for miles, and a great pub that does the best steaks I've ever had. The Inn's fine, too, and you'll get there in less than two hours even on a Friday night. Go for it, Moll, there's a good girl. And take someone new? S xxxx

P.S. The quest will continue later. The best is yet to come.

'What does he mean by new?' asked Dot. 'I'm new – take me!'

Molly frowned. 'I can't leave the kids. They exhaust my mum, and Edna can't manage overnight.'

'True. But you do need a break, he's right.'

'I had thought of asking Tom to look after them next time I got hauled away by one of Shaun's loopy schemes. He seemed keen to do it, and Max will do anything for him, but I'm not risking that now, not after the second letter.'

Dot thought for a moment. 'Okay, you can't ask Tom to hold the fort yet, so why don't you take him with you?'

'What? Are you crazy? He's probably not even

speaking to me. And anyway, who'd look after the kids and Marian?'

'Me. I'm their big sister, and it's my fault you're landed with the dog. I'm the obvious choice. Or don't you trust me?'

Molly could see that Dot was only half joking. She hugged her. 'Don't be daft, I trust you more than anyone. You're like my oldest daughter now, but my best friend, too.'

'I am?'

'Course you are. I can't believe I've not known you forever.'

'But... best friend?'

'Well, technically speaking, that would have to be Shaun; I've never been very good at getting close to women, especially after Kate and everything, but you make it seem so easy to be friends. Hey, don't cry. I didn't mean to set you off. And anyway, would Tom want to come away with me?'

Dot sniffed and reached for a tissue. 'Come on, Moll, you must know Tom would go anywhere if you were involved. Forget those letters, it's only for one night. You can pay the extra for two rooms if that makes you feel better. Go on, phone him. Do it now.'

Molly dug out her mobile and dialled. Tom answered before she had planned what to say, and for a moment Molly was speechless.

'Hello? Molly? Is everything okay?' His voice sent multiple shivers down her spine and she swallowed hard before answering.

'Tom, just hear me out before you make any decisions. I've had another clue. Could you be free to come to Peterborough with me for a night?'

'Peterborough? With you? Why?'

'Oh, well, if you're busy...'

There was a brief silence and then Tom laughed. 'Molly – beautiful Molly. You're asking me to go away with you for the night and you think I might be too busy? Are you crazy?'

His laughter was infectious, and relief made Molly giggle. 'I wasn't propositioning you – we can have two rooms. If you're not still angry with me?'

'I never was angry. Just frustrated.'

Molly was silent for a moment. 'I know how that feels,' she said eventually.

* * *

Two days later, as Tom drove them both west towards Peterborough, Molly was stunned at how quickly everything had been arranged. In the end, Dot had taken charge and rung the Majestic Inn, booked two rooms, and explained about the voucher and Tom's need for easy access. The children were delighted at this chance to have what Theo called a 'Dot-Fest' of films, dance music and pizza. She had promised them popcorn, too, and duvets downstairs; a proper sleepover.

Molly was light-headed with the freedom of it all. She had never spent a night away from the children before. Jake hadn't been one for romantic surprises and, even if he had, they would both have been too broke.

'Are you warm enough?' asked Tom. 'Put the heater on if you're cold.'

'No, why did you think I was cold? It's a gorgeous day out there.'

'You shivered, that's all.'

'I'm just excited and kind of nervous to be going away, just on a whim like this, with you.'

The silence after this remark lengthened until Molly wondered if she'd overstepped the mark. She hadn't meant to say that, it had just popped out. But it was true. The thought of spending all these unin-terrupted hours with Tom was exhilarating. They had never been properly alone for more than a few minutes up until now. Their date had almost gone badly wrong, and at home there were the constant distractions of children, Dot, and anonymous letters.

'Tom, I didn't mean…'

'I know what you meant. I feel just the same. As if it's the night before Christmas? Or the start of the school holidays?'

'That's it exactly.'

They drove in silence for a while, while the radio played old hits from the seventies and eighties. Suddenly, Tom turned up the volume.

'Listen. I love this one.'

'Why?'

'You'll see.'

As the music poured out of Tom's state-of-the-art speakers, Molly stretched luxuriously. She'd always found this old Pointer Sisters song unbelievably erotic. 'Slow Hand'. Everything she'd always wanted in a lover but never found. She blushed, realising that Tom was watching her out of the corner of his eye.

'Keep your eyes on the road,' she grinned.

'But don't you agree it's a great song?'

'Oh, yes, definitely.' Molly swallowed, with difficulty. Reaching for her water bottle, she drank half of it in one gulp, and hiccupped. 'Sorry, I'm so thirsty.'

'Well, we deserve a really good bottle of wine

tonight. There's a pub right next door to the place we're staying. I looked on the website. Are you hungry?'

'I don't know. I've got butterflies.'

'Don't be scared, Molly. It's only me.'

'I'm being silly.' She glanced across at Tom. His hands on the wheel looked amazingly strong and capable, and his sleeves were rolled up again to reveal those wonderful forearms that could probably be used for a stunt double; Aidan Turner, maybe? She looked at his hands again and imagined them sliding over her body, accidentally letting slip a little moan of excitement as the music wove its magic and she got further into her fantasy.

'You feeling all right, Molly? Am I going too fast?' Tom asked, cutting his speed slightly as he saw a village sign in the distance. 'I can't help wondering why I'm here, to be honest.'

'No, I'm fine, and your speed's perfect.'

'So, why did you ask me to come away with you? You seemed so edgy about us the last time we were together.'

'I'm not twitchy about you and me, Tom. I was just... er... thinking about seeing the sea.' She drank more water and stared out of the window.

'But we've just left the sea. We're heading inland.'

'Oh, yes, sorry. Must have been dreaming. I didn't sleep very well last night.'

Tom frowned slightly but said no more. The village was disappearing into the distance now, and the next song was ABBA. The sound of 'Dancing Queen' and the sight of the open road stretching out ahead caused them both to start singing, and the next few miles passed quickly as Molly threw herself into the songs that seemed to get cheesier by the minute. They worked their way happily through Tom Jones, The Monkees, and an obscure medley of Eurovision entries before they approached the outskirts of Peterborough, when Molly regretfully turned down the volume and got out the directions for the hotel.

'We're getting close now, Tom. Go right at the roundabout and then left straight away. Then just follow the road.'

'Have you been here before?'

'No, but following maps is one of my hidden talents.'

'Really?'

'Nope, just wrote it all down before we came away. I've had enough rows about directions to last me a lifetime.'

Tom laughed. 'And here we are. Well done, that's definitely earned you a starter as well as a main course. Can you get my chair out for me when I find a good place to park?'

They trundled through the foyer, Tom laden with their bags, and Molly doing a fine job of avoiding two small children who were blocking the doorway.

'You're great at this, Molly,' said Tom, as they reached the desk. 'Have you ever thought of being a full-time carer?' He grinned to show he was joking. Molly was about to reply but was distracted by the haughty girl looking across at them.

'May I help you?' she asked, looking at Molly.

'Yes, we've got two rooms booked for tonight,' answered Tom.

'Can I have your name, please?'

'Cavendish,' said Tom.

The receptionist ran a pointed nail down the list on her computer screen.

'No, sorry. I don't seem to have you here,' she said to Molly.

'Maybe it's in my name. Molly White?'

'Oh, yes, here we are. And another room for?'

'Mr Cavendish. Which is me,' said Tom, trying to make eye contact.

'Your rooms are just through there and up the stairs. Oh, wait a minute, I think yours,' she glanced down at Tom, 'is on the ground floor.'

'We would ideally like adjoining rooms,' Tom said, icily.

'I'm sorry, sir, that won't be possible. The lift is out of order. Excuse me, I have a queue waiting. Here are your keys.'

The receptionist looked over Tom's shoulder to the people behind him. Molly put a hand on his arm, feeling the tension in his muscles. 'Come on, we'll check yours out first.'

He allowed Molly to push him through a set of double doors and down a long corridor. The artwork was less than inspirational. She paused at number 23 and unlocked the door.

'Here you go.'

'Aren't you coming in?'

'Oh, do you want me to unpack your bag for you?'

There was an uncomfortable silence, and Molly realised how awfully wrong she had got this moment. After a few seconds she said, 'Anyway, I guess you'll want to settle in and so on. When shall we meet for dinner?'

'Come down in half an hour? I want to get changed, and I guess you do, too?'

'Right, I'll be down soon. Tom?'

'Yes?'

'Thank you for coming with me.'

Their eyes met and Molly felt the full force of his attraction. His blue eyes were full of longing and she could hardly bear to look at his lips, they were so immensely kissable. He reached up and touched her cheek.

'Molly, you are a stunningly beautiful lady, and on top of that, you're a lovely person. Even if you do say daft things sometimes.' He grinned. 'I can honestly say that there is nowhere in the world that I'd rather be at this moment. See you in half an hour. And don't be late.'

21

Molly slung her overnight bag over her shoulder and ran up the stairs two at a time. In ten minutes she was showered and dressed again, sitting at the dressing table with her up-ended make-up bag in front of her. First, she brushed her long curly hair until it crackled with electricity and stood out round her head like a crazy halo. Then she took stock of her face. Her eyes glittered with excitement and her cheeks were already pink, so she satisfied herself with a dab of translucent powder on her nose, and a smudgy border of eyeliner along her eyelids. This was tricky to apply with clammy, trembling hands.

She sighed and looked again. Nope, not glamorous enough. She added smoky eyeshadow and a coat of brown mascara. Better. A quick slick of lip gloss and she was ready. Oh, wait – perfume. Molly stood up and sprayed herself liberally with her favourite scent, a light, woody cologne that made her feel sparkly and sensual. Rummaging in the heap of make-up, she found a heavy gold necklace and ear-rings, glad that she'd managed to pack some glitz.

As she stood in front of the long mirror, Molly assessed the finished picture. Even with her most critical head on, she had to admit that she looked pretty good tonight. She had brought a long black jersey dress because she could roll it up in her bag and it wouldn't crease. The neckline was gently plunging but not vampy, and the skirt came down almost to the floor. She slipped her feet into black ballet pumps – no need for tights tonight, but Molly suddenly wished she'd thought to bring stockings, or some really sheer black lacy hold-ups. No one was going to see what she was wearing underneath, though, were they? She met her own shining eyes in the mirror and raised her eyebrows at her reflected self.

Downstairs, she found Tom already waiting, looking good enough to eat. Dressed in his usual go-ing-out gear of black jeans and a smart jacket, he was waiting for Molly in the corridor outside his room.

'Oh, am I late?' she asked, glancing at her watch.

'No, I was just too edgy to stay put. Shall we go?'

Molly pushed Tom through the foyer, deliber-ately ignoring the receptionist, but Tom called, 'See you later, sweetheart,' as they passed the desk. She looked up vaguely and smiled at him for the first time, doing a double take when she noticed at last how gorgeous he was. Molly seethed.

'Don't you mind people being as ignorant as that woman was earlier?' she asked, as they bowled across the car park to the pub.

'Nah, I'm used to it. Some people are all gushing, trying to over-compensate, and then others, like Frosty the Snow-woman in there, don't even ac-knowledge you exist.' He shrugged. 'I don't much care either way these days. So long as the people I like treat me right.'

They settled into a wooden booth and Molly picked up a menu. Was Tom hinting that she needed to change her attitude to him? She hid behind the giant laminated pages while she pondered this one. He could wheel himself along in most places, but sometimes a bit of help was useful. He was obviously more than capable of doing everyday jobs, and she blushed when she remembered how she'd offered to unpack his bags. It was just that Jake had always expected her to do those things for him. How could she explain this without making her mistake even more embarrassing?

'Hey, come out from behind there, I'm getting lonely,' Tom said, tapping on the menu.

'Sorry, I was just thinking.'

'Well, don't. No more thinking tonight, do you hear? We're going to have fun. I'm ordering one of those huge sharing platter things, if that's okay with you? The one with the little crunchy bits of chicken and prawn, and dips? The picture looks amazing.'

'Oh, yes, that sounds yummy. I might just have that and then an enormous pudding instead of a main course. They've got a sticky toffee one with clotted cream.'

As they munched their way through the starter, squabbling amiably over the best bits, Molly at last began to unwind. The wine helped, and the cosy atmosphere of the pub. A log fire crackled away near Molly's side of the table, and after a while she leaned into the padded backrest of her bench, watching the flickering flames.

'You look a lot more relaxed now,' said Tom. 'I was thinking I'd have to fill you full of brandy to get you this chilled out.'

'Was I that bad?'

'Yep, pretty much. You've been worrying about those stupid letters and trying to keep everyone else happy. Tonight was a great idea of Shaun's, even though he can't possibly know about the letters. He must know you very well.'

'He does. I miss him loads. I'm still not sure how he managed to organise all these clues so quickly or how he gets them posted. The only person I can think of who might be helping with that is his neighbour, Suzie, but I don't want to put her on the spot by interrogating her. And I don't know why he did it at all, really.'

'Just to help you though the worst days, I guess. And to leave no questions about Jake unanswered? There are always things you want to ask after someone dies suddenly. My mum and dad pulled that one on me, too.'

'What happened? Tom, I'm sorry. Maybe you don't want to dig all that up.'

'It's okay. I don't talk about it often, but I'd like to tell you. They were both killed when their camper van plunged into a harbour in Yorkshire.'

'Oh, no! However did that happen?'

'They think my dad had a stroke. He slammed his foot down hard on the wrong pedal. I was eight – I was away at camp for a week in Whitby with my school at the time.'

There was a silence as Molly thought about the young Tom, so suddenly bereaved. Her heart ached for him.

'Now don't start feeling sorry for me; you're one of the few people who treat me like a normal human being,' he said, reaching for her hand. 'I was okay, after a bit. I went to live with my nan, and she filled me full of stew and dumplings and cake.'

'Were you... were you always in a wheelchair?'

'No, I was hit by a truck when I was fifteen. The doctors told Nan I wouldn't make it, but I pulled through eventually. Well, obviously I did or I wouldn't be sitting here with you. Nan didn't think she could cope with me after the accident, although she did in the end, bless her sweet soul.'

'And now she's gone, too?'

'Yes, Molly, but I told you not to look like that. It's an old sadness, not like yours.'

'That's a brave way of looking at it. Were you with anyone when you had your accident? It sounds horrendous.'

'I was with a crowd of my mates and my girlfriend. We were being stupid, messing around on the ring road after we'd been necking cider. The police had turned up at the local park to round us up for underage drinking, and we all legged it back over the main road, and a lorry was coming. We thought we had time to get across. They all made it, but I tripped and it just caught me. I was lucky not to be completely crushed, I suppose.'

'Oh, Tom. So, what happened with your girlfriend?'

'She stayed for a bit. I think she liked all the drama to start with. You know, the life and death stuff? But then it all got a bit sordid. I couldn't even go to the loo on my own. She soon disappeared when she realised I needed a nurse, not someone to give me love bites.'

'But you must have felt awful.' Molly paused when she saw Tom's expression. 'Sorry, I'll stop being so depressing now. Let's eat something disgustingly sweet and sticky – it's medicinal.'

Back at the hotel, Molly reached Tom's door and stopped. The moment to say goodnight had come far too soon. It was only half past nine and, thanks to the strong black coffee, she was still wide awake.

'Are you going to come in for a little while?' said Tom, gazing at Molly's feet. The tips of his ears were red, and she could see that the flush went right down his neck.

'Oh, go on then, but I don't make a habit of this sort of thing, you know.' She giggled nervously as she unlocked the bedroom door with a flourish and he wheeled himself inside, peeling off his jacket and throwing it over a chair.

'Phew, it's boiling in here,' he said, as Molly passed him his sticks. 'The window doesn't seem to open and the heating's fixed at some sort of tropical island setting. You'd better take your coat off. One of us will have to sit on the bed. Do you want the chair?'

Molly slid out of the chunky cardigan she'd been wearing as a coat, and kicked off her shoes. She sat down on the bed. After a moment or two, she leaned back against the pillows and stretched her legs out, wriggling her bare toes. 'This bed's really comfy, and it's massive,' she said, 'there's plenty of room for you, too.'

'You're not propositioning me by any chance, are you?' Tom swung himself round to the other side of the bed and made himself comfortable. 'Yep, you're right, there's plenty of space. And there's even a radio.' He twiddled with the controls until the peaceful sound of an old Marvin Gaye song swelled around them. 'It's weird, but this keeps happening,' he said, turning on his side and leaning up on one elbow so that he was looking straight into Molly's eyes.

'What keeps happening?' she asked, willing herself not to look away.

'Music that fits the mood. First there was "You Do Something To Me", then "Slow Hand". And now here's "Let's Get It On". You've got to admit, it's spooky.'

'Hmmm. I guess there are lots of songs that would fit, though. It's not really that odd.'

'Name one.'

Molly sat up. She loved a pub quiz-type challenge. 'New or old music?'

'Either.'

'Right. An oldie first. The Stones – "Waitin' On A Friend". I love it. And you're definitely my friend. Your turn.'

'Okay. "I'll Be There For You", if we're on the "friends" theme. Now you.'

'"Bridge Over Troubled Water"? Too obvious, maybe. True, though; that's what you are to me just now.'

Tom blinked, and Molly wondered where he would take this next. She had a feeling that they were heading for deep waters. She slid off the bed and went to put the kettle on, but heard him sigh.

'You can't just resort to tea when things start getting interesting, Molly. Come back here,' he said, patting the covers beside him. 'Anyway, it's my turn again. What's the matter?'

Molly held up a hand. 'Sshhh. Listen. Turn the radio up.' The sound of a throbbing bass beat filled the room. Molly felt her body start to react to the music, her blood flowing faster, temples pulsing in time to the steady rhythm. 'It's Blur, isn't it?' she said. '"Tender Is the Night"?'

'Mmmm.' Tom nodded. 'I reckon this is one of the sexiest songs ever written.'

Molly sat down on the bed again, and turned towards Tom just as he switched all the brighter lights off. One lamp glowed in the sudden darkness as he held out his arms. She moved towards him, mesmerised.

As their lips came together and the music thumped in time with their heartbeats, Molly felt waves of desire crashing over her. Was it all going to be okay after all? She had to try to switch off the voice in her head that said she was rubbish in bed and she'd never, ever get the hang of letting go. It was fine when she was by herself – she could usually play around and give herself a kick or two, or at least until thoughts of her mother crept in. Good girls don't do that sort of thing, her mother had said, when the subject had come up, so to speak.

Instinctively, she kissed him back, their bodies coming together as if they'd been waiting for each other. She felt his excitement and slid her hands under his shirt, shuddering as he began to explore her curves. It was a moment or two before Molly realised that the strange tinny sound was her phone ringing. Tom gasped as she pulled away from him.

'Molly – no. Leave it,' he groaned, reaching for her. But Molly's maternal instincts had already dived into panic mode.

'Hello, is that you, Dot?' she said anxiously, without checking the display.

'Oh, Molly, no, it isn't Dot. It's me, Edna. I'm sorry to be calling you at this hour.'

'Edna, what's happened?'

'Well, dear, as you know, I'm not usually one to make a fuss.'

'Just tell me. Please.'

'It's just that I saw you drive away with that young man, so I knew you weren't here, and there's the loudest music you ever did hear coming from next door. Is there someone responsible in charge, dear? I'm only telling you in case someone reports you to the police.'

Weak with relief that none of her children were in danger, Molly gradually managed to pacify her neighbour and eventually rang off. 'I'm just going to have to phone Dot. I'm really sorry, Tom.'

Tom clenched his teeth as she keyed in her home number. 'That interfering old bat. Why did she have to ring you tonight? Wouldn't the morning be soon enough?' he moaned. But Molly's attention was on Dot.

'Yes, I know you wouldn't play it too loud, pet, but maybe just turn it off now? It must be bedtime, surely? Okay, see you tomorrow. Love you, bye.'

Molly turned back to Tom, and sighed. 'I suppose you're annoyed that I answered the phone.'

'No, but...'

'You are. You think I should have just ignored it, don't you?'

'Well, she had no business making trouble for Dot, did she? And what are you supposed to do? You're miles away.'

'She was probably only worried that everything was okay. She's a mum herself. You don't understand what it's like to have kids.' As soon as the words were out, Molly could have bitten her tongue off. Tom glared at her, eyes like blue ice. She tried not to look at his rumpled shirt, now fully untucked from his jeans, and his flushed face.

'No, I don't suppose I do, not being a father,' he

spat out. 'Oh, well, best to find out these things before it's too late. There's no point in me having anything to do with your family, because there's no way I could ever understand how a *mother* feels.'

Molly got up, furious with herself for being so tactless but irritated beyond belief that he could expect her to ignore the phone when she'd left Dot with so many responsibilities. 'Look, I'm going to bed. There's no point in talking about this. See you in the morning.'

'Molly, don't go. You can't just keep running away every time something goes wrong.'

She heard him still calling her as she ran down the corridor towards the stairs, and the angry tears started to fall before she'd even reached her room.

* * *

Tom watched Molly leave, wishing more than he ever had in his life that he could get up and run too. He so needed to be able to chase after her, carry her back over his shoulder if necessary, and either make love to her until she begged for mercy or finish the row off properly. He looked down at his wasted legs and cursed the stupid fifteen-year-old boy who had thought he could outrun a truck.

22

The next morning, Molly woke with a splitting headache. She had tossed and turned for most of the night, tortured by the thought of being so close to Tom and then throwing it all away. How could she have been so stupid? She should never have picked up the phone. But deep down, Molly knew that she could never have ignored a call from home, and if Tom couldn't accept that fact, they might as well give up on each other.

Surely he must understand her need to know the children were safe? What mother could leave a late-night call unanswered when she'd left her family at home? Her anger flickered again. She wasn't going to just take all the blame for last night's fiasco – Tom would have to meet her halfway if he wanted her enough. But did he? And could she ever be the sort of woman who would satisfy him and make him feel whole again? Was that what she really wanted? The thought of last night's passion burned in Molly's mind and made her feverish and restless. She jumped out of bed.

After showering for as long as she could stand the steam and the piping-hot water, the ache in Molly's head and neck began to ease. With a couple of paracetamol tablets and a cup of strong black instant coffee inside her from the hospitality tray, she felt almost human. It was time to face Tom. She had never been able to stay cross for long and she fervently hoped he would be the same. As she knocked on his door at half past eight, she put on her best smile.

'Come in if you're a ravishing brunette and you bring ambrosial food,' shouted a muffled voice.

'Well, the brunette bit's right,' she answered, opening the door. Tom was sitting on the edge of the bed, fully dressed – to Molly's relief. The sight of him wearing only a sheet might have pushed her right over the edge after the disturbingly erotic dreams she'd had when sleep had finally come.

'Are we friends today?' he asked, grinning up at

her and making her heart flip. Her hand seemed to reach out of its own accord to touch his rough cheek, and he held it and kissed her palm.

'I haven't shaved,' he said. 'I can't see myself properly in the bathroom mirror here. Sorry.'

'No problem, designer stubble's fine by me. Are you ready to eat?'

'Starving – let's go.'

The snooty receptionist wasn't there this morning, but a beautiful young black girl was in her place.

'Hi, guys, breakfast's being served over at the pub when you're ready. Would you like me to ring your order through? The menu's on the table over there. Or you can just go and see what takes your fancy when you've had some coffee.'

Molly could see the girl eyeing Tom curiously, but in a flirty way rather than as an oddity to be looked down on. 'Let's just go over now,' she said.

'Why are we in such a rush?' asked Tom, as Molly propelled him back to the pub.

'What do you mean?'

'You couldn't wait to get out of there. Why?'

Molly concentrated on catching a waiter's eye and finding somewhere to stow the chair. When they were seated, she realised Tom was still waiting for an answer. 'I just didn't like the way that receptionist was looking you up and down, if you must know.'

Tom snorted. 'You're not telling me you're jealous? Molly White, gorgeous, witty and, above all, able-bodied, jealous of a woman eying up a cr—'

'No, don't you dare say that word. We weren't going to mention the letters.'

'I wasn't. Oh, forget it, you're being ridiculous.' Tom's lips were set in an angry line now. So much for sorting things out, thought Molly, she'd just ruined everything.

She drank some of the scalding coffee that the waiter had just placed in front of her and wondered how to resurrect the day. Maybe she'd just wait and see what happened next. She was too tired for an argument this morning. In her limited experience, large plates of delicious food sometimes worked for men when any amount of sweet talking failed.

To Molly's relief, when he'd demolished the best part of a full English breakfast, Tom looked up, smiled and said, 'Well, what do you want to do now? Have we done enough bickering yet? Shall we start again and go somewhere fun?'

* * *

Half an hour later, they were spinning around one of the nearby lakes, on smooth, easy-to-navigate paths, with the morning sun warming their backs. There was plenty of room for Molly to walk beside Tom and the water park was almost deserted.

'Was this always here? It's beautiful,' said Tom, gazing around at the sparkling water and the wild birds that were swooping and skimming the ripples. His heart lifted at the sight. He was in this terrific place with the woman of his dreams – his *Lady in Red*. She was tricky, unpredictable, and hard to get close to, but she was the only person in the world who'd ever been able to make him feel this over-whelming love and desire. Life couldn't get much better than this, could it?

'I think I remember Shaun coming here from when he was about ten; it used to be a quarry, I think,' answered Molly. 'There's a caravan park be-hind the trees. You can go on a boat trip over there, look.' She pointed to where a narrowboat was moored under the trees.

Tom idly watched a young couple walking along the shore of the lake, holding hands. As Molly turned to see what was making Tom look so sad, the man picked the girl up in his arms and swung her round. She squealed and he put her down gently, kissing her before carrying on up the tiny beach.

'What's up, Tom?'

'Sometimes it's hard to think I can never do that with you.'

'Thank God for that, I've never liked being picked up. If you tried to do that to me, I'd give you a black eye.'

He laughed. 'You can joke, but I mean it. I'm not like Jake. There are so many things I can't do.'

'Look, Tom, whether or not you can pick me up and twirl me around like an Olympic skater, it's no good talking like this.'

'We've got to face facts.'

'I *am* facing facts. I'm a mum with four children and now I've got a stepdaughter and a mad dog to go with them. And who said I wanted you to be like Jake? You're two very different people.' Molly avoided Tom's straight blue gaze. She carried on walking and he followed.

'Look, Molly,' Tom said, when they'd covered the next few metres in complete silence. 'I'm not trying to push Jake out of your head, but I don't think you're completely pole-axed by grief any more.'

Molly blushed. 'So you're saying I should be over Jake dying by now? Just be able to move on? And what would the kids think of that? What would my mum say?'

'Don't put words into my mouth. And anyway, why does it matter what people think? This is about us, isn't it?'

'Of course it matters. We don't live in a bubble. My family mean everything to me. If you don't understand that, our whole relationship is totally pointless.'

Molly turned and began to walk back towards the car at a great pace, and Tom had no choice but to trail after her. Well, he'd completely messed that one up. They might as well head for home.

* * *

It was lunchtime when Tom's car pulled into Molly's driveway. Max saw them coming from the front garden and flung himself on Molly as she climbed out of the passenger seat.

'Mum, I thought you weren't coming home till tonight? Dot's taking us to the cinema in a minute. I was just waiting for the others to get ready. They're taking ages. Can we still go? Hi, Tom,' he added belatedly, as Tom reached for his sticks.

'Why don't we all go?' Tom asked, looking over at

Molly. She shrugged, suddenly shattered. How could she stay awake throughout a whole film? She'd had trouble keeping her eyes open on the way home, but she'd hated the thought of dropping her guard. The silence between them had been frosty, and sleeping didn't seem an option.

'Wicked! Yeah, Mum, let's all go, we can go in both cars then. We were going to catch the bus. Then we were going to go to that new pizza place up the road for tea. Go on, Mum, pleeeeeease?'

'Oh, I don't think so, Max. There's the ironing to do.'

'Right, I get the message,' said Tom, bitterly. 'I'll get back home now. I won't see you all for a while, because I've been invited to see one of my old university friends in Somerset.'

'You didn't mention it earlier.' Molly felt an unexpected pang of disappointment.

'No, because I didn't decide until today if I should go. Sasha said she'd cover for me if I needed her; the shop's not very busy at the moment. But my friend's been asking me to go for ages. I guess I ought to go and catch up with the gossip. I think she said there's going to be a bit of a reunion in Bristol.'

'She? Your friend's female?' Molly could hear the waspish note in her voice but she didn't care.

'Yes, her name's Lena. We were always good mates but I haven't seen her for years. She lives in some sort of hippy commune now, doing lots of yoga and eating tofu burgers and whole grains and such-like. She was always a bit of a character at uni... sort of like a young Naomi Campbell.' Tom passed Molly her bag and swung himself back into the driving seat, throwing his sticks into the passenger side with what seemed like unnecessary force. He waved to Max and Moll, and drove away before Molly could argue.

Oh, God, this was turning into a really horrendous day. Molly longed to get in her car and speed after Tom, to follow him home and spend the whole night in his arms. She should have told him how she felt while there was a chance, but she had hardly been sure of her feelings until she had seen his car disappearing down the road. She ought to have leaned into his car and whispered, 'Please don't go, Tom. I'm still half afraid to be alone with you but I can't imagine my life without you any more.'

But it was too late. Molly would just have to get used to the fact that Tom had gone, and worse still, he had gone to be with another woman – a gorgeous, probably willowy and graceful model-type from his past. Tortured by the beginnings of a burning jealousy, Molly, shoulders bowed, went into the house.

23

It was nearly two weeks before Molly heard from Tom again. The Easter holidays were over and she was back at work, finding her job even more soul-destroying than usual, when her phone pinged.

'You've got a message, Miss. Somebody loves you, but it ain't me,' said the spotty thirteen-year-old who was currently refusing to play any of the instruments on offer.

'Thanks, Clyde. I'll look at it in a minute. Now, what about a clarinet?' Molly asked, holding up a full-colour picture of an orchestra in full flow. 'Look, here's one. You haven't tried a clarinet yet, have you?'

'Oh, piss off,' said Clyde, knocking over Molly's music stand as he left the room. She began to pick up her sheet music, and then stopped. Enough of this dismal job. It was time to leave the abuse behind her. Only that morning, Molly had received a letter in the post that had shocked and touched her. It seemed that Jake *had* taken out a small life insurance policy, after all. The firm in question had only just been notified of her husband's death, because the address on the policy had never been updated. They apologised for the unfortunate delay and were sorry to intrude on Molly's grief, but would appreciate the early provision of a certified copy of Jake's death certificate. On receipt of this, they would generate a bank transfer for the sum of fifty thousand pounds.

Molly had almost called in sick this morning. She had the beginnings of a cold and both Max and Hattie were under the weather, too, but she had pulled herself together enough to know that she oughtn't to let her schools down. Now, however, she knew beyond doubt that she could not stand this job for a moment longer. Fifty thousand pounds would act as a buffer for a while, and it would give her a chance to think about what she could do next to earn some decent money.

Molly felt the familiar pang of guilt when she thought about the children and all her responsibilities. She never seemed to get it right these days. She was sure she shouldn't have sent Max and Hattie to school today. If Jake had been around, he would either have insisted she stayed at home with them or have arranged cover for himself so that he could look after them for at least part of the day. It was too hard juggling childcare and a job where she was completely unappreciated and never respected. Scraping her belongings together, she marched down endless corridors and through the reception area with a fiery glint in her eye.

'Excuse me, you haven't signed out, Mrs White,' she heard the school secretary call, but Molly was already over the threshold.

Driving down the coast road, she switched on the radio and began to sing at the top of her voice. Okay, she wouldn't be able to live on the money forever, but it was enough to let her start again doing something she wanted to do. What would that be, though? Maybe she could resurrect her book and start sending it out again. With a pretty thorough rewrite, it might be publishable.

Suddenly, Molly remembered that she had received a text just before her big exit. She pulled into a layby and reached for her phone.

Molly, you are invited to a private
viewing at the gallery tomorrow
night. Bring the whole family.
Champagne and canapés
available. Or fizzy wine and posh
nibbles anyway. New exhibition by
largely unknown artist, i.e. me.
Please come. Tom xx

Molly's heart lurched. She had tried so hard to
put Tom and his trip to see Lena out of her mind,
and to concentrate on getting the house straight
during the holidays. Since Easter, she and Dot had
painted the living room and made huge inroads into
the garden-tidying jobs. Sam, Theo, Hattie and Max
had also been pressganged into helping, bribed with
yet more takeaway pizza and garlic bread. Suddenly,
everywhere was looking much more respectable.
Molly was beginning to feel as if she would be happy
to stay in the house now. And with the cheque on its
way, she would be able to make a few more changes.

Despite the whirl of activity, thoughts of Tom had
refused to go away, even when Molly had been at her
busiest and had fallen into bed each night exhausted
from her efforts. His exhibition tomorrow would be a
test of how she felt. They would all have to be there;
it was only polite, she reasoned. And she would buy

something new to wear. A skinny black pencil skirt to show that she was down to her personal ideal weight, thanks to all the gardening and bursts of sadness. And maybe a soft silky shirt that would make her feel sexy and feminine; she was sick of living in jeans and old sweatshirts.

Molly shook herself. She would call in town and see what she could find, there was just time before she picked Max and Hattie up from school. She did a neat U-turn and headed for Ferrymead shopping centre.

* * *

Tom stared at his phone. It had been an hour since he'd sent the text and there was still no answer. Would Molly come to the gallery tomorrow? If she didn't, then he might as well give up hope of ever being with her. Tom had rung Dot earlier to see how the land lay, but she hadn't been very encouraging.

'Look, Tom, you went away and left Molly high and dry, and you told her you were going to be spending time with some Naomi Campbell lookalike. How did you expect her to feel?'

Tom sighed. 'When you say it like that it doesn't sound great, but Lena was never anything serious.'

'Bloody hell, man. What difference does it make if it's serious or not? You were with her, right? Getting close and personal in the depths of the countryside?'

'Well, if you put it like that... but Molly was more interested in finding out how you lot were coping without her than being with me when we were in Peterborough.'

'Christ! Do you realise how pathetic you sound? Molly's a mum first and foremost, and a wonderful one. Would you have her any different? If you would, you've picked the wrong woman.'

'I wouldn't change a single thing about her. I... I'm mad about her, Dot. I love her. There – I've said it out loud at last, but please don't say anything to her. You've been brilliant about keeping all this to yourself so far, it really means a lot to me to be able to talk to you in confidence. But now what shall I do?'

Dot was silent for a few seconds and then took a deep breath. 'Just text her, okay, Tom? Ask her to the gallery and I'll do my best to persuade her to come if she seems to want to get out of it. And then it's up to you.'

Tom checked his phone again. Still nothing. He was beginning to fully understand that the week with Lena was going to be very hard to put behind them, but it had been an eye-opener in so many ways. Lena had made it clear that she was more than happy to help Tom to find out if he was a fully functioning male.

'You know I've always fancied you, don't you, honey?' she'd breathed, after their second bottle of Scrumpy. 'Come on, let's just go to bed and see what happens. If this Molly person is worth her salt, she'll be glad I've done the research for her.'

Tom had let Lena strip him and enfold him in her duvet, had kissed her with as much passion as he could muster and then, to his shame, had closed his eyes and pretended she was Molly. Afterwards, he hadn't been able to meet her eyes, but Lena had just laughed and said, 'There you go – you've had a full MOT, and now you can go ahead and shag her senseless. And I bloody hope she appreciates what I've done for her by sending you back. I could quite easily keep you here, you know.'

Tom had felt a heady, exultant pride in his battered body. He had satisfied a woman who was a self-confessed expert in her field. Lena had issued an open invitation to him to return if things didn't work out with Molly. Tom didn't know if he could cope with all those seeds and grains, though, and he'd never been a fan of tofu. And in any case, she just wasn't Molly.

* * *

The next night, Molly was ready for the exhibition way too early. The others had been delighted with their invitation, and Dot had also decided she'd need something new to wear, although Dot's idea of new usually meant 'vintage'. She'd been scouring the charity shops of the little seaside town and had unearthed a beautiful long black velvet dress with a white crocheted collar. It clung to all her slender curves, and Dot had added huge gold earrings and a few chains and beads. Her hair was now short, fairly spiky, and curling around her ears. She had decided to remove her dreadlocks last week after an unfortunate incident with Marian and a pot of white emulsion paint. Dot's new black hair had made Hattie and Theo stand back in amazement.

'What's up, guys? It's hideous, isn't it? You hate it, don't you?' Dot had wailed.

'N-n-no, I don't hate it. But you look even more like Dad and Sam now,' Hattie had said sadly.

'That's not a bad thing, though, is it?' Molly had soothed. 'It's lovely to see the likeness, surely?'

Hattie and Max had started to cry simultaneously, and Molly had been reminded that their grief was still very raw. As she'd hugged them both, she had wondered why her own pain wasn't sharper, not to mention why she was so excited about seeing Tom later. Did it mean she hadn't ever cared enough for Jake?

At the gallery later that night, a buzz of excitement filled the air. Tom sat near the front door, welcoming his guests with a smile and a chilled glass of bubbly. His eyes lit up when he saw Molly and he murmured, 'God, you're beautiful.'

She looked at him searchingly. 'Did you have a nice time with Lena?' she asked.

'Yeah, great, thanks, always good to catch up with old mates.'

'I bet it was.' Molly moved further into the gallery, catching her breath as she saw the new canvases ranged around the walls. The children followed her, Max giving Tom a high five as he passed by. When they were all inside, Tom closed the door and locked it.

'Oh, no, does that mean we have to buy something before we can get away?' asked Dot, draining her glass and helping herself to a refill.

'No, it's just that all the invited guests are here now. The press are over there and there are a few lecturers from the university. The others are previous customers and so on.'

'Are you making a speech?'

'Nah – let's eat Sasha's canapés now, shall we?
She's been working in the kitchen all day.'

By the time Molly got to speak to Tom again, she
was beyond words. The pictures were glorious; passionate explosions of colour and light that were
worlds away from his previous offerings for the
tourist trade. Pride of place had been given to the
back view of Molly, but not many people seemed to
have realised who had been the inspiration for the
painting. Molly was much more glamorous tonight,
with her hair swept up and her new skirt and high
heels emphasising her streamlined figure.

'So, what do you think of them?' Tom asked, as
he finally caught up with Molly by the portrait.

'You must know that they're all stunning. And as
for this one – well, I never expected to be in an exhibition,' she said, blinking back the tears that had
been threatening ever since she'd walked through
the door.

'Have you had any more boxes? You know I
meant what I said about looking after the kids for
you?'

'Nothing yet. There must be one soon – it's been
ages. But I expect you'll be too busy now.'

'Busy? What do you mean?'

'With Lena.'

'Oh, come on, Molly. You know Lena's just an old friend, don't you?'

'So you didn't sleep with her last week, then?'

There was an agonised pause, and then Molly turned on her heel and began to round up the family.

'Hey, where are you going?' he called, as she herded Max, Hattie, Theo and Dot towards the door.

'Need to get this lot to bed,' she flung over her shoulder.

'Hang on a minute, I'm not ready to leave yet. It's not my bedtime,' protested Dot.

'Well, you stay then. We're going.'

Dot looked from Tom to Molly and back. 'Well, I might stay for another glass of fizz. I haven't seen all the pictures yet,' she said.

'Suit yourself,' said Molly, and left with her grumbling children in tow.

* * *

Tom flexed his shoulders and sighed deeply. The night had been a resounding financial success. He'd sold three paintings and got two more commissions. The reporter from the local paper had promised him a good write up, and he'd been asked to do a guest lecture at the university. Even so, his heart was heavy. Sasha and Dot were in the kitchen clearing up the last of the debris and having one last glass of champagne, but Tom longed for his bed and oblivion.

'Can I get you anything, boss?' shouted Sasha, over the sound of water gushing into the sink.

'No, it's okay. I'll have a coffee in a minute when you've finished, if you're making one.'

'For you, Picasso, anything,' said Dot, ruffling Tom's hair as she passed to collect the empty bottles.

'Wait, Dot – don't go. I need to talk to you.'

Dot paused and looked down at him. She frowned. 'Actually, you don't look so great, for saying you're tonight's big star. Let me just drop this lot in the recycling bin and I'll be back with the coffee, okay?'

She was back within five minutes, carrying a loaded tray.

'Where's Sasha?' Tom asked, peering into the kitchen.

'I told her I'd finish off in a minute. She looked shattered.'

Tom took a steaming mug from Dot and held it in both hands, breathing in the fragrant steam. She had thoughtfully put a half bottle of brandy on the tray and he sloshed a hefty measure into his coffee, offering it wordlessly to Dot.

Dot helped herself and then sat back, kicking off her heavy boots and putting her feet on the arm of another chair. 'Come on then, Tom, spill the beans. What's gone on tonight with you and Molly, and why has she gone off in a huff?'

Tom flinched. He thought for a moment.

'Do you want the straight answer, or the bullshit version?'

'Which do you think, Tom?'

'Right, here goes. You already know I love Molly more than I've ever loved anyone in my life. I fancy her like mad and I want to be with her, but I was worried that I might be impotent.'

'Okay. I'm glad I went for the straight answer... I think. Why is she so furious then?'

'Because I went off to see my old friend Lena last week and told her about the problem.'

'You told her about Molly?'

'Yes, and the... other issues.'

'Blimey, Tom. You told this old female friend about the fact that you didn't know if, to be frank, you could get it up? And were you and Lena ever a bit more than friends? By that I mean, has she ever come on to you, at all?'

'Well, yes, a long time ago, but I thought it would be good to talk to a woman about it.'

'Oh, you did, did you? And you didn't think that someone who was an old friend and had possibly always had the hots for you might see that as something of a challenge?'

'Um, no.'

'So, to cut a long story short, you had few a mad passionate nights with your old girlfriend, and now you're wondering why Molly's not impressed?'

'It was only the last night that it actually happened, but I'm starting to get the point. This isn't going to be an easy one to get over, is it?'

'That's putting it mildly, Tom. More coffee?'

They sat together in the aftermath of the party, taking turns to eat the leftover blinis. And Tom wondered, not for the first time, how he could ever have got this so wrong.

24

The next box arrived when Molly had almost forgotten to look out for it. She'd begun to think that Shaun had finally run out of steam, but she'd been so preoccupied with Tom's treachery that the boxes seemed less important than usual.

The postman was leaning on the doorbell when Molly came to the door, dishevelled and wearing only a bath towel.

'Thought you wuz out,' he said tersely, handing over the parcel.

'No, I've been decorating again, and I needed to get the paint out of my hair. You're very early today,' Molly answered, pulling up the towel to make sure she was decent.

'Must be hard, being on your own, like?' he said, eyeing the towel. 'Could always come round and give you a hand if it all gets too much. If yer know what I mean?' He winked, and Molly felt slightly sick.

'No, thanks, I'm fine, and if you ever make that sort of comment to me again, I'll report you to your superiors and make sure you get suspended,' she said, shutting the door firmly and rushing back upstairs to get some clothes on. But the parcel was too tempting to leave, and she found herself picking at the sticky tape before the postman's van had even left the drive.

This box was less flashy than its predecessors. It was square and chunky, with a pattern of sage-green grape vines over a parchment-coloured background. It looked sophisticated and tantalising, like a special gift from Harrods or Fortnum and Mason.

Molly eased the lid off and peered inside. She could smell something spicy and rich. It reminded her of Christmas, and for the first time she felt a twinge of excitement at the thought of the next festive season, with or without a man in it.

The pale green envelope felt like an old friend, and Molly drew out the sheet of notepaper with a shiver.

Hello, bestest buddy – welcome back from (possibly sunny) Peterborough – hope you're feeling more chilled now. Did you decide to take someone new with you? If so, you might want to hijack them for your next mission. Onwards and upwards, as they say. This one's a biggie. Don't go on your own.

Molly's fingers trembled slightly as she reached for the second piece of paper. Would she ever get used to the thrill of this quest? This poem was longer than the last.

> *So, you're now in the mood for*
> *   romance,*
> *And where better to find it than*
> *   France?*
> *Take a look at the map*
> *(But don't get in a flap)*
> *And find out a bit more while there's*
> *   chance.*
> *You may find that this quest takes*
> *   you far*
> *To the land where the oompah*
> *   bands are.*
> *There are shorts made of leather*

A hat with a feather,
But don't settle for less than the star!

Love you more than crunchy locusts, sorry
about the crap poetry! S xxx

Molly looked down at the poem and tried not to cry. Shaun must have jumped several years ahead in his imagination, to a world where Molly was moving towards a new relationship and had someone to cosy up with. France. Oompah bands? You wouldn't find those in France – surely they were in Switzerland, or Bavaria, or somewhere like that? And romance? Pah! But this must somehow be linked to the photograph album in the other clue. The leather shorts were a definite link, surely? What did it all mean? Why was this place so important to Jake and Shaun?

She checked to see what else was in the box, and found a tightly folded map of an area to the east of Bordeaux, with an X clearly marked over a village in the middle of nowhere. On the back was written an address, and the words *Find Tante Maria and ask her about Marcel. Lederhosen optional.* Great. Don't get in a flap? Shaun was asking her to set off to a place that she'd never heard of, with the possibility of an even more complicated quest involving leather garments, taking an unknown companion, to find out – what exactly? She tipped the box up angrily and a small carton fell out. It had a picture of a plum tree and the words 'Prune Capital of Europe' in gold letters on the lid. Inside was a layer of glistening purple prunes. Did Shaun think that bereavement had caused constipation?

The map still lay on Molly's lap, and she looked at it more closely. She could see that Shaun had drawn an aeroplane over a line from England to Bordeaux, and another line to the X had a train drawn next to it. Not a straightforward trip then. Molly realised that she had accepted the challenge already.

But how could she manage to get away? And how much was all this going to cost? The cheque from Jake's insurance was long cleared, but Molly had it earmarked for a whole list of things, and she'd still got to decide how she was going to support the family. The re-read of her book had convinced her that it was better than she'd remembered, but there was a lot of work to be done on it. And even if it did get published, it wasn't going to make her fortune. Well, she'd worry about all that later.

Molly reached for her phone, thinking that only a few short months ago Dot's number had been unknown to her.

'It strikes me you've only got two options, if you don't count asking your mum or Edna to babysit,' said Dot, sounding less than pleased to have been woken up.

'Go on then, what are they?'

'Take me to France and leave Tom in charge of the kids, or vice versa.'

'But I can't ask Tom now, can I? Not after what happened. I'm guessing he told you how we parted and why?'

'Yes, he did, and I think you're totally over-reacting, to be honest, Molly. I mean it isn't as if you two are romantically involved, are you? I know he'd love to move in and look after the gang, but it'd be better still if you invited him to go with you.'

'And why exactly would that be better?' Molly could hear herself snarling. The tension in her shoulders was building and she had already bitten off one of her best nails. She imagined Dot's face falling, and added hastily, 'Okay, no. We're not involved, exactly, but I kind of want to be. I'm just not sure if I'm ready.'

'Even more reason to ask him, because whatever else is going on inside your head, you two are friends. There doesn't need to be any more to it than that. Stop acting like a sulky teenager and give him a

call. I'm free to step in at your house – I can just as
easily go to work from there, and Sam can come over
and help if I need back-up with dog walking and
stuff.'

'Well...'

'Do it, Molly. Just imagine – France in May. It's
absolutely the best time to go.'

'Who says so?'

'I was watching one of those programmes when
people decide to move house and then hate all the
ones they show them. They were going to live in the
Dordogne, this couple, and I'm sure it was filmed in
May. You won't need your cardigan collection.'

'What's that supposed to mean?'

'Well, you do like to cover up, don't you, Moll? Let
it all hang out – get a few strappy tops and let the sun
get to your body. You can cope with this now.'

'Can I?'

There was a short silence, then Dot said, 'Yes, you
can. You've changed a lot in the last few months.
Haven't you?'

Molly massaged her neck with one hand and
thought about this. She knew she was growing
stronger – making the decision to climb out of the
rut and leave her job, standing up to creeps like the
postman, being firmer with Max's tantrums, and so

on. But inside, she felt as if she was still the same person she'd been throughout her marriage – sometimes unsure of herself, often worried, and never completely happy with her appearance.

'How have I changed, Dot?' she asked, holding her breath. It was like waiting for a school report.

'Oh, come on. You must know you look great – confident, better dressed, less likely to cry at the drop of a hat. You're still a bit of a wimp underneath, though, aren't you?'

'Hmmm, I suppose so.'

'You know so. All you need to do is to bite the bullet and let Tom get closer to you. It doesn't have to be another long-term relationship, you know. Sometimes things can be just right for now. Anyway, I need to get dressed. Speak later, love you.'

Molly shivered. This felt like a huge step to take. Life with Jake hadn't been perfect by anyone's standards, but she was beginning to miss him more now than she had in those first dreadful weeks. It seemed as if distance was making their relationship clearer. He often appeared in her dreams – not doing anything in particular, just being Jake. Sometimes she woke up crying, lost in the big bed and overwhelmed by sadness, but other mornings her first sleepy thoughts of the day were warmer and more positive.

More than anything, Molly wished she could have just a little while to talk to Jake, to ask him about Kate, about his relationship with Dot's mum, and especially his feelings about Dot herself. There were so many questions, and it was too late to wonder if things could have been calmer and more loving between them if she'd understood him better.

She finished dressing and padded downstairs to see if anyone was looking for breakfast yet. It was Saturday, and the sunlight flooding through the kitchen window made it seem even more like a day off. Molly flicked the kettle switch and gazed out at the sun-dappled garden. The grass was neatly mown, thanks to Sam's efforts last weekend, and the old bench that leaned against the apple tree was moss-flecked and inviting. No sounds came from upstairs, so there was time for some spoiling.

Molly ground a handful of coffee beans in Jake's little machine, sniffing the scent rapturously as she tipped them into the pot. The boiling water hissed as she poured it over the grounds, and she added her favourite china mug and a couple of digestive biscuits to the tray. The grass was still wet with dew as she made her way barefoot down the garden, and the birdsong flowed over her, filling Molly with a wild sense of possibilities just out of reach. She sat down on the bench and wriggled her toes in the grass. The delicious smell of coffee mingled with the earthy garden aromas.

Suddenly, she knew she needed to get away, to see different places, and – more to the point – to be with Tom. And when she came back, the future must be tackled. An idea had been growing in her mind; a way of working from home that would bring in cash but still give her time to write. It would be good to spend more time here. This house was feeling more like her own place now and less like limbo, but the spring sunshine and the trees bursting with tiny buds filled her with anticipation. France, with Tom. Could she? Should she?

Why the hell not?

25

The engine noise was too deafening for them to hear each other speak, but Tom could see that Molly was muttering under her breath. He looked out of the window as the runway disappeared and felt her fingers close around his as the plane left the tarmac. As the ground fell away, she sighed and relaxed into her seat.

'Oh, I hate that bit, don't you? I feel as if I should hedge my bets and say a quick Hail Mary,' she breathed.

'I'm always relieved when the plane makes it up into the air. I can never help thinking about the weight of it and how weird the whole flying thing is.'

'I guess it's too early for a gin and tonic?' Molly

was still pale, although her colour was gradually coming back.

'Not at all – we're on holiday, aren't we? And I think we're going to need a drink. We've got no idea what will happen when we get to France, or even if we'll just have to keep on travelling.' Tom grinned, coasting along on a surge of mad excitement at the thought of being with Molly. He still hadn't got over the shock and delight of her call asking him to join her on the trip.

'But why? Wait, I'm not saying I won't come,' he'd said as she'd begun to babble, 'but we hardly parted on good terms last time, did we? And now you want me to set off with you to a mystery place, not knowing how long we'll be gone?'

'I know it sounds mad, but Dot thinks you're the best person for the job. I don't know who else to take.'

The ungracious reply sent Tom's soaring heart plunging back into his boots. Oh well, at least she's asked me, he thought. And as his nan had been fond of saying, 'You have to be grateful for small mercies in this world.'

The previous week had been chaotic, with Molly throwing out endless orders to Dot, writing lists, phoning Sam several times a day, and generally panicking for Britain. Tom had tried to reassure her that Dot was quite capable of running the show for much longer than four days, but Molly's mothering instincts were well developed, and she had found it almost impossible to let go of the reins.

When he had tried to pay for both their flights and train tickets, Molly had become even more agitated. So they had eventually agreed on Tom funding absolutely everything for the whole time they were away, and then halving the final bill later.

At last, however, everything that could be organised had been timetabled to within an inch of its life. And, issuing heavy threats to Theo, Hattie and Max about good behaviour, Molly had finally allowed herself to be bundled into a taxi. Her anxiety levels had soared to new heights when she had realised that Tom was going to have to abandon his wheelchair at the bottom of the aeroplane steps and haul himself up using the power of his arms.

'Well, how did you think I was going to get in the bloody plane?' he'd snapped as she had clutched his sleeve, looking up at the towering staircase in horror.

'I don't know. I didn't give it a thought. Can you do it?'

'Of course I can do it! What's the alternative? Grow wings?'

At the sight of her crestfallen face, Tom had felt his irritation drain away, and by the time they were settled in their seats, he had even managed to give her a hug. She'd responded with unexpected enthusiasm, surprising the grumpy lady who had taken the aisle seat in their row and making her tut loudly.

Now, as the stewardess began the slow progress down the gangway, Tom sighed happily. First an ice-cold drink and maybe a sandwich, and before they knew it they'd be landing in France. He squeezed Molly's hand. 'This is going to be so much fun,' he whispered, loving the way Molly's curly hair flowed down her back and the tantalising glimpse of cleavage that appeared when she wriggled her shoulders to get comfortable.

'I hope so,' Molly responded.

'You still sound worried. Are you expecting problems? Shaun wouldn't give you anything too awful to deal with, surely?'

Molly wrinkled her nose. 'It's a mystery to me, this one. The holiday in the photo album must have happened a year or so before Jake and I got together, by the look of their ages in the picture by the beer garden. I don't see how anything that happened so long ago can be relevant now, do you? And why are we going to France, if the mystery place was in Austria or Switzerland or Germany?'

'Shaun obviously thinks there are things you need to know, so let's just play it by ear,' said Tom, 'and I've never been to any of those places.' He smiled up at the stewardess and she smouldered back at him, touching his hand casually as she passed him his gin. Tom could feel Molly's annoyance and couldn't help being flattered that she was jealous. It was a long time since he'd felt so alive. Meeting Molly had unlocked something inside that was unfolding and developing every day, and the steamy encounter with Lena had fired him up even more.

'Did I tell you I've decided to advertise for pupils?' asked Molly, startling Tom out of his thoughts.

'Pupils?' Tom had a sudden vision of Molly dressed in a Miss Whiplash outfit, opening her front door to a queue of clients in anoraks.

'Yes, piano, clarinet, flute. I've made a few enquiries and I can make much more money working from home than I ever could in schools, without getting kicked or sworn at. I don't know why I've never done it before.'

'Oh, music lessons.'

'Of course music, what did you imagine? I don't know how to do anything else.'

'It's a great idea. You'll need Instagram and a website. Maybe the local paper would do a bit of a feature?'

Molly laughed. 'You can be my agent, Tom. I'll need some help with all that.'

'I'll do that with pleasure, if you promise to forgive me for the thing with Lena.'

There was a silence, and Tom thought he'd gone too far. But there was no way they would ever get anywhere if he couldn't say what he was thinking. And more than anything, Tom wanted there to be a future for them, together. He held his breath and waited for her response as the plane began its descent.

After a moment, Molly turned in her seat so that she could look straight at Tom. Her clear, green eyes were sparkling with tears, but she was smiling.

'I know I was silly about Lena,' she said, getting the name out with difficulty, 'but I wanted to be the one to show you that you were definitely a real man, whatever doubts you had. I've got so many problems of my own... erm... in that area.'

'You're being a bit coy, aren't you, Molly? "In that area?" You sound like a Victorian heroine. What are you really trying to say? You're not telling me you don't like sex?'

Molly blushed and the grumpy lady on the end of their row looked interested. 'It's not that I don't like it,' she hissed under her breath. 'It's just that I'm not very good at it, I suppose.'

'Who told you that?'

'Nobody. I can put on a good show.'

Tom had the vision of Molly in thigh-high boots, complete with whip again. He shook his head to rid himself of the picture. 'Sex isn't a competition, sweetheart. You don't get extra marks for a perfect performance.' The lady next to Tom nodded thoughtfully and Tom half turned his back on her to face Molly. 'What's this got to do with me and Lena, anyway?' he asked.

'I guess I kind of thought we could work things out together, and that you might be feeling insecure, too. I understand, though, and don't ask me any more questions now.' She held up a hand to stop Tom interrupting. 'Let's concentrate on reading my guidebook. Forget Google, I always go old-school when I'm on holiday. I do love a map and some local info.'

Speeding through the vineyards of Bordeaux on a local train, Tom felt himself unwinding even more.

The sun shone down through ancient, twisted branches – blazing through the train windows, warming his face and making dappled shadows on the passengers' faces. Tracks wound here and there between the rows of vines, and the sky was a deep, rich blue with only the occasional puffy cloud. If I painted this scene, thought Tom, everyone would think it was too pretty to be real.

They were heading for a little town about an hour to the east, so there was plenty of time to sit back and appreciate this interlude with Molly before she had to concentrate on Shaun's next quest. He began to mentally rewind their muttered conversation on the plane. It had thrown him completely. Surely someone this voluptuous and sexy wouldn't have any trouble in bed? He glanced across at Molly. At least their travelling companions were distracting her from any worries at the moment. Tom could see that she was as fascinated as he was by the other people in the crowded carriage.

All the seats were full, and some of the floor space was taken up by a group of teenagers with a couple of guitars between them. Some of the older passengers seemed to be getting tired of their chatter, not to mention the strumming and the French folk songs, but Tom thought it added the final touch to the adventure. How different from a ride on a train at home, with frazzled commuters and everyone absorbed in their phones or laptops.

He wanted the journey to go on for hours, or at least until it was time to take Molly out for a leisurely dinner, with a carafe of rough local red wine and something rich and beefy to eat. They would tear chunks from a rustic loaf to dip in their stew, and afterwards share a piece of delicious French apple tart, loaded with cream, and a brandy or two with their hot, strong coffee.

The scenery was gradually changing now from vineyards to row upon row of small fat trees. 'What do you think they grow here, Molly?' asked Tom, peering out of the window, enchanted by the view. 'Are they apple trees?'

'No, not apples – that's in Normandy. Don't you remember the clue?'

'Ah, prune trees?'

She laughed. 'Well, sort of. Plums. It tells you about it in my book. Apparently, this is the prune capital of Europe, there's even a museum of prunes.'

Tom pulled a face. 'Wow, really? You get to see old prunes in glass cases? And I thought the pencil museum that Nan used to take me to was as bad as it could get. Do you remember Jake coming here?'

Molly shook her head. 'We didn't get together until we were sixteen; this must have been the year before. His family often used to go off for long holidays, and mine never did. I was always really jealous. Jake had the sort of skin that tanned easily and he stayed brown for ages.'

The train wound on through the plum trees, and the singers moved on to sad, haunting melodies. Tom was deeply content. All too soon the outlook changed again as they pulled into a small town. He glimpsed a square surrounded by plane trees, and café tables with a sprinkling of early lunchers. Soon Molly was once again coping manfully with decanting his chair, both suitcases and their hand luggage, before the train rattled off again deeper into the heart of France.

Blinking in the sunlight, Tom and Molly sat on the platform and looked at the map again. The village marked with the X seemed to be fairly near to the town, but Tom had no idea how they were going to get themselves and their luggage there. A porter ambled by and Molly tapped him on the shoulder.

'Sorry to bother you, but do you speak English?' she said, giving him the benefit of her shiniest smile.

'Ah, *oui, madame*,' he replied. 'I speak vaire good Eengleesh. 'Ow can I 'elp you?'

Molly showed him the map and in no time he had organised them a taxi and was loading their cases into the boot.

'*Merci beaucoup*,' said Molly with an excruciatingly bad accent, as Tom gave the porter a large tip. 'You are very, very kind.'

The man beamed, and Tom sensed his puzzlement as he glanced from Molly to Tom. Was he wondering what such a beautiful woman saw in this wreck of a man? He wished he hadn't given the tip now, and resolutely looked away as the taxi drove off. Sighing, Tom told himself that if this was the shape of things to come, he'd better get used to it and stop feeling sorry for himself.

Their taxi meandered through fields and a couple of sleepy hamlets, and eventually it reached the outskirts of a larger village. An old stone church stood guard at the entrance to the village, with a magnificent graveyard next to it. Tom could see the sort of marble creations that would surround a much grander church at home, and each one seemed to be decorated with bunches of both real and artificial flowers, and topped with ornate photo frames.

The taxi driver muttered something unintelligible and Molly leaned forwards, handing him the map. He shrugged, and pulled up next door to a baker's shop. The striped awning cast a deep shadow, and a spindly wrought-iron table and two chairs sat under its canopy. Here sat the oldest lady Tom had ever seen. She was dressed in dusty black from head to toe, and seemed to be fast asleep. The taxi driver pointed to his meter and Tom parted with the relevant coins, once again adding a hefty tip. He would have to stop this, or their spending money would be used up by tonight. As the driver deposited Tom and Molly with their belongings on the pavement and drove away, Molly gazed at Tom in dismay.

'Now what do we do?' she whispered. 'We need to get a move on; we don't even know where we're sleeping tonight.'

The old lady gave a snort and opened her eyes. There was no alarm there, just an inquisitive sparkle.

'*Bonjour, madame,*' said Molly, and then added desperately, 'I don't suppose you speak any English, do you?'

'*Mais certainement, ma petite,*' answered the lady, getting to her feet with some difficulty, 'and I am sure zat you can only be Mme White? I 'av been expecting you for some time. My Shaun, he did not say quite when you would be 'ere.'

'*Your* Shaun?'

The lady smiled rather sadly. 'I am his Tante

Maria. Madame Maria Martinez. Come inside, both of you. It is time for coffee and maybe a piece of gateau. But I expect you will both be requiring some tea?' She smiled, and slowly led the way inside her house.

Molly raised her eyebrows at Tom in a silent question. He shrugged and began to wheel his chair into the darkness of the hallway. Thank goodness there were no steps. This was all very peculiar.

'I feel as if we've dropped right into the middle of an Agatha Christie novel,' whispered Molly as she followed him. 'I keep expecting Poirot to appear. Is she real? And is she the key to the mystery, or just the beginning of the search?'

'I think we're about to find that out,' murmured Tom.

26

Afterwards, Molly could never remember how the conversation moved so swiftly from cake to darker subjects, but in the space of half an hour it was obvious that the latest box had led them to very deep waters – and they were about to plunge in headlong, with no idea of the consequences.

Tante Maria made coffee for herself and a pot of English breakfast tea for Molly and Tom, before settling herself in an armchair in front of the gently crackling log fire. It was warm in the little room and Molly's eyelids began to feel pleasantly heavy as she sipped her drink. Tom looked very much at home, too, stretched out on the hearthrug making a fuss of the marmalade cat that had its cushion right in front of the blaze. Tante Maria smiled down at him.

'Ah, Cossette knows the best place to relax. The cat is always queen in my 'ouse.'

'Do you light the fire just for the cats?' asked Tom, undoing another button on his denim shirt and rolling his sleeves up. The heat from the fire was beginning to make him dizzy and he wondered if he could ask for some water.

'Oh, no, the fire is for me. When you get to my age, the evenings seem chilly even on days like this. The cats love it, too, though. It was the same when Shaun and Jake were 'ere, only it was Cossette's grandmother on the cushion in those days.'

Molly looked up sharply at the mention of Jake. So the old lady did know why they were here. She met the rheumy eyes properly for the first time and the two women exchanged a long look. The clock ticked on the mantelpiece, Cossette purred, and time slowed right down. Molly had the sensation of being on the edge of a precipice. She took a deep breath.

'Tante Maria... if you don't mind me calling you that?' There was a brief nod and a smile from the lady. 'I have come to see you because Shaun has left me a sort of treasure hunt, only now I'm suddenly not sure if it's treasure I'm going to find, or trouble.'

'You must tell me what Shaun has said to you.'

'Not much, only that I have to come to France, and then maybe on to somewhere where lederhosen are worn. I know it must all sound very odd. And I've got to find a star, and a hat with a feather. Does all this mean anything to you?'

The old lady was sitting very still now, her cheeks even more white and papery than they had when she slept in the sunshine. Molly leaned across and patted her hand. 'I'm sorry, I've upset you,' she said softly.

'*Non*, I 'av known zis was coming for some time,' said Tante Maria, 'and I am ready to talk to you. Shaun... he said you were beautiful and brave, and zat I must tell you the truth. It has been a long time to keep the secret, and I am very tired now.'

Molly waited. The silence became unbearable, and Tom began to move himself over to sit on a small wooden bench that stood further away from the fire, apologising for being so clumsy. When he was set-tled, the old lady sighed.

'Now we are all comfortable,' she said, 'and I am glad, because this will take some time. Your husband, Jake, and his friend, Shaun – who is the grandson of my English cousin, Katherine – came to stay with me when they were fifteen years old, the exact same age as my grandson, Pierre. It was a wonderful holiday –

my dear Katherine came, too, and we spent many happy hours reminiscing while the boys got to know each other better.'

Molly leaned forward. 'But in Shaun's photographs, there were four boys, and the background didn't look like this village. Have I got my wires crossed somehow?'

'Pardon?'

'I mean, was there another boy? And did they go to Austria or Germany, too?'

Tante Maria clasped her hands together but Molly could see that they were trembling. 'Yes, there was another boy,' she said. 'His name was Marcel.'

Tears were trickling down the parchment cheeks now, and Tom got to his feet, using his sticks to swing himself across to where the old lady sat. He lowered himself to the floor at her feet and took both her hands in his.

'You don't have to say any more now – don't upset yourself.'

'Yes, she does!' Molly sounded hysterical even to herself, but she was unable to control the feeling of panic that was filling her body, chilling her even though the fire was still warm. 'You must go on now, Tante Maria, you can't leave the story there. Who was Marcel, and what happened to him?'

Tante Maria freed her hands and fished out a tiny lacy handkerchief from a deep pocket in her dress. Mopping her eyes, she continued her tale. 'Marcel was a beautiful boy – golden-haired, blue-eyed, with the voice of an angel. He sang in the church choir and was just on the point of going to a new school in Paris where his voice could be trained properly.'

'And what has all this got to do with the other boys?'

It took a while for Tante Maria to speak, but this time Molly – intercepting a stern look from Tom – managed to hold her tongue. Finally, the old lady began to tell the story, haltingly at first but gaining speed as the memories washed over her.

'Shaun and Jake were handsome young men,' she said, 'very friendly and natural – and they quickly formed a very close friendship with Pierre; the three of them soon became inseparable. They spent their days cycling around the lanes and farm tracks, drinking cider and becoming tanned, fit, and fluent in a mixture of French and English... strange words... I don't know how to say it...'

'Do you mean slang?'

'Yes, I think that is the right term. It was almost like a secret language. Everyone made Shaun and Jake welcome. They were so handsome and charming, and Pierre was good-looking, too. Even so, Marcel was different. He was far more innocent than the others and he idolised them all. But it was your Jake in particular that he loved, Molly.'

Molly wrapped her arms tightly around herself. 'Carry on, please. I have to know all this.'

'Well, the boys had let Marcel join them on several occasions, and towards the end of their holiday had even persuaded Marcel's very protective mama to let him come on a camping weekend with them to a beer festival in Bavaria. They had not told her about the beer – selling the trip as a sort of nature walk – but they had planned to take the train and hitchhike, pitching their tents in farmers' fields and drinking as much beer as they could get.'

'And his mother agreed to this?' Molly's maternal instincts made her suspicious, but Tante Maria nodded.

'Marcel was hopelessly over-excited about the weekend, and his mother had always found it hard to deny him anything. He was her only son, born when she had long given up hope of having children. Marcel told everyone about the holiday – he nearly drove the other three boys insane with his constant prattling. I think they even thought about leaving him behind, but Shaun was too soft-hearted to do that when it came the time to go away together.'

'What do you mean, Shaun wouldn't leave Marcel out?' asked Molly. 'Are you saying the other two would have done it?'

A shadow passed over Tante Maria's face. 'I am afraid,' she said hesitantly, 'zat Jake and my grandson Pierre were not... not such kind boys. Of course,' she carried on, seeing the look on Molly's face, 'your Jake may have become different as he matured, but at that time...'

Horrified, Molly hugged herself harder as the story continued to unfold, chilled at the thought of the cruelty that was shouting out to her across the years. It was true, Jake had been many things – energetic, creative, charming, witty, generous when it suited him – but not kind-hearted.

As Tante Maria described the start of the adventure, with some of the neighbours and the boys' families coming out to wave them off, the older woman began to cry again. 'And they were all so young, so excited,' she wept.

'But why shouldn't they be excited?' asked Molly, dreading the answer.

'Because, although four boys went away, only three returned,' said Tante Maria, wiping her eyes again. Tom patted her knee and recaptured one of the veined, fragile-looking hands when she was ready to carry on. She smiled down at him.

Molly watched Tom as he tried to comfort the frail old lady, and knew that this was what Jake had been lacking; the deep vein of kindness that ran right through Tom like a seam of molten gold. The shock of Tante Maria's words seemed to be taking a while to sink in, but when the rest of the story followed, it was even worse than Molly had anticipated. Tante Maria sat up straighter and held on tightly to the handkerchief as she stumbled through the final part of the tragedy.

'It was bound to end in disaster, I can see that now. There was a terrible accident. Marcel... over-indulged at the beer festival, even though the boys said they had tried to restrain him. Pierre assured me that they did their best to curb Marcel's drinking. He was not used to alcohol – he had stuck to Coca Cola on the previous evenings in town.'

'Accident? He was hurt?' Molly asked, confused.

'Not exactly hurt, no. Marcel's mother was summoned very late on the final evening by the police, and got to the hospital just in time to say goodbye to her beloved son.'

'But what happened to him? How did he die?'

'There was an enquiry at the time. It was... how do you say it... inc...'

'Inconclusive?' finished Tom.

Tante Maria nodded. 'It seemed Marcel had an allergy that he had been aware of and had always been very careful to deal with. Apparently, for some reason he forgot about his problem and ate some salted peanuts. He reacted immediately and died very quickly.'

The three of them sat in silence, while the logs settled into a pile of dying embers. After a moment, Tom reached over to add sticks and stir the flames into life, and the spell was broken.

'I still don't understand why we're here,' said Molly. 'It's a terribly sad story but it was an accident. Teenage boys do silly things. They drink too much and forget to be careful. I could tell you a few things about my Sam that would make your hair curl.' She saw the old lady's bemused frown. 'I mean, that would surprise you.'

'Yes, of course. You 'av an English saying, "boys will be boys", and it is true.'

'So why do you think Shaun wanted us to come and find out about it?' Tante Maria was silent, and Molly's heart lurched. She sat forward. 'Wait a minute, Tante Maria. You don't think it *was* an accident, do you?'

'I don't know. Perhaps it was.'

'But the police must have looked into it at the time? Surely they would have found out if there was anything sinister about the whole thing?'

'Perhaps zey were looking in ze wrong place.' The old lady's accent was getting stronger as exhaustion took hold of her, and Tom sent Molly another warning glance.

'Tante Maria, we won't keep you, we need to go and find somewhere to stay for the night, but do you think that Shaun wanted Molly to investigate the accident in some way? Did he have doubts about it, too?'

'I don't know,' she said again. 'I think... possibly. He may have had guilty feelings. You will be staying here tonight, of course. My daughter, Paulette, will be home soon to cook dinner.'

'But we couldn't possibly stay with you, just out of the blue like that. You only met us today,' protested Tom.

Tante Maria held up a hand and Molly had a glimpse of the imposing woman she must have been in her prime. There was a fierce glint in her eyes even now. 'No arguments. Tonight you sleep 'ere, and tomorrow you catch ze train to Munich. Paulette will sort it all out on ze Interweb machinery.'

'Munich? Why? We only have a day or two, will we have time to get to Munich and home again, Tom?'

'Molly, you must go – Shaun expects it, I am sure. You need to speak with Pierre.' Tante Maria was flushed now, and Molly patted her arm, trying to work out how this change of plan was going to affect their timetable.

'But why is Pierre in Munich?' asked Tom. 'And couldn't we just ring him first? He might not want to talk about all this.'

'It is not possible. I do not have his telephone number. Sadly, we are estranged. He lives some distance out of Munich. Paulette will make everything right.' The old lady closed her eyes and Molly could see the conversation was over for now. It looked as if tomorrow was going to be even more eventful than today.

27

Munich Station, the next morning, was bursting with travellers and full of things that Tom would have liked to look at more closely. He had never had so much fun travelling before. Even though her mind was so preoccupied with Jake's past, Molly was still his ideal person to share an adventure with.

Even when she was obviously worried and under pressure, Molly never seemed in a hurry to get where she was going once the journey was underway, but was happy to look around her, watching the other travellers, and shamelessly listening to their conversations. As they waited on the platform for the local train that was going to take them deeper into

Bavaria, she handed Tom a baguette filled to over-flowing with ham.

'It's a good job we're not vegetarian, they don't seem to go in for hummus and suchlike here. Do you want some orange juice or shall I get you a beer?'

'Juice, please. I ought to keep a clear head. We need to sort out a hotel booking for tonight. Paulette was amazing, wasn't she?'

Molly nodded, biting into her own baguette with gusto. Tom thought she looked much better today. He'd been alarmed by her pallor the night before, as she tried hard to make sense of the horrors of the day. At last, Paulette had arrived, solid, bustling, and maternal. She had taken stock of the situation with one glance and begun to organise them all. The old lady had been dispatched to her room for half an hour's nap, and the rest of them had quickly got to the heart of the problem.

In a short time, Paulette had reassured them that they were welcome to stay and that her mother had insisted on a couple of beds being constantly ready ever since Shaun had been in touch with her. It would be no trouble at all to cook for four instead of two; in fact, she would invite her neighbours, Andre the baker and his son, around to join them and make her speciality – bacon and bean broth. Andre could then bring some of his famous walnut bread to go with it, and maybe his son would contribute one of their prize-winning strawberry tarts.

'Andre will be delighted. He is always trying to get his feet under my table. He doesn't get broth like mine very often. I think he would marry me given half the chance,' she grinned, 'but I am far too busy to be nursemaid to two grown men.'

Tom had been reassured to see Molly's colour coming back at this, and she was soon fully fortified by a glass of the gutsy red wine that he had been imagining on the train. The evening had improved as it had gone on. Paulette had gone to summon Andre, then quickly put together a huge pan of hearty soup, fragrant with chunks of gammon, onion and garlic, and loaded with every sort of bean imaginable.

'What are you putting into your soup, Paulette?' Molly asked, fascinated. 'Is there a recipe?'

Paulette had laughed. 'Recipe? Oh, no, just what my mother and my grandmother and their mothers before them have done.'

'Is it a secret?'

'Not at all, Molly. I had a ham hock already boiled, and I have added good stock, and then some herbs, chopped cabbage, and tins of beans and pulses – cannellini, haricot, borlotti, green lentils, butter beans – any you have. Of course, my mother soaked her own beans in her day, but I am a working woman and life is much too short for that now.'

Later, Tom had watched Molly blossom, trying out her schoolgirl French on Andre and his burly son, and talking quietly to Tante Maria when she joined them after her snooze. Molly's hair, unclipped from its slides, shone in wild curls over her shoulders, and her eyes were bright with enthusiasm. He wondered how she was feeling as she drew nearer and nearer to understanding what had made her husband develop into the man he had become.

What surprises – or shocks – would Molly face the next day? But that night, she had seemed content to let Paulette take charge – of the food, of the hotel and train reservations, and most of all, of the mood of the evening.

It seemed that the easiest way to get south of Munich to the very edge of Bavaria (Paulette had let her eyes slide over Tom's useless legs with practicality rather than sympathy) would be a flight from Bordeaux and a local train from Munich Station.

They discussed the possibilities, and Paulette assured them that she would be happy to drive them to Bordeaux if they could be up and ready to be off by 6 a.m. It would be a long day for them all, but she could combine the journey with a visit to an old friend for breakfast. *Voila* – everyone would be happy! She ignored their protests and served dinner. Conversation and wine flowed – the meal was one of the best Tom had ever eaten – and it seemed as if the four other people around the refectory table had known Tom and Molly for years, instead of having had two cuckoos dropped unexpectedly into their nest.

This morning, Molly had hugged Tante Maria tearfully before Paulette had bustled them into her car. The old lady looked frailer than ever today, and had clung tightly to Molly, wishing her luck. Tom was very grateful for Paulette's no-nonsense approach on the drive into Bordeaux. She chatted for parts of the drive but left time for their own thoughts, eventually saying an affectionate but unemotional goodbye, and wishing them luck.

'Whatever Pierre says to you both, remember this – they were just boys, and it was many years ago. Ring me if you need to talk. I am as keen as you are to know what really happened.' Sadness took her voice away for a moment, but she continued bravely, 'He was a difficult child in some ways, my Pierre. Delightful, funny, but perhaps not so loving as I might have wished. A self-contained boy in many ways. If we could have talked... But there it is. I wish I had done things differently.'

'Don't we all,' said Molly, with feeling.

Now, many hours later, as the little train pulled out of Munich Station, Tom knew that he and Molly were going to face some tough times. They both fell silent as the new landscape unfolded. This was chocolate box land. Chalets were scattered over the green hillsides, but distant mountain peaks still had a heavy coating of snow.

The sunshine sparkled on the river that flowed along beside the train track, and brightly coloured flowers filled all the window boxes. Sometimes a steeply wooded hillside would turn into a sheer drop, and the breathtaking views would make Molly grab Tom's hand and lean towards him. Tom loved the feel of her soft skin – she had pushed up the sleeves of her linen shirt and her bare arm brushed his every now and again, warm and enticing. The faint scent of vanilla wafted across to him when Molly moved, and her lips were just asking to be kissed.

He wondered, as he had been doing ever since their flight, what her problem was. Maybe if they shared a bottle of wine tonight he would pluck up his courage to ask her to explain properly. But they had more serious business to deal with first.

Once again on a station platform, a much smaller one this time, Tom and Molly looked at each other.

'Now what?' Tom asked, rubbing his ear and yawning. Tante Maria's cat had insisted on spending the night on his bed, and had got up every so often to chase an imaginary mouse, or to sit on his chest and rhythmically dig her claws into him.

Tom had given up on sleep after an hour or two, and had started reading a thriller that he'd bought at the airport. It was full of knife attacks and shooting, and by the end of the third chapter he had been more wide awake than ever. He'd fallen into a deep sleep just before dawn and dreamed of rescuing Molly from a marauding gang of drug dealers, but his phone's alarm clock had jangled him back into the real world at 5 a.m., ready to get on the road.

Molly sighed. She looked how Tom felt – rough. 'I guess we should make for the town centre and find a tourist information point. They'll have maps there. I've got the last address that Paulette was given by Pierre, but it's a while since she's heard from him and he's never answered any of her letters.'

'Did Paulette have any idea about what the *star* reference in Shaun's rhyme could mean?'

'Only that Pierre fancied himself as the star whatever he was doing. It sounds as if he had an ego the size of Jupiter as a boy. I can't wait to meet him, can you? He sounds lovely,' said Molly drily.

She wove through the crowded streets of the little town, steering Tom's chair as if she'd been doing it all her life. Every time they paused to negotiate a particularly tricky pavement or wait for a path to clear for them, she would pat his shoulder reassuringly. He was torn between liking the thought that she was aware of him and of feeling uncomfortably like the family pet.

Eventually, they reached what seemed to be the main square and found the familiar 'i' sign over a timber-framed chalet-style building, with riotous scarlet geraniums in its window boxes. Inside, peace reigned, and the cool, unhurried atmosphere was such a relief that neither Tom nor Molly could speak for a moment. The receptionist smiled a welcome and spoke to them in perfect, barely accented English.

'Can I help you? Are you looking for somewhere to stay?'

'Oh, yes, we are,' said Tom wearily, having an image of a huge four-poster bed and nothing to do but climb into it for a nap, 'but we've got some detective work to do first, unfortunately.'

'Really?' The well-plucked eyebrows shot up. 'Tell me more. How can I assist you?'

Molly handed over the crumpled address that Paulette had given her and the photograph of the four boys. 'We really need to find this man – his name is Pierre Deville but we haven't got much time to spare.'

'Goodness me, that does sound exciting,' the girl said, peering at the picture and the note, '...but this is easy. Everybody knows Pierre, although he doesn't live at that address any more. He married well, you know. He has certainly changed since this was taken – he looks so young in the photograph. And who are the others? Are you searching for them, too?'

'No, just for Pierre. But we didn't know about his marriage; that's the problem, we've never met him, and he's been out of touch with his family for some years now. We need to talk to him urgently,' said Molly, sinking onto a nearby chair and flexing tired shoulders. She reached for one of the leaflets about the town and began to fan herself.

'Can you tell us where he's living, and maybe a bit more about him?' asked Tom. He hoped the extra time resting would help Molly to recover her energy.

The heat outside was overpowering after the chill of an English spring, and he guessed it must be exhausting pushing him everywhere; he was no lightweight. Although he was slim-hipped, Tom had always tried to keep in shape by using the gym whenever he could, and the extra muscle power had developed considerably in his chest and upper arms over the years, making him heavier than he looked.

'Pierre lives in a *schloss* about ten kilometres away – it is quite hard to reach by public transport.' She leaned over her counter and put a beautifully manicured hand on Tom's arm. 'Now, don't look so worried. There is no need to be downhearted. I will find you a nice hotel, you can both go and have a little siesta, and maybe taste our local beer? And then this evening, Pierre will be here.'

She smiled at their astonishment. Molly said, 'Here? He'll just come to us?'

'Well, not here exactly. He will be in the beer garden just along the street at eight o'clock – he is the star of the band.' She raised her arms and made motions as if she was playing a trombone, with accompanying noises. 'You know what I mean. I believe you have the same thing in your country?'

'An oompah band?' asked Molly, stifling a grin.

'That is it. He is there several times a week. You

can go and watch them, and then perhaps see Pierre afterwards. Or would you prefer me to telephone him for you?'

'No!'

The receptionist looked startled at Molly's tone, and began to slide a fingernail down a list of hotels. 'I hope you don't mind me asking, but what is your price range? Modest, or a little more luxurious?'

'Oh, modest, I'm afraid,' answered Molly, but Tom interrupted her.

'We're not going to cut corners tonight – let's have a bit of luxury,' he said. 'No, don't argue, Molly. We both deserve spoiling now and again. I'd like a four-poster bed, how about you?'

'Two rooms?' asked the girl, dimpling at Tom. 'If you were only requiring one room, I could have booked you into the best hotel in the town, with a four-poster bed and a whirlpool bath. It has a beautiful shady garden, too. I am able to offer a special deal tonight. I have contacts there.'

Tom looked at Molly and raised an eyebrow. She giggled.

'He thinks he looks like James Bond when he does that,' she said to the receptionist. 'Oh, go on then, Tom. I wouldn't want to deprive you of your bit of luxury.'

The receptionist smiled. 'You will not regret it, and the hotel is very close to the beer garden. It is hard to say...' she looked again at the snapshot that Molly had left on the counter, 'but I am almost sure that the place in your picture is the one you will be visiting later.'

'I suppose one Bavarian beer garden looks much like another, though? I read somewhere that they always have conker trees around them,' said Tom, wishing she would just get on with it and book their room. The thought of being alone with Molly and having an exotic bath and a huge comfortable bed thrown in, was distracting to say the least.

The receptionist read his thoughts and reached for the telephone. 'Yes, you are right, up to a point, but if you look closely here, you can see a corner of the sign above the door. You will see later.'

The hotel was as good as Tom had hoped – better, because the girl hadn't mentioned the secluded patio outside their room where they could sit in the shade and order tall, slim glasses of chilled lager, beaded with condensation.

Molly sighed with contentment. 'I wish we didn't have to go hunting around for some bloke who sounds like quite a nasty piece of work, don't you? This place is perfect.'

'I know, but maybe we'll get all that over with fairly quickly, and then we can wander around the town, have something suitably Bavarian to eat, wallow in the whirlpool, have late-night drinks in this little garden?'

'Well, I'm going to have a bath now, and I want to check on everybody at home so I might be a while. I just hope I don't drop my phone in the water. I might even have another bath later, just because I can. Is that okay?'

'Absolutely. Take your beer with you and have a good soak. I'm going to sit in the sun and think about dinner,' said Tom. Which was really a lie, because all he could think about was Molly.

28

By quarter to eight, Tom and Molly were settled under a giant parasol in the courtyard of the Edelweiss Beer Garden. It was the biggest one of its kind in the town and it looked prosperous and stylish. The ubiquitous horse chestnut trees towered over the seating area, creating a sea-green cave, cool and refreshing after the heat of the crowded streets. There was a beer festival going on – the clerk at their hotel had told them that they were incredibly lucky to get a room tonight, and it was only possible because there had been a last-minute cancellation.

'Are you ready to eat?' asked Tom, reaching for a menu.

Molly shook her head. 'I can't... or at least not

until we've found Pierre and got it over with,' she said. 'My stomach's in knots. I don't know why. It was all so long ago, but I can't help feeling sick at the thought of what he might say.'

'Well, you won't have to wait much longer. I think this is the man himself. No, don't look now, he's behind you. Sorry, I sound as if I'm auditioning for a pantomime.'

Molly tried to catch a glimpse of the new arrival without actually turning round. 'Which one? Oh, yes, that guy with the fancy lederhosen and a cheeky feather in his trilby. Great legs, but does look a bit full of himself. You could be right.'

As she spoke, the man crossed to the little stage where a handful of musicians were already tuning up, and took hold of the microphone.

'Greetings to friends old and new, and welcome to our fiesta night. We bring you fun, laughter and music. Oh, and there may be beer, too!' He raised the stein that one of the waitresses had put into his outstretched hand, and held it up in a toast, as the diners and drinkers laughed.

'*Raus*, Pierre – give us a song,' shouted an elderly lady at the table right next to the stage. The audience took up the chant. '*Raus, raus, raus*, Pierre!' The man gave a bellow of laughter, downed half his beer, and signalled to the band to strike up their first tune. It was a well-known drinking song with actions that the crowd could copy, involving much slurping of beer. Tom and Molly watched in amazement, carried along by the rhythm and energy of the musicians.

Pierre was obviously in his element, playing the audience for all he was worth, teasing regular customers, flirting with a group of pretty girls and heckling the band mercilessly, his sparkling dark eyes scanning the crowd to see where more fun could be generated. The audience loved him, and when he finally came off stage at the interval, they howled for more. As Pierre passed their table on his way to the bar, Tom reached out a hand.

'Excuse me, I'm sorry to bother you,' he said. 'But could we have a word?'

Pierre looked down, taking in Tom's wheelchair and Molly's flushed cheeks in one glance. He took his hat off and bowed to them both. 'Do I know you?' he asked.

Molly gestured to the empty chair at their table. 'No, we haven't met, but I think we have some friends in common from a few years back. Jake, Shaun and Marcel? Although, to be fair, we never met Marcel. Your mother and grandmother send their love, though,' she added.

The man sat down heavily in the chair next to Tom. He stared at Molly in silence for a few moments, while the PA system blasted out an old ABBA song about the winner taking it all. His olive skin, tanned from many summers, was suddenly several shades paler. It was hard to see the young boy from the old snapshot in this charmer with the silvery wings to his once-black hair, especially now the smile was gone from his face.

After a while, Pierre stood up again. 'I am sorry, I can't talk to you now. I have only five minutes left of my break and I have an important telephone call to make. But if you wait behind at the end of the show, we could spend some time together over a coffee and perhaps a brandy? Or better still, meet me somewhere quieter.'

'Of course, we can see you're busy,' said Tom. 'Would you like to come to our hotel? It's the big one across the road.'

'Is it really? You have planned this visit for some time then? It is very hard to get rooms over there.'

'No, it was quite a sudden decision, but we'll explain later; we don't want to hold you up. We'll be in the hotel bar right after the show, okay?'

Pierre nodded, and began to weave his way towards the door. He clapped on his trilby, slipped back into his stage persona, and moved through the crowd, slapping a few people on the back as he passed, and exchanging the odd ribald comment. Molly saw him pause and glance back at her as he entered the bar building. His expression was un-readable.

Much later, as they sat in semi-darkness on the hotel terrace waiting for the barman to bring them a drinks menu, Molly rehearsed what she would say to the man who held the key to the story of Marcel. How much did he know? It was all so long ago. What was Shaun's involvement, and how much had Jake known about the tragedy? It seemed strange that nei-ther of them had ever discussed the French holiday or the Bavarian trip, but since her husband's death Molly had been forced to revise her ideas of their relationship several times. She had never expected so many secrets. Were all marriages like this? Was it only when one partner was snatched away that a full picture could be seen? She looked out at the twin-kling fairy lights that were threaded all around the trees in the garden. It was so pretty here. She wished she could enjoy it properly.

'Should we order Pierre a brandy, do you think?' asked Tom, peering through the open doorway to see if their guest was approaching. 'The barman's coming now.'

'No, let's wait until he gets here. It seems a bit presumptuous to choose for him. He shouldn't be long, surely? The band finished playing half an hour ago. I hope he didn't think we were rude coming out early. I just couldn't stand the noise any longer.'

'Me neither, there's only so much brass band music I can take. When they launched into "Una Paloma Blanca", I knew we had to leave. But we did wave to him, didn't we? And he definitely waved back.'

'I expect he'll be here soon then,' said Molly.

But Pierre didn't arrive soon; in fact, he didn't appear at all. After another twenty minutes, Molly went across the road to see if she could see him, but the bar was in darkness and there was no answer when she banged on the door. There seemed nothing else to be done but to go to bed.

Tom was furious with himself for taking his eye off the ball. He should have guessed this might happen and stayed until the end. Wearily, he allowed Molly to push him to the lift. At least they had the prospect of a night together, and who knew where that could lead? But just as Molly reached out to press the lift call button, the hotel clerk came bustling over, holding a key.

'Excuse me, sir, madam, but I have remembered that the receptionist from the tourist information said that you had originally asked for two rooms when I spoke to her earlier. She is my cousin, Sylvia. She was concerned that she had forced your hand in choosing this hotel.'

'Oh, no, there's nothing to worry about,' said Tom. 'We're fine, and she was only being helpful.' He glared at the man, willing him to go away. But it was no use, the clerk had clearly decided on his mis-guided mission of mercy.

'It was just that another room has become free at the very last moment,' said the man, beaming at them both. 'I can offer it to you for only 70 Euros, under the circumstances. I would hate to think that we had not been helpful.'

Molly looked down at Tom. 'I think I'll take it, if you don't mind?' she said. 'We could probably both do with some thinking time, couldn't we? And I don't think I'm going to sleep much, so I can read if I'm on my own.'

'I don't mind you reading,' he said. Even to him-self, his voice sounded plaintive, and she bit her lip.

'Here is the key, I will come up with you and help

to transfer your belongings. You must have the very best we can offer,' said the clerk, who had missed their conversation due to being distracted by a stray dog that was threatening to enter the building.

Tom seethed. Couldn't Molly see how much he wanted her to stay with him? He'd thought they were getting somewhere; she had seemed much more relaxed with him today, even though she was wound up about meeting Pierre. Where was he going wrong? Another wasted night, and still no nearer to having her in his arms. Tom could feel the tension in his shoulders as he tried to smile up at Molly. She was probably right; they had been living in each other's pockets this week. A breather might do her good. The last thing he wanted was to have a row tonight when they were both so tired.

Tomorrow, they would put all their efforts into finding Pierre. But when all this was sorted, Tom knew he couldn't wait any longer. He had to get Molly into his bed, whatever it took.

29

The next morning, it became more and more obvious that Pierre was not going to be as easy to track down as Molly and Tom had hoped. Molly, after tossing and turning for much of the night, felt crumpled and out of sorts. Several times she'd sat up in bed and decided to ring Tom's room to ask if she could change her mind and join him, but the second before pressing his room number on the bedside table, her nerve had failed her. The vision of disappointing him was too much to bear – of lying woodenly next to him while he wondered why she was such a frigid bundle of fear.

Was this going to be the story of her life? she wondered gloomily. Always frustrated, burning with sexual tension, never able to seize the moment in case she couldn't let herself go? Tom had been perfectly polite to her this morning, but the recent easy warmth between them was missing. She supposed she shouldn't be surprised – no man was going to put up with being turned down so often.

As she listened to Tom questioning their waiter, Molly reached into her bag for some painkillers. Her head was thumping, partly from last night's loud music and lack of sleep but mainly due to the generous quantities of beer that she'd managed to consume. Whatever Pierre had to say to them, it wasn't going to be good, she thought. How could such an old tragedy be dug up without some sort of backlash? Maybe they should just give up and go home. But Tom had other ideas, and seemed to have turned into a cross between Poirot and Miss Marple overnight.

'So, you saw the man we're looking for heading out of town at around eleven o'clock? Are you sure it was Pierre?' he asked the boy, who began to edge away nervously.

'I am almost sure. You must ask the manager,' he said, scooping up their plates and leaving swiftly.

'Stop it, Tom, you're scaring him,' said Molly, massaging her temples. She looked round for somewhere to get a glass of water, then gave up and shuddered as she swallowed her tablets with the dregs of cold coffee.

'He's done a runner,' said Tom, spreading butter on a roll with unnecessary vigour. 'How are we going to find him now? The only thing to do is to go to his house.'

'But we don't know where he lives, do we?'

'No, but that receptionist from the tourist information place does. She said he'd done well in life, or something like that. He lives five miles away in a *schloss*. That's a castle, isn't it? He must have married quite a bit above himself.'

Half an hour later, Tom and Molly were in a taxi being driven along a tree-lined avenue that wound up a steep hillside. The woods were so thick here that they couldn't get a decent view of what lay at the top of the hill, but as they turned the last corner, the little castle was revealed in all its simple beauty. Basking in the sunshine, it was clearly an important residence; not so large as to be daunting, but turreted and embellished like the home of a fairytale princess. Outside on the gravel drive sat a low-slung sporty Mercedes with the roof down. One door was open as if the driver had gone back to fetch something, and the great oak front door at the top of a flight of stone steps stood open a crack.

'Blimey,' said Molly. 'Pierre certainly did marry well.'

Their driver crunched to a halt, held the taxi door open for Molly and then got out Tom's wheelchair, expertly flipping it open and holding it steady for his passenger.

'Wait for us, will you?' asked Tom. 'We might not be long.' The man shrugged and got back into his cab, unfolding a newspaper and lighting up a cigarette.

'Now what?' whispered Molly.

Before they could make a decision, they heard a wild flurry of barking from inside the house, and a woman slid out of the door, closing it swiftly behind her. Not seeing them at first, she leaned against the door, eyes closed, a picture of elegance. Her clothes were understated – well-cut navy linen trousers and a fitted cream top, with a navy and cream striped jersey slung across her shoulders. Her feet were as long and slim as the rest of her body, and thrust into slightly scuffed tan loafers.

Discreet gold jewellery finished the picture: hooped earrings, thin bangles, and a delicate locket. Her hair was scooped up in an artlessly glamorous bun with just a few selected strands escaping. Molly guessed the woman to be in her early fifties but she could easily have been ten years younger or older than that. It was a timeless style, and one that Molly knew she would never be able to achieve, however hard she tried.

As Tom, Molly, and the now alert taxi driver gazed admiringly, the lady opened her eyes and glared at them. Her mouth was a disapproving line.

'Excuse me, we were just wondering...' Tom began. The woman glared.

'And what, pray, are you doing outside my house?' she asked in heavily accented English, coming down the steps and stopping on the last one so that she was still slightly above them all.

'Oh, erm... well, we wondered if we could speak with Pierre? I'm guessing he's your husband?' said Molly, as Tom seemed to have been struck dumb.

'Pierre? Are you saying you are acquainted with my husband? Is he expecting you?'

'Not exactly, but we arranged to meet him last night for a chat and he didn't show.'

'Show? I don't understand. You were in the show, too?'

'No, I mean he didn't turn up.' Met with another blank expression, Molly stumbled on. 'I'm sorry, I hadn't realised how much of my language was slang. Pierre was supposed to meet Tom and me. Oh, I'm Molly White, by the way. He was meant to be in the bar of our hotel after his performance. We waited for ages but he didn't come.'

Light was beginning to dawn on the older woman's face. Tom took a deep breath. 'Could we possibly talk to you instead? You may be able to help us. We've come a very long way to see Pierre. We've travelled from England through a great chunk of France and Germany, and now he's got away.'

'Got away? You make it sound as if Pierre is escaping from something?'

'I think that's probably true,' said Molly, deciding that frankness was the only way forward now, 'but if he is, we need to know why. And quickly. I have children at home who need me.'

'Ah, children. Pierre and I were never blessed with those.' She stared at them for a moment longer, and seemed to make a decision. 'Very well, come in. But I have to leave shortly. And you,' she addressed the stunned taxi driver. 'Go round to the kitchen and Antoinette will make you some coffee. Tell her to bring some for us. And do not discuss my business with her. Do you understand?' The man nodded and scuttled away.

In the parlour, which overlooked the sweeping valley and a river beyond, their hostess said, 'We will wait for Antoinette to bring the tray. She is very inquisitive and I would like this to remain between us.'

They sat in silence for a while, admiring the view. Tom looked exhausted, thought Molly. The steps had been hard for him. There was no handrail to haul himself up with, and the stone had worn unevenly to create a major tripping hazard. When coffee and dainty biscuits had been laid out in front of them by the maid, Molly leaned forward and said hopefully, 'So, is your husband here?'

'Alas, no. He did not return last night. I had just made the decision to go into town and make enquiries of his fellow band members. I telephoned the bar, but they thought he was heading for home when he left.'

Molly tried to find a tactful way to ask the question on her mind, but there wasn't one. 'Does your husband often stay out all night?'

There was a sharp intake of breath and Molly thought she'd blown it. Tom was frowning at her and the lady had gone white.

'Frau Deville, I'm sorry. We are enquiring about an incident that happened a long time ago. Pierre would have only been about fifteen years old. Three boys may have been involved and another young man died. His name was Marcel.'

Molly glanced at Frau Deville and was horrified at how she seemed to be ageing before their eyes. Tears were trickling down the beautifully made-up cheeks, and her shoulders sagged. As Molly watched, she put her hands to her eyes and wiped away a trail of mascara, then took out a vast cotton handkerchief and began to sob in earnest. Molly moved to sit beside her and tried to pat her arm, but she was roughly shrugged off.

'Why did you have to come here and stir up trouble for us?' Frau Deville spat, through her tears. 'There was no need. Pierre had almost forgotten, I am sure. He told me years ago of his holiday with Jake, Shaun and Marcel, but he did not want to say much about it; that was obvious. I didn't press him. He seemed distraught if ever he thought of that time.'

'I think you will have to tell me about it now,' said Molly. 'This has gone too far for us to go away and pretend we haven't seen you.'

'But I do not know what to tell you,' wailed the woman. 'Pierre told me very little. The boys were young. There was a mix-up. One of them ate one of our speciality almond pastries – they make them here in the town – it was late at night after they had all been at the fiesta for hours. He stopped breathing. The others called an ambulance. That is all I know.'

Molly and Tom sat in silence as Frau Deville gradually calmed herself, mopping away the signs of her outburst with the handkerchief. After a few minutes, she stood up and went over to the long mirror hanging over the fireplace.

'I look dreadful. Please excuse me while I go and freshen up. Please, have some more coffee. I will be back shortly.'

As she left the room, Tom hissed, 'I thought Marcel was supposed to have just had a handful of peanuts or something? Her story doesn't match up. Anyway, now you've done it, she'll be off like a shot and we'll have to take over the castle and live here forever.'

Molly laughed, breaking the tension. 'I wish. Couldn't you just see yourself living here? Waited on hand and foot, with that view to look at all day? And an endless supply of almond pastries? Mmm.'

'That was a tasteless comment, Mrs White. I had thought better of you.' Tom started to laugh, too, but they both sobered up quickly as they heard their hostess returning. She came back into the room and sat down, straight-backed and graceful as ever.

'I am very sorry for my unseemly outburst. The truth is, I have no idea where my husband has gone, and I don't know what else to tell you about the incident with the boy.'

'Do you think he'll come back soon? I mean, mightn't he have just gone away to think about things for a few hours?' Molly asked.

'I have checked his room. He must have come in and packed while I was asleep. He has taken his passport.' Frau Deville looked as if she was about to break down again, but mastered her emotions. 'We have never shared a room. I think I should make it clear, for the benefit of your enquiries, Pierre and I, we had... have a marriage of convenience.'

'I'm sorry, but I'm not quite sure what you are telling me?' Molly asked gently. There had been way too much confusion today already, and there was no way she was going to second guess what the most important pieces of the jigsaw looked like.

'As you have said, this is an old, old story, my dear. It is a tale of hearts broken and a life lost.'

Tom leaned forward and tentatively took one of the older woman's hands in his.

'We don't want to dig all this up just for the sake of it, but Molly is Jake's widow and Shaun's best friend. For reasons only known to himself, Shaun has given Molly a quest to find out about the story of the Bavarian trip.'

Molly nodded. 'I've been following Shaun's clues to find out more about my husband and this is where the trail has led us. Now we're well and truly stuck.'

'Clues? You make it sound like some sort of game.'

'Well, it almost seemed like that to start with,' said Molly, 'but now it's much more serious. Although to be fair, I've covered infidelity and a child born out of wedlock already, so I suppose death had to be the next step.'

Molly and Tom waited, sensing they were getting just a shade nearer to the heart of the matter. Frau Deville, now freshly powdered and tidied, looked like any other aristocratic lady. It was painfully clear that she would have liked them to leave, but Molly knew they would have to sit this one out to the bitter end or there would be no point at all to their trek across Europe.

'Is there anything, even trivial, that you can tell us before we try to find your husband?' asked Molly.

'All I can tell you,' Pierre's wife said reluctantly, 'is that Pierre was deeply in love with your friend Shaun. The story reminds me of one of those plays by your oh-so-famous playwright Mr Shakespeare, where everyone loved the wrong person.'

'Sort of like *A Midsummer Night's Dream*?' asked Tom.

'That is it exactly. From what I have been told, Pierre loved Shaun, Shaun loved Marcel, and Marcel loved Jake. It was bound to end in disaster.'

'But what happened? I'm getting the strong impression that Marcel's death could have been avoided,' Molly said. 'Frau Deville, if you know something about this awful thing, your conscience surely must tell you to speak, even after all these years? What about Marcel's family? And Pierre's mother and grandmother? Don't they deserve peace of mind?'

'What makes you think they would gain peace of mind from Pierre?' said his wife.

'Well, he was there. He knows exactly what went on that night. And I think you do, too.'

'Are you accusing me of something, Mrs White?' asked their hostess, drawing herself up and fixing Molly with an icy glare.

'You reacted very badly to our questions, didn't you? It's an old story – a tragic mistake. So why does it still upset you so much? And why should it be so distressing for Pierre to talk about something that happened so long ago and was clearly an accident?'

30

Back at their hotel, Tom and Molly reluctantly had to admit that they were at a dead end. They had dragged out their visit for as long as possible in the hope that he would suddenly come home, desperate for reassurance from his wife, and ready to reveal his part in Marcel's story. But they had known from the start that Frau Deville was desperate for them to leave. As noon approached, Molly had written down several addresses and phone numbers and begged Pierre's wife to contact them if there was anything to report. They found their driver asleep in his cab, and headed for the town with much relief.

'Okay, Molly, let's do lunch,' said Tom, 'and let there be champagne.'

'But champagne's for celebrations, and we still haven't found what we came for,' Molly protested, as she lowered herself onto Tom's four-poster bed. He had opened the double doors onto his balcony and was pleased to see that Molly's belongings had been re-deposited on the floor. The hotel clerk had signalled to them to stop as Molly pushed Tom through the foyer. He had explained that Tom's room was available for just one more night, but that the person who had previously been booked into Molly's had now appeared.

'I am so sorry,' the clerk said, almost wringing his hands in apology. 'But the lady in question is a very good customer and I do not wish to offend her. Will you be leaving today, or will you take the opportunity of one more night in the double room?'

'We'll stay,' said Tom. 'We've got plans to make. Can we order lunch in our room?'

'But of course. Just ring down when you are ready to order. And I will make sure chef sends you up a selection of his special appetisers as a token of our regard.'

Peacefully settled on their patio, Tom watched the waiter bring in a trolley of delights – a huge platter of cold meats and shredded cabbage made the centrepiece on the sheltered table, followed by little dishes of olives, slices of cheese, wafer-thin salami and pickles. There was a champagne bucket and two slender glasses, and a bowl of fresh fruit, generously studded with strawberries. Finally, the waiter produced another plate holding two fluffy almond pastries. Molly rolled her eyes at Tom.

'I suppose it was bound to happen,' she said, 'we couldn't avoid them forever, could we? Nemesis.'

They ate in silence, listening to the sounds from the street drifting over the hotel's hedge. Snippets of conversation, intriguing but too brief, followed each other in quick succession. Children laughed and squabbled, lovers talked intently, the elderly exchanged news, but none of the voices were there for long.

'I feel at the moment,' Molly said, 'as if I'm caught in a sort of kaleidoscope of happenings, bits of family dramas and old loves, and none of it making sense. What do we do now?'

'Have some more champagne and wait and see what tomorrow brings,' suggested Tom, holding out the bottle.

'But whatever happens, we'll need to head home in the morning, and we haven't got Paulette to organise us this time.'

'I'm sure the hotel will help,' said Tom, mellow

and relaxed. 'We can fly from Munich to London, I expect. Easy.' He smiled at Molly and was pleased to see that she was looking at him properly for once. The champagne had made her cheeks pink and her eyes were saying things he'd only dreamed of.

'Molly, let's have a siesta,' he said. 'I'm sleepy, are you?'

She smiled rather sadly. 'I am, but we need to talk. It's not as easy as that.'

'Look, I'm not asking you to swing from the chandeliers. I really am tired. Let's just get into bed and have a cuddle. I just want to feel you next to me. You can even snore if you like. We don't need to talk about it.'

'Can it really just be a cuddle?' she asked hopefully. 'Only, I really am a bit of a basket case when it comes to sex.'

'We'll just go and snuggle down. We've got all the time in the world to think about the rest of it. For now, we need to sleep. It's been a weird few days.'

Waking up two hours later, Tom realised that they must have fallen asleep instantly. He still had an arm around Molly, who was lying on her right side with her glorious hair spread across the pillow, breathing softly but making the occasional murmur in her sleep.

Tom leaned up on one elbow and feasted his eyes. She was so beautiful. How could he convince her that whatever issues she'd had with sex in the past, they could surely work them out together if they took things slowly? He wondered if it was all down to Jake, this fear of getting close to another man. Suddenly, dead or not, he wanted to punch the man. How could he have caused so much damage to a woman like this? Sensing him watching her, Molly opened her eyes.

For a moment, she stayed where she was, then rolled onto her back, stretching luxuriously. She had slipped into the bathroom and taken off her clothes before they'd settled down for a nap, and was wearing nothing but a thin silky robe, which now fell open to reveal the swell of her naked breasts. Tom caught his breath, feeling himself respond instantly to the sight, and wishing he hadn't stripped off to t-shirt and boxers. How could he have ever thought he wouldn't be able to make love to this wonderful woman?

'That was the best sleep I've had for ages,' Molly said. 'Have you been awake long? I think you were out cold before I even managed to close my eyes.'

Tom leaned over and kissed her before he could chicken out. She froze, but after a second or two, slid her arms around his neck and kissed him back, gently at first and then with increasing passion, until they were both breathless. Their hips pressed together urgently, as if their bodies had been waiting for this all along. Tom groaned.

'What's the matter?' Molly asked, moving away slightly and looking into his eyes. 'Don't you want this?' He could feel her nervousness, held at bay slightly by desire but still very much there.

'Nothing's the matter, it's just that you are so gorgeous and sexy and sensual, and I can't resist you much longer.'

'Oh,' she dimpled up at him, 'I thought you weren't enjoying it for a minute.'

'Did you? Really?'

Molly blushed. 'Well, no. You're obviously quite interested.'

'Interested? I'm desperate to get you out of that dressing gown and make love to you so hard you'll beg for mercy.' He saw the sudden panic on her face and grinned. 'But I'm not going to.'

'You're not?' Molly murmured. Was she relieved, he wondered, or was that a tinge of disappointment in her voice?

'Definitely not – that's it for today. Your body is a temple as far as I'm concerned, as they say.'

'But why?' The words came out as a wail. What the hell did she want from him? Tom battled with conflicting emotions for a moment and then sat up.

'Molly, you're driving me crazy, but I don't want us to make a cock-up of this.'

She began to giggle, and he turned to smile down at her as she lay amongst the pillows. 'Okay, I know that's a bad phrase to pick, but you know what I mean. When I talked about us making love just now, your eyes went from all soft and seductive to terrified in two seconds flat. That's not the response I'm waiting for, sweetheart.'

'But...'

'You're beautiful and desirable, and the best thing that's ever happened to me, but I'm in this for the long haul.'

'So what are you saying?' Molly's voice was barely a whisper.

Tom gritted his teeth and turned away from her, the better to resist. He hoped against hope that he was getting this right. He was going by his gut feeling, but it was so bloody painful. 'I'm saying that we'll wait until you look at me without any doubt in those green eyes.'

There was silence. Tom kept his back to Molly and waited.

'Oh. Right. Well, I think I'll just have a bath then,' she said after a couple of very long minutes. She levered herself off the bed, tying the belt of her robe in a tight bow and flicking her hair back over her shoulders as she swung into the tiny bathroom. He heard the water filling the enormous bath and ran his hands through his already tousled hair. That had been a tricky one. He had almost lost control there, but this was too important to rush. The waiting game was what he must focus on for now. Molly must be even more ready than Tom was before he would let himself go completely.

31

That night, Tom and Molly slept on opposite sides of the bed. Molly woke up every couple of hours and listened to Tom's almost silent breathing for a while. It was strange to feel so comfortable with someone and yet be so painfully aware of them physically. Her nerve ends were still tingling from the memory of his kiss, and the surge of disappointment she'd felt when he backed off was as sharp as ever.

She contemplated waking him up at six o'clock and asking him what was wrong with her and why could he resist her so easily, but he looked so peaceful that she made herself wait, propping herself up on her pillows to read her Kindle. Eventually, he stirred, stretched and opened his eyes.

'Morning, beautiful lady,' he said, his voice husky with sleep.

Molly swallowed hard. 'Tom?'

'Yes, love? Are you okay?'

'Is there something wrong with me?'

He yawned, opened his eyes fully, and looked up at her. 'In what way?'

'Well, I get what you said last night about waiting until you're sure I really want you, and all that.'

'I'm sensing a "but" coming next.'

'But if I'm as sexy as you say, how can you... I mean... why don't you...?' She broke off, unable to meet his clear blue gaze.

'You mean, why aren't I driven over the edge with lust and just forced to ravish you, like in the movies?'

Molly nodded.

Tom grinned. 'I guess I've had a lot of practice at self-restraint in my life. I usually keep my temper, I keep my own counsel, I'm a private kind of guy, and I don't give up easily.'

'Right. So you really believe that one day soon I'll stop being such a wimp and we'll just go for it?'

'Yup. And when we do, it won't just be the earth that moves, it'll be the entire sodding planet. If I didn't believe that, I'd have gone home by now. No, that's not true,' he added hastily as her face fell, 'I'd never leave you alone to cope, sweetheart, no matter what. Now, isn't it time we had some breakfast?'

At nine o'clock, when they'd reduced the table to a sea of pastry crumbs and coffee dregs, Molly tried one last time to get in touch with Pierre.

'I'm sorry, but my husband has once again failed to return home.' The clipped tones of Frau Deville were, if possible, even less friendly than yesterday.

'Have you spoken to him at all?' asked Molly tentatively.

'I really don't see why that is any of your business, but no, I haven't. When he telephones me, be assured that I will tell Pierre that you are seeking him. And now, I must excuse myself. Goodbye.'

Molly put the phone down and shook her head at Tom, who was now inside the room stuffing clothes randomly into the case. She remembered the struggle they'd had to manoeuvre both the wheelchair and the case being pushed ahead of it, and sighed. It was going to be a long day and they hadn't even achieved what they'd set out to do.

'What now? I ache all over today,' she groaned, joining Tom in the bedroom and slumping onto the bed. The series of broken nights were definitely catching up with her, and she suddenly longed to be home.

Tom reached for the phone. 'I'm going to ring the tourist information lady. I bet she'll help with flights and transfers. It's time we were in England,' he said.

* * *

Many hours later, at the end of a long day of travelling, Molly sat in her kitchen watching Dot make hot chocolate and thanking her lucky stars that everything had been reasonably straightforward. There had been one or two hiccups – the worst being the lack of wheelchair ramps at two of the stations – but at last they'd made it through Customs and grabbed a taxi home. Tom had been dropped off first, and Molly was already missing him badly.

She'd expected that in her own home she would be able to go back to the old routine fairly easily – single mum, busy life, hugs from the kids filling any gaps. But the thought of breakfast tomorrow without Tom was already filling her with gloom, and her eyes felt heavy and prickly.

'Are you going to tell me what's been going on?' asked Dot. 'You look terrible.'

'Cheers. Whereas you, my almost-daughter, look pretty good for someone who's been minding a gang of hooligans,' replied Molly, as Hattie and Max flew through the kitchen chasing Marian, who had a pair of socks in her mouth and was growling happily.

When the clamour had died away, Molly gave Dot a potted version of the trip, leaving out any hint of the passion that had been bubbling under for the whole time she had been away. When she'd run out of steam and was losing herself in the hot creamy chocolate, Dot asked, 'So now what?'

The simple question hung in the air. Molly shrugged. 'I don't know where to go from here. There's obviously something very fishy going on or Pierre wouldn't have done a runner like that. Guilty conscience, do you think?'

'Could be. I guess you're stuck until you can speak to either Pierre or Shaun.'

'I've tried Simon's phone, but it just says the number's unavailable.' Molly clenched her fists and banged them down on the table, startling Marian, who had been passing on her way to investigate her food bowl. Molly reached down and fondled the dog's soft ears. 'Sorry, Marian, it's getting to me a bit now. I just want to get this stupid quest done and settle down again to a quiet life.'

'Do you? I can't think of anything worse,' grinned Dot. 'Tell you what, I'll get the kids in bed and we'll open some wine and make a spider diagram.'

'Will we? Why?'

'It's the only way I've ever been able to plan anything. It always works. You go and put your feet up
on the sofa and watch some mindless junk on the
TV, and I'll be with you in half an hour. Off you go.'

An hour later, Molly and Dot were sitting on the
floor in front of a crackling log fire, each nursing a
large glass of merlot. They had lit the fire for comfort
– the evening wasn't really chilly but Molly suddenly
needed the reassurance of the homely flickering
flames. They had a huge sheet of paper and two
marker pens in front of them and Dot had begun to
plot out Molly's progress so far.

'Look, I'm putting the word "Jake" right in the
middle of the diagram, and then the spider's legs are
all the people who were involved in his life.'

She drew a line at a time and added a thought
bubble with a word in it at the end of each one. First
came *Molly* to which she added *Married, four children*.
As she worked, Dot methodically ticked the people
off the list she'd already made, occasionally adding
someone new that occurred to her. Molly began to
unwind – the fire, the wine, and the loving support
were at last working their magic. Surely together
they could see where to go next?

She looked down at the paper. On one of the legs,

Dot had written *Pierre*. She had followed this with the names of Shaun and Marcel, even though Shaun already had his own bubble. Molly drank some more wine and stretched her tired shoulders. She should stop now before she and Dot finished the bottle, or the headache that was threatening would be a humdinger of a hangover tomorrow.

What was she missing? There must be something really significant that had passed them by so far. Why had Pierre felt it necessary to disappear so swiftly? What had Shaun wanted him to say to Molly? She thought about Shaun – always in love, flitting from one man to another until Simon had managed to tie him down. Had he known he was gay when he took the camping trip? Surely he must have. Had Jake known? Four boys cooped up together. Had they shared a big tent or had they split into pairs, and if so, who had ended up sleeping with Shaun?

32

Crouching shivering and wretched over the toilet bowl at three o'clock in the morning, Molly thought this night would never end. She held on with white knuckles as she was violently sick again, and in the shuddering aftermath, began to cry in great heaving gasps. This couldn't just be a red wine hangover come early. What had she eaten that nobody else might have had?

She remembered the rather tired-looking sandwich that she'd bought somewhere along the way yesterday, and was sick again at the very thought of food; a horribly painful experience with nothing much left in her stomach.

Wrapped in her winter dressing gown and curled

up under an extra layer of quilt, Molly began to cry again, snuffling into her pillow so as not to wake the children. How was she going to get up in a few short hours and cope with the day? Dot was meant to be going back to work this lunchtime – she had already used up a good wedge of her holiday helping Molly with the quest. As she drifted into a fitful sleep, Molly knew there was only one real option.

* * *

Tom felt ridiculously flattered when he picked up Dot's voicemail the next morning.

'Tom, it's me – Molly's sick – actually throwing-up sick – and I've got to go to work in two hours. Can you help? I don't know who else to call. Her mum's gone off on some trip or other with a gang of OAPs and she won't let me ask Edna. Call me, Tom – please.'

The last word came out almost as a wail, and Tom, fresh from the shower and missing Molly already, felt like a knight about to leap on his charger. Of course he wasn't happy that Molly was ill, he told himself, but Sasha would be glad of the extra cash to mind the shop and he could easily take some work with him if he needed to spend a few days with the family. His heart leapt as he keyed in Sasha's number. He would pack up his watercolour pad, brushes and palette, and treat the whole thing as a working holiday. It would be good to explore a different type of painting – maybe he would even have a try at portraits.

He briefly imagined Molly naked, stretched out on her bed posing for him, and then shrugged off the image. She would be more likely to be huddled under a comfort blanket today.

Within an hour, Tom had left the shop in Sasha's capable hands – to her obvious satisfaction – packed his paints and a bag of clothes and was now sitting in Molly's kitchen getting his instructions from Dot. Max sat on his knee, pale and anxious.

'When will my mummy be better, Tom?' he asked, nuzzling into Tom's shoulder.

'We'll soon have her sorted,' Tom said, belatedly wondering how he was going to get up and down stairs to keep an eye on the invalid, who he could now hear trying to be sick again. Dot was ahead of him.

'I'm just going to get Molly settled on the sofa. This is the first time she's been sick for about an hour, so that's an improvement.'

'Is it?' asked Tom, listening to the strangled retching noises.

'Oh, yes, she was throwing up every ten minutes when I got up. She kept drinking water because she had a raging thirst, but it wouldn't stay down. I'm ringing the doctor as soon as she's comfy down here. He'll probably only say keep the drinks going, but small sips rather than gallons of it.'

'What about school for these guys?' Tom hugged Max closer and indicated Hattie, who was ploughing her way through a bowl of disgustingly sweet cereal.

'Dot rang in to say we'd be late,' she said, pulling a face. 'I've never been in the late book before.'

'You won't be in the late book, my pet,' said Dot. 'You've got a good reason to be a bit behind today. We'll get you there as soon as we can. You've both got all your stuff ready, haven't you?'

'Yes, but I really don't mind having the day off to help Tom,' said Hattie hopefully. Tom was tempted – another pair of hands would be a relief – but Dot shook her head.

'Tom'll be fine; he can ring Edna if he gets stuck. I've let her know what's going on, and I'll be back when I've picked you up after school. I'm only doing a lunchtime shift today.'

'Oh.' Hattie's face fell as Dot bustled out of the

room to organise Molly's temporary bed. Tom grinned at her sympathetically and she shrugged and finished her breakfast, slurping the last drops of milk in a way that Tom knew Molly wouldn't appreciate. He decided to keep quiet. The poor kids had enough to deal with; they were both pale this morning, and he hoped it wasn't a bug that was going to sweep through the lot of them. One he could deal with, but a whole household? He thanked his lucky stars for a strong stomach.

By midday, Molly was over the worst and was sleeping peacefully on the sofa under her fluffiest blanket. Tom sat in the chair opposite, with everything he needed spread around him – Dot had fetched him a small table and he felt a rare moment of complete happiness as he arranged his pencils in an orderly row. Picking up a 3b, he began to draw Molly as she lay half-hidden, face turned into her pillow. The mass of curly brown hair looked unusually bedraggled and there were dark circles under her eyes, but Tom knew that no other woman could ever look so beautiful to him.

He sketched her left hand, clenched around an edge of blanket, and carefully drew in her wedding ring, now firmly back in place after the brief moment of experimentation in the restaurant. When would she stop wearing it? He wondered how long it took to stop feeling married when your partner died. Would there ever be a time when Molly would be free? And even when she did, why would she choose to spend the rest of her life with someone who couldn't even walk her down the aisle? The bubble of happiness wobbled, but Tom resolutely carried on with his picture. This was going to be good.

* * *

The next day, Molly was beginning to improve slightly but Hattie, having come home from school with griping pains in her tummy, was now in the place of honour on the sofa. Molly revised her thoughts about the tainted sandwich – this was definitely a bug, and a very nasty one at that.

'I really need go back to bed now, Tom – if you can cope? Hattie needs my space down here and I've got to lie down; I feel terrible,' Molly said, collecting her book and favourite pillow. 'Edna said she'd pop round with some shopping later because Dot's got an extra shift today. Are you sure it's okay for you to stay a bit longer?'

Tom looked at Molly's washed-out face and wished he could magically make her better. 'We'll be fine, won't we, Hattie?' he said cheerfully. 'We'll watch some rubbish on the TV and I'll keep her supplied with little drinks of lemonade. That's what the doctor said.'

'Okay, well, if you're sure?'

'Off you go, but make sure you take some more water up there. Do you feel like eating anything yet? And you probably don't want Marian with you, do you?' said Tom, as the dog slunk out of the room hopefully.

Molly shuddered, shaking her head as she left the room. Hattie moaned slightly in her sleep as Marian crept back in, trying to look ill-treated, and Tom began to worry what he would do if Hattie started to be sick again. He'd worry about that one if it happened, he decided, and began to sketch the vulnerable little figure lying on the sofa, one bare arm and leg dangling over the edge. She looked very uncomfortable but Tom was afraid to move her in case she woke up – she had been tossing and turning for most of the night.

As his pencil scratched across the page, he heard the sound of the doorbell and cursed under his breath. But before he could move, the front door opened and a creaky voice shouted, 'Coo-eee!'

Hattie stirred when Marian let out a warning

'woof' but didn't wake up properly, and Tom put a finger to his lips as Edna shuffled into the room, carrying a Tesco bag.

'Just a few bits and bobs for the patient. Where is Molly, anyway?' she asked, peering at Hattie on the sofa.

'In bed, she needs to recover a bit. She's had a tough time with this bug.'

Edna sniffed. 'I see. Well, I'll put these away and then stay and help you.'

'I'm fine, thank you, Edna. Hattie will probably sleep all day if she's not disturbed,' Tom said.

'But *you* can't look after them all, surely?' Edna was wearing her most disapproving face now, and had begun to prowl round the room, plumping up cushions and picking up Hattie's discarded socks and teddy.

'I can manage,' said Tom, feeling his hackles rising dangerously.

'I'm not so sure about that. I don't know what Molly's mother would say, I'm sure.' Edna stood, arms folded, gazing at Hattie for a moment, and then seemed to notice what Tom was doing. 'You're drawing a picture of this poor defenceless child while she sleeps? Have you no respect?'

Tom stared. 'I'm an artist, Edna, this is what I do. What's respect got to do with it?'

'Well, if you don't know, I'm hardly the one to tell you. I'll be having a word with Molly later. This is all very worrying.'

'Worrying? Why?'

But Edna was already heading for the door, every bone in her body suggesting extreme disapproval. The dog growled deep in her throat as the front door shut behind Edna. Tom blew a loud raspberry, and then jumped as Hattie opened her eyes. 'Oh, sorry, love, did I disturb you?' he asked.

'No, I wasn't asleep. *She* woke me up. Then I kept my eyes closed because I don't like her.'

'Don't you? I thought Edna was part of the family these days?'

'She's never been part of my family. My dad didn't like her either. He said she was an interfering old bitch.'

'Hattie! Your mum wouldn't like you to use that word, surely?'

'It's okay if it's a quote – that's what my teacher said anyway. And he didn't like her, it's the truth. Dad said she spied on him through the fence. She once reported him to the council for trying to kill one of her massive trees. You know, those big Christmas tree-type ones?'

'The conifers? That's a bit daft, Hattie, why would an old lady do that?'

'It was true. She wouldn't cut its branches back and we didn't get any sun in our garden, so he drilled some holes in it and poured some of that black fence stuff in.'

'You mean creosote?'

'I don't know what it's called. But *she* saw him somehow. She never sleeps, Dad said, like a witch's cat. And then Dad said she was a trouble-maker and she was never happy unless she was upsetting somebody.'

'Right. Well, some people are a bit like that,' Tom said lamely. 'So anyway, Miss Hattie, you're sounding a lot better. Do you feel like a drink?'

'I'm starving. Can I have my breakfast now?'

'Hmmm, I'll go and see what there is in the kitchen. Edna was supposed to be bringing bread in the supplies bag. I think maybe a bit of toast to start with, till we see if you're really okay?'

As Tom pottered around the kitchen balanced on his sticks, he thought about what Hattie had said. He was aware of Edna's dislike of him, but had always thought it was something to do with his disability. Maybe she just hated men?

33

Three days later, Molly was in the garden filling tubs with geraniums, half-heartedly throwing a stick for Marian, and trying to think of easy ways to make it look as if someone cared about the place. At this time of year, Jake would have already had this place looking like a miniature Kew.

But Jake wasn't here, Molly reminded herself grimly, and if she didn't want to spend all her time out here digging, planting and tidying, she would have to find a way of simplifying the whole thing. She'd done her best over the past few weeks to keep it all in reasonable shape. There was too much of it, though, and the damned weeds kept growing.

Mowing the lawn could only do so much to improve the garden's appearance but Molly was still feeling too weak and shaky to do anything too heavy. Hattie seemed to have bounced back almost immediately, but Molly couldn't seem to shake off the wobbly after-effects of the bug. Either she was getting old, or she was just unfit, she thought miserably, pulling her jumper sleeves down over chilly fingers.

She had only just come outside, after waiting around for the postman for most of the morning and then resorting to a nap when it was obvious he wasn't coming. She was afraid of missing his ring at the door – there *must* be another box soon, although it was hard to predict when they would arrive because the gaps between them had been so random. Shaun wouldn't do anything that didn't have a big finish; he was such a drama queen. And the last box hadn't seemed like the end of a quest, had it?

It was so frustrating to be stuck. All the enquiries about Pierre had come to nothing. Shaun was completely out of contactable range, as far as she knew, and Simon's phone was always on voicemail. The leads that she and Tom had painstakingly followed had come to nothing.

Nobody seemed to know where Pierre had gone and Molly didn't know what she could try next. She jumped up, swaying slightly, as the phone in the hall began to ring.

'Hello?' Molly heard the woman on the other end of the line clear her throat in a business-like way.

'Mrs White? Am I speaking to Mrs Molly White?'

Molly sighed. Cold callers again. 'Look, I don't want any double glazing and my loft's already insulated. I—'

'Mrs White, this is Patricia Clamp from your local Children's Services office. I'm a family investigation officer and we need to speak to you quite urgently. Can I call round now? Is it convenient?'

'You need to speak to me? But why?' Molly asked, rubbing the back of her neck. She sat down heavily on a chair, exhausted by the brief spell in the garden.

'I'll explain when we arrive. We'll be with you in approximately thirty minutes. Goodbye.'

'We? Who's we?' Molly stuttered. The line was dead. She closed the garden door and went back into the kitchen to put the kettle on. Could this be something to do with school? She racked her brains to think why this Patricia Clamp person might want to see her. Had Theo been in trouble? But then surely the school would have been in touch first.

Half an hour of worrying did nothing for her state of mind, and by the time the doorbell rang,

Molly was more jittery than she had been since just after Jake's death. She opened the door to find two women on the front step. They were smiling brightly, and the shorter, grey-haired one was clutching a substantial briefcase.

'Molly White?' asked the taller, solidly built woman, holding out a hand to shake, 'I'm Beryl Stover.'

Molly took the outstretched hand limply, then remembered reading somewhere that a forceful handshake was crucial when dealing with people in authority. She grasped Beryl's hand more forcefully and noticed her wince. The silence lengthened and Molly wondered if Beryl knew she had a trail of something that looked like dried egg down her cardigan. Beryl frowned slightly and repeated her question.

'Oh, yes. That's me. You'd better come in,' said Molly, leading the way into the kitchen. 'Can I get you some tea? Coffee?'

'No, thank you – we're fine. It's just a few questions really, Molly. We won't keep you too long. Hopefully,' added the lady with the briefcase. 'Pat,' she said, holding out a hand.

'Pat what?' asked Molly, bemused. She looked at the hand. Why would the woman want her to pat it?

'No, *I'm* Pat,' said the visitor, exchanging a glance with her colleague. We've got a right one here, the look seemed to say. Molly tried to pull herself together. If only she didn't still feel so shaky. Pat concentrated on putting her case down on the table and flipping the catch, murmuring, 'May we sit down?'

Molly motioned them towards the chairs around the table. There was no way they were all going to cosy up together in the living room. This didn't look like an occasion for getting settled for a good long friendly chat. She decided to stay standing, but had to lean on the back of a chair for support. Sweat trickled down her back.

'I'll be as brief as possible, Molly,' said Pat. 'There has been an official complaint made. A very serious complaint, as it happens.'

Molly stared. Why did this woman have to keep saying her name? Was it meant to be reassuring? She was beginning to feel dizzy again, and suddenly longed for Tom to be here, ordering her upstairs for a nap, and sending someone up with a nice cup of tea. Pat cleared her throat.

'The issue is with your childcare arrangements, Molly. We have had a report that you have been leaving your younger daughter in the care of someone unsuitable and possibly unsafe.'

'Unsafe?' Molly burst out. 'You can't mean Dot? She's my stepdaughter, for goodness' sake. She's completely trustworthy. What on earth are you talking about?'

'No, Molly, not your stepdaughter. The complaint refers to a Mr Tom Cavendish. Apparently, he has been looking after your daughter Harriet quite recently, and has previously cared for all your children?'

'Of course he has. But who would complain about Tom? He's a good friend. What's he supposed to have done?' Molly was beginning to tremble. She wondered if she was about to be sick again. That would go down well, she thought, vomiting on a representative of the Children's Services Department.

'Unfortunately I can't tell you the identity of the person who made the telephone call,' said Pat, leafing through a sheaf of papers that she'd pulled from her case.

'Oh, yes, you can!' shouted Molly. 'I've got a right to know who would say something so poisonous... and... and... libellous, haven't I? This is my very good friend you're insulting here, you know?'

'I think what my colleague means is that the call in question was anonymous,' said Beryl. 'Although, to be fair,' she continued, pushing her spectacles up her nose and exchanging glances with a rather flushed Pat, 'information relating to these sorts of complaints is always highly confidential.'

'I bet it is,' spat Molly. She turned as the front door opened and children's voices could be heard in the hallway. 'Look, here's Dot. You can ask her about Tom. We all trust him. What's he supposed to have done, anyway?'

'If you could ensure that your children are out of the room for a short while, I'll explain,' said Pat. 'This won't take long.'

'You're absolutely right it won't,' said Molly, grabbing a pack of Kit Kats from the worktop to bribe Hattie and Max into the garden.

Several hours later, Molly and Dot sat side by side on the biggest sofa, sharing a family-sized packet of crisps. They had both been way too exhausted to cook tonight, but the children had eaten leftover pizza quite happily and were at last asleep. Theo was in her room watching Netflix on her laptop and Snapchatting as many of her friends as possible before her credit ran out, so they could at least talk for a moment.

'Okay, let me just get this straight. Tom is being accused of making inappropriate sketches of Hattie while she was asleep? When you were upstairs in bed ill?' said Dot, scratching her head.

'Yep, that's about the size of it. I told them that he was a painter, and that he draws pictures wherever he is, of whatever subject, but they weren't interested in a reasonable explanation. They were going round to see him straight from here, but they made me promise not to warn him.'

'Sod that, I'd have rung him anyway,' said Dot.

'I know, I felt the same, but I didn't want to make things worse. I thought he'd sound more innocent if he wasn't primed.'

'But he *is* innocent! You surely don't think there's anything in it?'

'What do you take me for, Dot? Do you think I'd leave the kids with anyone who was in the least bit dodgy?'

They crunched crisps for a while, both deep in thought, until Molly sat bolt upright. 'Dot! It must have been Edna. Tom said she came in with the groceries while he was minding Hattie. But... I thought Edna liked us.'

Dot pondered for a moment. Molly looked at her stepdaughter, seeing that the short mass of dark curls was awry and there was a frown between her eyes. She was so like Jake. Molly blinked. This was no time to get sentimental. Dot suddenly slapped herself on the forehead.

'Of course! How dumb are we? The letters. Edna must have written those anonymous letters.'

'But why would she do that? She's my friend.'

'I don't know why, but I'm sure it must have been her. This is serious, Molly.'

'No, it's not – anyone with any sense would know it's all a load of rubbish. Tom's the kindest, most trustworthy man you could ever meet. He would never do anything even the slightest bit weird.'

'Well, I know that, and you know that. But once a complaint's been made through the proper channels, the whole thing gets nasty. There has to be an investigation now.'

'How come you know so much about all this sort of thing?' asked Molly.

'There was something like it on *Eastenders* last week. Maybe that's where Edna got her idea from. I'm guessing that Tom's going to be under suspicion until he's proved not guilty of doing anything wrong.'

'Well, we'll just tell them about the letters.'

Dot sighed. 'They're bound to ask to see them, and I burnt them. That was really stupid, wasn't it?'

'Yes, pretty stupid. But I don't blame you; they were disgusting. Do you think Tom will ring us tonight? I thought he'd have been in touch by now. I've left him loads of messages. I was going to call him on the landline after the kids were in bed if he hadn't been in touch, but now I'm almost scared to talk to him.'

'I bet he's upset. I'd be devastated.' Dot chewed her lip. 'I'm going to phone him. Can I use your mobile? I can't be bothered to move.'

'It's on the blink. I'm going to have to take it back to the shop tomorrow. I realised this morning that I can't get texts, and it's suddenly started switching off in the middle of a call, saying the battery's dead. I've got five missed calls on it now and it won't even let me see what the numbers are. They might have been from Tom – there's no way of knowing. It's driving me mad.'

Molly curled up into a tight ball on the sofa as Dot reached for her phone. She heard Dot leaving a message after a moment or two, and her stomach clenched. 'No answer?' she asked unnecessarily, as Dot came back into the room.

'Nah. Maybe he's gone to bed.'

'It's only nine o'clock.'

'Maybe he's so drunk he can't answer the phone.'

'Oh, cheers for that, Dot. As if I didn't feel bad

enough already about dropping this on him. Shall I just go round?'

'Look, there's nothing we can do now, if he's in bed. Let's at least try to get some sleep. I'll make you some milky hot chocolate and you can borrow my new book.'

Molly headed for the stairs, grateful for the cosseting but unsure whether *Revenge of the Werewolf's Child* would do much to aid restful slumber. Oh, well, it was a nice thought. She trudged up the stairs, feeling about a hundred years old. She would ring Tom in the morning, and if he still wasn't picking up, she would go and see him at the shop. She had to say sorry. And she badly needed to see him.

34

At ten o'clock, Tom was hunched over a table in a motorway service station, drinking tar-black coffee and eating a bun. He had been driving for several hours when he'd felt his eyes closing alarmingly and had pulled off as soon as he could leave the M25. He had known that setting off tired and furiously angry was a mistake, but after the visit from Beryl and Pat, he had been unable to settle to anything. He would have to get away for a few days, but where should he go?

Casting around for a place to seek sanctuary, Tom briefly considered Lena then discarded the thought – he'd never get away with visiting her again if Molly let him into her life properly. And anyway, the idea wasn't appealing. Only Molly would do for him now, but would he ever get chance to show her how much he loved her now that this added complication had put another spanner in the works?

Dot and Molly's increasingly frantic voicemails had finally driven him to turn off his phone, at least until there was time to stop driving and think properly. He shuddered at the memory of the interview with the social workers, feeling branded and smeared by their veiled accusations. What could he say to Molly now? Did she think he'd been doing something creepy and wrong with Hattie, too? The messages had all sounded positive and worried, even affectionate, but Tom's confidence was at rock bottom.

Grabbing his sticks and balancing them across his knees, Tom wheeled his chair towards the cloakroom. He'd better take advantage of the facilities while there was a chance; at least the doors would be wide here. The cloakroom in the B&B might not be very user-friendly. He sighed, wondering if all the bustling non-wheelchair users around him had any idea of the amount of planning it took to go to the loo in strange places.

As he sped down the last stretch of motorway, Tom imagined he could already smell the sea. This would normally have given him an immediate burst of joy. Although he'd lived within striking distance of the beach for some time, he always loved to explore a new coastline, and this one was uncharted territory for him. As a child, he had very rarely been brought to the south coast – his parents had been big fans of the glorious, windswept beaches of Northumberland, and his nan had thought holidays were a waste of money. But as his speedy little car ate up the miles, Tom knew this wasn't an adventure – it was an escape.

Sasha, summoned at short notice, had shrugged and agreed, as always, to mind the shop for as long as she was needed. And Tom, with a heap of random clothes and other basic essentials stuffed into a bag, left before she could ask too many questions.

'What about Molly?' she'd shouted after him as he swung himself into the driving seat. 'Have you told her where you're going?'

Tom cursed himself for having confided his feelings for Molly to the ever-romantic Sasha. She was now dropping so many casual questions that he'd been seriously tempted to tell her to mind her own business, which might not be a tactful way to deal with the subject.

'If she rings, tell her I was called away. A bit of

mystery's always good in a relationship,' he yelled back through the open window. Sasha grinned and gave him a thumbs up as he drove away, waving until he was out of sight.

The block of ice that was currently surrounding and crushing his heart began to thaw for a moment, but then he remembered Beryl and Pat, and set his jaw. They had said that their investigations might take weeks. What was he meant to do in the meantime? They had also recommended unofficially (ha!) that he should stay well away from Molly and her family.

Tom felt despair creep into his soul. How had he let this happen? Was it his fault? Surely a man could draw a picture of a friend's sleeping child without this craziness?

As he approached Hove, Tom turned his SatNav's sound back on and listened to the bossy lady telling him where to go. He was quite attached to her most days, but today she was getting right up his nose. Pulling into the tiny car park as instructed, he bagged the only disabled space and wondered how long it would be before he could fall into bed. Exhaustion made him clumsy as he laboriously got out his chair and wheeled himself and his small amount of luggage into the entrance hall.

Tom scratched his head, and then rubbed a hand over his bristly chin. He must look a complete wreck. He'd flung on his oldest leather jacket, and his jeans were paint-spattered. Oh well, this wasn't about the way he chose to dress.

The receptionist was dealing with a phone call. She looked down at him and raised her eyebrows, miming being with him shortly.

'Can I help you, sir?' she asked, finally putting the phone down after what seemed like an unnecessarily long conversation.

'I rang earlier to book a room – Tom Cavendish.'

'Ah.'

'Is there a problem with that?' Tom could feel his muscles tensing and a pulse starting to throb gently in his neck. Not now. Please, not now. Couldn't she see how knackered he was?

'Well, no – but the person who took the message obviously wasn't aware of the full circumstances.'

'Meaning?'

'Now, there's no need to take that tone, sir – I'm only trying to help. It's just that you've been booked into the top floor.'

'And you're going to tell me that there isn't a lift, right?'

'You didn't say you needed a ground-floor room when you telephoned.'

'I think you'll find I did. Look at me, woman. Am I going to risk being given a room in the bloody attic?'

'I'm calling the manager, sir. He doesn't allow his staff to be spoken to aggressively.'

'Well, bully for him.'

Tom's jaw ached with the effort of suppressing his rage as the receptionist disappeared into a back room. She returned almost immediately with a jowly man in a grey suit who held out a hand to Tom.

'Good evening, Mr Cavendish, there seems to have been a mix-up. How can I help?'

'You can start by giving me a room that I can get to, maybe.'

'But I'm afraid if you didn't specify your requirements when booking...'

'Of course I specified... oh, forget it.'

He turned and wheeled himself out of the hall, almost demolishing an occasional table and a vase of silk flowers on the way out. He could hear the manager calling after him, but kept moving, getting his chair stashed away and manoeuvring his sticks to get himself into the driving seat in record time. At least they weren't following him – there was no way he could have resisted letting rip completely if it had come to a stand-off, and the only time he'd really let go in a fight he'd broken the other man's nose.

Driving back along the coast towards Brighton, Tom pulled into a side road to ring Molly but managed to resist the temptation. She would only tell him to come home, and he knew that some time on his own was what he needed to clear his head. Sitting thinking about Molly for a moment brought something she'd said into clear focus, though. It had been when she was describing Matt and Gordon's wedding. She had talked about their Brighton B&B and Tom had asked if there were any photographs of the big day (purely to see what Molly had looked like with Jake). There had been a shot of Matt and Gordon in the centre of a laughing group outside a pretty townhouse.

When he'd met Matt on Boxing Day, he'd mentioned that their place was in the Kemptown area. Tom was pretty sure that if he could find roughly the right place, he would recognise it from the photo. Keying the word Kemptown into his SatNav, Tom joined the stream of night-time traffic again and passed the pier. The thought of finding a familiar face was reassuring, and at least he could be sure of a helping hand to get to bed.

There were crowds of holidaymakers still out and about, some of them hunting in packs. Tom heard a gang of women shrieking as he wound his window down to get some air – they were all wearing pink sparkly Stetsons and cowboy boots, and the one in the middle had a short veil, and a sash saying 'Bride-to-Be'.

Soon, the bossy lady was directing him into a network of parallel streets, lined with rows of small hotels and bed and breakfast establishments. He drove up and down for several minutes and was just about to give up when he spotted the place. It was three storeys high and was painted in crisply contrasting blue and white, with a striped awning over the door and huge hanging baskets filled with pink petunias.

To his amazement, Tom saw that there was a disabled parking space right outside the door of the B&B and it was, blessedly, empty. He parked and looked up at the sign. There was a number to ring and he punched it into his phone, too exhausted to waste energy getting out of the car to enquire if there was a room available.

35

Life without Tom was turning out to be very dull, thought Molly, as she hurled washing into the machine and wondered what to make for dinner. Dot was preoccupied with the workmen who were mending a burst water main right outside the house, and had spent most of her spare time this week nipping in and out with trays of tea and Molly's best biscuits. There was only one worth looking at among them, but Dot was making the most of the male company and had challenged herself to get his phone number by the end of the day.

She'd said she'd be working tonight, so Molly would be alone with the children again. Everything felt so dull without the prospect of a text, or a call, or even a surprise visit from Tom. Where could he have gone? Sasha didn't seem to know, and his phone switched to voicemail every time Molly tried to ring. She was having to use Dot's phone to try to text him, and she hadn't yet got round to getting a new one. That must go to the top of the list of things to do, she decided, grabbing her bag and getting ready to do the school pick-up.

'Dot, I'm off now. I'm going to call into town and get a new phone if this one can't be fixed,' she yelled, as she climbed into the Land Rover.

'Okay,' came back a faint voice from the pavement at the front of the house. Dot was on the hunt again.

Later that night, when the children were safely in bed if not asleep, Molly was sitting with her brand-new phone, trying to make sense of the complicated instructions, when she heard a light tap at the front door. Delighted to be distracted from the struggle, Molly jumped up. It must be somebody who knew the children might be sleeping and wouldn't risk waking them. She peered through the spyhole and saw Edna's face, distorted by the glass, peering right back at her.

'I just wondered if you'd like a few magazines, love?' said her neighbour, stepping into the hall without being asked and heading for the living room. Molly followed, feeling a wave of rage start to build up as she watched the jaunty little figure making herself at home in the most comfortable chair.

'Are you mashing a cuppa, Moll? I'm as dry as a bone,' asked Edna, helping herself to a Jaffa Cake from the box that Max had almost emptied earlier. 'I've just finished my ironing and I thought you might like a bit of company. Evenings are no fun when you're on your own, are they? I saw young Dot leaving, and that man friend of yours hasn't been around much lately, has he?'

Suddenly, the accumulated annoyances of living next to this busybody of a woman became too much for Molly. 'Yes, well, you know why Tom hasn't been here recently, don't you, Edna?' she said, seeing the small blue eyes behind their bottle-bottom glasses narrow as Edna considered her reply.

'I don't know what you mean, I'm sure,' she said quickly, taking her glasses off to polish them on her blouse. 'What you do and who you invite into your house is your own business, isn't it, dear?'

'I thought it was, but you seem to have made it yours, don't you?' asked Molly, through gritted teeth. She moved closer to Edna and folded her arms. 'You've been quite busy lately, haven't you?'

'What are you burbling on about?'

'Letters, Edna. Anonymous ones. Full of spite and venom. Am I ringing any bells yet?'

Edna pulled her cardigan more closely round her plump body. 'I think you must have gone a bit funny in the head, Molly. What in heaven's name are you talking about? I could report you for threatening behaviour if you carry on like this.'

'Report me to Children's Services, do you mean? That won't be a problem because you've already got their number, haven't you? You rang them only last week. What did you think would happen? Did you realise that Tom would be so distressed that he'd leave, and nobody would know where he'd gone?'

'No, I'm sorry, dear. You've lost me. Your young man's gone away, did you say? Probably for the best, though.'

'For the best? Don't you realise that Tom's in a very vulnerable position, Edna, thanks to you? Because you spelt out the fact that he's disabled, only you used a nastier word, didn't you? If he harms himself, if he's so depressed he...' Molly's voice died away and her anger with it. All she could think about was Tom, alone somewhere and deeply hurt by this evil woman's accusations. Her eyes were full of tears as Edna got up to leave the room, but she managed to reach out a hand to stop her neighbour.

'Oh, no, you don't, I haven't finished yet. You're going to put things right before tomorrow's over.'

'I'm not sure what you're trying to say, Molly. It sounds to me as if you've been watching too many soaps again.'

The fury came back, blessedly filling Molly with new energy. 'You are going to ring those people and you are going to tell them that you made a dreadful mistake when you made those accusations.'

'And why would I want to do that?' Edna's chin came up and she spat out the words. 'He was just using you – a poor young widow; he was only after your money. I was trying to help, that's all. What use could he be to you? I can mind the kids, you don't need him.'

'Is that all this was about? Your pathetic jealousy?'

'Don't be ridiculous. I'm not jealous of that chancer.'

'Chancer? Tom's a good man who cares about me... about us all.'

'Ha! That's what you think.'

'It is indeed what I think, Edna, and it's also what the Children's Services people need to think. So tomorrow, you're going to make that call and apologise for wasting their time. You're going to say you made a terrible mistake in ringing them. And that you lied about what you thought Tom was up to. You knew he meant no harm, didn't you?'

'Humph. And what if I don't?' Edna's eyes were downcast now and she was trying to edge towards the door again, but Molly stood firm.

'Well, if you don't do that, I'll be forced to tell them about the large amount of money you've got stashed away in that extra bank account of yours. The one in your brother Laurence's name? And then they will, I'm sure, be keen to let the benefits fraud squad in on the secret. Because you've been making false claims for years, haven't you?'

'How... how did you know about that?' Molly felt a pang of guilt as the colour drained from her neighbour's face, but she told herself that Tom's wellbeing was at stake.

'I've known for a week or two now. Laurence came round here one day when you weren't at home, didn't he tell you?'

'You're making it up. Why would he come here?'

Molly smiled. 'He was worried, Edna. He'd been having some very strange phone calls from his bank. He needed someone to talk to and he could tell I was a safe pair of ears. And I wouldn't have said anything, Edna – or not without talking to you first, anyway.'

'You expect me to believe that?'

'Yes, I do. I'm your friend, or I thought I was, and I was trying to find the right moment to discuss it with you. But this changes things. So, are we singing from the same hymn sheet now? You will make that call, won't you?'

Molly stood back and allowed Edna to scuttle into the hall. The older woman's face was a mask of anger and she refused to meet Molly's eyes as she nodded her agreement. Molly closed the door behind Edna, her whole body shaking. How was she going to let Tom know that the heat was off? And would the authorities drop the case just like that, on the strength of one call?

Hearing a wail from above, Molly began to climb the stairs, exhaustion in every step. It occurred to her that she hadn't thought about Jake for some time. Did that mean she was unnatural? An uncaring widow? Sod it, she was too tired to worry about that now.

Max was sitting up in his bed with tears pouring down his face. 'Mummy, I don't like the dark,' he said, wrapping his arms around her neck and wiping his damp face on her hair.

'Neither do I, pet. Let's put your little night light on and I'll read you a story, shall I?'

'Can't Dot do it?'

'Dot's at work, Max. Won't I do?'

'Well, if Dot's at work, Tom can come up and draw a picture with me. I don't get bad dreams when Tom's here.'

Molly sighed. This was going to be a long night.

* * *

Much later, in the haven of her own room, Molly undressed slowly and looked at herself in the long mirror. She stood sideways and sucked in her stomach, putting her shoulders back so that her outline was curvy but without any droopy bits. As the cool night air from the open window drifted across her body, Molly watched her nipples harden and wondered what Tom would say if he could see her now. She felt slim and immensely desirable for the first time in years. It was definitely time to tackle her fears and all those feelings of inadequacy. If only Tom would come home. She heard Max begin to wail again and reached for her dressing gown.

36

The next day, a rapping on the door woke Molly from the light doze she'd fallen into after Max had finally been coaxed off to sleep. He had been awake off and on all night, and had only given in to exhaustion at around six o'clock. She sat up and blinked at her bedside clock. Half past eight already? Why hadn't her phone alarm gone off? Thank goodness it was Saturday, she thought, as she leapt out of bed and dragged on her dressing gown. The postman was turning to leave as she wrenched the door open, and seemed reluctant to come back.

'Overslept, did we? I've rang the bell five times,' he said, eyeing Molly's wild hair and rather grubby bare feet. He turned back reluctantly and was met by Marian's wet nose in his crotch. 'Bleedin' dog,' he muttered.

'I think she likes you. She must be able to see past that bluff exterior,' said Molly.

'Huh?'

'Never mind.' Molly reached out to sign for the parcel, immediately lifted out of her gloom. At last – something to do that didn't involve worrying or childcare. As she made a diversion to the kitchen to make tea, she heard the first stirrings from Hattie's room and Theo rushing to beat her sister into the bathroom. Molly cursed under her breath. How come a furiously ringing doorbell didn't wake her daughters, but the click of the kettle going on worked every time? When was she ever going to get time to open the box?

She could feel its hard edges through the wrapping paper, and itched to rip it open and read the new letter. Molly pushed the box into the cupboard under the sink just as Hattie breezed in. It would just have to wait until the kids were all busy.

Much later, with Theo heading for the beach and the younger two parked in front of a favourite Disney film with the dog, Molly retreated to her bedroom and closed the door. Then she changed her mind and opened it a crack, just in case Max and Hattie had a sudden urge to demand food or had some other random need.

With the paper in shreds on the floor, the most stunning box of them all was revealed. This one was bigger than all the others and was a deep golden colour with tiny sparkly diamante studs all over. A silver and gold striped bow finished off the sumptuous effect. It was almost too beautiful to open, but by now Molly's curiosity had reached fever pitch and she fumbled with the ribbon until she could get the lid off. Inside was a cloud of fluffy white swansdown and the obligatory envelope, thicker this time.

Molly paused. The biggest and best – could this be the final clue? She didn't know whether to be thrilled or sorry that the quest might almost be over. The one thing she was sure of was that it would all be so much more fun if Tom was here. Determined to play by Shaun's rules, she tore open the envelope before even putting a finger into the swansdown.

Molly, my loveliest, most trustworthy friend, by now you'll know all of my secrets and most of Jake's to go with them. I just hope you still love both of us.

What did he mean? Light dawned as Molly realised that Shaun must have expected them to have solved the previous clue properly by now. She read on, desperately hoping that he would help her out here.

So, do you begin to see why your marriage to Jake wasn't a bed of roses? Over the years, I've watched you watching him, if you know what I mean, and I've ached to wipe that puzzled look away. Because no one could be really happy with a man like Jake. I know we both cared about him, there was never any question about that, and I think you thought I was always secretly in love with him. But I wasn't, Moll. I knew him too well for that and I knew what he was capable of. As you will, too, by now.

No, no, I don't, thought Molly, running her fingers through her hair in frustration. If only we'd found Pierre – he must be the key.

Anyway, this is the last clue. The final one of what I've been thinking of as the Magnificent Seven. It's always been a magical number for me and I'm guessing it will be for you, too. When I was getting all this ready for you, I lined the boxes up in front of me on the table and tried to imagine how you'd feel about each one and what it could tell you. By now, if everything's gone to plan, you'll have a new daughter (because knowing your mothering instincts, you won't be able to shut Dot out). You'll have made your peace with the gorgeous, feisty Kate and she'll have spilled the beans; you'll have realised that shagging the headmaster was a big mistake; got your first four-legged friend; had some fun in Peterborough. I'm hoping you'll have found Pierre, and that you've understood at least some of the reasons behind what happened.

Are you happy or disappointed that you've nearly reached the end, Moll? I hope the boxes have taken your mind off the pain and that you're beginning to get used to life without Jake. I also hope that you can forgive me. I can't wait to see you again. We've got so much to talk about. I need to know if you've found some sort of love interest. Molly, I know all about your problems in the sack.

Molly sat bolt upright, horrified. Her cheeks burned, and she felt an overwhelming urge to hide. What did Shaun really know? And how the bloody hell did he know it? Did he think she was frigid, or just useless at sex? Oh, God, this was awful. She forced herself to read on.

But Molly, none of it was your fault. You've only ever slept with Jake and that tosspot Robin, haven't you? Yes? Well, I rest my case. But maybe by now you've found someone to take charge of giving you some five-star loving. I bloody hope so, it's about time. I'd volunteer for the job myself but I haven't really got the qualifications. Anyway, I'll let you get on with the clue. Think of me as I lie on the beach, beer in hand, with a hot surfer on the horizon and the prospect of throwing another prawn on the barbie. See you in September, or maybe October if the fun's still happening.
Yours, as ever,
Shaun xxxx

The poem was always on a separate piece of notepaper, but this time the paper was clearly hand-made, thicker and fancier than the usual type, and with a golden border. Molly thought Shaun must have used a fountain pen for this final clue, and his writing was even harder to read than usual, festooned with so many whirls and swirls, but at last she managed to decipher it.

Now your quest is at last at its end,
And I hope your poor heart's on the mend,
For your final delight,
I decided you might,
Like to celebrate with a good friend.
If you're wondering when, why and where
Find the clue and just stand still and stare,
You must go to Cloud Nine
And then look at the sign
But make sure that you get yourself there.

(And that means within the next week – this is urgent!)
PS Best frock on for this one. Maybe show

a bit of cleavage? You know what they say; if you've got it, flaunt it. And wear your present – it's for the future.

Cloud Nine? Sign? Had Shaun really lost it this time? Molly carefully lifted out the swansdown to reveal a beautiful butterfly necklace, shimmering and delicate. It was the palest shade of turquoise, with a slim silver body and antennae. She gasped – it was the most ravishing thing she'd ever owned, apart from the dragonfly brooch. All these years without glamorous presents of jewellery and then two in a row.

Was Shaun just sending her something pretty to give her pleasure, she wondered, or was it significant? Was she the butterfly emerging from a very long time in a chrysalis? It was a lovely thought but Molly had never felt less like this stunning creature. She glanced across at the mirror on the dressing table. Her hair was lank and she had dark shadows under her eyes. She needed tea, and quickly.

Downstairs, listening to the children squabbling about whose turn it was to hold the TV remote control, Molly put the kettle on and thought hard about Shaun's letter. Something was bugging her but she couldn't put her finger on what it was. She fished it out of her pocket and re-read it twice. The second time she got it – the phrase about Kate spilling the beans.

What could Shaun have meant by that? Kate hadn't told her anything she didn't already know, had she? It was no use. Her mind felt full of custard today. She would have to ring Kate, but she'd be at work by now. Should she wait until later? No, Kate could talk any time – that was a perk of being the boss.

'Molly?' Kate answered on the second ring. 'What's up?'

'Oh, Kate, I'm not sure how to put this, but you remember the day I came to see you?'

'Well, of course I do, I'm not senile. Molly, is this important? I'm just about to sack someone.'

Maybe ringing during the working day hadn't been such a good plan after all. Molly took a deep breath. 'Yes, I think it is important. I've had a letter from Shaun today.' There was a silence. 'Kate? Are you still there?'

'Yes, I'm here. What did he say?'

'Well, it was a bit weird really. He seemed to think you were going to tell me something when I came to see you.'

'Did he?'

Molly stood up and began to pace the kitchen. She waited. After a few moments, Kate said, 'Okay, I knew it would have to be said sometime. I was going to tell you that day. When Shaun came to see me, he told me to do it. But I didn't want to.'

'Kate, you're scaring me. What's the matter? You're not ill, are you?'

Kate gave a short bark of a laugh. 'No, nothing as straightforward as that. It's something I should have explained when you were with me. It's even more difficult over the phone. Shaun said it would change your life.'

'Really? Just say it, Kate, please, whatever it is.'

'Right. It's just that I lied when I said that Jake and I had a great time in bed.'

The significance of this didn't strike Molly for a moment. Puzzled, she said, 'So you mean you don't like sex much either?'

'What? No, I love sex. It's just that Jake was rubbish in bed.'

Molly was unable to speak. Her body felt icy cold, and the room swam in front of her.

'Molly? Are you still there? Molly – answer me. I'm sorry, I knew I should have told you before. He was a nightmare. Rush, rush, rush – never gave me time to get in the mood, and sometimes he actually hurt me. I loved him, Molly – I always have and I always will, but being in bed with him was no fun at all.'

Molly began to smile. She replaced the handset, went out into the garden and laughed until the tears poured down her face and her ribs ached.

37

Still hiccupping and wiping her eyes on the back of her hand, Molly wandered down the garden path followed by a completely over-excited Marian. She was bemused; filled with a crazy sense of relief, as if she'd been given a reprieve from a terrible illness or some life-changing good news.

As the dog bounced amongst the bushes, Molly pottered happily around, picking a strange assortment of flowers and foliage, feeling the grass under her bare feet already getting warm in the morning sunshine. There had been a heavy shower of rain the previous night and everywhere smelled fresh and clean. There wasn't much to choose from in the garden at the moment, but back in the kitchen

Molly created an enormous – if somewhat crazy – arrangement in at least ten shades of green with a few spikes of japonica and some apple blossom thrown in.

She put the earthenware jug in the middle of the kitchen table and stood back to admire it. A little bubble of leftover relief burst into a giggle. This was her celebration bouquet. If Jake had been a disaster in bed, how could she be blamed for failing to get into the swing of things so often?

She remembered the feeling of impatience that Jake carried everywhere with him, even into their bedroom. And Robin – well, he'd just been a bit too gentle, now she came to think of it. Sort of apologetic. She'd thought it was because he was a kind, caring man. But he'd been totally under Lydia's thumb for years, so he was always likely to have been less than dynamic between the sheets. It wasn't all Molly's fault. It really wasn't.

Molly was jolted out of her growing euphoria by Hattie bouncing into the kitchen.

'Wow, Mum! Those flowers and stuff are ace! You should do that sort of thing more often. Can you show me how to make one?'

Molly smiled down at her daughter and ruffled her curly hair. 'Nobody's ever said anything about my flower arrangements before. Do you really like it?'

'Yeah, it's like a bit of the garden's come inside. I don't like those flash ones you see in shop windows and at weddings and stuff.'

'Me neither.'

'Hey, maybe if you can't find anyone to teach music to, you could do things like this – you know, for people like us.'

'What sort of people are we then, love?'

'Well, a bit different, I s'pose. Anyway, I'm starving, is there any cake?'

Back in the garden, Molly thought about what Hattie had said as she sat on the bench drinking her tea. It was good to feel as if she'd got another talent, apart from keeping the family fed and getting a few notes out of children who would rather be messing around on their phones. And she could obviously make decent cake, if the speed at which the batch of brownies and the flapjacks had disappeared this week was anything to go by. Maybe she could even have great sex?

None of these skills seemed very likely to make her fortune, unless she retrained as a high-class lady of the night, but it was encouraging to feel a bit more positive about herself for a change. And now she'd got – as Shaun had reminded her – another daughter to love, and one who was willing to help in lots of practical ways, too. If Tom would only show up, life would be pretty good.

When Dot returned much later, breezing into the kitchen after the others were finally in bed, Molly hugged her hard.

'Hey, what's all this about?' Dot said, grinning as she flopped into a chair. 'Are you after a babysitter?'

'Well, probably, but I don't know when I'm going out or where I'm going.'

'Right. Okay, let's get this straight, you want me to sit for you on an unspecified night while you go somewhere that you haven't decided about yet? I like the flower arrangement, by the way. Did you do it? Didn't know you were into that sort of thing.'

'Thanks, yes, I did and yes, I am, when I think about it. It's not that I haven't decided the details about going out, I just don't know where the party is. Here, have a look at this.'

Molly poured Dot a mug of tea, slid the greenery to one side, and pushed the package and the letter across the kitchen table to her. She bit her lip as Dot read, then leaned forward to admire the necklace for about the twentieth time. Dot raised her eyebrows.

'Phew! This is gorgeous. But the poem's complete gobbledegook to me.'

Molly sighed. 'Me, too. I've read it so many times I know it off by heart but it still doesn't tell me where to go.'

'What do you think he could mean by Cloud Nine? Is it a secret code or something? Think, Molly. What do those words mean to you?'

Molly sat down opposite Dot, closed her eyes and concentrated. The house was very quiet. The only sound came from the radio in the corner that was playing a late-night medley of chilled-out music. She realised that what she was half listening to was an old Beatles song. The words swirled around in her brain, teasing her with something that stayed just out of range. Cloud Nine. What had that got to do with the Beatles? Suddenly, it came to her.

'George!' she shouted, making Dot jump so much that she spilt tea all over her shirt. Marian started to bark wildly, obviously convinced that this must mean a walk was imminent.

'Sshhh, you stupid dog, the others'll wake up. And why are you yelling random men's names, Moll? I wish you wouldn't. This shirt was clean on this morning,' said Dot, dabbing at her front with a tea towel.

'George Harrison. He sang about Cloud Nine, I'm sure he did. I'm going to look for the CD.'

Molly headed for the music collection in the next room, which Jake had once sorted into categories, having refused to even contemplate using Spotify. Unfortunately, only he had understood how each one fitted. Molly had tried to get him to explain his system but it seemed to be based on which CDs he liked best. The first section was music from his early years, pure nostalgia. Sixth-form music, she thought sadly, remembering how she and her friends used to hang around the common room, loving the idea of being able to make coffee whenever they felt like it and flirting outrageously with any boys available.

'Have you found it?' whispered Dot, coming into the room behind her. 'Shall I check on Spotify?'

'No, I want to listen to it on CD, like Jake did, but can't remember how much he liked George,' Molly replied.

Dot looked blank, and Molly continued to rummage, finally unearthing the album she wanted in a section labelled 'Ace solo artists who used to be with great bands'.

'Here it is, let's play it,' said Molly, sliding the CD into the machine and turning the volume up as much as she dared. 'Shut the door, Dot. I don't think it'll wake them. From what I remember, it was one of the quieter tracks.'

Music flooded from the speakers and Dot and Molly subsided onto the floor, listening hard. After the fourth play through, they looked at each other in despair.

'I can't see what he's getting at, can you?' asked Dot.

'No, but it must be on here somewhere, maybe like a sort of code. I'll try again in the morning. I need to sleep now.'

'You could Google it next – no, let me do it, I'm quicker.'

After a few frustrating minutes of scrolling through hairdressers, party planners and other unconnected businesses all called Cloud Nine, Dot shrugged and gave up. 'Don't suppose you've managed to get hold of the wanderer yet?' she asked.

'Nope.' Molly heaved a huge sigh. 'But when I do, I'm going to tell him that if he ever goes away like this again, I'm going to have to kill him.'

'Right. Well, that'll stop his gallop,' said Dot. 'Hey, I'm just assuming I can stay here tonight – is that okay? I'm too tired to go home,' she added, heading for the stairs with the dog hot on her heels.

Molly grinned. She was glad Dot preferred being

here, but not really surprised. When they had called in at Dot's house on the day they'd adopted Marian, she had been amazed that anyone could live in such tidiness. Molly had decided it must be the legacy of an organised mother – Dot was programmed to eliminate mess and clutter at her own home, but she didn't seem to have a problem with it here.

Following Dot up to bed, the words and plaintive melody of George's song were still going round and round in her head. Cloud Nine. She wished she was there.

38

On Monday morning, Molly decided to be proactive for a change. Instead of just letting things happen to her as she'd always done in the past, she would put her saggy leggings in the bin where they belonged, wriggle into her tightest jeans, and go out into the world. It was high time she took charge of her own life and stopped just going with the flow.

She thought about the day she'd walked out of her job. That hadn't been a conscious decision, just a reflex action, so it didn't count as part of her new, dynamic character. The quest had been a big part of her routine for the last months, but that had been orchestrated by Shaun. Even getting a dog had happened without Molly needing to do much. She would start by insisting that everyone walked to school instead of having the lift that they usually whined for. It would only take twenty minutes if they went through the park, and they'd all feel better for the fresh air.

Half an hour later, chivvying Max, Hattie and Theo out of the house with Marian pulling hard on her lead, Molly seriously considered giving in and just bundling them into the car.

'I hate walking to school, you know I do, Mum. You get there all hot and sweaty,' grumbled Hattie. Theo just glared at Molly and Max rolled his eyes.

'I think I'm getting a stitch,' he said, dragging his feet.

'Don't scuff your school shoes, Max. Hattie, you're going to have to speed up if you want to get there to-day. And Theo, if you look at me like that once more I'm confiscating your phone.' Did other people's children make this much fuss about a short stroll in the sunshine? At least the dog was enjoying herself. Molly hardened her heart and ignored the moaning, marching along in front of them with Marian until they realised they would have to trot a bit faster if they were going to make it to school before lunchtime.

Once the younger two were safely delivered,

Molly waved Theo on her way to the college further up the hill and turned back with Marian towards the town. She would go to Tom's place first and see the goth girl – maybe she would be able to get a message to him. But when Molly reached the door of the gallery, everywhere was in darkness, and a note on the door said that due to family commitments, the shop would be closed today and possibly tomorrow, too. Why couldn't Tom just get in touch? Where was he, for pity's sake?

Sighing, Molly moved on. The next call on her list was the newspaper office, where she put a carefully worded advertisement in the next night's *Express*. Time to start the next part of her career – music teacher and voice coach. It was years since she'd sung in public, but Molly's talents had covered a wide range of musical styles when she'd been at school and college. She remembered singing karaoke at someone's party when she and Jake had only just got together. Everyone had said she had a great voice, although Jake had warned her never to show him up like that again.

This done, Molly took a diversion through the stationery shop and treated herself to a fabulous, glossy red and black striped notebook and some gel pens. It was time to make a list, or even a full-scale life plan, and then the book would come in handy when she started writing again. After this, she suddenly longed for strong black coffee. Her head throbbed with worrying about Tom, and she was beginning to understand what heartache really meant – her chest was literally sore whenever she thought about him, and her heart thumped uncomfortably if she let herself dwell on his disappearance. The thought of a moment's respite was irresistible.

The only place that you could get proper freshly ground coffee in this town was at Jake's Bistro, but Molly wasn't sure if she could face the staff yet and there was the dog to consider. Marian had been very good so far in the shops that were dog-friendly and had collected several new fans by putting on her best cute face and holding her head on one side flirtatiously, but the bistro had a strictly 'no animals' policy. Molly shook herself; she really needed to get herself in there and stop being afraid to face Jake's workplace.

Maybe Marian would be happy enough outside if Molly could beg her a bone from the kitchen. Even after all these months, everything to do with the running of the place was being done *for now* with Louisa firmly holding the reins. No big decisions had been made. Everyone who worked there was being amazing about carrying on without their former boss, but the time of reckoning must be fast approaching, thought Molly. She'd mainly dealt with Jake's business affairs over the phone or online in the last months, and had only had the odd meeting with the temporary manager at home to make sure things were ticking over.

Louisa always made Molly feel vaguely scruffy. Her straight auburn hair was never messy, and even looked great scraped back in a French plait for work. Louisa's organisational skills were legendary, and Molly knew they must soon have to have a serious talk about the future of the bistro – they couldn't go on like this for much longer. The cooking was shared between Louisa and a part-time chef at the moment, with several waiters and waitresses on a rota. Would Louisa want to run the place indefinitely? Molly wasn't at all sure if this town was big enough for Louisa and her ambitions to flourish.

The walk through the town and along the promenade only took fifteen minutes. Molly would have been happier if it had taken twice that long. With shaking hands, she looped Marian's lead through the hook provided outside the door, then took a deep breath and entered the bistro. Inside the little restaurant, the warm smell of baking ciabatta was tantalising. Molly smiled a greeting to Louisa, who was dealing with an irate customer.

'Look at this ridiculous bill. You've charged me for a full continental breakfast and I only had a croissant and some fruit. It's a rip-off. I want to see the person in charge here,' the man said, standing up to make his point.

Louisa straightened to her full height and looked him in the eyes. 'I *am* the manager, actually,' she said, 'and I think you'll find if you check our menu that a continental breakfast entitles you to your choice of food from the buffet.'

'But I only...'

'What you choose is entirely up to you, sir. It's still the same price.'

'Well, I'm going to have some more then.'

'Please do, I'll fetch you a clean plate,' Louisa said sweetly, turning her back on the man to go to the kitchen. She bared her teeth at Molly in a hideous grin. Molly snorted. She had never seen Louisa in action, although Jake had always said she was scary.

Molly settled herself in a window seat, ordered

coffee from her favourite waitress, asked if any juicy bones were available, and waited for Louisa to return. When she did, she was carrying a large white china plate and a fresh pot of tea.

'There you go – enjoy,' she said, waving the man towards the breakfast buffet.

'Oh... er... thank you. So, there won't be any more to pay?'

'Certainly not. Try the apricot Danish, they're melt-in-the-mouth,' Louisa said with a beaming smile. She turned to Molly. 'I'll join you, if that's okay? I haven't had a minute since we started at half seven.'

'Lovely. I wanted a chat really, but I thought you'd be too busy.'

They both watched the man coming back to his seat with a loaded plate. He had managed to cram three pastries, a bread roll, butter and jam, and a few small cheeses onto it, and was gazing at it with a delighted expression.

'You were brilliant then, Louisa,' said Molly. 'I'd have been tempted to hit him with a tray.'

'It was nothing, love. After dealing with the boss, that one was a pussycat.' She broke off, putting a hand up to her mouth. 'Oh, God, I'm sorry. I forgot for a minute who I was talking to.'

'It's fine. I don't have many illusions left about Jake. He must have been a pig to work for.'

Louisa laughed. 'Not a pig, no. You just needed to read him carefully. His moods would change so fast it was hard to keep up with him. He was incredibly talented in the kitchen, but if anything went wrong he was as hard to handle as a stroppy toddler.'

'Do you miss him, Louisa?'

'As a boss or as a person?'

'Either. Both?'

Louisa blinked hard and looked out of the window at the expanse of beach exposed by the low tide. Molly thought, not for the first time, what incredible luck Jake had had in finding a spot with a view like this, but then remembered that luck hadn't really come into the equation. He had trawled the internet for weeks while they were still in Leicestershire and had made numerous forays to the east coast, coming back either elated or dejected by turn.

Eventually, he'd secured this place by happening to be in the estate agents just as it went on the market, and making an offer without even viewing it. Molly had been horrified at the risk he'd taken but, as usual, Jake's impulsive nature had served him well.

Aware that Louisa still hadn't answered her question, Molly began to wish she hadn't pried. She had always suspected that Louisa was closer to Jake than she ought to be, but what good would it do to know for sure?

'I'm sorry, I shouldn't have asked you that. Ignore me, Louisa,' she said.

'No, it's okay, you've got a right to know. Yes, I miss him desperately, in every way. We were never more than friends though; I hope you believe me when I say that. Jake didn't feel that way about me. If he had, I don't know what would have happened.'

'You're very honest.'

'There's no point being anything else now, is there? Anyway, let's talk about you, shall we? It's safer.'

Their coffee arrived, and it was just as good as Molly had expected. The biscuit was crisp and buttery and the aroma of freshly ground coffee beans revived Molly's flagging spirits, taking away her sadness at the pain that Jake had left behind him. They drank in silence for a while, content to let the gentle background music flow over them. Molly recognised an old jazz compilation of Jake's and had a pang of nostalgia for the nights when he'd been relaxed and easy to be with, sipping wine and telling her about his day. There had been good times, and she mustn't let herself forget a single one of them. After a while, Louisa shook herself and smiled.

'It's great to see you in here, Molly, and you're looking fabulous. Have you done something to your hair? I can't put my finger on what's different.'

Molly looked at Louisa doubtfully. Did she mean it? The woman who made Kate Moss look beefy thought Molly looked good? 'No, I guess I'm just feeling a bit better about myself,' she answered, fighting an urge to get out her little mirror and check herself out. 'I've lost some weight – not loads, but everything fits better.'

'It's what my sister calls "The Bereavement Diet". She lost over a stone when her husband died but she's put it back on now, plus a few more pounds.'

'Has she? Why?'

'She met someone else. Happiness sometimes doesn't go with skinny, does it? Although, if you're newly loved-up, it tends to work.' Louisa met Molly's eyes and grinned. 'If you know what I mean?'

'Erm...'

'Look, it's none of my business, it was just that my friend Lynne saw you in the Italian restaurant with that gorgeous artist bloke from the gallery. I just wondered if you'd been consoling yourself in the best possible way.'

Molly blushed to the roots of her hair. How many other people were talking about her, if the jungle drums had already been busy? This was awful. What if the children heard rumours? She could guess what people would say – probably comments along the lines of 'husband not cold in his grave before she was looking for a replacement' or similar. How long was she expected to wait, though? What would be considered a decent interval? And surely that decision was up to Molly? She drank the last of her coffee and worried.

'Molly, don't look so crushed. I wouldn't have said anything if I'd thought you'd be upset. I was just pleased for you if it was true. It was what Shaun hoped would happen.'

'Shaun? What's he got to do with it? Have you spoken to him? I thought he'd left his phone at home, the snake.'

'Hey.' Louisa held up a hand. 'Calm down. It was ages ago, before he went away. We had a drink together after I'd closed up here. I think he kind of knew that you needed to meet someone a lot less high maintenance, and the sooner the better. He was very drunk that night. I've never seen Shaun like that. He kept talking about forgiveness.'

'Did he? Who needs to be forgiven?'

'I think he meant himself, for some reason. He was rambling a bit, kept mentioning someone called Marcel and saying he never meant to do it.'

Horrified, Molly stared at Louisa, who was beginning to clear the table.

'But... but it couldn't have been Shaun. We thought it was Pierre...'

'What was Pierre?' Louisa sounded distracted. The restaurant was beginning to fill up with lunchtime customers. 'I'm going to have to go, Molly. We'll talk soon. I've got a few plans I'd like to run past you. I've been trying out one or two new ideas to get more of the evening trade in. Have a look at the sign. I put it up just after we lost Jake, but of course you won't have seen it.' She nodded to the wall behind Molly and bustled away.

Molly turned slowly and stared. The words were in bright red – why hadn't she noticed them before?

Cloud Nine Party Nights!
Do your spirits need a lift? Do you love to eat wonderful food, drink champagne and listen to cool jazz?
Come and join us on Cloud Nine; the second Saturday of every month

Next party night: 10 June at 7.30 p.m. –
booking essential

So 10 June was the day that Shaun had planned for Molly to party all night, wearing something revealing and sporting his butterfly necklace? She did as Shaun had instructed, and stared at the sign some more. How had he ever expected her to guess this clue? Although he'd probably thought she'd be in and out of the bistro all the time, keeping an eye on things. He wasn't to know that she'd opted out of everything to do with the restaurant. There were only a few days left before the big night. She must find Tom, and then they could carry on working on the mystery of Marcel.

Molly's stomach churned when she remembered Louisa's words. Could they have been blaming Pierre for Marcel's all-too-sudden death when it was Shaun who was responsible? It seemed impossible. Shaun had never even been able to squash a spider. He had the kindest heart of anyone that Molly had ever known.

She stood up to leave, catching Louisa's eye and waving as she negotiated the busy tables. If Louisa was prepared to stay on, this place could be a gold mine, thought Molly. Jake had been a great chef and a charismatic host, but his volatile moods had made him too unpredictable to be a business success. And he'd had such a low boredom threshold that if a scheme hadn't immediately taken off, he would just ditch it and move on. As she left the bistro, Molly suddenly remembered the rest of the clue. She was meant to be meeting someone here at the party. Who on earth had Shaun lined up for her?

39

Tom could see through into the hotel bar, and could just make out a figure sitting alone by the window. He waved, and the man got up and came towards him, opening the door and standing aside politely as Tom wheeled himself in.

'Thank you for coming to meet me at such short notice, Tom.' The voice was just as charming as he remembered, deep and heavily accented.

'Hello, Pierre. It's good to see you at last. I was surprised to get your message, though, and even more so to hear you were in England. I thought you would have contacted Molly, not me, though?'

Pierre shrugged. 'Of course I should have done

but I think this kind of conversation is better man-to-man, don't you?'

'I'm not so sure about that, but anyway, I couldn't believe it when I heard you'd travelled across to Newhaven. I'm so glad you called, there are a lot of mysteries to unravel.'

'Absolutely. I decided that this sort of conversation is easier in person and I had some important business to do in London so it seemed a good idea to combine the two things. Can I get you a drink? I chose this hotel quite randomly when you told me you were in Brighton, but it seems comfortable enough.'

'God, yes. I'd love a pint, thanks, Pierre. I've not had a drink since I got down here because I thought I'd better stay in complete control. I've been doing a lot of thinking. But meeting you calls for something stronger than fruit juice.'

Pierre waved Tom over to his original table. 'You go and settle yourself and I will bring the drinks. This place is so confusing. There are very many flavours here, and some of them look more like coffee than beer. I myself am drinking a good German lager. How about you?'

'Excellent. Lead me to it.'

The bar was softly lit, and Tom had a fleeting vision of bringing Molly here and drinking champagne in one of the cosy alcoves, before taking her to bed. One day, he promised himself, but then remembered with a lurch of his stomach that he wouldn't be able even to see her when he got back, let alone whisk her away for a weekend of wining, dining and passion.

At last the two men were seated at the window table, and Tom took a hefty gulp of his ice-cold lager. Setting down his now half-empty glass, he looked across at Pierre, who was staring out of the window into the darkness of the hotel's garden, a melancholy look on his face.

'So, Pierre, where do we begin? Maybe you could start by telling me why you ran away from us so suddenly?'

Pierre sat up straighter, eyes flashing. 'I want you to know that I did not run away, Tom. I merely distanced myself for a while. I had some thinking to do.'

'Hmm. And have you finished now?' asked Tom dryly. This was like watching a carefully rehearsed play. There was something deep about Pierre, not to mention a large dash of arrogance in the way he met Tom's enquiring gaze as he gave his answer.

'I have come to a few conclusions, yes.'

There was a silence that seemed to go on for far

too long. Tom raised his eyebrows. 'Are you actually going to share them, or shall I go to bed? I'm knackered, to be honest, mate. It's been a stressful few days.'

'Oh, I am sorry, Tom. It is just that I am finding these long-ago thoughts very hard to deal with. Let me get you another beer and I will start at the very beginning.'

'A very good place to start,' murmured Tom, as Pierre set off again for the bar. He was beginning to feel spaced out and slightly crazy. It had definitely been a bizarre week.

Returning with two brimming pint glasses, Pierre settled himself again and took a deep breath. 'Perhaps I could ask you for a contribution first,' he said. 'What exactly did you and the beautiful Molly think about the extent of my involvement in Marcel's story? I'm sure you must have discussed it at length.'

'We... erm... well, we thought you must have been largely responsible for his death, to be perfectly honest.'

'And why would you reach that decision, if you don't mind me asking?'

Tom met Pierre's steady gaze and was surprised to find no anger there now, but a haunting sadness in its place. 'I think it was the way you left so abruptly, really,' he said with a shrug. 'You can't blame us for finding that suspicious, can you? Your wife said she had no idea where you'd gone, and all our enquiries came up with no trace of you. It was definitely an escape.'

'Yes, it was in a way, but not because I am guilty of murder, which is what you have been thinking, I am quite sure.'

The harsh word shocked Tom, although it was spoken softly. Even in their late-night discussions, he and Molly had never actually used the term 'murder' and had tried to be fair about making assumptions about the Marcel affair. He took another reviving swig of beer and stretched his tired shoulders.

'I reckon you need to do some talking, Pierre. If you start now, we might just get to bed before dawn.'

Tom listened intently as Pierre started to tell his story, falteringly at first but gaining in confidence as he got into his stride. Afraid to speak in case he interrupted the flow, Tom sat as still as he could. The babble of voices around them had almost died away and the room was fairly quiet now. The barman was polishing glasses and the receptionist had come in to help with wiping tables down. Please don't let them try to throw us out until he's finished talking, thought Tom desperately, I can't wait any longer to hear this.

'...so we four boys finally arrived in Bavaria,' said Pierre, 'and that was when everything began to go wrong.'

'But you'd been such good friends in France, hadn't you?' prompted Tom. 'What happened to spoil things?'

'Love happened, Tom. It has a habit of getting in the way, don't you find?'

'You'd better tell me the rest before they call last orders. I was just about to go to bed when you texted to say you were on your way from the port. Go on, what's love got to do with it? Oh, no, now I'm turning into Tina Turner.'

'Tina who? Ah, you mean the "River Deep, Mountain High" lady. I like her songs. We sing "Simply the Best" in the beer garden. She is very popular in my country.'

'Never mind that, just tell the story, Pierre.'

'Right. Love. The eternal triangle, or in this case, square. We were all passionate boys growing into even more passionate men. None of us had ever loved a woman, although from what I gathered, Jake had started to make a few conquests back in England. I knew even then that women were never going to be... how do you put it... my scene? I fell deeply in love with Shaun. He was slim, edgy, glamorous. I adored him.'

'And did he feel the same?'

A shadow passed over Pierre's handsome face. 'Sadly, he did not. Shaun had become besotted with Marcel, who was just as slim but with the blond curly hair of a Botticelli angel.'

'And Marcel?'

'The whole thing was a disaster, with everyone loving the wrong person. Marcel loved no one but Jake. He followed him everywhere.'

'How did Jake feel about that?'

'Irritated, but also flattered, I suspect. He used Marcel. Oh, not in a lewd way,' Pierre said, seeing the look on Tom's face, 'just as a servant – to fetch and carry for him, to provide food, to give him money for drinks when we could persuade anyone to buy them for us, you know the sort of thing? Gradually, the heat level rose, both within the group and with the weather. It was thundery and very, very hot during that August. Tension began to mount.'

Pierre fell silent and Tom sent an agonised glance over at the barman, willing him to find some more glasses to wash. 'So what about you, Pierre? What did you think of all this random love and lust?' he asked.

Pierre grimaced and held out both hands, palms uppermost. 'I was distraught. I loved the person whom I have always loved – Shaun. No one else would ever have satisfied me once Shaun had hold of my heart.'

Tom looked at the man sitting opposite him and wondered how he could ever have thought him arrogant. There were tears in Pierre's brown eyes, and the hand that he passed over his face was shaking slightly. 'And Jake?' Tom asked.

'As usual, Jake cared only for himself. He was charming, witty, vivacious, dynamic, but also selfish and sometimes cruel.'

'I just can't understand how Molly could ever have wanted to marry a man like that.'

'What you have to understand, Tom, is that men like Jake are essentially actors. They can make you feel very special, and they can make you think that they care about you. Was theirs a happy marriage?'

Tom shrugged. 'I thought so, but I'm beginning to realise there's a lot more that Molly needs to come to terms with. I think she feels guilty for not missing him more. But carry on, tell me what happened next.'

'As far as I know, there were no physical relation-ships between any of us. I suspected that Jake had feelings for other men himself but was fighting them by being sarcastic.'

Tom frowned. 'Really? I got the impression that Jake was relentlessly straight.'

'Maybe. Maybe not. He was forever needling Marcel about the crush the boy had on him, and teasing Shaun for not being more manly. As for me, he left me alone. I could always stick up for myself, and I tried to do the same for Marcel and Shaun if necessary.' Pierre fell silent, staring into space. Tom coughed.

'Sorry, Tom, I was miles away. Our holiday was drawing to a close by this time and I felt as if I was living on the edge of a volcano. On the last night of August, there was a huge fiesta in the town. There were rival bands playing their music, dozens of food stalls, beer flowing like water. Somehow we managed to get very drunk, even though we were not allowed to buy our own beer.'

'Of course. You were all still very young, weren't you?'

Pierre nodded ruefully. 'Shaun was the worst. He was dancing on the tables whenever he could get away with it, and he kept trying to kiss everyone –

male and female. We had made friends with some of the local boys who were older, and I think they were just playing a game of seeing which one of us would be sick or collapse first. But then things started to go badly wrong.'

Tom settled himself in his chair and took another gulp of beer. This was probably going to take some time.

40

Molly sat on the sea wall and thought about Shaun and Tom. She was desperate to see them both again. Why did everyone she loved keep going away? This was getting ridiculous: first Jake, then Shaun, and now Tom. She sat up straighter as she realised that she'd automatically grouped Tom with the other two most significant men in her life. And now she couldn't even text him, with her phone constantly on the blink. She had been borrowing Dot's mobile every now and again to try and get in touch, but Dot had taken it with her today.

The beach was getting busier as the afternoon wore on, and Molly watched as a family with a mum, dad, and twin baby girls settled themselves on the pebbles near the promenade. The young parents had hauled their double buggy to a fairly flat spot between them and now the man was unbuckling one of his daughters to show her the sea.

'Look, Nina, I'll take you paddling in there when you're bigger and then we can go on the pier and catch some crabs,' he said, lifting her high into the air. 'Now, you go to Mummy and I'll get your sister out so she can have a look.'

He passed the baby to the woman, who had been gazing up at them adoringly, and bent to pick up his other daughter. Molly felt tears trickling down her cheeks as she saw the immense tenderness in the way the man handled his little girl. Had Jake ever been like that? Yes, he had, come to think of it. He had been the only one who could get Sam to stop screaming in the middle of the night. And when Hattie had been doubled up with colic, Jake had soothed her by laying her across his knees and gently massaging her back. Hold onto these memories, she willed the young mum on the beach. Keep them safe, you might need them one day.

Getting out her new notebook and pens, Molly decided this was as good a time as any to start her plan. She opened the book and wrote on the first page 'Molly White – Part Two'. Then she began her list. She cheated to start with, by putting down some of the things she had already done so that she could have the pleasure of ticking them off.

1. *Leave dead-end job.*
2. *Put an ad in the paper for pupils.*
3. *Finish getting the garden sorted.*
4. *Decorate the bathroom and get the leaky shower fixed.*
5. *Sell the car and buy something cheaper to run.*
6. *Talk to Louisa about possibility of a partnership in the bistro.*
7. *Buy a dress and shoes for the party.*
8. *Get hair cut properly – not with nail scissors.*
9. *Find a way to get Tom home.*
10. *Have amazing sex (with Tom, so number 9 essential).*

She put down her pen and took a few deep breaths to stop her heart pounding. Some of these things were easier than others. She ticked the first two items and put half a tick by the third. The rest might need a bit more time and thought, and as for the last one... Molly's cheeks burned at the thought.

Had she moved far enough forward to do it? It was one thing feeling good about her body, but entirely another letting someone else see it, with its tracing of stretch marks, random freckles, and small birthmark in the shape of a cheese wedge. Well, unless she could find Tom, she could forget number ten, because there was no way she was jumping into bed with anyone but him. Tom would definitely be worth waiting for, Molly was sure.

She looked at her watch. The lunchtime rush at the bistro should be dying down now. Maybe there would be a chance to work on number six. Jumping down from the sea wall, she took a last look at the happy family on the pebbles, now with a baby each and playing some sort of Pat-a-Cake game, and set off for the restaurant.

Louisa was just coming to the end of her shift by the look of it – she'd taken off her apron and was standing by the window staring out at the beach. Molly waved and she looked startled for a moment, then opened the door wide.

'I didn't expect to see you again today. Is everything all right?' she asked.

'Yes, no problem. I wanted to ask if you had time for a chat – business this time,' Molly added hastily, seeing the expression on Louisa's face.

'I'm just leaving, shall we go somewhere for a drink? Or do you want to stay here and eat?'

'I need to be outside somewhere because of Marian. Why don't we call at the deli and get a picnic, then we can go on the beach?'

Sitting on the stones eating crab sandwiches and drinking freshly squeezed orange juice, Molly wondered why she didn't take her lunch to the beach more often. Even with the hopeful seagulls wheeling around their heads waiting for crumbs, it was a very peaceful place to be. As if reading her thoughts, Louisa said, 'We should do this regularly – you know, have a working lunch and talk about the business.'

'To be honest, I wasn't even sure if you'd want to still be part of it all with Jake gone,' said Molly, glancing sideways at the younger woman, who had finished her sandwich and was now tackling a huge slab of fruit cake.

'Are you kidding? I love being in charge.' Louisa reddened and bit her lip. 'Sorry, Molly, I didn't mean anything by that.'

'I know you didn't. And I'm so glad you feel that way, because I wanted to see how you felt about the two of us joining forces.'

As they ate their way through the enormous bag of food that Louisa had chosen – and Marian helped by eating the crusts – Molly outlined her plans as briefly as possible. If Louisa could come up with ten thousand pounds to give the bistro a bit of a facelift and get some promotions going, Molly would put up the same amount and set up a business partnership, sharing the profits and paying Louisa a higher wage to cover the extra responsibility. They would have planning meetings every week to update each other, and they would be responsible jointly for hiring and firing of staff. It was a rough plan at the moment, Molly could see that, but Louisa's eyes were sparkling before she'd even got halfway through it.

'This is brilliant! It's much better than I'd hoped for. I was thinking you might shut the place and I'd have to find another job, and here you are offering me a stake in it.'

'But can you manage financially? I don't want to put you in a difficult position if you can't get hold of any cash.'

'I've got some savings in a building society account that I was going to use to go on a round-the-world trip, but I'd so much rather do this. It's a fantastic opportunity. Jake would never let me have a say in the way he ran the bistro and I've always had lots of ideas. Maybe some of them were a bit off the wall, but I'm sure one or two would have been worth a listen.'

Louisa blinked and rubbed her eyes. Molly patted her arm. 'You don't have to tell me, I know what he was like,' she said soothingly. 'We've got Jake to thank for finding such great premises and starting the ball rolling, though. Now it's our turn to make this town sit up and take notice.'

The two women sat looking out to sea as the dog galloped off to find some action near the water. Molly had a feeling that this was going to be the first of many such times. Why had she always thought Louisa was a difficult person to get along with? Looking back, it was probably because Jake had given her a bad press. Molly got out her notebook, ticked number six and looked doubtfully at the next task on the list.

'Louisa?'

'Yes?'

'You don't fancy coming shopping with me for a foxy dress and some killer heels, do you?'

'Funny you should say that, I was going to do that very thing this afternoon. I need something impressive for the next Cloud Nine party. This one's going to be the best yet. When do you need your dress for?'

'The same night. It's a long story. Come on, we'll

have to drop Marian off at home first, but if we hurry up there'll be just time for a quick shop before I do the school run.'

'Great. What are we waiting for?' Louisa whistled the dog and stood up, brushing crumbs from her smart work trousers. 'I want something short, tight, and black to wear, and I want some amazing bling to go with it. What about you?'

'I haven't got a clue. It's so long since I bought a dress, I'm not even sure what size to try on.'

'You look like a perfect twelve to me. I can see you in a sort of fifties number, with a tight waist and a big skirt. You want quite a low neckline to show off your cleavage, too.'

'That's what Shaun told me to get.'

'Shaun? How does he know you're coming to our party night?'

'Like I said, it's a long story. I'll tell you sometime when we've both got a glass of wine in our hands.'

They scrambled back up the beach still calling Marian, who was killing a discarded flip flop. If only Molly could find Tom, just to talk to him for a while, today would be shaping up into something pretty good. But without Tom... Molly shivered. Life without Tom just didn't bear thinking about.

'...and it was then that Jake had his big idea.'

'Go on,' said Tom.

Pierre clasped his hands together. 'This is the hard part, Tom. Jake knew of Marcel's unfortunate allergy to nuts and he devised a kind of Russian Roulette.'

'I don't understand. I thought Marcel ate something with nuts in it by mistake.'

'No, I'm afraid it was much worse than that. Jake stole some coarse pâté from one of the stalls and found half a loaf discarded on a table. Then he asked one of the local lads to go into his mother's kitchen and get a packet of ground almonds. Shaun went, too, but he was staggering by that time.'

Tom's face must have given his feelings away again, because Pierre flushed before carrying on. 'Jake mixed the almonds with some of the pâté and spread it on the bread and put some un-doctored pâté on the rest. Then he cut it all up into small chunks and told us we were going to play a little game.'

'You don't mean you all had to pick a bit of bread and eat it? But that was...'

Pierre nodded sadly. 'Yes, a matter of life and death. In Jake's defence, I'm sure they didn't realise what a serious allergy it was. I think they assumed Marcel might come out in a rash or at worst have swollen eyes, or something like that.'

'Really?'

'I... I hope that was the case. We were all very drunk and Marcel could never refuse Jake anything, even though I think he suspected the risk he was taking. He knew Jake very well by this time and still worshipped him.

'For a while, I thought it was going to be okay. Shaun was even less aware of what was going on than I was, but after a few rounds of the game he seemed to suddenly realise the danger that Marcel was facing. It was too late. As Shaun jumped up to stop him, Marcel selected his last piece of bread. He was unconscious within seconds, but he was aware of what was going to happen just before his eyes closed. I'm sure he knew he was dying. I will never forget the look on his face.'

'But how did you ever get away with it? Weren't the police involved?'

'Yes, of course. But we were popular in the town, and we told the other boys that Marcel had eaten one of the special almond pastries that were on sale everywhere. We said we had tried to stop him but that he was showing off to impress us. That was all Shaun could come up with at such short notice. He'd sobered up very quickly at that point.'

'Yes, I guess that sort of thing would have a sobering effect.'

'The police believed our story, and the evidence that everyone gave was in our favour. And it wasn't until Marcel's mother arrived the next day and came to talk with us all that I realised fully how stupid Jake's plan had been and how reckless I had been to go along with it.'

'You are surely not telling me that Jake deliberately set out to murder an innocent young boy, whose only fault was to love him? Was he really so evil?'

'Not evil. No, certainly not that. Manipulative, impulsive, mischievous, foolhardy – but I am sure that he didn't think his game through to the possible conclusion. Jake always relied heavily on luck.'

At last, Pierre ran out of words and the barman signalled to Tom that he really would have to leave the bar now. As Pierre wheeled him to the door, Tom's mind was reeling. He knew that tomorrow he would have endless questions to ask, but for now all he wanted was sleep. At least Pierre's story had taken his mind off Beryl and Pat for a while.

His stomach lurched as he remembered what was to come when he went home – as he surely must, and soon. But was he ready to face the prying eyes? If the local paper had got wind of the accusations – and it was quite likely that they had because one of their reporters was a neighbour of his in the shopping street and didn't miss a trick – it would be very hard to face everyone.

* * *

The next day, the warm breezy weather had gone and torrential rain appeared as if from nowhere. Tom's plans for bowling along the promenade and getting some fresh air to clear his head had to be put on hold. He sat in the dining room of the B&B and wondered what to do with himself. Matt and Gordon, bustling backwards and forwards with loaded plates of bacon, eggs, sausages and mushrooms, were not very encouraging.

'The forecast's terrible,' said Matt, giving Tom a toast rack full of golden-brown slices and topping up his coffee. 'The last time it set in like this, we had rain for three weeks solid. How long did you say you were planning to stay with us, Tom?'

Tom didn't answer. He thought about his chilly, uncomfortable flat at home. The bed here was bigger and more comfortable than his own, and the breakfast that his host had just placed in front of him looked wonderful. But he was itching to see Molly.

'So, Tom. Why was it you came down here without letting Molly know you were leaving town?' asked Matt. 'I was a bit confused last night. Are you trying to avoid her for some reason?'

'Not exactly. I just needed a bit of thinking time.'

'It's just that Gordy and me... well, we thought you two went really well together, and we were kind of hoping you'd make a go of it, you know?'

Tom shrugged hopelessly. What should he do?

He wasn't sure how to amuse himself if it was going to be pouring with rain. He could move fairly quickly in his chair, but the rest of the population always seemed hellbent on standing in his way on wet days. They would let their umbrellas drip on him and then suddenly decide to shelter in groups just when he needed to get past them. He picked up his knife and fork. At least he could enjoy the moment.

After breakfast, Tom sent Pierre a text:

> Have you eaten yet? Do you want to meet up?

The reply came immediately.

> Just finished, will call for you in ten minutes.

The rain was still coming down by the bucket-load when Tom and Pierre finally made it onto the promenade. Pierre was surprisingly good with the wheelchair. He wove in between the soggy tourists with practised skill and soon had the two of them installed in a coffee shop in The Lanes, settling Tom at one of the best tables and fetching two dark, fragrant espressos. The two men drank in silence for a while, staring mournfully out at the few sodden tourists.

'I thought England in June would be hot and sunny,' said Pierre at last, draining his cup.

'It sometimes is,' Tom replied defensively, 'but you might need to give it time.'

'How much time?'

'Three weeks?'

'You are having the joke with me, surely?' Pierre sighed dramatically and slapped both hands down on the table, causing the lady on the next table to choke on her croissant in surprise.

'Apparently not. How are you planning to spend the day?'

'Heaven only knows. I really want to see your beautiful lady and talk to her about the past, if that were possible. But I'm sensing a problem with you and Molly. Do you want to talk about it?'

'How long have you got?'

Pierre laughed. 'Unfortunately, my friend, I have all day. I am not one for the wet weather walking. Go ahead, unburden yourself.'

So Tom ordered more coffee and poured out his story. He left nothing out, and Pierre leaned forward, chin on hands, listening to every word. When

Tom eventually ground to a halt, Pierre's eyes were sad.

'So, in a nutshell, you love this woman very much but you feel that she is holding back, and you thought it was just because of her troubled feelings about sex. But now you've had time to think, you wonder if she's hesitating to commit to a man in your condition? And now there is the complication of the accusations about your trustworthiness?'

Tom nodded. 'I can't go back there if the situation is so uncertain, but I want to see her more than anything in the world.'

'Then you must fight for her. All women love a man who is prepared to suffer for their love.'

'Suffer? How will being charged as a paedophile help my cause?'

'It won't come to that – you are innocent. Some interfering busybody with nothing better to do has made complications. Probably a woman, I have to say. Any ideas who that could be, Tom?'

Tom shrugged. He didn't even want to say Edna's name. 'You're right, Pierre, I've got to face up to it. I can't stay down here getting hyperactive on strong coffee and feeling like a loser, can I?'

'Indeed not. So, let us check out of our respective establishments and head for Norfolk. I am fortunate that you are here to give me a lift instead of battling with your English rail system, which never seems very reliable. And who knows? Maybe the sunshine will get there before us.'

As they set off, Tom's heart was racing. It could have been the caffeine causing it, but he had a strong suspicion that it was the thought of seeing Molly again.

42

Tom drove homewards with a lighter heart than he'd had for weeks. Pierre, in the passenger seat, was silent for the first part of the journey, but when they were well on the way he cleared his throat and turned towards Tom.

'So, my friend, have you decided how you are going to produce your happy ending?' he asked.

Tom stretched his tired shoulders. 'You make it sound like a magic trick,' he said, playing for time. 'It's not going to be easy.'

'No, but it can be done, with forethought,' Pierre answered. 'And you must not waste any more time. You are still young, and so am I.'

'If you can call thirty-five young?'

'Most definitely I can.'

'What would your own happy ending be then, Pierre? How would you go about finding that?'

Pierre shrugged. 'This is not about me.'

'But what about your dreams?' persisted Tom. 'You can't just give up on happiness, surely? You could live for another fifty years. Are you never going to tell Shaun how you really feel about him?'

'I owe a loyalty to my wife, even if we do not love each other. I have to talk to her before I can make any life-changing decisions,' said Pierre, 'and we need to make a more immediate plan for you. We will go straight to Molly's house and you can declare your love.'

'But I've told you about the problems with the authorities. I can't just walk back in and pretend nothing's happened. It's bad enough people looking at you because you're in a wheelchair, without them pointing and muttering about child molesting.'

'Hmm. I see what you mean. Well, we must just play it by ear. Maybe something will occur to you.'

'Yeah, and maybe pigs will fly.'

'What? Why would they do that, Tom?'

'Never mind. Let's listen to some music now. I need to think.'

* * *

Tom and Pierre pulled up outside Molly's house just as the whole family reached home. Molly, Dot, and the children had, for once, all arrived at the same time and they were all playing a crazy game of hopscotch as they came down the street. Tom could hear their giggles as he opened the car door, and it occurred to him that he had never heard Molly laugh like this before. She turned and saw him as she finished rummaging for her key, and her face lit up. Tom had never really understood what that phrase meant until now but, seeing the sparkle in her look, his heart felt as if it would explode with love.

'Tom! Where have you been?' shouted Max, flinging his arms around Tom's waist as he struggled to stand upright.

'Give the man a break, mate,' said Dot. 'You'll have him on his back.'

Tom looked at Molly and could see his own thoughts reflected in her shining eyes. Something was radically different here. Pierre unfolded himself from the passenger seat and Molly gasped in delight.

'You found him – you found Pierre.'

'It was more that he found me, really,' said Tom. 'Can we come in?'

Dot had already prised the keys from Molly's hands and let the children into the house. Max and Hattie were dancing round the garden shouting 'Tom's home' at the top of their voices, and Theo had sensibly put the kettle on.

'Does everyone want tea?' she asked. 'And I could quickly make some scones, if you like? I know how,' she carried on, seeing Dot's doubtful expression.

The kitchen was getting crowded now, and Tom lowered himself into a chair with relief. Pierre joined him, blinking around as Max and Hattie returned to forage for crisps, arguing fiercely about who should have the last packet of Monster Munch. Theo shouted at them to shut up and started to crash around getting baking ingredients out. Molly was counting out mugs as Dot made the tea, thinking aloud about what she could get out of the freezer for dinner.

'We could have some of that beef casserole,' she bellowed above the din, 'or what about some haddock and prawns? You could make your fish pie.'

'But we haven't got any parsnips,' Dot yelled back.

'There are plenty of potatoes, though. I'll go and see what I can find.'

'Is it always like this?' Pierre whispered. Tom nodded happily.

Much later, with the children safely upstairs in their pyjamas and the spare bed made up for Pierre, peace finally reigned. Dot had left for her evening shift at the pub, and Tom, Pierre and Molly settled themselves in the garden. The rain had cleared at last, and the air was still pleasantly warm. Molly had dried all the garden chairs, lit candles, and opened another bottle of wine. At last she ran out of jobs to do. She sat down with a deep sigh between the two men, and refilled their glasses.

'Right, guys, you've both got some talking to do,' she said.

Tom thought for a moment. He was still reeling at the information that Edna had been 'persuaded' to call off the witch hunt. The case was going to be dropped and no further action would be taken, according to Molly. He wondered if that was the reason for her new bubbliness.

Since he and Pierre had arrived, Molly had hardly stopped smiling, and she had even been singing as she'd laid the table and got the children settled with their homework earlier. Now she was stretched out on a lounger with her eyes half shut, a look of complete contentment on her face.

'I'm not asleep, boys,' she said softly. 'Come on – spit it out. What have you got to tell me?'

Pierre leaned forwards and put his elbows on his knees. 'I think this is my story, Molly, although it involves many people and impacts on many lives.'

As Pierre described in vivid detail the four boys who had lived and loved all those years ago in France, and told of the long-ago night when a game had turned into a tragedy, Molly grew pale and reached for Tom's hand. Tom could hear her ragged breathing as she struggled to stay calm and not to interrupt the flow, but the shaking of her body gave her away. He tried to send his love through their clasped hands as Pierre drew his story to a close.

'...and I have not seen Shaun since that day when he and Jake left for England. He would not speak to me for those last days when the police were questioning us and everyone was so distraught.'

'Surely you don't think Shaun has blamed *you* all these years for Marcel's death?' asked Molly, standing up to put her arms around Pierre as his tears began to fall in earnest.

'I think we blamed ourselves to a great extent, as well as each other. Except Jake, of course. He refused to take any responsibility for his actions, even when talking to me. I am sorry to speak ill of the dead, especially as Jake was your husband and the father of your wonderful children, Molly.'

'So whose fault did Jake think it was?' asked Molly, paler than ever now.

'As always, anybody's but his. He laughed it off and said it had just been a game – a joke that had backfired. He made it sound as if the three of us planned it together and must keep quiet to save each other's skins. Which, to my shame, we did.'

Pierre was crying quietly, his handsome face contorted with long-ago grief. Tom patted his arm, overwhelmed all over again at the selfishness of Molly's husband. He could see no way to ease Pierre's guilt, unless Shaun could be persuaded to talk to him. But Shaun had very cleverly passed the responsibility for all this to Molly.

43

The day of the Cloud Nine party started badly. Pierre had now been staying with Molly for over a week. This had been good in many ways – he played with Max, lent a hand with the cooking, helped Molly to design a plan for a more easily maintained garden, and generally added a much-needed male presence in the house. But on the day of the party, Tom's frustration at never being able to get Molly alone and her own feelings of pent-up desire reached fever pitch.

Tom had arrived early to make sure that Molly had time for a leisurely bath, and to snatch a few minutes with her before the evening began properly. He found that Pierre had all this in hand and was holding the fort cheerfully, entertaining Max, Dot and Hattie with a game of crazy golf in the garden. Molly was already bathed and sitting in the kitchen painting her nails when Dot ran through the house to let Tom in. Her hair flowed down her back in a soft curly waterfall, and she smelt of her favourite cologne – fresh and yet deeply sensual.

'Oh, hi, Tom,' she said, rather offhandedly. 'I thought you were meeting us at the bistro?'

'Well, I could have done. It would have been a damn sight easier for me,' he snapped back.

'Why didn't you then? We'll be going there in less than half an hour. Pierre's ordered a taxi big enough for all of us. You can leave your car here and share it if you like?'

'I thought you might need some help with the kids.'

'No, it's okay. Pierre's got it covered, I think. I'm just going to get dressed.'

'Right, well, if I'm not needed, I'll see you there.' He turned and made his way out of the room as quickly as possible. That was the trouble with using sticks, it was very hard to make a sharp exit. In the event, he demolished a small table and almost broke the window in the door before he made it to his car.

Molly didn't come after him, and Tom seethed all the way to the bistro.

* * *

Molly watched Tom go, filled with a stomach-curdling mixture of tenderness, irritation, and pure lust. He looked so wonderful tonight, obviously fresh from the shower, wearing new straight-legged navy trousers and a striped shirt that exactly picked up the deep blue of his eyes. Did he have any idea what he was doing to her, making no move to get her into bed when she was now more than ready?

After a moment or two of wallowing in self-pity and grumpiness, Molly felt a jolt of shame. Bloody hell, even to herself she was sounding like the worst sort of spoilt bitch. Why should Tom do all the work? What if he'd been feeling as shy about them finally getting it together as she had? It was time she took some action herself. Molly stood up and squared her shoulders, heading for the garden. She needed to talk to Dot and Pierre. And then she had a phone call to make. She would need her credit card for this one.

The party was in full swing when Molly's taxi arrived at the bistro. She craned her neck to see Tom through the crowd, but he was nowhere to be seen, so she concentrated on greeting all the staff and looking round to see who else she knew. Max and Hattie had been allowed to stay up late tonight, but Dot had volunteered to take them home whenever they got grouchy, so Molly let them mingle. They were in their element, with all Jake's old colleagues making a fuss of them and giving them titbits of new recipes to try.

Molly gazed around, waving to acquaintances, seeing a lot more of her friends than she was expecting, and sinking a large glass of prosecco in the meantime. Where could Tom be? He'd left her house ages ago. A sudden fear hit her, making the wine acidic in her stomach. Maybe he wasn't going to come at all. Maybe she had put him off by being so nasty. Molly cursed her bad temper. All her careful planning would come to nothing if Tom didn't turn up.

In those moments of panic, Molly at last knew for sure how deep her love for Tom had become. If he wasn't going to turn up, she didn't want to be at the party either. She turned to check the entrance one more time and froze. Squeezing through the crowd was a slender, elegant figure dressed entirely in black and carrying the biggest bunch of lilies that Molly had ever seen. She opened her mouth to call his name but only a croak came out. He walked towards her, beaming.

'Hello, gorgeous, have you missed me?' said Shaun.

44

Dropping the flowers, Shaun wrapped Molly in the tightest hug she had ever experienced. Tears ran down their faces; it was impossible to decide which tears were hers and which were Shaun's.

'You b... b... bastard,' stuttered Molly eventually. 'I don't know where to start with telling you how pissed off I am with what you did to me. You left me, then you sent me on this bloody quest, and now Tom's gone, just when it was all going to be so lovely.' She began to cry properly, great gasping sobs that hurt her chest and turned her into a snotty mess. Shaun held her close and cried with her until they were both spent. As they calmed down, Molly noticed that, unsurprisingly, a crowd had gathered. At the forefront of this was Louisa.

'Look, the staff room is empty, guys. Why don't you both just pop in there and sort things out? I'll send your other friend when he comes in from playing Frisbee with Max, okay?'

Louisa ushered Shaun and Molly into a tiny room full of bags and shoes. It smelt of ancient cigarette smoke and perfume. Molly wrinkled her nose.

'Well, go on, Shaun – you start. I want some answers from you. Why did you really set me the quest? It can't have been just so that I'd get to know Jake. And why are you home so early from your trip? You weren't supposed to be back until October.'

'Aren't you pleased to see me?'

'You know I am. Now, talk.'

'What did the girl mean by your other friend? Did you actually find yourself a bit of a love interest, Moll? If so, my work here is done.'

Molly stamped her foot, something she hadn't done since primary school. 'Just get on with it, Shaun, before I have to slap you.'

Shaun grinned. 'Okay, okay. Here goes. I'm not really back early because this was always when I meant to come home. I wanted to be here for the end of the quest. I only said October to give myself a bit of breathing space, in case things were complicated out there.'

'So where's Simon?'

'Ah. Well, actually, Simon and I split up three months ago. I've been travelling with a gang of Dutch guys since then. Don't look so worried, Molly, we'd been on borrowed time for ages now. It was bound to happen. Now, what was your other question?'

'You know very well what it was. Why the boxes?'

'Did you not find it helpful to go back through your past then? Aren't you a different person for doing it?'

'But why couldn't you have just talked to me? Why all this secrecy? You could have told me about Marcel years ago.'

Shaun held Molly's gaze steadily. 'And would you have listened? If I'd just told you about Bavaria, and all the parts that made up Jake's complicated personality, and his black side? You'd have just thought I was doing it for my own benefit.'

'I don't know what you mean.'

'Yes, you do, Molly. You'd have thought I wanted Jake for myself, wouldn't you?' Molly blushed and looked down at their hands, fingers closely entwined. Her knuckles were white – she must have been hanging on to Shaun for all she was worth. She made an effort to loosen her grip, but couldn't bring herself to let go completely. He carried on after a moment or two.

'You know I'm right. You would have thought I was trying to put you off him. And I thought about doing that sometimes, when Jake was being even more horrible than usual. But the kids adored him, even though he could be a difficult sod. He was a good dad on the whole, wasn't he? And you know him a whole lot better now, don't you?'

'I guess so. I'm beginning to understand what made him tick. But Shaun... did Jake mean to kill Marcel?'

'Who can tell? I hope not. He was always one for weird jokes, and sometimes he had no sense of danger. I'm as sure as I can be that he didn't realise how drastic Marcel's allergy was, and neither did I. Jake also seemed to think he was immortal – you remember his driving?'

Molly shuddered. 'You're not kidding.'

'Yup. So maybe he just didn't take the possibility of death seriously enough, for himself or his friends? I've thought about it a lot, as you can imagine, and I still don't know. But whatever happened then, and I don't want to sound smug, aren't you better for the quest? Haven't you changed? Improved?'

Molly thought for a minute, torn between exasperation and the growing realisation that she *was* different. Stronger, more self-confident, happier in her own skin than she'd ever been. She thought about her plans for the future, her feelings for Tom, and all her hopes shimmering and waiting for her. Shaun watched her with a faint smile on his face, one elegant, black-jeaned leg crossed over the other, swinging his foot as if he was doing nothing more taxing than waiting for a train.

Molly opened her mouth to speak, to tell Shaun that he might, just possibly, have been right to do things his way, but at that moment the door swung open and Pierre's burly figure was outlined against the background of the restaurant. Shaun stopped, stared incredulously and then leapt to his feet, flinging his arms around Pierre, who rocked on the balls of his feet, almost bowled over.

'Pierre, you old sod – what the hell are you doing here? Oh, I've missed you so much.' Shaun began to cry again, burying his face in the soft cotton of Pierre's shirt. Pierre's arms instinctively circled Shaun and the two of them stood together, Shaun's head only reaching Pierre's chin. They looked as if they belonged together.

'Of course I'm here. Where else would I be?' said

Pierre huskily. 'When Molly came to find me and described your quest, I knew you would be needing me very soon. I told you back then that you only had to say the word and I would find you. I love you, Shaun.'

'But – your wife?' Shaun sounded like a small boy whose toy car might suddenly be taken away from him.

'I will of course have to go back and explain to her. But I don't flatter myself that she will care too much, and she certainly won't be surprised. So long as I don't try to claim any of her money.' He grinned down at Shaun. 'Can you keep me in the manner to which I am accustomed, as you English like to say?'

'Not a chance,' said Shaun. 'But I have got a really amazing idea for a new business. It involves you, Molly. It's a winner, I promise.'

Pierre cleared his throat. 'And me?'

'Of course you, too, you silly man.'

Molly was beginning to feel decidedly in the way. She sensed that Shaun was desperate to start the long process of filling in the last years. Maybe his love for Marcel had just been a young boy's dream? Was Pierre going to be the one for Shaun, after all? Her heart ached with a bizarre mixture of joy in their reunion and longing to feel the same sense of coming home with Tom. Where on earth could he be? She tapped Pierre on the shoulder, snapping him out of his state of bliss.

'You guys, there's someone I need to see. And if everything goes to plan, I won't be home tonight. You'll be staying with us, won't you, Shaun?'

Shaun nodded. 'I hope so. And if Pierre is there, too, there's nowhere else I'd want to be.' They gazed at each other lovingly and Molly began to feel slightly queasy. She had to get out of here. Shaun was so preoccupied he hadn't even registered her possible assignation.

'Right, I've already cleared it with you about looking after the kids, with Dot to help you, Pierre. I'm sure Shaun will be useful, too.' There was no answer. 'Look, please just listen to me, you two,' she almost shouted. Both men turned towards her, as if trying to wake up from a particularly wonderful dream. 'You will go home at a reasonable time, won't you?' Molly tried again. 'Dot's in charge really, but if you join her, I'll feel as if every angle's covered.'

Shaun shook his head. 'I don't get it, Molly. Where will you be?'

'There's someone I really need to see.'

'What, all night long? Who is it?' Both men were looking interested now. About time, Molly thought.

'He's a friend at the moment. I hope he's going to be a whole lot more than that by the end of the night.'

'Ooh, Molly, you did it. I knew you could if you tried,' said Shaun delightedly. 'What's he like? What's his name? Is he hot?'

'He's lovely – kind, funny, strong, caring, and his name is Tom. I think he's extremely hot, now you come to mention it. What would you say, Pierre?'

Pierre raised his eyebrows. 'Oh, yes, he is sizzling. If I wasn't already spoken for...'

Shaun punched him on the arm, and Molly could see that it was only half in fun. She wondered if Pierre was aware of Shaun's jealous streak. If he didn't know about it now, he soon would. She looked around for the large shoulder bag that she'd dropped by the door.

'Right, I'm off. I'll see you guys later – if things go badly – or ideally, I'll be back after breakfast.'

Pierre and Shaun had already turned back to face each other as Molly left the room. She wondered if she should write a quick 'Do Not Disturb' sign for the door, but then decided that she had more urgent things to think about. Going back into the main restaurant, the wall of sound hit her. Jazz music played in the background and everyone seemed to be talking and laughing at once.

She scanned the room for Tom, but there was no sign of him anywhere. Dot caught her eye and gestured to the children, who were eating their way through a plate of garlic bread. She gave Molly a thumbs up and mimed the word 'Tom?' Molly shrugged and pointed to the door, weaving her way through the crowd to the entrance lobby. Maybe he was waiting for her out there. But there was no sign of Tom near the door, or anywhere around the edges of the building where the smokers were congregating for a quick cigarette.

Molly's stomach clenched and her heart began to pound uncomfortably. He wasn't coming, was he? She had driven Tom away with her horrible self-centred bad manners. She slung her bag over her shoulder and started to walk along the promenade, tears prickling her eyelids. Suddenly, she spotted a familiar figure sitting on a bench near the pier, with his wheelchair parked beside him.

'Tom?' she shouted, beginning to jog towards him – not an easy task in heels. The man turned. Thank goodness. He was here. 'Why didn't you come to the party?' Molly gasped, as she reached Tom's bench. 'I looked for you everywhere.'

'I was going to come, but I needed to think.'

'And what did you have to think about that was more important than spending the evening with me and the kids?' Even to herself, Molly sounded petulant. She took a deep breath to steady her heartbeat and sat down next to him. 'I'm sorry for being a bitch,' she said, taking his hand and twining her fingers in his. Tom looked down at their joined hands in amazement and then back at Molly.

She met his gaze. 'I know what you're thinking. It's something I'm not very good at, showing affection. I can do it with the children but it's harder with adults.'

'Why's that, do you think? Are you wary of me?'

'N... no, not exactly wary. Just shy, I guess. Not sure how you'll react, or if you want me to touch you.'

'Come off it, Molly, you can't really be unsure about that. You know how much I want you, don't you?'

She nodded. 'I do now, and I also know that I feel the same about you, and it's about time I told you how I feel instead of expecting you to be psychic or something. Look, let's go for a drink and we can carry on with this. I'm only just getting started.'

'Okay, but don't you want to go to the party? Where shall we go, if not?'

'No, I don't need to go back. We'll go to the Grand Hotel.'

'Okay.' Tom's expression was impossible to read, but at least he'd agreed to come with her, thought Molly, as he climbed into his wheelchair and they headed for his car.

The hotel foyer was cool and opulent, with shaded pink lighting and ornate chandeliers. Tom wheeled himself across the thick carpet, and whistled in amazement. 'Wow, this place is like a high-class brothel. It's fantastic. Do you come here often? I've always wanted to say that to someone.'

Molly giggled. 'I've peeped in before, but I've never been for a drink. Let's go through to the bar. There should be a table in the window for us.'

'Should there? How did that happen?'

'You're being a bit dim for a bright sort of bloke, Tom. It happened because I booked it.'

'When?'

She blushed. 'Earlier today, when I realised it was time I made a move. Call it girl power, if you like.'

Sure enough, the best table in the bar held a reserved sign and a champagne bucket complete with condensation-beaded bottle and two tall flutes. As they approached, the barman moved towards them, gliding across the room as if on well-oiled castors.

'Mrs White?' he asked, with a discreet bow. Molly nodded, suddenly lost for words. She could see Tom's grin out of the corner of her eye.

'I'm just... erm... nipping to the loo,' she mumbled. 'I just need to... um...'

Tom raised his eyebrows, but settled himself at the table and waited. Molly was soon back, still pink in the face, and as she approached, the barman opened the champagne with the smallest of pops and poured them each a drink. He moved away as Molly lifted her glass.

'What are we toasting?' asked Tom.

'Our first night together?'

'Oh. Right. And that will be... when exactly?'

Molly took a gulp of champagne and hiccupped slightly. 'Tonight, actually.'

'Molly, what do you mean? I feel as if I've dropped into some sort of parallel universe where you keep saying everything I want you to say.'

'I've booked a room here for tonight, if that's okay with you?' Molly felt her face reddening all over again, the bright blush making her so hot that she had to fan herself with a handy menu. Was she really doing this? Molly White, inept lover and sensible mummy? With a pack of three condoms now nestling in her handbag? Propositioning a gorgeous man? And making things happen for a change?

'Can we take the champagne upstairs now?' asked Tom, motioning the waiter over. 'Only, if this is going to turn out to just be a dream, I want to get to the good bit before I wake up.'

Their room was small, almost filled with the enormous king-sized bed. The barman put the tray of champagne down on the dressing table and left quickly, not meeting their eyes.

'I bet he thinks we're having an affair,' said Molly, wondering why this thought filled her with heady excitement rather than her usual embarrassment.

They looked at each other for a long moment. Molly reached out and switched on the radio. 'We need background music,' she said, listening to see what it would be.

Tom's slow smile told her that it was appropriate, and she moved towards him, kicking off her shoes as the sweet sound of an old love song from the fifties filled the room. They stood face to face in the narrow space at the end of the bed, with Tom still balanced on his sticks. Molly slipped her arms around his waist and he bent to kiss her, gently at first. As the kiss deepened, Molly moaned slightly and Tom broke away. 'Why have you stopped?' she said, drawing back.

'Don't panic. It's just that I want to hold you properly and I'm trying to work out how I can do it. If I get rid of one stick, I can get closer to you.' He dropped a stick on the floor and she felt his right arm encircle her, pulling her close. They kissed again, deeper this time, harder. Just as Molly was beginning to think she was going to have to tear Tom's clothes off if he didn't hurry up, they began to sway slightly. Tom reached for the wall to steady himself but Molly's legs were so weak with longing that she crumpled under his weight, pulling Tom down on top of her on the bed.

They landed with a bounce, bumping heads, and then lay still. Molly waited to see if anything hurt. Realising they were both in one piece, she started to giggle hysterically, and Tom joined in, holding her close as they laughed themselves into a state of near exhaustion.

'Are you okay?' Tom gasped, when he could get control of his breathing.

'Yes, my legs just went from under me. I couldn't stand up.'

'Welcome to my world,' he said, which for some reason set them both off again.

At last they were able to calm down, and lay in each other's arms, peacefully.

'Well, that's one way of breaking the ice,' said Tom. 'How are your legs now?'

'I'm not sure. I think you might need to check if anything's broken,' said Molly, heady with relief that they were actually here together, with champagne at the ready and no interruptions.

Tom pulled back to look her in the eyes. 'You're very forward tonight, Mrs White. Do you often ask strange gentlemen to check your legs over for damage?'

'No, I can honestly say you're the first, in more ways than one.'

'What do you mean?' he asked, sliding a hand under her skirt and upwards to a point where he halted. An expression of delight came over his face. 'Molly, you're wearing stockings,' he breathed.

'Yes, I rather thought I was,' she dimpled up at him, wriggling to get more comfortable. 'I bought them specially for the occasion.'

'For the party?'

'No, you silly man, for you.'

'But how did you know I love women in stockings?' he asked, spellbound by the soft flesh at the top of her thigh.

'Call it a lucky guess,' she said. His breathing became ragged as he explored further, and Molly gave herself over to complete bliss. After a moment, he stopped. Molly opened her eyes wide.

'What's wrong?' she asked, unable to keep the anxiety out of her voice.

'Nothing's wrong, my love. I just want to do this thing properly. We've waited so long, and we've got all night. I'm going to undress you very slowly and then we're going to have a champagne break.'

'Do I get to undress you, too?'

Tom refused to meet her eyes. 'I'd kind of rather you didn't see me like that just yet. That's why I need the champagne.' Molly frowned, puzzled, and he carried on bravely. 'Think about it. My legs aren't a pretty sight. The scars never really faded much, and I hate how weedy they look.'

Molly wrapped her arms around him more tightly and thought fast. She knew she should have anticipated this, but she'd been so preoccupied with her own hang-ups that she hadn't given Tom's even a moment's consideration.

'Okay, this is the deal,' she whispered into his ear, kissing his neck to reassure him. 'You are easily the sexiest man I've ever met, let alone been to bed with.

There is nothing about you that doesn't completely turn my legs to jelly.'

'Yes, I noticed that,' he grinned. She slapped him lightly. At least he could joke about it now, maybe she was getting somewhere. 'Right, as I was saying, this is what I'm going to do. Just this once, you can take off all of your own clothes and slide under the bedclothes. I won't look, I promise.'

'That sounds safe enough.'

'It is. But first, you have to drink a whole glass of champagne and strip me naked very, very slowly. And while you're doing that, you have to kiss every last bit of me, very, very thoroughly.'

Tom's voice was hoarse as he answered, 'You strike a hard bargain.'

'I certainly do. I'll get the champagne.' She poured deftly and handed Tom a brimming glass, lifting her own in another silent toast. They drank deeply, finishing their drinks in record time. The DJ on the radio was playing one of Molly's favourite songs now. The mellow sound of Elton John singing about sacrifices flowed over her, as she climbed back onto the bed and lay down, opening her arms to Tom. He began to unbutton her dress, kissing his way down her throat until she moaned with anticipation.

'More champagne?' he asked in a low voice.

'No, don't stop,' she answered.

And Tom didn't.

* * *

Sunshine was creeping through the crack in the curtains when Molly woke the next morning. She rolled over onto her back and watched the dust motes floating around in the air above the bed, putting off, with delicious anticipation, the moment when she would turn to Tom and kiss him awake.

The bed was enormous, and she wriggled blissfully as she remembered the night before and the final realisation that she was not only completely normal, but as Tom had gasped, 'bloody amazing in bed'. She rolled over, unable to wait any longer, and saw Tom's eyes open. For a second or two, he lay without moving, and then he turned and his deep blue gaze took her breath away.

'Tell me this is really happening,' he murmured.

Molly laughed, and sat up in bed. She swung her legs over and stood up in one fluid movement, intensely aware of her nakedness but totally relaxed.

'I've got something for you,' she said, rummaging in her handbag.

'I was kind of hoping you had.'

'No, not that. Well, yes that, but not yet. It's a present, kind of.'

Molly handed over a small red leather jewellery case. Tom's eyes widened. 'It's okay, it's not a ring,' Molly said. 'In fact, it's not jewellery at all, it's just that I've always kept it in there. Go on, open it.'

'Is this the last little box for a while, do you think?' asked Tom, as he opened the lid. He picked up a tiny bundle of silk and unwrapped the smooth grey stone that lay at its centre. It was almost a perfect heart shape.

'I found it on the beach years ago,' said Molly. 'It's my lucky charm. But I don't need it now – I want you to have it.'

'You're giving me your heart,' Tom whispered. 'Do you even realise how brilliant that makes me feel? Hang on, where are you going?' he said, as Molly got up again.

'I won't be long. I'm just going to get dressed and go downstairs for a minute.'

'Why? Don't go – we can order breakfast up here. I want you to come back to bed. I haven't finished with you yet,' he grinned.

'Oh, I'm going to, don't worry. It's just that I need to visit the downstairs cloakroom again. A pack of three doesn't seem to last long with you around.'

Tom laughed, and stretched his arms above his head. 'Did I mention how I feel about you, at all?' he asked, as Molly slid into her clothes.

'Only a few hundred times, but I don't mind hearing it again,' she said, sitting on the edge of the bed.

'Okay, here goes. I love you more than I've ever loved anyone in my entire life,' Tom said, reaching for her hands and holding them gently. Molly leaned over and kissed him, her lips lingering on his. He slid his hands up her arms and began to pull her towards him.

'Hold that thought,' she said, wriggling out of his grasp. 'I'll grab some clothes and be back in less than ten minutes.'

As the door slammed behind her, Molly kicked off her shoes and ran down the corridor. Ten minutes? Who was she kidding? She could do it in five. There was a lot of catching up to be done.

* * *

MORE FROM CELIA ANDERSON

Celia Anderson's next title is available to order now here:

https://mybook.to/CeliaBackAd

ABOUT THE AUTHOR

Celia Anderson is a top ten bestselling author of women's fiction. She writes uplifting golden years fiction for Boldwood.

Sign up to Celia Anderson's newsletter and get a FREE short story!

Follow Celia on social media:

ALSO BY CELIA ANDERSON

Life Begins at 50!

A New Lease of Life

Dancing Under the Moon

Living the Good Life

Here Comes the Sun

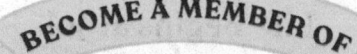

Boldwood

Boldwood Books is an award-winning fiction publishing company seeking out the best stories from around the world.

Find out more at www.boldwoodbooks.com

Join our reader community for brilliant books, competitions and offers!

Follow us
@BoldwoodBooks
@TheBoldBookClub

Sign up to our weekly deals newsletter

https://bit.ly/BoldwoodBNewsletter